ACCLAIM FOR BETH WISEMAN

Need You Now

"You may think you are familiar with Beth's wonderful storytelling gift but this is something new! This is a story that will stay with you for a long, long time. It's a story of hope when life seems hopeless. It's a story of how God can redeem the seemingly unredeemable. It's a message the Church, the world needs to hear."

— Sheila Walsh, author of *God Loves Broken People* and *Song of the Brokenhearted*

"Beth Wiseman tackles these difficult subjects with courage and grace. She reminds us that true healing can only come by being vulnerable and honest before our God who loves us more than anything."

— Deborah Bedford, best-selling author of *His Other Wife*, *A Rose by the Door*, and *The Penny* (co-authored with Joyce Meyer)

The Land of Canaan Novels

"Beth Wiseman writes with a masterful hand that reaches the recesses of the soul. Her capability for understanding the human condition exceeds traditional empathy and moves the reader to both introspection and exhilaration. Characters connect, transform, and redeem, making for a must 'one sit' read. Wiseman's comprehension of grace and redemption plays out in the subtle confines of the everyday and teaches the reality that new life is possible for all."

— Kelly Long, best-selling author of *Sarah's Garden*

"Wiseman's voice is consistently compassionate and her words flow smoothly."

— *Publishers Weekly* review of *Seek Me With All Your Heart*

"In *Seek Me With All Your Heart*, Beth Wiseman offers readers a heart-warming story filled with complex characters and deep emotion. I instantly loved Emily, and eagerly turned each page, anxious to learn more about her past—and what future the Lord had in store for her."

— Shelley Shepard Gray, best-selling author of the Seasons of Sugarcreek series

"Wiseman has done it again! Beautifully compelling, *Seek Me With All Your Heart* is a heartwarming story of faith, family, and renewal. Her characters and descriptions are captivating, bringing the story to life with the turn of every page."

— Amy Clipston, best-selling author of *A Gift of Grace*

The Daughters of the Promise Novels

"Well-defined characters and story make for an enjoyable read."

— *Romantic Times* review of *Plain Pursuit*

"A touching, heartwarming story. Wiseman does a particularly great job of dealing with shunning, a controversial Amish practice that seems cruel and unnecessary to outsiders . . . If you're a fan of Amish fiction, don't miss *Plain Pursuit*!"

— Kathleen Fuller, author of The Middlefield Family novels

ALSO BY BETH WISEMAN

Need You Now

The House that Love Built
(Available April 2013)

The Daughters of the Promise series

Plain Perfect

Plain Pursuit

Plain Promise

Plain Paradise

Plain Proposal

The Land of Canaan series

Seek Me With All Your Heart

The Wonder of Your Love

His Love Endures Forever

Novellas found in

An Amish Christmas

An Amish Gathering

An Amish Love

An Amish Wedding

An Amish Kitchen

Seek Me With All Your Heart

and

The Wonder of Your Love

Two Land of Canaan Novels

BETH WISEMAN

THOMAS NELSON
Since 1798

NASHVILLE DALLAS MEXICO CITY RIO DE JANEIRO

Published in Nashville, Tennessee, by Thomas Nelson. Thomas Nelson is a registered trademark of Thomas Nelson, Inc.

Thomas Nelson, Inc., titles may be purchased in bulk for educational, business, fund-raising, or sales promotional use. For information, please email SpecialMarkets@ThomasNelson.com.

ISBN 978-1-4016-8755-7

Library of Congress Cataloging-in-Publication Data

CIP data is available.

Printed in the United States of America

12 13 14 15 16 17 QG 6 5 4 3 2 1

Pennsylvania Dutch Glossary

Aamen—Amen

ab im kopp—crazy, off in the head

ach—oh

aenti—aunt

boppli—baby or babies

Budget, The—a weekly newspaper serving Amish and Mennonite communities everywhere

bruder—brother

daadi—grandfather

daed—dad

danki—thank you

Deitsch—Dutch

dochder—daughter

dumm—dumb

eck—special place for bride and groom at the corner of the wedding table

Englisch—a non-Amish person

fraa—wife

Frehlicher Grischtdaag—Merry Christmas

grossmammi—grandmother

guder mariye—good morning

gut—good

hatt—hard

haus—hause

kaffi—coffee

kapp—prayer covering or cap

kinner—children or grandchildren

lieb—love

maedel—girl

mamm—mom

mammi—grandmother

mariyefrieh—tomorrow morning

mei—my

mudder—mother

nee—no

onkel—uncle

Ordnung, The—the written and unwritten rules of the Amish; the understood behavior by which the Amish are expected to live, passed down from generation to generation. Most Amish know the rules by heart.

Pennsylvania Deitsch—Pennsylvania German, the language most commonly used by the Amish

roascht—roast

rumschpringe—running-around period when a teenager turns sixteen years old

schee—pretty

schtinkich—stinks

sohn—son

Wie bischt—How are you?

wunderbaar—wonderful

ya—yes

Seek Me With All Your Heart

A Land of Canaan Novel

Beth Wiseman

THOMAS NELSON
Since 1798

NASHVILLE DALLAS MEXICO CITY RIO DE JANEIRO

One

Emily stood behind the counter of her family's country store, watching as the tall man walked down each aisle, the top of his black felt hat visible above the gray metal shelving. First thing that morning, he'd strolled in and shot her a slow, easy smile, white teeth dazzling against bronzed skin. He moved slowly, sometimes glimpsing in her direction.

Emily twisted the strings on her apron with both hands and tried to slow down her breathing. Her heart pulsed against her chest as she glanced out the window toward her family's farmhouse in the distance. *Where is Jacob?* Her brother knew she didn't like to be left alone in the store, and he'd promised to be right back.

Their community was small, and all the members in the district knew each other, which was the only reason Emily agreed to work in the shop. But this Amish man was a stranger. And Amish or not, he was still a man.

Emily jumped when the man rounded the bread aisle toting a box of noodles in one hand and a can in the other. With the back of one hand, he tipped back his hat so that sapphire blue eyes blazed down on her. As he approached the counter, Emily clung to her apron strings and took a step backward.

"How come everything in this store is messed up?" Tiny lines creased his forehead as he held up a can of green beans with a large dent in one side. Then he held up the box of noodles. "And this looks like it's been stepped on. It's mashed on one side." He dropped them on the counter, then folded his arms across his chest and waited for her to answer.

He towered over her. Emily stared straight ahead, not looking him in the eye. The outline of his shoulders strained against a black jacket that was too small. Her bottom lip trembled as she turned her head to look out the window again. When she didn't see any sign of Jacob, she turned back to face the stranger, who looked to be about her age—maybe nineteen or twenty—which didn't make him any less threatening. His handsome looks could be a convenient cover up for what lay beneath. She knew he was not a married man since he didn't have a beard covering his square jaw, and his dark hair was in need of a trim.

He arched his brows, waiting for her to respond, looking anything but amused. Emily felt goose bumps on her arms, and chills began to run the length of her spine, even though Jacob had fired up the propane heaters long before the shop opened that morning.

"This is—is a salvage store." Her fingers ached as she twisted the strings of her apron tighter. "We sell freight and warehouse damaged groceries." She bit her lip, but didn't take her eyes from him.

"I can't even find half the things on my list." He shook his head as he stared at a white piece of paper. "What about milk and cheese?"

"No, I'm sorry. We mostly have dry goods."

He threw his hands in the air. Emily thought his behavior was improper for an Amish man, but raw fear kept her mouth closed and her feet rooted to the floor.

"Where am I supposed to get all this?" He turned the piece of paper around so she could see the list.

Emily unwrapped the strings of her apron and slowly leaned her head forward. She tucked a loose strand of brown hair underneath her *kapp*.

"What'd you do to your hand?"

Emily glanced at her hand, and a blush filled her cheeks when she saw the red indentions around her fingers. She quickly dropped her hand to her side and ignored his comment. "You will have to go to Monte Vista for most of those things. People usually come here to save money, just to get a few things they know we'll have for a lesser price."

"That's a far drive by buggy in this snow." He put both hands on the counter and hung his head for a few moments, then looked up as his mouth pulled into a sour grin. With an unsettling calmness, he leaned forward and said, "Just one more thing I can't stand about this place."

Emily took two steps backward, which caused her to bump into the wall behind her. "Then leave," she whispered as she cast her eyes down on her black shoes. She couldn't believe she'd voiced the thought, and when she looked back up at him, the stranger's eyes were glassed with anger.

"Please don't hurt me." She clenched her eyes closed.

David couldn't believe what he'd heard. "*What?* Hurt you? What are you talkin' about?" He'd never hurt anyone in his life. He walked around the counter and reached his hand out to her, but she cowered against the wall.

"I'm sorry. Whatever I did, I'm sorry. Please, don't cry." He touched her arm, and she flinched as a tear rolled down her cheek. He pulled back and said softly, "Please. Don't cry. Look . . ." He showed her his palms, then backed up and got on the other side of the counter. "I'm leaving. Don't cry."

He rubbed his forehead for a moment and watched her trying to catch her breath to stop the tears from flowing. She swiped at her eyes and sniffled, then looked up at him. He noticed a scar above her left brow. A deep indentation that ran nearly to her hairline.

The bell on the front door chimed, and David looked away from the woman and toward the sound. An Amish fellow around his own age stepped inside. He glanced at David, then took one look at the woman against the wall and hastily rushed over to her. He brushed past David, almost pushing him, and touched the woman on the arm.

"Are you all right?"

"I didn't do anything, I promise." David watched the young man wrap his arm around her and whisper something in her ear. "I mean, I guess I acted like a jerk, but I never meant to . . ."

The fellow waved a hand at him and shook his head before turning his attention back to her. "Go on back to the *haus*."

David's eyes followed the young woman as she scurried out the door, her chin tucked. Through the window, he saw her trudge through the snow toward a white house on the other side of a picket fence, her brown dress slapping at her shins as she hugged herself tightly. David pointed to a black wrap hanging on a rack by the door. "She forgot her cape," he said and looked out of the window again. He wondered what exactly had just happened.

"I'm Jacob." The man walked closer and extended his hand to David, who forced a smile.

"I'm David, and I'm real sorry. I came in here in a bad mood, and I guess I must have scared her or something." He dropped his hand and shook his head. "But I sure didn't mean to. Really. I'm just real sorry."

Jacob peeled off a snow-speckled black coat, walked to the rack, and hung it beside the forgotten cape. He turned to face David. "It's not you. My sister just gets like that sometimes. I try not to leave her alone, but I heard one of the horses in the barn kicking at the stall, and I was gone longer than I should have been."

"Is she . . ." David wasn't sure how to ask. "*Ab im kopp*?"

Jacob chuckled. "*Nee*, she ain't off in the head." His expression grew serious. "She's just . . . I reckon she's just going through a *hatt* time right now."

The bell on the door chimed again, and David saw a small girl enter. She was bundled in a black bonnet and cape and was breathing hard. "Are you the one who made Emily cry?" She thrust her hands on her hips and drew her mouth into a frown. David opened his mouth to answer, but Jacob cut in.

"Betsy, what are you doing out here? You're supposed to be helping *Mamm* get those jams labeled so she can carry them to Abby's bakery later. Does she know you ran over here?"

The child untied the strings of her bonnet, pulled it off, then tucked loose strands of blonde hair beneath her *kapp*. "I reckon this is more important." She folded her small arms across her chest as her hazel eyes bored into David. "What did you do to Emily?"

"Betsy, he didn't do nothing. Now, get on back in the house." Jacob stacked papers on top of the counter, dismissing the child.

Betsy walked to David, her hands landing back on her tiny hips. She squinted her eyes and pursed her lips together. "I want you to know that if your behavior instigated this outpouring of emotion from my sister, it would be best for you not to visit us here again." She nodded her head once, but David was too stunned to say anything. *The women in this family are crazy.*

"Just pretend she's not here," Jacob said as he walked to the girl. He gently grabbed her by the arm and led her to the door. He pulled the door open. "Put your bonnet on and go home, Betsy."

Betsy stood in the doorway as snow powdered her black cape and the threshold of the shop. She plopped her bonnet back on her head, tied it, then lifted her chin. "I will be going back to tend to Emily, and I suspect you should be heading to your own *haus*." She spun around and slammed the door behind her.

David cocked his head to one side and watched Betsy from the window. "How *old* is she?"

"Seven." Jacob shrugged, then sighed. "And a handful."

David scratched his chin and finally pulled his gaze from the window. "I have a sister who is seven, but she doesn't talk like that." He paused. "I don't know many Amish folks who talk like that, even us older ones."

"*Ya*, Betsy is special. She's a real pain most of the time, but *Mamm* and *Daed* let some *Englisch* people give her some tests, and they said she's what they call gifted." Jacob pushed a button on the cash register, and the drawer swung open. He filled the slots with bills as they talked. "Betsy's been reading since way before other *kinner* her age. I reckon she thinks she knows everything." He chuckled. "Sometimes I think she does, too, using them big words and all. She does math real *gut* too."

David nodded. "Oh."

Jacob slammed the cash drawer shut, then smiled. "In case you were wondering, *mei mamm* is normal."

David laughed. "*Gut* to know. Are those your only siblings?"

"No. I got a younger *bruder*, Levi. But he works with *mei daed* doing construction and installing solar panels."

David had noticed that lots of the Amish homes in Canaan used solar panels, something you didn't see a lot of in Lancaster County. "How'd your *daed* and *bruder* get into that?"

"*Daed* knew he was going to need to find an outside job here since farming is going to be a challenge, at least in the beginning." Jacob shook his head. "Can't believe that there's only three months of frost-free weather here." He paused with a sigh. "Anyway, *Daed* planned ahead and learned about these solar panels before we moved here."

David nodded again as he considered whether or not his family might benefit from solar panels.

"And me and Emily take care of the shop, and 'course *Mamm* has the house to tend to . . . and Betsy, which is a full-time job when she ain't in school." Jacob scratched his forehead. "What 'bout you? Where'd you come from? I haven't seen you around here."

David sighed. "We moved here. Yesterday. We're not even

unpacked, but my stepmother wanted me to pick up a few things."

"You don't sound happy about this move." Jacob sat down on a stool behind the counter and eyed David skeptically.

"I'm not, really. I mean, my whole family and everything I've ever known is in Lancaster County. In Pennsylvania. My great grandfather left us some land, so we moved." David shook his head. "Although . . . I reckon I don't know why. This is nothing like Lancaster County. It's—" He stopped when he realized he might offend Jacob if he went on.

"It's all right." Jacob took off his hat and ran a hand through wavy brown hair. "You ain't tellin' me anything I don't know. We moved here from Middlefield, Ohio, three months ago. It's real different here for us too."

"What made your family move?"

Jacob shrugged. "Needed a change." He pulled his eyes from David's and his forehead wrinkled as he went on. "And Levi's got asthma. The weather is better here for him. Less mold, which seems to trigger it."

David suspected there was more to it than that, but he just nodded.

"Lillian, my stepmother, was wondering where the school is for my sister. I have two sisters, but only Anna is old enough to go to school. She's the one who's the same age as Betsy. Elizabeth is almost five, so she won't start until next year."

Jacob grunted. "There ain't no schoolhouse. Hoping to build one soon, though. Right now, the young ones are getting their schooling from Emma Miller, the widow around the corner." Jacob pointed to his right. "Big blue house on the next road to the right. She teaches them in the barn."

"In the barn?"

"*Ya*. She's got a *gut* setup out in her barn. All the young scholars have their own desk, and it's all heated with propane. It's just until we can get the school built. Widow Miller is sick; otherwise Betsy would be in school today." Jacob chuckled. "Bet *Mamm* is hoping she gets well real soon."

David had almost forgotten about his list from Lillian. "I better pay for these couple of things, then head to town for the other items." He reached into his pocket and pulled out a five dollar bill.

"There's a singing here on Sunday, if you're interested." Jacob handed David his change. "It won't be nothing like what you're used to, I'm sure, and there ain't a whole lot of people who attend, maybe only ten or fifteen, but you could meet some folks. There will even be a few single girls coming. How old are you, anyway?"

"I just turned twenty."

"And you ain't married yet?"

David forced a smile. Marriage wasn't in his plans. "No."

"I'm getting married in December." Jacob grinned again. "Adding another crazy woman to my life. Beth Ann's her name."

David watched Jacob's eyes light up when he said her name—his new friend was happy about this. "Congratulations."

"*Danki*."

David picked up his small bag with the noodles and green beans, and then extended his other hand to Jacob. "Nice to meet you, and please tell Emily that I'm not some psycho or anything." He chuckled, but stopped when he saw the color fade from Jacob's face. "Did I say something wrong? I just don't want her to think I'm—"

Jacob waved his hand. "Nah, it's okay. I can tell you're a normal guy." Then he stood up and headed toward the back of the shop. "See ya 'round," he said over his shoulder. "Come Sunday, if you feel like it."

David opened the front door of the shop and walked toward his buggy. The snow had stopped, and he glanced across the white terrain between the shop and the house. Movement on the front porch caught his eye. *Emily*. He stopped for a moment, then pivoted on his foot and headed in her direction. He'd never made a woman cry before today.

EMILY'S FACE FLUSHED with embarrassment as she watched him walking toward her. When was she ever going to feel—and act—normal again? She reached up and touched the scar on her forehead. *Never*.

The screen door slammed behind her, and Vera Detweiler joined her daughter on the porch.

"Who is that handsome fellow comin' 'cross the yard?" *Mamm* smoothed the wrinkles in her brown apron. "I don't recognize him."

"I'm going in the *haus*." Emily started to step around her mother, but felt a hand on her arm.

"Emily. That's rude. Is this young man coming to see you? Did you meet him at the shop?"

Emily wiggled free of her mother's grasp. "*Ya*. But he's not very friendly, and I'd rather not talk to him."

Mamm's lips thinned. "Emily, how are you ever going to find a man and get married if you keep running away from everyone?" She softened her expression. "You must move past what happened."

The man was nearing earshot, so Emily didn't have a chance to respond.

"*Guder mariye.*" *Mamm* waved from the front porch. Emily didn't think there was much good about this morning at all.

"*Guder mariye* to you." He stopped in the yard and looked up at Emily and her mother. "I just wanted to come apologize to Emily." He shoved his hands in his pockets, and with his shoulders hunched forward, his gaze landed on Emily. "I'm sorry for the way I acted back there." He nodded toward the shop. "I'm just having a really bad morning. I didn't mean to scare you."

With renewed humiliation about her behavior, Emily looked away from him. When she turned back to face him, his gaze was still on her. "It's all right," she mumbled, casting her eyes to the ground, wishing she'd never have to see him again. *Not much chance of that if he lives here.*

Her *mamm* carefully eased down the porch steps, then extended her hand to him. "I'm Vera Detweiler."

"David Stoltzfus. We just moved here yesterday from Lancaster County." He latched onto *Mamm's* hand, glanced at *Mamm* for a moment, then looked up at Emily.

Mamm turned her head and smiled. "That's my daughter, Emily."

As David's hand dropped, he nodded in Emily's direction. "*Gut* to meet you. And again, I'm sorry for the way I acted. I'm not normally like that."

Emily drew in a deep breath and was about to speak when *Mamm* cut in.

"Come into the *haus*. Let me get you some hot *kaffi*. You can tell us about your family."

Mamm started back up the porch steps and then turned around to see if David was following her. He hadn't moved. *Good. Maybe he'll just head back to wherever he came from.*

"Come in, come in," *Mamm* coaxed with a wave of her hand. "We're such a small community, we're always anxious to meet new members."

Emily held her breath, but David smiled and moved toward the steps. *Mamm* waited for him at the doorway and held the screen door for him to follow her in. Emily trailed slowly behind them.

"Emily, you keep David company while I go get us all a cup of *kaffi*. I have some on the stove." *Mamm* smiled in a way that made Emily self-conscious, and she waited until her mother turned before she rolled her eyes.

"Uh, I can go if you want." David arched his brows, holding his hat in his hands. "I saw the eye rolling thing." Then he grinned.

Now that she was feeling safe inside with her mother, she allowed herself to notice the well-defined, boyish dimples on either side of his striking smile. Back in Middlefield, she might have responded to his good looks, but she was wiser now and knew that looks were deceiving.

"*Mamm* asked you to stay, so stay." Emily pointed to the rocker in the corner of the room. She waited for him to sit down before she eased onto the couch across the room from him. She folded her hands in her lap, sighed, and then watched David tap his foot nervously against the wooden floor.

"So . . . Jacob tells me that there is a singin' here on Sunday."

Thanks a lot, Jacob. Emily forced a smile. "*Ya.*" She strained to see around the corner and into the kitchen. *Mamm* was placing three cups on a tray. "I reckon there won't be many people here. It won't be anything like you're used to, I'm sure." She turned back to him, narrowed her eyes, and frowned. "No outside games or anything. And mostly younger teenagers."

"*Kaffi* for everyone." *Mamm* hummed as she sauntered back into the den, then placed the tray on the coffee table. Emily wondered how much more transparent her mother could be. "*Ach*, I forgot the creamer. I'll be right back." *Mamm* scurried back to the kitchen about the same time Emily heard tiny feet jumping down the stairs. Betsy stopped at the bottom of the stairs and folded her arms across her chest.

"What are *you* doing here?" Betsy glared at David, who sat up a little taller when he saw her.

"Besty, *Mamm* invited him for *kaffi*. This is David Stoltzfus."

"Betsy and I met earlier." David smiled. "Although we weren't properly introduced." He stood up and extended his hand to Betsy, who ignored the gesture. She squinted her eyes and pressed her lips firmly together before she veered around him and plopped onto the couch beside Emily. David returned to the rocker as Betsy slid closer to Emily on the couch, then placed a protective hand on her sister's knee. Emily's heart was heavy as she put her hand on top of Betsy's. *I wish Betsy didn't know something bad happened to me.*

"Here we go." *Mamm* returned carrying a white creamer in the shape of a cow, a trinket *Mamm* said her grandmother had given her. Emily disliked the creamer, and it embarrassed her every time her mother used it. When *Mamm* walked toward him, David held out his cup, and Emily stifled a grin as he eyed the cow.

"Interesting creamer."

Mamm raised the tail end so that milk spewed out the cow's mouth and into David's cup. *Mamm* thanked him, although Emily wasn't sure David's statement had been a compliment.

"So where are you living? What homestead did you purchase, David?" *Mamm* sat down in the other rocking chair in the far corner.

David finished taking a sip of his coffee, then set the cup down on the table between him and *Mamm*. He shook his head before answering. "I don't know who owned it before, but it's a real mess. Needs lots of work."

"Where 'bouts is it located?" *Mamm* crossed her legs as she sipped her coffee.

"If you head north toward that bakery that's on the corner . . ." David pointed to his right. "I can't remember the name of it, but you turn on that street." He scratched his forehead for a moment. "My family lives in the two story *haus*, the one that badly needs new paint. And my *Aenti* Katie Ann and *Onkel* Ivan moved into the smaller *haus* on the property."

Betsy leaned forward and narrowed her eyes at David. "You bought that old place?" Betsy's voice squeaked as she spoke.

Emily watched David's cheeks redden. "*Ya*, I know. It's in real bad shape. But we plan to start painting, and . . ." David let out a heavy sigh. "My stepmother, Lillian, 'bout fell over when we pulled in last night and she found out that there ain't no indoor bathroom. Just an outhouse."

Mamm set her coffee cup down and kicked her rocker into motion. "You said your stepmother?"

Since divorce wasn't allowed, Emily knew David's mother must have died, and she felt a wave of sympathy as she recalled the death of her grandmother two years ago.

"*Ya*. Lillian is great. *Mei mamm* died when I was eight, and *Daed* married Lillian about three years later." He paused and the warmth of his smile echoed in his voice. "Everyone loves Lillian. She's been a great stepmom, and I have two sisters now. Elizabeth is almost five, and Anna is seven, same age as Betsy."

"I look forward to meeting all of them." *Mamm* returned the smile and then turned to Betsy. "I'm sure Betsy will be anxious to meet Elizabeth and Anna."

Betsy's eyes sparkled with mischief and grew rounder as she spoke. "Lizzie at my school said an evil witch used to live at that house."

"What?" David cinched a brow and leaned forward.

"Betsy!" *Mamm* glared at her. "That's enough!" She turned to David. "I apologize for *mei maedel*, David." She faced off with Betsy again. "Where in the world do you hear such nonsense, such silliness that is not proper talk?" Then their mother straightened in her chair as she folded her hands in her lap. "I reckon to have a word with Magdalena about this." She turned to David. "That's Lizzie's *mamm*," she said as she cringed. "They're from Missouri." Then she shrugged, as if that explained it.

Canaan was home to Old Order Amish families from Pennsylvania, New York, Indiana, Ohio, Michigan, and Missouri. Folks had slowly been settling in this southern part of Colorado for about seven years. From what Emily had learned over the past three months, some were buying land at cheaper prices than in their home state. Others said there was a shortage of land where they lived. And she'd recently met an older man and woman who left their Order in Indiana because they disagreed with the way their bishop was running the community. Then there were those folks who seemed to be running from something—like her own family. She instantly wondered which category David and his family fell into.

"David, how did you come to purchase the property?" *Mamm* tilted her head to the side as the tiny lines above her brows became more evident.

"My great-grandfather purchased it." David shrugged. "I don't think he ever saw the place. He bought it off a computer at the library before he died. *Mei daed* said Grandpa Jonas bought it mostly for the land, but said we'd have lots of work to do on the houses." He shook his head. "But I reckon none of us knew it was gonna be this much work."

Betsy chuckled. "That's for sure."

Mamm pointed a warning finger in her direction. "Be quiet, Betsy." Her mother turned back to David and took a deep breath. "Well, as you know, we're all about hard work, and I'm sure the community will pitch in and help."

David's mouth tipped up on the left side as he nodded. "We might need some help. I know *mei daed* and Lillian would appreciate it."

Betsy crossed her small legs, pressed her lips together, then peered at David. Emily recognized the expression and feared Betsy was about to disobey their mother again.

"Lizzie said there are snakes in the basement that the witch collected, and I'm not going to that house." She shook her head back and forth.

Mamm bolted upright from her chair, and Betsy's face twisted into a frown. "Betsy! To your room. Right now. You are being rude." Their mother pointed to the stairs as her face turned a bright shade of red. "There is a load of clothes on my bed that needs folding. Tell David good-bye."

Betsy huffed and then stood up. She gave a quick wave in David's direction; then she stomped across the room to the stairs. *Mamm* waited until Betsy was out of earshot before she turned her attention to Emily.

"Where does *mei dochder* come up with this silliness?" *Mamm* sighed. "I will most surely be havin' a talk with Lizzie's mother."

Emily shrugged, and *Mamm* turned back to David. "I apologize for Betsy. We continue to scold her for making up such outrageous stories. Betsy is a smart girl, but she has a big imagination." She took a deep breath and stood taller. "I'm sure that you and your family will make the *haus* into a wonderful home. And I'm sure the community will help you."

David nodded with a half-smile, then stood up from the rocker. "I best be going. I've still got to go to Monte Vista for some supplies."

Emily wasn't surprised by his desire to get out of their house. He probably thought they were all a bit *ab im kopp*. He'd witnessed Emily react like a crazy woman earlier in the shop, and Betsy said there were snakes in his basement left there by an evil witch. Emily couldn't help but grin. Maybe he wouldn't come around too much.

But then there was *Mamm*. Always trying to make up for her family's actions by running her perfect household with a smile on her face. Always perfect, always happy. It never mattered what happened, *Mamm* carried on as the ideal *fraa* and *mudder*, with her flawless *haus* and her ability to pretend that everything was good . . . all the time. Betsy often made that difficult, but three months ago it had been Emily who challenged her mother to face tragedy and still keep a smile on her face.

"Wait right here." *Mamm* jumped up and scurried toward the kitchen. Emily drew in a breath and blew it out slowly as she avoided David's eyes on her. *Don't look at me.* She wanted to reach up and cover the scar on her forehead, but doing so would only draw attention to it, so she fought the urge, leaned into the back of the couch, and kept her eyes down.

"Guess I'll see you Sunday." David smiled as he spoke, and Emily felt her chest tighten.

Her mouth dropped open slightly, but she quickly snapped it shut. After a moment, she said, "You won't like the singings here. Hardly anyone comes." She shook her head as she stood up and faced him. "I wouldn't waste your time."

"Jacob said there will be some single ladies here."

Emily locked eyes with him for the first time since he'd arrived. Nervously, she moistened her dry lips and shrugged. "Maybe." Then she looked away as her stomach churned, wishing he'd just leave and not come back. She knew his type. Charming and good-looking—but deceitful, which could cause a girl to let down her guard.

She shivered as a brief flashback threatened to squeeze her throat shut and leave her breathless, a feeling she'd had more than once.

"But *you* don't want me to come on Sunday?" He rubbed his chin for a moment, then dropped his hand and fumbled with his hat.

Emily was relieved when *Mamm* walked back into the den.

"Here, David. You carry these things to Lillian." *Mamm*

pushed a large, brown paper bag toward him. "There are three loaves of bread, some pretzels, and a batch of my famous oatmeal cookies." She smiled as David stood and accepted the bag. "And you tell Lillian to stop by anytime. And not to panic. We will all help you get things together at your new home."

"*Danki*, Vera. I know Lillian will be real appreciative." He moved to leave, *Mamm* following. Emily was relieved when he was almost out the door.

He turned around before he pulled on the handle. "See you Sunday, Emily." An easy smile played at the corners of his mouth. Emily bit her bottom lip, then forced a smile.

"*Gut, gut.*" *Mamm* gazed at him as if he were the answer to all her prayers.

Emily began to calculate. *Today is Wednesday. Four days.*

Four days to find an excuse not to be at her own house during the singing.

Two

Lillian held little Elizabeth's hand as they waited outside the outhouse for Anna. Elizabeth had no qualms about venturing across the front yard to their primitive accommodations, so Lillian couldn't understand why her older daughter refused to make the trip by herself.

"Anna, are you almost done?" Lillian sighed and fought to tamp down her building anger about this move. She knew Samuel thought it was best for all of them, and she struggled not to question God's will, but as she stood outside the boxlike structure with a half moon carved on the wooden door, she just shook her head.

"It's stinky in here, *Mamm*."

Lillian leaned her face closer to the door. "Then you best hurry, no?" She smiled down at Elizabeth; then she gazed across the snow-covered flatlands of their new home. She raised one hand to her forehead to block the sun's glare. It was amazing how there could be so much snow on the ground and yet the sun was blazing down on them. It felt much warmer than Lillian knew it to be. She lifted her eyes to the mountains that surrounded them in every direction. Samuel said to think of it as the Promised Land, a place where they'd start anew and get out of debt. Every time she thought about their home in Lancaster County, her eyes watered up. Now was no exception.

She couldn't fault her husband, though. After David's kidney transplant five years ago, Samuel had struggled to keep up with everything. Samuel's shunned brother, Noah, had donated one of his kidneys to David and had paid for most of the expenses related to the transplant surgery, the larger invoices that would have put a strain on the community health care fund. However, medical bills continued to trickle in long after the surgery, and David's medications cost over a thousand dollars a month.

"But isn't that what the health care fund is for?" she'd asked Samuel when she found out he'd taken out a mortgage on their home. Her husband didn't feel comfortable extracting additional funds for follow-up care because several of the elderly folks in their district were receiving chemotherapy for cancer. Samuel also refused to allow his brother to continue paying the bills.

"Anna, aren't you done yet, *mei maedel*?" Lillian knocked on the door.

"Almost."

Elizabeth let go of her mother's hand and reached down into the snow, piling a mound in her hands. "Elizabeth, don't do that." Lillian gently eased her up and brushed the snow from her black mittens. "We don't know what's underneath all this snow." She glanced around the yard and focused on a pile of tin lightly covered in white powder. Junk. Everywhere.

The door swung open, and Anna jumped out, her cheeks a rosy shade of red. "It's cold and stinky in there. When is *Daed* going to make us a bathroom?"

Not soon enough. "It's the first thing on *Daed's* list." Lillian reached for Anna's hand, and the three of them made their way back to the house, following the path that had been formed from prior trips to the outhouse today. As they crossed the yard, she looked to her left to see Katie Ann sweeping the porch of their home. The smaller house was about a hundred yards away, and from what Lillian had seen of it the night before, it was in much better shape than this oversized shack they were living in. But Samuel said that Katie Ann and Ivan didn't need this big house since they didn't have any children.

Lillian pulled on the screen door, pushed the door to the den open, and felt the musty smell of lingering water rush up her nostrils. Samuel temporarily repaired the leaky roof earlier that morning, but it was going to take a long time to rid the house of the dingy odor.

"Where do we hang our capes, *Mamm*?" Anna stared up at Lillian, batting her inquisitive eyes.

Lillian sidestepped a pile of boxes to her right. "Somewhere in all this mess, there is a hat rack. We'll run across it. See if there are any pegs on the wall in the kitchen." She pointed to her left. "And be careful where you step, Anna. Some of those boards in the kitchen feel loose. Step very carefully, honey, okay?" Lillian shook her head and grumbled. *This house* must *be safe for my children.* Her life back in Lancaster County was luxurious compared to this.

"Here you go, sweetheart. Let me help you." Lillian untied the strings of Elizabeth's bonnet, then removed her cape. They both followed Anna into the kitchen.

"No pegs, *Mamm*." Anna held up her small black cape and bonnet.

Lillian sighed. "Here, give it to me. We'll just put it here for now." Lillian draped the items over the back of Samuel's chair at the head of the table. At least their table, two backless benches, and two arm chairs were in place in the kitchen. She glanced at the box on the kitchen counter, the one with the broken plates inside, and supposed that if those were the only things damaged, she could live with it. The moving company had done an excellent job overall, but loading the buggies into the moving vans had been challenging. And Samuel had been visibly relieved when the horse trailer finally pulled up to their new house with his long-time horse, Pete, and two others inside.

"What's that?" Anna pointed to an electrical outlet in the wall.

"It's for electricity, like the *Englisch* use."

"Why's it here?"

Lillian smiled at her beautiful daughter whose prayer covering was on crooked. *So many questions.* She leaned down, straightened the *kapp*, and tucked Anna's light brown strands beneath the covering. "The people who lived here before weren't Amish, so they had electricity in the house. We won't be turning it on, but those outlets are all over the house." Lillian looked at the light bulb dangling from a cord above the kitchen table. She pointed to it. "See. They had lights."

"It stinks in here too, *Mamm*." Anna clamped her nostrils closed with her fingers.

Elizabeth copied her sister. "*Ya, Mamm. Schtinkich.*"

Lillian put her hands on her hips and sighed. She could either get upset or just try to go along with things and know that their lives were in God's hands, and that His will would be done. She leaned down and tickled Anna and Elizabeth, bringing forth loud giggles. "Everything stinks to you two this morning, doesn't it?" Lillian pulled both her girls into a hug and basked for a moment in the comfort of family, promising herself that there would be no more worrying. She had her husband and children, and they were all healthy and safe. So much to be thankful for.

"I love you both. It won't be like this forever." Lillian eased out of the hug. "Your *daed* should be home from town soon. He went to buy some plumbing supplies, and David should be back from the grocery store before long also." She walked into the den, Anna and Elizabeth following, and picked up two boxes of old pictures from her former life, before she'd converted to the Amish faith and married Samuel. "I'll be right back. I'm going to go put these things in the basement."

IT WAS THREE hours later when David turned into the driveway of what was supposed to be their new home. He grimaced as he maneuvered the buggy to the left of an old tractor partially covered in snow and blocking part of the driveway. The snow had stopped shortly after he left the Detweilers' place, and the trip to Monte Vista hadn't been as bad as he'd feared. It was longer than he cared for, but most of the snow on the roads had been cleared, pushed into mounds on either side. Now the sun shone brightly atop the glistening snow that surrounded their house.

Why here? He knew land prices were high in Lancaster County, and that farmland was becoming scarce there, but his father had plenty of land for all of them. It didn't make any sense. He unhooked Buster and led the animal to one of the four rundown barns on the property, his black boots sinking to his ankles in the snow as he walked. Shaking his head, he couldn't believe that his *daed* had sold their home in Lancaster County so quickly to make this move, despite David's many objections. And why did Lillian go along with it? David recalled the look on her face when they pulled onto the property yesterday. He thought she might cry. Then she saw the outhouse, and David knew that it was only a matter of time before Lillian would convince his father to move back to Lancaster County. It had to be. At least he hoped so. Without his own money, David had no other choice but to live here too.

After he secured Buster, he started to walk toward the house when the sound of hoofbeats made him turn. His father was pulling up the driveway. As he waited, he scanned the yard around the house, much of which was covered in snow. But even the snow couldn't hide the litter. A pile of tires, some old chairs, and a whiskey barrel were visible beneath a thin layer of white, and to his left was a pile of tin. So much debris to be carried off. Then there was the house. Badly in need of a new roof, new floors, and some insulation. In his upstairs bedroom, he had actually felt the frigid wind blowing through the cracks in the walls last night. Even the bathroom was poorly put together. It had a tub and sink with running water, but no toilet. *Why?* Wouldn't it have been just as easy to put in a commode?

"How was your trip to town?" Samuel trudged across the yard with a smile stretched across his face.

"It's a long way to Monte Vista from here." David met his father in the yard and took two large plastic bags from him. His father balanced long white pipes across his shoulder, and David could see more of them hanging out of the back of the buggy.

"After you put those bags in the house, can you go get the rest of those pipes and haul them upstairs?"

"Sure, *Daed*." David eased his way up the porch steps ahead of his father, then into the den.

"Samuel, is that you?"

"It's both of us, Lillian. *Daed* is coming in behind me." David held the door as his father wound through the threshold with the plastic piping still draped over his shoulder.

"Where's the toilet?" Lillian met Samuel at the doorway.

His father put the piping down, then stroked his dark beard and grinned. "Toilet? I must have forgotten that."

Lillian slapped her hands on her hips. "You better not have returned to this house without a toilet, Samuel Stoltzfus!"

Samuel pulled her into a hug and nuzzled her neck. "Or what?"

"No more meals until me and the girls have a toilet in this house! Do you hear me, Samuel?" She eased him away, but *Daed* grabbed her face in his hands and kissed her.

David shook his head. "Stop it. Not in front of your *sohn*." He couldn't help but grin. His father and Lillian were as happy and affectionate with each other as the day they'd gotten married. David regretted that he'd never have that, someone to love for a lifetime.

"Where are Anna and Elizabeth?" David set the bags on the floor with a thud, hoping to break up the smooching going on. "H-E-L-L-O?" He knocked on the wall beside him.

"*Ach.* Sorry, David." Lillian grinned at David briefly, then turned back to Samuel and pushed him away. She put her hands back on her hips. "Where's my toilet?"

"In the back of the buggy, *mei lieb*." Samuel scooted past her. "Where are my girls?"

Lillian relaxed her arms at her side and smiled. "The nicest woman came by earlier. Her name is Vera Detweiler, and . . ."

"*Ach!* The groceries." David moved toward the door. "I got everything on your list, and that woman you mentioned, I met her too. She sent some bread and stuff for you."

"She told me. She said she decided to come by and see if she could help me with anything. She brought her little girl, Betsy." Lillian laughed. "When she got here, Anna and Elizabeth were running around the boxes like wild animals. We talked for a while, and then she offered to take them to her house to play with Betsy so I could get some unpacking done."

David turned around before he walked out the door. "Her daughter Betsy is nothing like Anna and Elizabeth."

Lillian moved closer to the door, her forehead wrinkled. "What do you mean? Vera seemed very nice, and Betsy is seven, like Anna."

"Seven going on seventeen." David grunted. "She's some sort of whiz kid. A bit of a smarty pants."

Lillian cocked her head to one side. "I didn't notice that about Betsy, but then she didn't really say too much." She looked toward the basement door. "Although she was rather obsessed about seeing our basement. I finally showed her, even though her behavior seemed to embarrass her mother."

David shook his head as Lillian pushed a box out of the way with her foot.

"Well, Anna needs friends. I don't think Elizabeth will have any trouble making friends when she gets into school next year, but Anna doesn't warm up to people as quickly as Elizabeth. It will be good for her to have a new friend here, to help her get adjusted in her new school. Can you go pick up the girls around three at the Detweilers' house?"

David took a deep breath. *I've been traveling half the day*. "*Ya*, I reckon so." He turned to walk outside, and as he started down the steps, he heard Lillian yell, "*Danki!*" Back at the buggy, he draped four plastic bags over his wrist and carried Vera's goodies in the other arm. Is this what he'd always be, their running boy, with no family of his own? No. As soon as he could get a job and save some money, he was heading back to Lancaster County. He would purchase a place of his own, and at least he'd be around other family and his friends in the beautiful place he'd been raised.

He thought about Anna and Elizabeth, and his stomach churned with anxiety. It would be hard to leave them, even harder than leaving his father and Lillian. When he was almost to the front porch, loud voices caught his attention, and he turned toward the smaller house on the property. He couldn't make out what was being said, but Uncle Ivan and Aunt Katie Ann were definitely having words. Probably about living in this place. He'd never understood why his aunt and uncle wanted to make the move here either. This community wasn't nearly as well-kept as Lancaster County. The mountains were nice, but the homes weren't as attractive or bright as those in his hometown of Paradise. To give Canaan credit, Amish families had only begun settling here six or seven years ago, as compared to Lancaster County where generation after generation had lived, making it a draw for tourists. That's one thing he didn't miss. Tourists.

His father said that this move to Canaan represented new beginnings for all of them. But why did they need a new beginning? Everyone had been happy where they were.

He opened the front door, wound around the boxes in the den, and put the groceries on the kitchen table.

"*Danki.*" Lillian began unloading the store-bought groceries; then she opened Vera's bag. "That was so nice of Vera. I really like her." She pushed a box to one side and placed the items on the cracked blue tile that covered the counter. She turned to face David. "What did you think about the rest of Vera's family?"

David shrugged. An image of Emily's face flashed before him. He'd never seen a woman look so scared, but inside her house, she'd looked comfortable—yet she'd given him the cold shoulder. Last thing he was interested in was going to a Sunday singing, but he'd made sure to tell Emily he would be there. Why? Just to bug her? It was obvious she didn't want him there. *Lord, what is wrong with me? Please help me to shed all this bitterness.* She was a strange girl, but it wasn't like him to go out of his way to make someone uncomfortable.

"I didn't meet Mr. Detweiler or Levi, the other son. I met Jacob, though. He seems like a nice guy. And I met the older daughter, Emily. I guess she's close to my age." David grabbed a soda from one of the bags, then held up his hands when Lillian frowned. "There's no tea or anything, so I bought these with my money." He'd only bought a couple of cans, but he knew that he needed to be more watchful of the small amount of money that he had. Once he had a job, he could start adding to it, and then get back home.

"It's not the money. They're just bad for you." Lillian thrust her hands on her hips and stared down at a large, white ice chest filled to capacity. "We have to get a refrigerator we can hook up to the propane." She pointed to the antique in the corner. "Don't even open that refrigerator. I already made that mistake. The contents are unidentifiable, and it smells foul."

"I'll haul it out."

Lillian smiled. "That would be great. Can you handle it by yourself?"

"Can you handle the smell?"

His stepmother giggled. "All I can do is laugh." She glanced around the kitchen with its cracked countertops, cupboard doors with chipped blue paint that were hanging by a single hinge, and possibly worst of all, the blue and gold striped wallpaper. "If Bishop Ebersol could see us now."

"Why'd you let *Daed* talk you into this?"

Lillian quickly turned away from him and ran her hand along a gas stove that had been there since way before David was born. Probably before *Daed* and Lillian were born. With her back to him, she shrugged. "Your *daed* thinks this is the best thing for us."

"How can it be? I mean, look at this place, Lillian. It's a wreck inside and out. Why would *Daed*—"

Lillian spun around, her eyes pleading with him. "David, we've been through all this. Please try to make the best of it."

He let out a heavy sigh. "I will, but I just don't understand why we have to."

"We are hard workers, David. We will make this place into a beautiful home." Lillian shoved a box out of the way with a hard push of her foot, and then she forced a smile. "Now, tell me about Emily. Vera said she's nineteen. Is she nice?" Lillian grinned mischievously. "Is she pretty?"

David thought about Emily's big brown eyes and how her cheeks flushed a dark pink color when he spoke to her.

"She's pretty enough, I reckon. But she's . . . different." David pulled the bench out and straddled it. "She went nuts when I was in the store, acted like I was going to hurt her or something."

"What?" Lillian sat down in the chair at the end of the table. "Why would she think that?"

David pulled off his hat and ran a hand through his hair. "I was a bit of a jerk." He watched Lillian's expression sour. "But, Lillian, trust me. It was nothing to make her go all crazy the way she did."

They sat quietly for a moment as Lillian twisted the strings on her *kapp*. Finally, she said, "Vera said they moved here from Middlefield, but I got the impression she wasn't telling me the whole story, about why they moved."

David scowled. "Is that so odd? I'm sure you and *Daed* aren't telling *me* the whole story about why we moved here either." He raised his brows, and Lillian looked away. She stood, then turned to the counter and began to nervously shuffle items around. *I'm right.*

"Well, I'm glad you're going to the singing on Sunday. It will be good for you to meet some people your own age." Lillian kept her back to him as she spoke.

"I guess."

"*Ach*, cheer up. Don't sound so gloomy." She twisted her head around and smiled. "Maybe Emily is someone you'd like to get to know better." Then her expression turned thoughtful, followed by a shadow of annoyance. "Maybe you can show her you're not such a scary guy, although I can't imagine why an Amish girl would be scared of an Amish man. It's not our way to be aggressive."

David thought about the scar that ran from Emily's brow to her hairline. "I think someone must have been aggressive with her before."

"Why do you say that?" Lillian leaned against the counter facing him and crossed her arms against her chest.

"She's got a scar that runs from here to here." He slid his finger from his brow all the way up to his hairline.

"That doesn't mean she's been hit. Accidents happen on farms all the time, you know that."

"I reckon." He paused. "But it would explain the way she acted around me."

"Hmm . . ." Lillian turned back around and busied herself by pulling plates out of boxes. "Uh-oh. This is Katie Ann's box." She held up a large, white serving bowl. "This stuff is all hers. Can you run it over there, maybe after you get that smelly refrigerator out of here?"

"That's me. The runner boy." David pulled himself off the bench. Lillian walked over, leaned up, and kissed him on the cheek. "I love you, David. Everything is going to be all right. I promise."

"I know." He eyed the old refrigerator and sighed.

KATIE ANN STEPPED out of the way so Ivan could pass her in the den. Once again, they'd spoken harshly to each other over a subject that wasn't worth arguing about. Ivan couldn't find any suspenders and had insisted that Katie Ann didn't pack them. She knew she had.

Eventually a silent truce emerged, and they resumed the unpacking.

"Where do you want this box?" He stopped a few feet from her and heaved the box up to get a better grip.

"In the extra bedroom." She pointed down the hall and

watched him march that way. He hadn't stopped working all day long, barely even ate any lunch. She didn't have much food to offer since their arrival last night, but she'd scrounged up some bread she'd brought with her and opened a jar of peanut spread. "No, not that bedroom." She edged toward the hallway. "That's the baby's—" She stopped herself. "I mean the sewing room."

Ivan didn't even turn around. He just kept going toward the room across from their bedroom. His broad shoulders disappeared around the corner. She waited.

When he never came out of the room, she tiptoed down the hallway and peeked around the corner. Her husband of almost twenty years was sitting in a chair next to the treadle sewing machine, surrounded by boxes. His elbows were propped on his knees, and his hands covered his face.

"Ivan?"

He looked up at her with tired eyes. "I'm just resting for a minute."

"We don't have to do all this today. Maybe we could take the buggy to town and have supper out. I'll do a full round of shopping tomorrow and stock up on everything we need, no?"

He nodded, then slowly stood up. "That sounds fine." He walked toward her, stopped and patted her arm, then moved out the door.

She rubbed the spot where his hand had just been and fought the buildup of tears in her eyes. She'd been so angry for so long, and now when she tried to put the past behind them, Ivan was as distant as she'd been before they moved.

Please, Lord, bless our new start. Help us to find each other again, to love each other the way a husband and wife should. Give me strength, Lord.

She left the room, but not before turning around and having a good hard look at her sewing room, with all the items necessary to make it just that. Her treadle machine, her comfy chair, baskets of yarn, boxes of material yet to be unpacked . . . Yes, everything to make this into a perfect sewing room. But all she could see—all she'd desired to see for so long—was a baby crib, a dresser with changing table and diaper bag hanging nearby, and tiny little clothes hung neatly on the pegs. But as she neared forty, her vision remained just that . . . a vision. She closed the door.

Her longing for a baby and her struggle with depression had almost cost her their marriage, but she couldn't reconcile that with what Ivan had done. Somehow she had to find balance, solace, and a way to move forward in her life without a child. A way to mend her marriage. A way to forgive Ivan.

When she walked into the den, Ivan was opening the front door. Her nephew, David, walked in toting a box.

"*Mamm* said this is yours." He handed the box to Ivan, who set it against the wall beside a lot of other boxes yet to be unpacked. Katie Ann watched David scan the den, then lean around and peer into the kitchen. "Wow. Nice place compared to ours." He grinned.

"Tell Lillian that I will help her with that big *haus*. I know there is much to do." Katie Ann moved toward David and touched his arm. She could still see him as a teenage boy, sick from kidney failure, which had been the scariest thing her family had ever gone through. And look at him now. A tall, handsome young man.

"I think if *Daed* can just get her a toilet put in, she'll be okay." He chuckled.

David was of marrying age now. She hoped he'd find someone special to share his life with. The thought made her mentally cringe in contrast with her own marriage.

"Does Samuel need me to come over now and help him put in a toilet? Let me get my jacket." Ivan reached for his black coat thrown over the couch nearby.

"But . . . but I thought we were going to supper." Katie Ann didn't miss how fast Ivan put his jacket on and practically pushed David back toward the door.

"I'm sure Lillian has something to eat over there, no?" He turned his attention to David as he reached for his hat.

"Sure. Not much. But we won't go hungry." David eased his way out the door, but then stepped back in. "Katie Ann, you wanna come?" Katie Ann stared at the back of Ivan. He continued down the snow-covered sidewalk without even turning around. She forced a smile. "No, David. But *danki*. I think I'll eat a sandwich and unpack some more boxes."

"Okay." He turned and followed Ivan, closing the door on his way out.

Katie Ann stood on shaky legs, looking at the door. How dare he treat her like this? How dare he blame their discord completely on her? She wasn't the one who had been unfaithful.

Three

Emily finished folding a load of clothes she'd piled on the bed, then she headed downstairs to check on Betsy and her two new friends. The youngest Stoltzfus girl was entertaining herself with some of Betsy's building blocks, but Anna was sitting cross-legged in front of Betsy, her eyes wide.

"The Bible doesn't say that," Betsy was saying. She flung her hands in the air. "It says for God so loved the world that He gave His only begotten Son, not *forgotten* Son." She shook her head as she pushed the Bible in Anna's direction. "See?" She pointed to the middle of the page.

Betsy had read the Bible three times cover to cover, but the biggest problem with being a seven-year-old who knew everything was that other seven-year-olds did not.

"Betsy, are you being sweet to your new friends?"

Her little sister sighed, then tipped her chin upward to meet Emily's eyes. "Of course."

"I'm thirsty." Anna rubbed her eyes as she spoke.

Betsy sat up taller. "We're almost done. 'For God so loved

the world, that he gave his only *begotten* Son, that whosoever believeth in him should not—' "

"Betsy! Get your friend a drink if she's thirsty." Emily put her hands on her hips. "Be nice." It was no wonder Betsy had trouble making friends. Her younger sister was sensitive, protective of those she loved, but entirely too smart for her own good and often misguided in her attempts to form friendships.

Betsy closed the book and slowly rose from the floor. "I'll be right back." She padded across the wooden floor in her black socks, but before she reached the kitchen, she turned to face Anna. "Do you know how many days it takes to form a habit?"

Emily glanced at Anna while straightening some magazines on the small table next to the rocker, curious what Anna's response would be to Betsy's off-the-wall question.

Anna's sweet little face flushed red, and she tucked her chin. "I don't know."

"Betsy, does it really matter?" Emily plopped down in the rocker and sighed. "Go get your friends something to drink. I put some paper cups and a small pitcher of tea on the table for you and your friends earlier."

"Twenty-one days." Betsy gave a nod toward them. "It takes twenty-one days of doing a particular task before it becomes a habit." She spun around on her heels and headed toward the kitchen.

Emily feared Betsy was never going to make real friends.

"I like Betsy." Anna's face glowed. "She's *so* smart."

Emily stifled a grin. "*Ach*, she's smart all right." She put her elbows on her knees and leaned closer to Anna. "So, how do you like your new *haus*?"

Anna bit her bottom lip for a moment. "We don't have a bathroom."

"That's what I heard from your brother." She leaned back in the rocker. "But isn't your *daed* going to put a toilet inside the house?"

"I think so." Anna leaned back on her hands.

Five-year-old Elizabeth walked to Emily's side. "It's stinky in the bathroom in our yard." She put her hand on the arm of the rocker.

Emily patted Elizabeth's hand, smiling. "I'm sure your *daed* will have you an indoor bathroom very soon, no?"

A knock at the door sent Emily's pulse racing. She'd heard her mother say earlier that David would be coming to pick up his sisters. Both girls raced to the door, and Anna pulled on the knob. "David!"

Emily stood up and walked toward the door and watched as both girls wrapped their arms around their brother's legs, squealing and carrying on as if they hadn't seen him in days or weeks. David leaned down and pulled them into a group hug. *He seems like a good man.*

"Did you girls have fun?"

Anna pulled away from him and stood tall. "Did you know that it takes twenty-one days to form a habit?" Her bright blue eyes sparkled.

David looked Emily's way for the first time, smiled, then looked back at Anna. "Is that so?"

Emily shrugged, looked at David briefly, but quickly pulled her gaze away. "A little something she learned from Betsy."

Betsy entered the room toting two paper cups. "Here." She offered one to Anna and one to Elizabeth.

"*Danki*," they both answered as they eased away from their brother and accepted the drinks. David was watching his sisters, so Emily allowed her eyes to drift in his direction. She jumped when she heard the back door slam and turned to see her mother lugging in two logs from the woodpile out back.

"Going to be cold tonight." *Mamm* stopped when she saw David, and her voice oozed as she spoke his name. "David, how *gut* to see you. I see you've come for the girls."

David narrowed the gap between them. "Here, let me." He lifted the logs from *Mamm*.

"Why, *danki*, David." Her syrupy tone evoked an eye roll from Emily. She watched David place the logs in the carrier next to the fireplace.

"David, do we have a toilet yet? Did *Daed* make us a bathroom?" Little Elizabeth tugged on her brother's pant leg.

David scooped her into his arms. "*Daed* and *Onkel* Ivan are working on that right now."

"*Yay!*" Anna jumped in the air.

Betsy crossed the room and stood right in front of Anna. "Next time we will go over Corinthians, and—"

"Betsy, I'm sure Anna doesn't want to have Bible study every time she comes over." Emily frowned at her sister, but Anna reached out and grabbed both of Betsy's hands. To Emily's surprise, Betsy didn't pull away and instead just smiled.

"I don't mind." Anna faced Betsy as the girls swung their hands from side to side. "I like to learn things from Betsy."

Betsy's face lit up, and it warmed Emily's heart. But this would mean seeing David more, and that was something she was confused about. His sisters clearly adored him, and he'd certainly won over her mother. But that made him all the more dangerous for her to be around. If he truly was a good person, someone she could care about, then there would be nothing but heartache in it for her. She was damaged. Ruined for any man. She reached up and touched the scar on her head, wishing instantly that she hadn't. When she pulled her hand down, she glanced at David. His expression was filled with pity, and that's one thing she didn't need.

"Excuse me." She turned to head up the stairs.

"See you Sunday, Emily."

That's what you said this morning, yet here you are already. She didn't turn around.

VERA WATCHED AS David loaded Anna and Elizabeth into the buggy, and she wondered what really had brought his family to Canaan. Lillian had said they all needed a fresh start, but Vera recognized the hesitancy in Lillian's voice. How many times over the past three months had Vera responded this same way when someone questioned their move from Middlefield? She waved from the porch as David and the girls pulled out, then she headed back inside to see that Emily had returned from upstairs. Her daughter was curled up on the couch, her legs tucked beneath her, with the familiar sense of sadness in her expression that kept Vera up at night. She sat down beside Emily.

"Where's Betsy?" Vera tucked one leg under herself and twisted to face Emily.

"She went upstairs. She said she was going to read a book."

Vera sighed. "I hope it's one we've approved." She shook her head. "That *maedel* just can't seem to soak up enough knowledge, but I don't want her reading about the wrong things."

They sat quietly for a moment, and Emily was far away, in a place that didn't exist until three months ago, and Vera longed for a way to make everything the way it was before.

"Do you know what I think we need?" She gave Emily a quick pat on the leg, then stood up. "We need a slice of snitz pie with a big scoop of ice cream on it." She shrugged. "So what if it's snowing outside. Pie and ice cream sounds *gut* just the same."

"I don't want any, *Mamm*." Emily continued to stare into nothingness, and Vera recalled a time when Emily thought there wasn't an ailment that snitz pie and ice cream wouldn't cure.

"Are you sure? Because you know when your *daed* and Levi get home, they're going to dive into the rest of that pie, and we'll be lucky to get any at all."

"I'm sure." Emily tucked her bare feet beneath her dress as she stayed curled up on the couch.

"You need socks on, Emily. I'll go get you some." Vera turned to head up the stairs.

"*Mamm*, I don't need socks. I don't need pie. I'm fine." Emily straightened her legs out and put her feet on the floor. She gazed up at her mother. "I'm going to go upstairs and take a bath before Levi gets home and hogs the bathroom."

Emily stood up, and Vera watched her trudge up the stairs as if taking a bath was her most dreaded chore. That's how Emily approached everything these days.

Please, Lord, let her forgive, forget, and move forward.

Though she tried to keep it out of her mind, Vera found herself thinking about what had happened to her daughter. It made her weak in the knees. And at those times she allowed herself to visualize it, she felt nauseous and angry beyond anything that God would approve of. With each wicked image of her baby girl being taken advantage of in such a way, Vera found herself having thoughts that were not in line with her upbringing, which was something that kept forgiveness just out of her reach.

AFTER HER EARLY bath, Emily closed the door to her room, thankful that she didn't share a room with Betsy, as she'd done in Middlefield. This house was no bigger than the one back home, but was laid out in such a way that five small bedrooms allowed each one of them to have their own space.

She laid down on her bed and cupped her hands behind her head, knowing she didn't have long before it would be time to help her mother with supper. Her stomach rumbled at the thought of food, but she already knew that once she sat down to eat, she wouldn't feel hungry anymore. The image of James sitting across from her at the diner would always slam into her mind, and she'd lose any appetite she'd worked up.

She recalled how flattered she'd been when James asked her to go on a real date. What she wouldn't give to go back in time. Her first mistake had been to lie to her parents about her whereabouts. She'd never lied to her folks, or anyone, prior to that. But she knew her father wouldn't have approved of her missing her Uncle Abram's birthday supper to go on a date with James Miller or anyone else. That's why God had punished her. For lying.

Emily recalled her words exactly. "*Daed*, I'm sick to my stomach. I'm not going to be able to go tonight." Her mother had come into her room shortly after, toting a tray with chicken soup, crackers, and hot tea, which only added to her building guilt. But it was James Miller. She had to go. And it was only a few blocks walking distance to the small diner where they'd planned to meet.

She clamped her eyes closed and fought the onslaught of images dumping into her thoughts. A simple kiss. Her first kiss. A kiss that went terribly wrong.

Every horrible detail was carved into her mind.

She repeated the words she'd said over and over since that night in September.

"I forgive you, James. I forgive you."

Hopefully someday she would mean it.

But she would never tell. She'd never tell who her attacker was. The policemen had questioned her over and over again and said there would be a meeting in front of a judge to decide what would happen to the person who'd hurt Emily. She wasn't sure she heard everything the policeman said that day, but she did hear the part about how she would have to tell a roomful of people what James did to her, and that was more than she would be able to bear. And what would James's parents think? Would James be shunned? Neither Emily nor the members of their small district would have been able to endure it. So she told yet another lie. "I took a walk to get some fresh air," she'd said. "And . . . I didn't know him . . ."

Emily heard her father and Levi talking with her mother downstairs, so she slowly rose from the bed to go help with supper. On her way down the stairs, she bumped into Levi coming up. As usual, he avoided looking at her. Was the scar on her face so repelling that her own brother couldn't look at her? She'd even overheard their mother speaking to him about his attitude, saying that he needed to act as normal as possible and to stop looking so sullen.

That was *Mamm's* answer. Pretend it didn't happen, and it will eventually go away.

Emily didn't think so.

When she entered the kitchen, her father was removing his black coat and black felt hat, both dotted with melted snow. He turned in her direction.

"*Mei maedel*, how was your day?"

Emily found her father's question so sincere. He wasn't avoiding her pain.

"It was *gut*, *Daed*." She smiled, knowing it was a partial lie, but justified her words with the fact that parts of the day had been bearable. Emily tried to stay upbeat around her father. She knew that he was devastated about what had happened to her. He never tried to hide his pain, and he silently understood hers. But she chose not to hide her misery from her mother. Maybe just once, *Mamm* could talk to her about it, comfort her, tell her that she wasn't the ruined woman she knew herself to be. Instead, always laughter. Always happy. And Emily resented her mother more and more each day.

Everyone knew Betsy was coming when the china in the cabinet began to rattle. She hopped down the stairs, both feet hitting each step at once, and then skipped across the den to the kitchen.

Betsy knew something bad had happened to Emily. It was the first and only time Betsy had ever seen a police car, and everyone was crying. Besides Emily, Levi had cried the hardest, even pounding his fist into the wall. *Daed* had overlooked Levi's aggression in light of everything.

"I'm going with Emily in the car with the lights!" Betsy had screamed that night as she clung to Emily's blue dress.

That was the last thing Emily remembered before she passed out and woke up at the hospital. She threw the blue dress in the garbage two days later.

"Emily, did you hear me?" Her mother slapped her hands to her hips.

"Huh?"

"Please put the chow-chow, jams, and jellies on the table." *Mamm* shook her head, then pointed to the bread on the counter. "Betsy, can you put the butter bread on the table, please?"

Emily realized that she'd come downstairs too late to help with supper preparation. She used to love cooking for others, but since she wasn't fond of eating these days, the cooking wasn't as fulfilling as it used to be. Just the same, her parents expected her to help with the meals, and she shouldn't have been late.

Levi came downstairs a few minutes later, and everyone took their seats. Emily sat next to Betsy on one wooden bench, Levi and Jacob across from them on the other bench, and her parents at opposite ends of the table in arm chairs that her father and Levi had built.

"Let us pray." The family bowed their heads.

Once they'd all prayed silently, her mother picked up a large pan of meatloaf. "Levi's favorite tonight." She smiled at Levi as she passed him the casserole dish, a glimmer of hope in her eyes that perhaps Levi would try to be happy, but once again he let her down.

Emily wanted to scream at him. *Why are you so unhappy? Nothing happened to you! Stop acting this way!* But she reminded herself that she didn't have the exclusive right to be miserable. Maybe there was something going on with Levi that no one knew anything about. Maybe he was more upset about leaving Middlefield than he'd let on.

"I have news." Their father lifted his brows and glanced around the table as he let *Mamm* spoon some potatoes onto his plate. "We have enough money in our community fund to start construction on the new schoolhouse when the weather clears, and I have six people in our community committed to helping out on Saturdays." *Daed* shook his head. "If we were in Middlefield, gathering workers wouldn't be a problem, but there just aren't very many of us here. But a nice *Englisch* fellow volunteered to head up the project. He's been a carpenter all his life, so we're in good hands." Then *Daed* smiled, as was his way. Her father always recognized the hardship of a given situation, but then he'd find a way to make the best of it. Emily was sure that her father believed he could turn anything bad into something positive. She knew it frustrated him that he couldn't do this for her. But Emily found *Daed's* approach to life endearing. It was as if he was saying, "I'm sorry something bad happened to you. I care, and I love you. It's okay to feel it, and I'm going to do my best to keep things going around here."

She recalled a time when she wasn't much older than Betsy. It was the first year she'd helped her mother plant a garden, and Emily had insisted that they have watermelons, something they usually didn't plant. She could still remember her father's excitement when the first sprig of growth popped through the soil. They all worked hard to avoid pride, but her father had kept Emily's first watermelon on display on the kitchen counter for so long that it almost became inedible. He showed it to everyone who came to visit.

"*Mei maedel* grew this. It's the finest watermelon I've ever seen," he'd said. Emily could still recall how proud she felt, and within a few years, she was completely in charge of the garden. Jacob did the tilling, but Emily did all the planting and harvesting, and her appreciation for the soil paralleled her father's. Many evenings they sat on the front porch after supper, and Emily would tell him about her garden, and her father would talk about the plentiful crops he had going in the fields. Working the land brought a profound sense of stewardship and close connection to God. Emily wondered if she would capture any of those precious moments in this new place when spring arrived.

In Middlefield, her father and brothers had worked the land full-time, but here in Canaan, *Daed* and Levi also had the construction and solar panel business they would be tending to, in addition to farming. Jacob was to tend the store with Emily and split his time in the fields. *Daed* said these changes were necessary until they knew how their crops would fare in this new climate.

"There's a new family in town, Elam." *Mamm* sat up taller. "They have a daughter, Anna, who is Betsy's age, another daughter who is five named Elizabeth, and . . ." Her eyes twinkled with hope. "And a young man named David who will be coming to our singin' this Sunday. He's Levi's age, I believe." She smiled in Emily's direction.

"He seems like a *gut* fellow." Jacob reached across Emily and began to spoon potatoes onto his plate.

Emily glowered at him. "I could have passed you the bowl." She leaned back as his arm came much too close to her glass of milk.

Jacob didn't react to her comment and instead piled another heap of potatoes on his plate. "Maybe he'll help us with the schoolhouse. I'll ask him Sunday when he's here."

Emily saw Levi scowl, but he didn't say anything.

"The mother's name is Lillian." Her mother shifted her weight in the chair. "And listen to this! She actually converted from the *Englisch* world about eight years ago, then married David's father, Samuel." *Mamm* cocked her head to one side and pressed her lips together. "So interesting. I've never known anyone who came from the other side."

"I'm teaching the girls about the Bible." Betsy raised her small chin and smiled at their father.

Emily remembered Betsy's Bible lesson with Anna. "Betsy, why don't you just behave like a normal little girl, play and have fun when you have friends over?" She knew the question was harsh, and there was that word again—*normal.* When Betsy's mouth fell into a frown, she softened her tone. "I mean, I'm sure Anna and Elizabeth's parents teach them about the Bible at their own home. Maybe they'd like to put a puzzle together or play a game?"

Betsy scrunched her face into a pout. "You can't learn much by doing that."

"Sometimes you just need to have fun, Betsy." Emily took a small bite of meatloaf.

Levi grunted as he reached for a slice of bread. "Maybe you oughta take your own advice."

Emily slammed her fork down. "You're not exactly running around here all happy, Levi. Maybe you best not tell me how I'm supposed to feel, or act, or be . . ." She felt tears building in the corners of her eyes.

"That's enough," *Mamm* warned each of them. "This is not proper behavior for the supper table."

Jacob pushed his plate back. Her oldest brother didn't like any type of confrontation, and Emily saw him cringe before he quickly bowed his head in silent prayer, then excused himself. "I'll go get the horses secured in the barn. Supposed to be real cold tonight, I heard."

"That's what I heard too." *Mamm* pointed toward the den. "I already hauled in some extra logs."

Emily watched as Jacob pushed his chair in and left the room. She'd never been as close to Jacob as she was to Levi, but all that had changed recently. When Levi withdrew inside himself for reasons none of them could understand, Jacob had stepped in and seemed to silently understand Emily's pain. He was much like their father in that regard.

She didn't hear much of the rest of the conversation. She picked at her food, but for once, there was no ugly replay going on in her mind. Instead, she was thinking about David Stoltzfus. A handsome, single man. And, apparently, a nice person. But Emily knew that she needed to avoid him, not get close to him. She reached up and grazed the scar with her finger. What would someone like David Stoltzfus want with her anyway?

Just the same, she planned to avoid the singing on Sunday somehow.

DAVID HAD NEVER seen a group of women so excited about a commode before.

Lillian rushed to Anna and Elizabeth the minute they walked

in with him. "We have a bathroom in the *haus, mei maedels*!" She pointed toward the stairs. "Go see!"

Anna and Elizabeth squealed all the way up the steps as Lillian followed.

"Glad to make the women folk happy." His father rounded the corner from the kitchen toting a steaming cup in his hand. "We just got here yesterday, but they made it clear that it was their first priority." *Daed* chuckled, then surveyed the den. Boxes were everywhere, but David knew his father was looking beyond the obvious clutter. "Lots of work to do on this *haus*, son."

David sighed. "Where do we start?" He scanned his immediate surroundings. Wooden floors rotted in places, cabinet and screen doors barely on their hinges, and chips of blue paint falling from the wood-planked walls. He could even feel cold air from outside seeping between the cracks as they stood there.

"Tomorrow I think we best start caulking these walls. We're gonna have a hard winter to go through, and best to get things weathertight before we worry about the looks of the place."

David nodded. "Sounds *gut*." He looked toward the kitchen. "I don't smell any supper," he said in a whisper.

"Lillian said she can't cook in the kitchen with all the clutter, so we're having ham sandwiches. It's all laid out. I'm sure we'll eat after Anna and Elizabeth both try out the new toilet."

David rubbed his belly and looked around. "*Onkel* Ivan go back to his *haus*? I thought he might stay for supper."

"He went home, mumbling something about taking Katie Ann out to eat." *Daed's* brows furrowed as he walked closer to David. He lowered his voice. "I think your *aenti* and *onkel* are having some problems. We need to offer extra prayers for them."

"What do you mean 'problems'? In their marriage?" That seemed unlikely to him, but his father nodded. David stared at a spot on the floor. "Is it serious?"

"I don't know. Ivan won't talk to me about it, but I've sensed unhappiness between them for a while now." *Daed* rubbed his forehead. "I think that's the reason they wanted to make this move with us, for a fresh start."

"That makes sense." David lifted his chin, putting him almost eye to eye with his father. He couldn't resist asking, "You and Lillian havin' trouble too? Is that why we had to make this fresh start?" He knew good and well that his father and Lillian were as happy as any married couple could be, but this was his roundabout way of getting the truth, he hoped.

"David, I know you don't believe that, and we've been over this a hundred times. There needs to be enough land for everyone, and prices are—"

"I know, *Daed*. That's what you keep telling me." He ran a hand through his hair; then he shook his head. "I'm gonna go get cleaned up for supper."

David walked up the stairs to his room. He eyed the bed, dresser, and nightstand he'd brought from Lancaster County, then glanced at a rolltop desk that had been left in the far corner of the room by the prior owners. It was a battered piece of furniture that badly needed refinishing. He tossed his coat and hat onto the bed, since there was nowhere else to hang them, and wandered down the hall to the bathroom, glad the girls had cleared out.

He inspected the new toilet. One toilet was better than no toilet. Maybe they'd get another bathroom put in downstairs soon. He twisted one lever of the antique faucet, and cold water slowly trickled out, splashing onto the rusted porcelain below. Then he turned the other lever, hoping for hot water. After a couple of minutes, he gave up and ran his hands under the droplets, gasping as he brought a handful of icy water to his face. He picked up a green towel draped across the sink and patted his face dry.

He could hear everyone gathering in the kitchen downstairs, and his stomach rumbled full force.

LATER THAT NIGHT David popped a handful of medicines into his mouth, the same thing he did every night and every morning. That's the way it would be for the rest of his life, however long that would be. He swallowed the four pills with a glass of water and thought of the conversation he'd overheard between his father and Lillian five years ago. He'd only been home from the hospital about a week, and his fifteen-year-old mind hadn't really considered what he'd been through.

"I don't care what the doctors say," he'd heard Lillian say. "Ten years is only the average time that a kidney will last."

Hearing those words had been difficult. Not just about the kidney transplant, but realizing that his chances of living a full life had been cut short. He'd decided on that day that he was not going to get married. He remembered when his mother died and how that destroyed his father. He wanted to avoid inflicting that type of hurt on someone. When he heard Lillian speak his fate, he came to terms with it. He'd accepted God's will, and he planned to be the best man he could be, void of any long-term goals or commitments.

He turned up the lantern on his nightstand and glanced

around at all the boxes he had yet to unpack. Hard to believe they'd only arrived last night. Today had been a full day. He thought about Emily and the way she'd reacted this morning. He picked up the bottle of prednisone on his nightstand. The doctor had warned him that his new dose was fairly high and could cause him to be unusually irritable. He set it down and decided he would watch out for any signs that the medication was causing him to be bad-tempered, even though he didn't really think his conduct should have been enough to make Emily cry. Maybe Sunday he'd learn more about her.

Four

EMILY HELPED BETSY INTO THE BACK SEAT OF THEIR covered buggy, then reluctantly crawled into the front seat with her mother, bumping her head on the metal enclosure as she got in. She rubbed the spot, wishing she didn't have to attend Sister's Day.

"It will be *gut* for you to be around Beth Ann and the other girls, Emily." *Mamm* got comfortable in the seat, then flicked the reins until the buggy began to slowly pull forward. "I was going to ask Lillian to join us for Sister's Day, her and the girls, but I reckon she probably has too much to do."

"All Beth Ann does is talk about hers and Jacob's wedding plans." Emily sighed. "I'm sick of hearing about it."

"Beth Ann is going to be your brother's *fraa*, your sister-in-law. You should be sharing in their happiness. Their wedding is only a month away, and it will be a joyous occasion." Her mother sat up in the seat and smiled. "Even if it is a bit of a whirlwind courtship."

Emily still couldn't believe that Jacob was marrying Beth Ann after only knowing her three months, but everyone loved Beth Ann, and Jacob was happy.

Mamm picked up the pace and guided the buggy down the

cleared driveway. Emily had heard her brothers shoveling snow early that morning.

"I think Beth Ann is going to be a *gut mamm*." Betsy leaned forward between Emily and their mother. "I hope they have *kinner* right away." She leaned back again. "You know, in nine months after their wedding. That's how long it takes for a baby to grow inside the mother's womb."

Emily snapped her head around. "Don't you think we know that, Betsy?"

"You don't have to yell at me!" Betsy opened her mouth and let out an ear-piercing scream, which she was known to do when she was mad. *For someone as smart as Betsy*, Emily thought, *she can certainly be an immature brat.*

"Betsy! What have I told you about that screaming?" *Mamm* turned her head to face Betsy. "I will not have that, *mei maedel*. You cannot just scream like that when you are mad. Do you hear me?"

Betsy let out a heavy sigh. "Yes, ma'am."

"I don't know why the three of us just can't have a nice day and everyone be in a *gut* mood and get along, as it should be." *Mamm* shook her head, then sat up taller in the seat and lifted her chin. "This will be a *gut* day, and we will all be happy, no?" She glanced back at Betsy before raising her brows in Emily's direction.

"*Mamm*, you can't force happiness on everyone around you." Emily pulled her eyes away and folded her arms across her chest, squeezing tight in an effort to warm herself.

They rode silently for a while, and as *Mamm* turned a corner, Emily gazed past the flat, snow-covered San Luis Valley toward the Sangre de Cristo Mountains to her east. She closed her eyes and envisioned herself climbing to the top of one of the peaks. At around eleven thousand feet, she imagined she'd be nearer to heaven and would feel closer to God.

It was a silly thought, but she longed to climb the mountains just the same.

"I'm glad we don't live in that house where the witch used to live." Emily turned around in time to see Betsy pointing to the homestead that David and his family now owned.

"Betsy!" *Mamm* groaned. "Do not refer to the Stoltzfuses' home in that manner again, and especially don't use those words in front of the other women today." *Mamm* put the reins in one hand, then rubbed her forehead with her other hand. "There is no such thing as witches."

Emily made the mistake of giggling.

Mamm yanked back on the reins and slowed the horse, then came to a complete stop as they neared a stop sign. "Do you think this is funny, Emily?"

Emily shrugged. "*Ya*, I guess I do."

"You are being disrespectful, both of you." *Mamm* twisted her body in the seat to face Emily, then looked back and forth between Emily and Betsy in the backseat. "I want this to be a *gut* day."

"Why does every day have to be a *gut* day for you, *Mamm*?" Emily threw her hands in the air. "I don't always have *gut* days, but Betsy did something I thought was funny, so I giggled." She paused, raised her brows. "But unless the happiness is on your terms, in your perfect little world, then it's not all right."

Emily had never spoken to her mother like that before. *Mamm's* eyes rounded, her lips pressed tightly together, and she took a deep breath. "Emily . . ." She breathed in again. "Our Lord would not approve of the way you're behaving, and—"

There was a calmness in her mother's tone that only caused Emily to react even more harshly. "He wouldn't approve of the way *you* act either, *Mamm*! How can you always be happy after what happened to . . ." She glanced at Betsy, whose bottom lip was quivering. Emily let out a heavy sigh. "I can't always be happy, *Mamm*."

"We need to pray, girls." Her mother bowed her head.

Emily shook her head as she opened the door of the buggy. Like so many other times in the past three months, she didn't want to talk to God. There were no cars anywhere in sight on the rural road, and she stepped out of the buggy. "I'm not going."

Mamm raised her head as her eyes grew wide. "Emily, you get back in this buggy!"

"I can't do it today, *Mamm*! I just can't! I don't want to go be around Beth Ann and everyone else, to have to smile and pretend." She bent at the waist and held her stomach for a moment, then rose up when she heard her mother's door slam.

Mamm rounded the back of the buggy. "Emily, please just get back in the buggy."

"I can't." Emily moved slowly away from her mother. "Not today."

"How will I explain your absence at Sister's Day?" *Mamm* thrust her hands on her hips, atop her heavy black coat.

Emily's jaw dropped. "I can't believe you, *Mamm*. You just don't get it! And all you're worried about is how to explain why I'm not there?" Emily kept easing backward, then turned and started walking briskly back home, trying to avoid patches of snow still left on the asphalt.

Her mother called after her, and Emily could hear Betsy screaming again, but she just kept walking, the frigid wind burning her cheeks, tears streaming down her face.

DAVID WAS GLAD to be working outside, feeling the sun on his back. His father and Lillian had decided to take Anna and Elizabeth with them to town this morning before getting started on the caulking or resuming the unpacking. He lifted his black boot high, then sank it into fresh snow and stopped to put his hand to his forehead. To the west stood the San Juan Mountains, capped in white, with sparse sprigs of greenery on the lower peaks. Though he wasn't thrilled about his new home, the massive mountain ranges in every direction were awe-inspiring, and he liked the way the sun blazed down from blue skies, making the snow glisten like glitter for as far as he could see.

He pulled on the barn door, then pulled again. When it wouldn't budge, he leaned down and hand-shoveled snow until the door opened enough for him to squeeze through the opening. Benches and tables that they'd brought from Lancaster County were stacked on one side of the barn. He doubted they would need half of the tables and chairs whenever it came their turn to hold worship service. His father had already told him that there weren't many folks in the area, and only a few families made up the district here. Because of that, David felt a sense of isolation. Despite the beauty of the mountain ranges, he found himself struggling not to see the high peaks as borders of entrapment.

On the other side of the barn, there were a few boxes that he needed to bring into the house, and in the corner were some rusted tools and empty barrels left by the prior owner. He glanced around the rest of the barn, surprised by how clean it was in comparison to the house. *Maybe I'll just live out here.* He grinned to himself as he made his way to the horses stabled on the far side.

Pete, his father's horse, had been around for as long as David could remember, and his own horse, Buster, was a fine animal that David received for his sixteenth birthday. Jelly Bean—named by Anna, who preferred that food over any other—was their newest horse, but not yet buggy broken.

"Hello, Jelly Bean." David stroked the horse on the snout, then checked the water and feed for all three. He glanced around the barn again and decided some of the old debris outside could be stacked in the barn for now.

He made his way back into the yard to start hauling some of the junk inside, things that Anna and Elizabeth might get hurt on. That's when he saw a girl walking down the street.

Emily?

EMILY KNEW SHE would be reprimanded when her mother returned home from Sister's Day later this afternoon, and she regretted the way she'd spoken to her, but she was so tired of pretending that she was happy. She'd been raised to believe that everything was God's will, even the really bad things. But she just couldn't wrap her mind or heart around how God's will could include what had happened to her. She prayed at every meal and during their devotion time, but something had changed. Her communion with God was not the same.

She pulled her black coat tighter around her. It was starting to snow again, so she pulled the rim of her black bonnet down and tucked her chin to avoid the cold flurries showering her face. She folded her arms across her chest and clutched her elbows, shivering as she walked down the road. She thought of Sister's Days back home in Middlefield. About once a month the women would gather, visiting and canning, quilting, or perhaps even cleaning house for someone who was unable. It was always filled with laughter and fellowship, and she couldn't remember ever missing the occasion. But that was when she had her entire life ahead of her. Today it would have been too much to listen to Beth Ann recite every detail of her upcoming wedding.

James's face flashed in her mind, like a scary picture she couldn't erase. She closed her eyes tight for a moment but couldn't seem to shake the vision. She could almost feel his hands on her, the intrusive way he touched her in places that were not appropriate. She'd asked him nicely not to do that following the kiss they'd shared, but James hadn't listened. She remembered pushing him away from her in his car. Then James had looked at her, and Emily would never forget the way that his eyes had shifted, rounding into balls of anger as he'd grabbed her by the arm and pulled her toward him.

If there was anything to be thankful for, it was the fact that she'd blacked out certain details of the next few minutes. Her next memory was of running as fast as she could on shaky legs, gasping for breath as she cut across a field beneath a barely moonlit sky. Then she'd run through dark trees toward home. She cringed as she recalled the doctor stitching up her head, a permanent reminder of that night. But even more painful was the news he delivered when he was done.

A tear trickled down her cheek as she relived that evening

at the hospital. She heard the doctor saying to her parents, "I'm so very sorry. Emily was raped."

Emily wasn't familiar with the term. Her father left the room without looking at her, and with tearful eyes, her mother tried to explain what the word meant. What little detail her mother offered was enough for Emily to understand that she was no longer fit for marriage. *Mamm* didn't say that, but Emily knew it to be true. When Emily asked if she had sinned or gone against the teachings of the *Ordnung*, her mother assured her that she hadn't. But Emily knew that no man would want her now. Since then she couldn't seem to find the peacefulness that she'd always felt in her heart. She knew that fear and worry blocked the voice of God, but she'd stopped seeking Him. She was afraid she would be alone for the rest of her life, with no husband or children, and worry about the future consumed her. Her prayers lately were mechanical, simple, and without the heartfelt connection she'd once treasured.

She kicked a rock in the road, then blew out a deep sigh and watched the frigid air cloud in front of her. She wanted to talk to God the way she used to. But God had allowed this to happen. It was His will that she was damaged, with little hope for the future.

Movement to the right caught her eye. She lifted her hand above her brow to block the bright sun and drizzling snow. She found the combination of warmth from the sun and cold from the snow all around her to be odd. She squinted until she made out the person walking toward her. *David Stoltzfus.*

She tucked her chin, pulled her bonnet lower on her forehead, and picked up her pace.

"Emily!"

Hugging her coat tighter around her, she walked even faster.

He yelled her name again, and as she cut her eyes in his direction, she saw him crossing the yard toward her. "Wait!"

She let out a heavy sigh between her chattering teeth, turned toward him, and waited.

"What are you doing?" He stood on the inside of a wooden fence that surrounded the property. "Why are you walking in this weather?" David pulled his own black coat tighter around him, and Emily could see his teeth chattering also.

"I—I just am. *Mei mamm* and Betsy went to Sister's Day, and I changed my mind about going." She forced a smile. "Nice to see you. Good-bye." Then she headed down the road.

"Wait!" David trudged slowly through deep snow until he was at the gate. He pushed it open and walked toward her. "I'll hitch up my buggy and take you home. It's startin' to snow real hard now."

Emily stopped. "No. It's not much farther. I'm fine." She turned toward the road again.

"You don't look fine. I reckon you're freezing to death."

"I have to go." She'd only taken a few steps when she heard him coming up behind her. She spun around and faced him. "Are you going to follow me?"

"*Ya*. I guess so. I can't let you walk all the way home by yourself. So I reckon I'll have to freeze to death too, to make sure you get home all right."

He smiled, and his dimples added a childlike quality to his expression, which she found adorable. She resisted the urge to grin and put her hands on her hips. "Well, that's the silliest thing I've ever heard."

"*Ya*. It is." He tipped his black felt hat down to block the falling snow. "So you should just let me give you a ride home. I can have Buster hitched to the buggy in no time."

She was chilled to the bone, and the thought of David following her all the way home was embarrassing. "Fine."

"Go in the *haus* and get warm. It won't take me long. I think Lillian left some *kaffi* on the stove."

"Are your folks home?"

"No. But just go in and help yourself." He pulled the gate open for her to walk ahead of him. She stopped.

"I—I don't think it's proper for me to go inside your *haus* without anyone home."

"It'll be just fine." He reached out and took her arm to coax her through the gate.

The feeling of his hand on her arm jarred her. She jerked away from him and took a step backward. "Stop it. I've changed my mind. I'm going to walk." She spun on her heel, but he spoke up before she even took a step.

"Emily!"

She turned to face him again.

His eyes were kind as he spoke. "I don't know what happened to you, but I promise you a thousand times, I will never hurt you. Do you understand me? Never. You're safe here."

Emily lowered her head. "I don't know what you're talking about."

He didn't step forward this time as he spoke. "A fellow doesn't have to be too smart to figure out that something bad happened to you, or I figure you wouldn't have got so upset at the store."

She opened her mouth to defend herself. Maybe it was the soothing tone of his voice or the gentleness in his eyes, but she paused for a moment, then realized how her behavior gave her away. She sighed. "I can't talk about it."

David walked toward her again. This time she didn't back away. "You don't ever have to talk about it. I just want to be your friend. I don't know anyone here." He paused before speaking softly, "Go get something hot to drink. I'll be out here getting the buggy ready. Just meet me outside when you're warm."

"Okay." By now, her cheeks were so numb they burned. She slid by him and started toward the house while he went to the barn.

Once she'd eased her way up the front porch steps, she pulled open the screen door, which was hanging by one hinge, then pushed the heavy door open. She could smell coffee, but the soothing aroma was mixed with a stale odor that caused her to grimace. In the kitchen, she took in the blue and gold wallpaper, a couple of cabinet doors also hanging by one hinge, and the many boxes still left to unpack. *So much work to do.*

She found a travel mug with a lid, similar to what her family used during cold weather. Then she helped herself to the coffee on the stove. The warm liquid helped to stifle the shakiness that consumed her entire body. She found another mug, filled it up, and secured the lid.

Outside, she approached David, carrying both cups.

"Ready," he said when he saw her.

"I brought you some too." She handed him one of the cups.

He smiled as he accepted it. "*Danki.*"

She walked around to the other side of the buggy, climbed in, and saw a portable heater on the floor.

"That will keep your feet warm," David said as he backed the buggy up. She leaned down and flipped it on.

David waited until they were on the road before he said anything. "It's a mess in there, huh?" He nodded over his shoulder toward the house.

"It will just take some time, that's all."

He laughed. "A lot of time."

Emily smiled, enjoying the sound of his laughter. Her heart felt a little lighter, her burdens not as heavy at the moment. "I'm sure *Mamm* will set up a Sister's Day for Lillian so we can all help her get the place in order."

David nodded. "I know Lillian would be grateful for any help."

"I really could have walked," she said as David pulled into her driveway less than five minutes later. "I told you it wasn't that far. Barely worth the trouble of hitching the buggy up."

"A couple of miles in this weather feels like more. I don't know about you, but I'm having trouble with the altitude. I reckon I couldn't have lived with myself if I'd gotten word later that Emily Detweiler was found frozen in her boots." He grinned, and Emily felt her face flushing.

"Well, I'm used to the altitude, but *danki* for the ride." She pushed on the door and stepped out, then turned to face him briefly.

"You're welcome."

As she walked up the path to her house, she knew one thing had changed. She no longer wished to avoid David by not attending the singing. A thought that excited and terrified her.

Five

EMILY PULLED A CLEAN BLUE DRESS OVER HER HEAD. THE singing would begin soon, and she found herself thinking about the tender way David had talked to her the last time she saw him. *"I don't know what happened to you, but I promise you a thousand times, I will never hurt you. Do you understand me? Never."* And she wanted to believe him. She knew in her heart that James had been an exception, that most men were not like him, but letting her guard down didn't come easy. On the flip side, what if David Stoltzfus was the most wonderful man on the planet, his character a mirror of his handsome looks? Then she would only set herself up for heartache because marriage won't be in her future. Just the same, she couldn't help but look forward to seeing him.

Mamm hadn't said much to Emily when she'd returned home from Sister's Day with Betsy. Emily knew she was mad, but as was *Mamm's* way, she'd quickly recovered and made it her business to make sure that everyone around her was happy, including Emily. So, in light of her guilt over the way she'd behaved, Emily faked happiness for her mother's sake for a few days.

"Emily!" Hop, hop, hop up the stairs, then Emily's door bolted open. "*Mamm* said to come downstairs. People are starting to get here." Betsy pointed one toe forward as she put her hands on her hips.

"I'm coming, Betsy." Emily sat down on the bed and quickly tied her shoes. "Who's here?"

"Hannah, Beth Ann, Edna, Leah, Amos, and . . ." Betsy rolled her eyes. "That David Stoltzfus person."

Emily stood up and put her hands on her hips. "Now, Betsy, stop that. David is Anna and Elizabeth's *bruder*, and they are your friends."

"He made you cry." Betsy's bottom lip curled under.

Emily walked to Betsy and squatted down in front of her. She cupped Betsy's chin in her hand. "Betsy, he didn't mean to. Sometimes I'm just too sensitive."

"Do you think David Stoltzfus is a *gut* man?"

Emily thought for a moment, about how she'd thought James was the best man in the world. She could spend her life in fear and worry, or choose another path, one God would prefer. "I'm going to choose to believe that David Stoltzfus is a *gut* man." She kissed Betsy on the cheek. "Come on. Let's go downstairs."

When Emily hit the bottom stair, she could hear voices in the kitchen. She rounded the corner to find David surrounded by all the single women—Hannah, Edna, and Leah. All three ladies were seeking a suitor in this small community, and Emily knew David could have his pick of any of them. She approached the group slowly and greeted everyone.

"*Mamm* has everything set up in the basement," she said. "There's plenty of food, games set out, and Jacob set up the shuffleboard table. I think he's down there playing with Levi."

She stretched out an arm toward the door leading downstairs. "So, please, everyone make yourselves at home."

"Come on, David." Hannah latched onto David's elbow. "I've been here before; I'll show you the way." Hannah batted her eyes at David.

David eased out of Hannah's grip and gave her a soft smile. "You ladies go on ahead. I need to talk to Emily for a minute." David winked at Emily when their eyes met, and Emily felt one knee give beneath her.

Hannah's face twisted with disapproval, and she gave a begrudging nod. David waited until everyone was out of earshot, then walked closer to Emily and said, "Let's take a ride in the buggy after the singing."

Emily's defenses piqued. "I can't."

"Just a short ride."

Footsteps rounded the corner. "She said she *can't*." Levi positioned himself in front of David. "Didn't you hear her?"

"Stop it, Levi. It's fine." Emily gently touched Levi on the arm, but he jerked away, eyed David, and headed out the kitchen door.

David arched his brows. "I reckon people from Middlefield are more aggressive than where I come from in Lancaster County. What was that about anyway?"

Emily shrugged. "*Ach*, just ignore Levi. He's been overprotective since—" She bit her lip, but David seemed to be waiting.

When she didn't go on, he said, "It's okay, Emily. You don't have to tell me. Now or ever. But just know that you're always safe with me. I promise."

She smiled. "Maybe just a quick ride after the singing later."

David smiled. "*Gut*."

David hung around until all the guests had left. Hannah Kauffman had been as flirty a girl as he'd ever met. She was from Minnesota. He'd never met any Amish women from Minnesota before.

Hannah was only seventeen, and she didn't behave like most of the Amish women he knew. She spoke softly, but she was also a bit bold, touching him constantly on the arm and never leaving his side. With her silky, black hair and big green eyes, David was sure any fellow would jump at a chance to spend time with her. But she just wasn't his type. Emily was more—

He recognized the thought and quickly pushed it aside. Emily had issues. And David knew he had his own problems. But the prospect of friendship with Emily interested him. He'd been taught his entire life that a person's looks didn't matter. He was human, though. He liked the way she walked, light on her feet with her hips swaying naturally. Her eyes were a warm brown, and when her lids slipped down, as they did when she seemed embarrassed, her long lashes brushed against high cheekbones.

"Emily will be right down." Vera came down the stairs smiling. "That's so nice that the two of you are going on a ride. Do you have a heavy blanket?"

"*Ya*. And a heater." David returned the smile, anxious for Emily to get downstairs. He'd only talked to Vera a few times, but she always left him feeling as though she was secretly plotting a wedding.

David looked up when he heard footsteps. "I won't be gone long, *Mamm*." Emily buttoned a thick black coat as she spoke, then tied her bonnet.

"Take your time." Vera smiled; then she turned toward her husband when he entered the room. David had met Elam Detweiler earlier that evening. "Elam, these young people are heading out. Remember when we were that age?"

David felt his face redden, and he glanced at Emily and saw her cheeks doing the same.

Once they were outside and walking through the snow toward the buggy, Emily said, "I'm sorry about *mei mudder*."

David opened the door for her. "About what?" He knew, but he wanted to hear what she'd say. He walked around to the other side and got in, then turned toward her.

Emily shrugged. "You know . . . the way she acts."

David smiled. "*Ach*, you mean the way she's already planning our wedding."

Emily avoided his eyes and bit her lip as the moonlight shone through the buggy and onto her flushed cheeks. She nodded. "So silly."

"*Ya*, it is."

Emily reached up and dabbed at the scar above her brow, then left her fingers there as if trying to hide it. Most women her age were looking for a husband, but David didn't want her to think that her scar had anything to do with the boldness of his statement.

"We barely know each other," he added with a smile.

She pulled her hand down but stared straight ahead. David flicked the reins and moved the horse into action, and they slowly trotted down the driveway. When they pulled onto the main road, he reached in the backseat of the buggy and pulled out a big brown blanket.

"Here." He handed it to her.

Emily took it, then reached down and clicked on the battery-operated heater. She draped the heavy blanket around her shoulders, wrapping her arms tightly around herself.

Emily fought the chill that ran from her head to her toes, unsure how much of it was from the frigid air. This was the first time she'd been alone with any man, outside of her immediate family, since her date with James.

Before she could stop herself, Emily said, "I'm not even sure why I came with . . ." She cut her eyes in David's direction and saw him raise his brows.

"Not sure why you came with *me*, no?" He grinned.

Emily turned straight ahead, sat taller, and folded her hands atop the blanket. She shrugged. "I figured you'd rather take Hannah, or maybe Edna, for a ride." Emily wished right away that she hadn't made the comment.

David turned his head toward her and grinned again, but then his expression soured. "I reckon those two are lookin' to be courted." He paused. "I got no plans to date anyone."

"Why?" She gritted her teeth and silently reprimanded herself for asking the question.

David shrugged. "Just not in my plans."

Emily's curiosity was piqued. Why wouldn't someone as handsome and seemingly kind as David Stoltzfus not be looking for a wife at his age? Maybe he was just telling her that, so as not to hurt her feelings. "I understand."

He turned toward her, captured her with his clear blue eyes, then turned and faced forward again. "I doubt it."

He'd mumbled it, but Emily heard it just the same.

"What about you?" David eased the horse onto Jenson Road. "Guess you don't have a boyfriend?"

"Why would you just assume that?" *What's wrong with me?* She blasted herself again for speaking every little thing on her mind.

"Whoa, don't get upset."

"I'm not upset." She'd said it louder than she intended. "I'm not upset," she repeated but more quietly this time.

"I reckon if you had a boyfriend, he would have been at the singing. Right?"

Emily didn't say anything for a moment. She folded her arms across her chest, shivering, despite the heater and the blanket. "Where are we going?" It wasn't like they could drive to town for coffee. It would take much too long to get to Monte Vista, especially this time of night and with the temperature dropping.

David rubbed his forehead. "I don't know. I didn't plan too *gut*." He glanced at Emily. "I'm sorry, Emily. This was a bad idea. Not the best weather for a ride."

"I'm all right. The heater is keeping my feet warm." She forced a smile. *No, you didn't plan very well.*

David shook his head. "This is the worst ride I've ever taken after a singing. It's cold. There's nowhere to go. I don't know what I was thinking."

Emily imagined David had carted a lot of pretty girls home after Sunday singings, as was customary if you were interested in the possibility of a romance. He'd said that was not the case, but still, his criticism about tonight stung.

"Then just take me back home. I don't want to be thought of as the worst ride you've ever had after a singing."

David slowed the buggy, and even in the dim moonlight,

she could see him frowning. "Sorry. That's not what I meant, Emily. It's not you. There's just nowhere to go and it's so cold."

"Then just take me home."

They came to a gravel road on their right, and David turned the buggy onto it. "Let's at least get off the main road. Maybe we can just sit and talk, if we don't freeze."

Emily's stomach started to churn, and she fought the vision of her and James in his car in Middlefield. David was nothing like James. He couldn't be. She'd seen him with his sisters. She'd never known much about James. Only that he had incredible good looks. Of course, David did too. She took a deep breath.

David cut off the lights in the front of the buggy, and Emily gasped. "It's too dark." Her heart began to beat hard in her chest. "Turn the lights on."

"But look how pretty it is. It's a full moon. You can even see the tops of the mountains over there, and—"

"Turn the lights on!" Emily slapped her palms against the dash of the buggy. "Now! Turn the lights on!"

Click. The headlights illuminated the gravel road in front of them. "Okay, okay! They're on." David twisted in his seat to face her. "I'm sorry, Emily." His teeth were chattering, but his eyes clung to hers. "It's just . . . pretty out here. I mean, the full moon and everything. I didn't mean to scare you."

He swung his arm over the seat, and Emily slid sideways into the buggy door. "No," she whispered.

"I'm getting a flashlight I have in the backseat." David slowly pulled a small black flashlight across the seat between them. He flicked it on, then shined it near the side of her face. "Are you crying?"

"No." But she knew she was on the verge.

David shone the flashlight on the floorboard of the buggy and lowered his head. They were quiet for a few moments. He took a deep breath and looked at her. "Emily, I don't know what happened to you, but I reckon it was something bad, and it must have been at the hands of someone bad." David paused, and Emily could feel his eyes searching for hers. She finally looked at him, and their eyes locked. "If we're going to be friends, you gotta stop being so jumpy around me. Emily, I will never hurt you." He shook his head. "This was probably a bad idea. Here I've taken you out in the middle of nowhere on a cold, dark night. I'm sorry."

He sounded so regretful that Emily instantly felt the need to make him feel better. "It's all right. You can turn off the headlights."

"Are you sure? Because I can leave them on."

"No. The flashlight is *gut* enough." David turned the lights back off, and they both looked outside. "You're right." Emily stared straight ahead and strained to see into the darkness. "You can see the mountain tops." She smiled as she imagined a stairway winding around the mountain, leading all the way to heaven. "Someday I'm going to climb one of those mountains."

When she turned to face David, he had a dreamy gaze on his face. "You should smile more. You're so pretty, but—"

But what? She reached up and touched the scar.

"I don't even notice that scar, Emily."

She quickly dropped her hand. *But what?*

David smiled. "You were the prettiest girl there tonight . . ." He paused, still holding the light toward the floorboard of the buggy. "But I don't have any interest in dating you. I hope we can be friends."

"I reckon I don't want to date you either." It was true. Or

at least it was true until he said he didn't want to date her. *Why didn't he?*

"*Gut.* Then we'll be friends," he said. Then his forehead creased. "Why don't you want to date me?"

Emily chuckled. "I guess where you come from, everyone wanted to date you. Well, I'm not one of them."

Her laughter didn't invoke the playful response she'd expected. Instead, David pulled his eyes away from her, and his face grew solemn. "I didn't really date back home."

Emily scowled. "I find that hard to believe. Someone as good looking as . . ." Emily faced forward on the seat, and she could feel her entire body flushing from head to toe. She was determined not to look at him.

"Emily?"

She didn't turn his way. "*Ya?*"

"This is *dumm*, no? We're both freezin'." David clicked the headlights on and then took the reins. "I'll take you home." He paused as he motioned the horse into a slow trot. "I guess I was just wanting to get to know you better."

Emily didn't say anything, and her teeth wouldn't stop chattering. The windshield and winter roll-downs didn't keep out the cold very well. They were quiet the rest of the ride back.

David's breath clouded the air in front of him as he turned into her driveway. "I'll see you on Thursday."

"Thursday?" Emily sat taller. "But that's Thanksgiving Day."

David turned his head toward her, his own teeth knocking together. "Didn't your *mamm* tell you that she invited us to Thanksgiving? My *Onkel* Ivan and *Aenti* Katie Ann too."

He faced forward again, but even in the darkness she could see him smiling. *Mamm* had never invited anyone who wasn't in the family for Thanksgiving. But then, back home there were lots of family for them to gather with. Emily scowled. Was her mother really trying that hard to play matchmaker?

David pulled the buggy to a stop in front of her house. It wasn't snowing anymore, but the cold night air was brutal, and Emily took a deep breath before she reached for the handle on the buggy door.

"I'm sorry about tonight." David offered a forced smile. "Next time we go out, I'll plan better."

Emily shrugged. "It's all right." She pulled the door open and jumped down. "Bye." She slammed the door and headed through the frigid air toward home, hugging herself as she trudged in ankle-deep snow. But she'd heard him loud and clear. *Next time we go out* . . .

DAVID STABLED HIS horse and walked briskly toward the house. He could see a faint light coming from his parents' room and assumed they were already reading in bed. Elizabeth and Anna would be asleep by now, so he tiptoed up the rickety porch steps and carefully pulled the screen door open. He jiggled the brass knob on the door until it opened, then made his way through the den to the kitchen.

He jumped when he entered the kitchen, not expecting to find someone sitting on one of the long benches. In the darkness, all he could see was the silhouette of a woman wearing a bonnet.

"Lillian?"

"It's *Aenti* Katie Ann, David. I'm sorry I startled you." She stood up about the same time David reached for a nearby lantern. As he lit it, he heard her sniffling. He held the light upward and saw dampness shining against his aunt's cheeks. She quickly turned her head away from the light and dabbed at her eyes.

"What's wrong?"

Katie Ann bit her bottom lip for a moment, then clasped her hands in front of her. "I—I don't have any milk. Ivan likes warm milk at bedtime. I thought maybe Lillian had some." She paused with a shrug. "I think it's terrible, warm milk. But it helps Ivan to sleep."

David studied her face in the dim light for a moment. He'd always thought Katie Ann was the prettiest woman in their family. She had deep brown eyes that were softened by tiny little lines at the corners, and her full smile lit up a room. Or, it used to. The past couple of years, Katie Ann just seemed sad all the time. David pointed to one of the large ice chests on the floor. "There's some milk in that chest. *Daed* is supposed to be getting a propane refrigerator tomorrow." He grinned. "Otherwise Lillian is going to go bonkers, I think."

Katie Ann pressed her lips together and walked to the ice chest. "I just need a small amount for Ivan. I'll go to market tomorrow." She flipped the latch and quickly located the milk. David watched her fill up a small container, but when she poured too much, it spilled over the side and onto the floor. "*Ach!* No." She set the carton of milk on the counter, then her small plastic container, which sloshed milk on the counter and onto the floor. "I'm a clumsy woman." Her voice cracked as she reached for a towel and began to dab the floor.

"Here, let me." David squatted down beside her and gently reached for the towel. He swiped the rag across the jagged wood. "I don't think anyone would notice a spill on this old floor." He offered her a comforting smile.

Still squatting, Katie Ann covered her face with her hands. "I should have been more careful." She sniffled.

"*Aenti* Katie Ann, it's no problem. Really." David touched her arm, then slowly stood up as she did the same. "What's the matter?"

She shook her head. "I reckon I'm tired. I need to get this milk to Ivan." She reached for the plastic container she'd brought. "I'm sorry."

David leaned against his hand on the counter. "There's no problem, *Aenti* Katie Ann. But are you sure you're all right?"

"*Ya, ya.*" She waved her free hand in the air. "*Danki*, for helping me clean the mess on the floor, and thank Lillian for the milk." She moved toward the door.

"Did you bring a lantern?" David raised the light in his hand slightly.

"No. But the moon is almost full, and I'm just going across the way a bit."

David extended his arm and offered her the lantern. "Here, take this one. I'll get it back tomorrow."

"I really don't need it. I walked over here without one."

David shrugged as she pulled the door open, then pushed on the screen. "I'll see you later, David." Katie Ann didn't turn around as she made her way down the porch steps.

He watched her until she'd made it safely to her own house, then he closed the wooden door. His heart ached for his aunt. And his uncle. Something was going on with them, and it had been for a long time.

He thought about Emily as he tiptoed up the creaky stairs

to his room. He didn't want to date anyone, but when Emily said she didn't want to date him, he'd felt an uncomfortable jab in the heart. He shook his head and grunted. He didn't need to take on whatever problems Emily had. He had enough worries of his own.

He put the lantern on his bedside table, pushed an unpacked box out of the way with his leg, then sat down on his bed. He popped the usual pills in his mouth and followed them with a glass of water. Then he lay back, folded his hands behind his head, and crossed his ankles. Shadows from the lantern danced on the ceiling overhead as he tried to focus on prayer. He tried to recall the last time he'd actually heard the voice of God in his mind, felt the words in his heart. His chest hurt for a moment when he realized that he couldn't remember the last time. He'd been so angry for the past few months, ever since he found out about this move. Fear, worry, and anger. All emotions that blocked a man from hearing God. He took a deep breath and closed his eyes.

Dear Lord,

Please help me to get rid of the anger in my heart about this move and accept it as Your will for me. I pray that this will be a good move for all of us, at least until I can save enough money to return home, to Lancaster County. Lord, I pray for my new friend Emily. I fear she's been hurt in a bad way, and ask You to wrap Your loving arms around her and comfort her. And extra blessings for Aenti *Katie Ann and* Onkel *Ivan.*

KATIE ANN HANDED Ivan a cup of warm milk that she'd heated on top of the stove.

"You didn't need to go out in this cold just to get me some milk." Ivan accepted the cup, blew on the hot liquid, then took a sip.

"I don't mind." She sat down beside Ivan on the couch and put her hand on his knee. It was a big gesture for her, since she'd avoided any contact with him since the day she saw him kiss the *Englisch* woman Lucy Turner. Ivan set his cup down on the table next to the couch, picked up his Bible, and pulled the lantern to the edge of the table. He didn't even notice that she was making an effort. She gingerly ran her hand back and forth across his knee, and she thought about how long it had been since they'd been intimate. Nearly six months. She'd given up conceiving a child long before that, and tonight wasn't about that. She wanted to feel close to her husband again, to somehow move past the pain they'd inflicted on each other.

Katie Ann knew that her failure to give Ivan a child had weighed more heavily on her mind than on his. Repeatedly, Ivan had told her that it was just God's will for them not to have a family, and that they would be happy, just the two of them. More than once, she'd screamed at him, told him she could never be happy with just him, with no children of her own—a real family. And she'd meant it. For years, she and Ivan had drifted apart. Conversation was kept to a minimum, and each had their own interests. Unfortunately, his included Lucy Turner.

When Ivan didn't respond to her tender caresses, Katie Ann eased her hand away from him. Her eyes drifted to his face, and if he would only look at her, he'd see the longing in her eyes. But he didn't raise his eyes from the Bible. *Look at me, Ivan.*

She yawned, covered her mouth, then mumbled, "I'm tired. Are you ready for bed?"

They seldom went to bed at the same time anymore. Ivan often stayed up reading in the den until long after Katie Ann was asleep, and that had been fine by her. But in this new place called Canaan, she hoped for a new beginning, a chance for them to renew their love and start fresh. Perhaps now that she had accepted her life without a child in it, maybe she could shed the anger she felt and be close to her husband again. And forgive his intimate encounters with Lucy. Ivan promised her that all he'd shared with Lucy were several lunches and a few stolen kisses. But she still felt betrayed.

"I'm going to read for a while yet." Ivan didn't look at her.

"Fine." She abruptly stood up. She walked around two boxes still needing to be unpacked, then marched up the first two steps before she swung around and walked back down. "Ivan . . ."

He lowered the Bible and raised his brows. Katie Ann fought the resentment bubbling to the surface by taking a deep breath. She wasn't quite ready to give up. "Maybe—maybe you'd like to come to bed now?" She paused, her eyes pleading with him. "With me." She was hoping Ivan couldn't see her flushed cheeks in the dimly lit room. She bit her bottom lip and waited for an answer.

"I'll be up shortly." He offered her a weak smile, then buried his head again in the Good Book. She was humiliated, but determined to stay hopeful. She turned and hurried up the stairs.

After a quick bath, she pulled a tube of store-bought lotion from the top drawer of her nightstand. A vendor at the Bird-In-Hand market back in Lancaster County sold the flowery scent, and it was a luxury she'd finally allowed herself. She spread it generously up and down her arms, careful not to get the purple cream on her long white nightgown. Vanity and pride were forbidden, but on this night, she wasn't thinking about those things. Tonight she wanted to smell—and look—good for her husband.

When she was done, she lay down in the bed and pulled the covers snugly around her neck. The small propane heater on her nightstand did little to warm her. She needed her husband for that. She closed her eyes and envisioned the last time they made love, but when the image blurred, she realized that for years it had never been about the lovemaking, only the baby making, which never happened. Tonight she wanted it to just be her and Ivan, without thoughts of conception, or of stolen kisses with Lucy Turner. And she knew that if she was truly going to open herself up to a new beginning with her husband, she was going to have to forgive Ivan for his indiscretions. So she waited.

And waited. As her lids grew heavy, she glanced at the clock. It had been over an hour since she came upstairs.

KATIE ANN OPENED her eyes seven hours later, and even in the darkness of the early morning, she could see that Ivan was not beside her. *Did he even come to bed last night?*

She dressed, then went downstairs carrying her lantern. Her heart was heavy as feelings of hopefulness about this new beginning seemed to be slipping away.

"I didn't hear you come to bed last night." She was surprised to see the coffee already made and Ivan at the kitchen table, casually sipping from his favorite green mug and reading *The Budget*—as if he hadn't a care in the world.

Ivan pushed his reading glasses up on his nose. "Do you remember Edwin Yoder, my cousin from Sugarcreek?" He kept his head buried in the newspaper.

Ivan usually scanned the general updates to see if anyone he knew had posted a memo about current events, then he would read through the obituaries. In many ways, *The Budget* was their only way of keeping up with relatives who didn't live nearby, and of course, both she and Ivan were interested in the happenings back in Paradise.

She nodded her head in response to his question, even though he'd ignored her comment. She poured herself a cup of coffee and joined him at the kitchen table. "*Ya*, I remember him. It's been years since we've seen him and his family."

Ivan pulled his glasses off and rubbed his eyes. "He's dead. Died of a heart attack recently."

"*Ach*, no. I wonder why we haven't received word from Sarah. Maybe a letter is on the way." Katie Ann shook her head. "We should pray for the family."

"*Ya*." Ivan bowed his head with her, then he looked up and took a deep breath. "He wasn't much older than I am."

"I know."

"Just goes to show you that you should live each and every day to the fullest."

Katie Ann bit her bottom lip for a moment and she twisted her coffee cup in her hands. "That's what I want us to do, Ivan. Live each day to the fullest." She smiled as she set her cup down on the table.

"We are." Ivan put his glasses back on and once again buried his head in the newspaper, reading about what people in Amish and Mennonite communities across the country were doing. Didn't he see what was happening right here, in his own home?

"Ivan?"

"*Ya.*"

She waited until he put the paper down on the table and gave her his full attention. "I love you."

"I love you too."

Then why can't you look me in the eye when you say it?

"I reckon I'll start breakfast. What would you like? I can scramble us some eggs, or I can just make us some *kaffi* soup." She stood up from the table and put on her apron.

"It doesn't matter to me."

Does anything matter to you? "Eggs I guess, then." She walked to the refrigerator and found a few eggs, then began cracking them into a bowl. "I'll be glad when we have our own chickens again. These store-bought eggs are nothing like fresh eggs. The yolks are light yellow, just not fresh. I can always tell the difference, can't you?"

He gave a nod. "Uh-huh."

"What are your plans today? With this weather, I reckon we can finish unpacking."

"*Ya*. We can do that."

She fought the knot in her throat and swallowed hard as she stirred the eggs. "Or . . ." She spun around to face him. "We could do something that we haven't done in years."

"What's that?"

Katie Ann wanted to yank the newspaper away from his face, but instead she took a deep breath and blew it out slowly. "We could just—just stay in bed all day. Remember when we were first married, the day everyone was snowed in? No one could get out, and we just stayed in bed all day." She waited for him to look at her. When he didn't, she boldly went on. "We just made love all day long."

"We're not snowed in."

Her eyes welled with tears. "Look at me, Ivan."

He folded the paper, placed it on the table, then folded his hands on top of it. "Why are you yelling?"

"I'm not yelling. I just want you to look at me." Egg dripped from the wooden spoon and onto the floor as she spoke.

Ivan put his glasses on the table and for the first time this morning, he looked into her eyes. "What is it, Katie Ann?"

"I'm asking you if you want to spend the day with me. Like—like we did that day we were snowed in so long ago." She held her breath.

"We're not snowed in and—"

"I know that, Ivan." She put the spoon on the counter, then moved a few steps toward him. "And I know there is much work to be done around here. But I'm asking you if you want to spend the day together . . ." She paused as she blinked back tears, which only made her feel pitiful and ridiculous. But she pressed on. "Just you and me. Making love all day."

Ivan raised his hand to his forehead, and Katie Ann wondered if he was going to rub the skin off as his hand went back and forth. "I thought we'd been through all this, that we were going to stop trying to have a baby. It's just not in God's plan, Katie Ann."

She sat down across the table from him. "I'm not talking about trying to make a baby, Ivan. I'm talking about a husband and wife spending the day together, just loving each other." She reached for his hand, then squeezed. "This is a new beginning for us. I want to spend time in your arms, in this new place, in our bed."

Ivan raised his shoulders, then dropped them slowly. "Okay."

Katie Ann felt like she'd been punched in the gut. She wasn't asking him to perform a mediocre chore, but to love her the way she longed to be loved. Instead, his response signified about as much excitement as hauling the trash to the burn pile. She let go of his hand and sighed.

"What now? I said okay." He raised his brows, the irritation in his voice evident.

"Forget it, Ivan. Just forget it." She eased out of the chair and went to the stove. After she dumped the eggs into the skillet, she stared out the window at the snow falling in heavy blankets all around them. They didn't need mounds of snow to keep them isolated from the world, or each other. They'd managed to isolate themselves from each other a long time ago. Out of the corner of her eye, she saw her husband reading the newspaper.

Six

Emily woke up Thanksgiving Day missing her friends and family back home in Middlefield. It would be the first Thanksgiving she'd ever had without her aunts, uncles, cousins, and grandparents. But *Mamm* had put the turkey in the oven the night before, the way she'd always done, and this morning the aroma filled Emily's mind with recollections of holidays gone by. Times when her heart was filled with peace, her future hopeful.

She rolled onto her side in the bed and snuggled beneath her quilt as her thoughts turned to David. She hadn't seen him since Sunday, but *Mamm* had said his family would be arriving in time for the noon meal. Emily knew she needed to crawl out of bed, get dressed, and go downstairs to help with preparations. *Just a few more minutes.*

Her heart fluttered when she thought about seeing him. He'd quickly gone from someone she feared to someone she wanted to know better, and that frightened her. She'd been focused on healing and establishing new goals for herself, and to develop a crush on David Stoltzfus would hinder her progress and set her up for much heartache. David could have any girl in the community he wanted, and Emily knew she was unworthy of his affections.

She thought about how attentive he'd been at the singing on Sunday, the way she caught him gazing at her when he thought she wasn't looking. But he'd said he didn't want to date her, so she was worrying for nothing. She threw back the covers and sat on the side of her bed. Then she recited her morning prayer, the same way she'd done her entire life.

Good morning, Lord. You are ushering in another day, untouched and freshly new. So here I come to ask You, God, if You'll renew me too? Forgive the many errors that I made yesterday and let me try again, dear God, to walk closer in Thy way. But, Father, I am well aware I can't make it on my own, so take my hand and hold it tight, for I can't walk alone.

In the past, she would have followed the prayer up with personal devotion and one-on-one communion with God, but she climbed out of bed instead. She tried again to recall the last time she'd heard the tiny voice that she knew to be God. Flashes of James were almost instant, and she fought to steady her heartbeat as she put on a dark green dress. She smoothed the wrinkles and realized that she hadn't heard the voice since before the attack. *Seems like God should be here for me now, more than ever.*

She pulled on her black tights, then sat on the bed to tie her shoes. A flurry of mixed emotions filled her head this morning. She was looking forward to seeing David, but apprehension raced through her every time she allowed herself to fantasize about something more than friendship with him. He'd made it very clear that friendship was all he had to offer, and that was all Emily had to give.

She tied her prayer covering and went down the stairs to find Betsy sitting at the kitchen table while her mother was scurrying around the kitchen.

"Emily, you're late. I need some help in here." *Mamm* spoke the words as if she was scolding Emily, but a smile was stretched across her face. "Now, come over here and test this dressing." *Mamm* pulled the oven open and scooped a spoonful from inside the cavity of the turkey. She pushed the spoon toward Emily's mouth.

"Wait, *Mamm*. It's hot." Emily leaned her face away while *Mamm* blew on the spoon.

"Here, try it now."

Dressing had always been her mother's specialty, and she'd made it every year for as long as Emily could remember, for both Thanksgiving and Christmas, and for their entire extended family. Lots of families in Middlefield had adjusted their traditions over the years, opting to have something other than turkey for Christmas, since they'd just had it for Thanksgiving. Plus, weddings were always in November and December, and turkey roast was served after the ceremonies. Emily was sick of turkey by Christmas each year and wished her mother would consider a change in tradition. Not *Mamm*. She wouldn't hear of it. "It wouldn't be Christmas without turkey and dressing," she'd said.

"*Gut*, no?" *Mamm's* left brow lifted as she waited for Emily to finish chewing.

"*Ya, Mamm.* It's fine." Emily rolled her eyes. "It's always fine."

Her mother breathed a sigh of relief, then returned to the stove and began stirring some green beans in a pot.

Betsy looked up from a book she was reading. "I'm going to be vega . . . vegetarian when I am a grown person."

Emily grinned as she pulled apples and oranges from the refrigerator for a fruit salad. She glanced to the left so she wouldn't miss the reaction from her mother.

"Betsy Ann, you will do no such thing." *Mamm* spun around to face Betsy, her hands on her hips. "What are you reading? I reckon it's not from the approved list."

"*Ya, Mamm*. It is." Betsy's big brown eyes grew round. "The boy, Ben, in this book is a vegetarian." Betsy nodded her head once for effect. "It's more healthy to be one of those."

Mamm shook her head. "It wonders me, is nothing safe in this world anymore? A *gut* Christian book about a ten-year-old boy who finds the Lord, and yet . . . he has to be a vegetarian?" *Mamm* slapped her hands down to her sides. "Not for you, Betsy. You would miss meat. And meat has protein. It's *gut* for you."

"I'm gonna be one anyway." Betsy closed the book and stood from the table. "When will everyone be here?"

"Around eleven is what Lillian said." *Mamm* turned to Emily. "Lillian said that she thinks David has sure taken a fancy to you. Evidently, he has mentioned your name several times, and—"

"We're just friends, *Mamm*." Emily knew that her father would reprimand her for taking such a sharp tone with her mother, something she'd been guilty of too often lately, but she could see her *daed* and her brothers through the window, shoveling the snow from the sidewalk. "Don't push about this."

"He just seems like such a nice young man, Emily. Maybe you should give him a chance." *Mamm* lowered the fire under the beans.

"David Stoltzfus has no interest in dating me, so you're wasting your time being hopeful about something developing between us." Emily didn't look up as she chopped the apples into small cubes.

"Now, Emily . . ." *Mamm* sighed as she turned to face Emily. "You don't know that. You are a beautiful young woman, and Lillian said he speaks fondly of you."

Emily took a deep breath, stopped chopping, and faced off with her mother, determined to squelch her mother's misdirected thoughts. "David told me straight to my face that he doesn't want to date me, that all he wants is to be friends. And, *Mamm* . . ." Her tone sharpened. "That's all I want too. So please just drop it."

"I don't like him anyway." Betsy padded across the wooden floor in her socks, still toting her book as she headed toward the den. She stopped once to look at Emily and scrunched her face into a scowl. "He made you cry."

"Betsy, we talked about that." Emily's voice grew louder as she spoke, but Betsy didn't turn around.

"I will not have such talk, Betsy. Do you hear me?" *Mamm's* voice carried into the den, and a faint "Yes, ma'am" breezed into the kitchen.

Emily resumed chopping the apples and hoped her mother would drop the subject of David. "It's cold in here." She twisted to look at the propane heater in the corner of the kitchen. "Is the heater on high?"

"I think so. But it's mighty cold outside, and this house isn't insulated as well as it could be." *Mamm* walked to the window and peered at her father, Jacob, and Levi, then she leaned down and checked the heater. "It's on high." *Mamm* walked to the refrigerator and pulled out a tub of butter. "I bet it's really cold at the Stoltzfus *haus*." She shook her head as she added butter to the boiled potatoes. "You should see that place. So much work to do. I reckon the cold air is just seeping through the cracks in the walls without insulation."

Emily didn't mention that she'd already seen the inside of the Stoltzfus home the day David gave her a ride home on Sister's Day. She thought about how unprepared David had been for their buggy ride this past Sunday—and how cold it had been. In her former life, she would have offered a guy like David a portion of her blanket to cover his legs. She'd spent the last three months so afraid of everything and everyone, particularly men, so she couldn't understand why she'd felt safe with him on a cold, dark night—but not comfortable enough to share the blanket. Especially with a man who told her straight out that he had no interest in dating her.

DAVID HELD ANNA on his lap in the back of the buggy as Elizabeth sat next to him. He felt ridiculous traveling this way, his parents carting him around. Back home, he would have taken his own buggy, but Lillian had insisted they all ride together on Thanksgiving.

"This is so nice of Vera to invite us for Thanksgiving." Lillian smiled at David's father, but then she scowled. "I can't imagine having to cook the Thanksgiving meal in that new *haus* of ours." She paused as she shook her head. "One of the cabinet doors fell off this morning when I opened it to unload some things."

Daed patted Lillian on the leg. "*Mei leib*, there is much work to do, but someday it will be a fine home." He smiled, raised his brows. "It sure is big."

"A big mess." Lillian glanced over her shoulder and smiled. "But we are all together and have much to be thankful for."

David readjusted Anna on his lap and avoided Lillian's eyes for fear he'd blurt out an angry comment and ruin her day. *As soon as I can, I'm going back to Lancaster County.*

His father eased into the Detweilers' driveway and maneuvered their gray buggy next to the Detweilers' black one, which was almost completely covered in snow.

"Why do they have black buggies and not gray ones like us?" Elizabeth leaned her face closer to the plastic weather protector on her side of the buggy. "And their *kapps* aren't like ours either."

David had recognized some of the obvious differences when they first arrived. There were only a few buggies on the roads, but he'd noticed the black ones. And prayer coverings in Lancaster County were heart-shaped in the back, unlike the ones Emily, Betsy, and Vera wore, which were squared in the back.

"Some things might look different, but our belief system and dedication to the *Ordnung* is the same, Elizabeth," *Daed* said before he stepped out of the buggy and began to tether the horse. David waited until Lillian got out of the buggy; then he pushed the seat forward. He set Anna on the ground and then helped Elizabeth out.

"I hope the Detweilers like my candied sweet potatoes."

David held out his hands toward the casserole dish Lillian was carrying. "Here, I'll carry that."

"Okay, *danki*." Lillian handed the dish to David. "I'll get the loaves of zucchini bread out of the back." Lillian walked to the back of the buggy. "Girls, go on up to the house, and no running."

David followed Anna and Elizabeth up the sidewalk. He turned around when he heard hooves clapping against the freshly cleared driveway. It was his Uncle Ivan and Aunt Katie Ann. Thank goodness they were coming, even though it still didn't seem like Thanksgiving without the rest of his extended family. Anna and Elizabeth knocked on the door, and a moment later Vera swung the door wide.

"Come in, come in. Warm yourselves by the fire." Vera motioned the girls inside, then turned to David. "Hello, David. Here, I'll take that for you."

David handed off the sweet potatoes. "*Danki* for having us." He glanced past Vera and could see Emily walking toward them.

"We're so glad to have you all. Make yourself at home. I'm going to go put this on top of the stove to keep warm." Vera headed off to the kitchen, brushing past Emily on her way. David noticed something different about Emily right away as she approached him. She looked . . . happy. She was smiling and her expression was welcoming.

"Hi." David nervously stuffed his hands into his coat pockets.

"Hi. Do you want me to take your coat?" Emily held out her hand, so he pulled his hands from his pockets and began unbuttoning. Emily turned toward Elizabeth and Anna. "Girls, Betsy will be down in a minute, or you can go upstairs to her room."

Anna and Elizabeth quickly shed their coats, hung them on a rack by the door, and headed upstairs—leaving David and Emily alone. She moved closer to him, which, for reasons he couldn't explain, made him nervous. He stared at her, mesmerized by the gleam in her eyes and the way the light from the fire glimmered and danced across her ivory skin—which took on a blush the more he gazed at her.

He stopped staring and quickly took off his coat, and she looked away as she accepted it and hung it on the rack. Avoiding his eyes, she was instantly back to the Emily he'd first met—timid, nervous. David silently blasted himself for making her feel uncomfortable, but being around her was scrambling his logic, making him consider what-ifs.

"Sorry about the other night, after the singing." He placed his black felt hat on the rack by the door, alongside his coat.

Her face brightened. Then she giggled. "You mean that cold, dark ride in the middle of nowhere with only a blanket and portable heater?"

David smiled back at her. This woman could transform herself back and forth quicker than anyone he'd ever known. Timid and afraid one minute, then glowing, beautiful, and poised the next. He couldn't help but wonder, and be angry about, what happened to strip her of the qualities she must have possessed on a full-time basis some time ago.

"*Ya*. I'll plan better," he whispered as he felt his own cheeks take on a flush just as his father and Lillian came into the room.

Lillian brushed past David and went straight to Emily, a smile stretched wide. "You must be Emily. I've heard so much about you."

Careful, Lillian. David knew he'd mentioned Emily's name more than he should have the past few days. Something else that puzzled him. He glanced at Emily to see her smiling. He wasn't sure if it was from Lillian's comment, or just because everyone seemed to smile in Lillian's presence. She had that effect on people.

"*Ya.* I'm Emily, and I've heard much about you also." Emily offered to take Lillian's coat at about the same time Vera walked back into the room, followed by Elam, Jacob, and Levi. *Onkel* Ivan and *Aenti* Katie Ann walked in, and Vera made introductions. Then she suggested the men warm themselves in front of the fire while the women put the finishing touches on the meal.

David took a seat next to his father on the couch. Elam and Jacob each sat in a rocker on the other side of the room. Levi stood near the fireplace with his arms folded across his chest, and Uncle Ivan stood nearby.

"So, Samuel . . ." Elam began. "I hear there is much work to do at your home."

Samuel nodded his head, then grinned. "I reckon that is an understatement." His father shook his head. "I should have traveled this way before I moved *mei* family here, and tried to do some work before we made the trip."

"We're a small community, but I know everyone will pitch in to help you. You can count on me and my boys." Elam nodded toward Jacob and Levi, then smiled. "And that brings me to another point. I know your girls will be starting school soon, and I don't know if you've heard, but we don't have a schoolhouse. Classes are being taught in a barn right now."

David's father nodded. "I did hear that from Lillian."

"Plans are to start construction on a new schoolhouse when the snow begins to clear. And I know you have your hands full with your own place, and—"

"Count David and me in," his father interrupted. "We're available to help."

Elam nodded. "We will work some on the schoolhouse and some on your place as the weather allows. We have an *Englisch* fellow named Arnold who will lead us with the project. He's a fine carpenter."

David watched his father nod, then he glanced around the room at the Detweilers' cozy den. It was much smaller than the den in their current home, and smaller than the den they'd had in Lancaster County. He wondered how they could possibly hold worship service in such a small house, but then he remembered where he was. Probably weren't more than forty or fifty people in the district here.

"We haven't met the bishop," David said, glancing from his father to Elam.

"He's a fine man." Elam sat up taller, but Levi grunted. Elam turned toward his son, then narrowed his brows and cut his eyes sharply at him. He turned back to David's father. "He's a bit strict, but a *gut* leader in our small community."

"We had a strict bishop in Lancaster County too," David said as he glanced at his *daed*, who nodded.

"*Ya*, Bishop Ebersol was firm, but he was also a *gut* leader."

David's chest tightened at the mention of Lancaster County. He wondered how *Mammi* Sarah Jane was doing, and Noah and Carley, and Mary Ellen, Linda, and all his other relatives he'd been forced to leave behind.

EVERYONE RAVED ABOUT *Mamm's* dressing. Everyone but Emily. She couldn't bring herself to enhance her mother's zestful spirit, something that Emily resented more with each passing day, as if nothing in their world had changed. Maybe nothing in *Mamm's* world had changed, but it certainly had in Emily's.

"Lillian, these sweet potatoes are so *gut*. I must get your recipe." *Mamm* took another bite of the candied yams.

Emily figured *Mamm* was secretly wondering if everyone liked Lillian's potatoes more than her dressing. Emily helped herself to more of the potatoes, intentionally bypassing a second helping of dressing. She tried to feel guilty about her attitude toward her mother, but nothing.

"Betsy, don't you like turkey?" Lillian eyed Betsy's plate, filled with dressing, potatoes, candied yams, cranberries, green beans, and everything except for turkey and ham. "Anna and Elizabeth love turkey." Lillian looked at her plate piled high with turkey and giggled. "We all do."

Emily liked Lillian right away. She'd barely spoken to the woman, but there was something about her. David had said everyone loved Lillian, and Emily could see why. Her smile made you want to smile along with her.

"I'm a vegetarian." Betsy sat taller, her expression serious.

Emily watched as Lillian nodded. "I see."

"Betsy is not a vegetarian." *Mamm* put her full fork down on her plate. "Betsy, get you some turkey or ham. You've always liked both."

"Not anymore." Betsy shook her head. "Not since I've turned vegetarian. Now I don't eat meat. I will have less chance of having coronary artery disease, gallstones, cancer . . ." Betsy took a deep breath and continued. "Particularly colon cancer, and kidney stones, and high blood pressure."

Emily cupped her hand over her mouth, wondering if *Mamm* might pass out, then she glanced around the table. Most were stifling a grin. Except for her mother and Levi.

"Betsy, you ain't got a clue what you're talking 'bout." Levi frowned as he reached for another roll.

Mamm forced a smile. "Betsy likes to read, and sometimes she takes things to heart." She leaned toward Betsy who was seated on the bench to her right. "I'm sure Betsy will be back to eating meat by the end of the week. Right, sweetheart?"

"No, *Mamm*. I'm done with all meat. It will help keep my bowels regular, too, I reckon."

Emily burst out laughing. Hard, gut-wrenching laughter that almost caused her to spew her food. Everyone looked shocked at her outburst—except for Lillian, whose eyes were watering in her effort to control herself. But Emily wasn't sure if Lillian was tickled about Betsy or Emily's inability to contain herself.

"Betsy!" *Mamm* said in a loud whisper. "What is wrong with you? That is not proper talk for the dinner table."

Emily glanced at David. His eyes were wide as he glanced around the room, finally locking eyes with Emily. Embarrassment flooded over her. She looked down at her plate and pinched her lips together.

"I'm going to be a vegetable too!" Anna said proudly.

"VegeTARIAN." Betsy shook her head. "Not a vegetable!"

Mamm forced another smile, but Emily was sure that her mother was ready to yank Betsy from the table and cart her out to the woodpile for a spanking. "That's enough, Betsy. Eat your—your vegetables." *Mamm* lowered her chin.

Emily glanced around the room again, her gaze landing

on David last. Their eyes met for a long moment, then David winked at her. Slow. Intentional.

She felt her left eyelid wink in response, as if it had a mind of its own. She quickly looked away, unable to fathom why she would act in such a forward manner—so flirtatious, so completely unladylike, and in very poor taste.

And yet the way David smiled at her sent her heart to racing in a way she hadn't felt since she was on her date with James, and her visions of that night plowed to the front of her mind. James had seemed like a good man too. How could she trust David? How could she trust anyone?

Emily excused herself from the table and rushed out of the room.

Seven

DAVID SILENTLY CHASTISED HIMSELF FOR WINKING AT Emily. He finished off the last of his turkey and dressing in one fork load, knowing he'd been the one to cause her to bolt from the table. However, she'd returned the gesture by winking back, which was confusing. Emily baffled him, for sure.

After the meal, all the men retired to the barn while the women gathered in the kitchen. His father and Elam each puffed on a cigar, something David only saw his *daed* partake in on holidays. Uncle Ivan, David, and Jacob stood near them, but Levi leaned against the far wall, one foot propped up behind him. David noticed him holding an inhaler and caught Levi glaring at him several times. It was quite clear that Levi didn't like him, but David wondered if Levi liked anyone. He was a sour fellow, unlike Jacob, who was always friendly. But today Jacob seemed antsy, and David suspected he was ready to head to Beth Ann's house. He'd mentioned several times throughout the course of the day that he would be going there this afternoon.

David shivered along with the rest of the men inside the cold barn as they all stood around sharing jokes.

"I've got one," David said as he recalled a joke he'd heard in Lancaster County. "A man once asked God, 'What's a million years to You?' God said, 'A second.' Then the man asked God, 'What's a million dollars to You?' God said, 'A penny.' The man asked God, 'Can You do me a favor?' God said, 'Sure,' so the man asked God, 'Can You give me a penny?'" David smiled. "God said, 'Sure. In a second.'"

They all laughed, and even Levi grinned.

Ivan was standing right beside David, across from the rest of the men, so David was pretty sure he was the only one who heard the vibration coming from Ivan's pocket. He watched his uncle discretely reach into his pocket and silence the noise before excusing himself. *Why is* Onkel *Ivan carrying around a cell phone?*

None of David's family had cell phones when they were in Lancaster County. He knew plenty of Amish folks who did, but mostly because their businesses required it. In some instances Bishop Ebersol had allowed it, but David had never known his uncle to need a cell phone.

EMILY CARRIED SEVERAL glasses to the kitchen. Her mother, Lillian, and Katie Ann were chatting as she placed the glasses in the sink.

"Martha is her name," *Mamm* said to Lillian and Katie Ann. "She's an *Englisch* woman who lives alone. Sometimes I take her homemade bread and such, so I thought I'd run her a plate of food later."

"I'll do it, *Mamm*," Emily said. Martha was the crankiest *Englisch* woman Emily had ever met, but it would get her out of the house. This silly flirting and winking with David had her stomach upset. "I'll take Martha a plate."

Her mother raised a brow. "Really? Hmm. That surprises me, Emily. But all right."

Lillian straightened in her seat at the kitchen table. "Nonsense. We'd be glad to carry Martha a plate when we leave. There's no need for Emily to have to hitch the horse to the buggy."

"Or Ivan and I can drop off the food to your friend," Katie Ann added.

"No, really. I don't mind." Emily paused, hoping to sound convincing. "Besides, *Mamm* will tell you, Martha is a bit, well . . . grouchy."

"She's right." *Mamm* shook her head. "Martha is difficult sometimes. In the three short months we've known her, I don't think the woman has ever smiled. She's different than most folks around here, *Englisch* or Amish." *Mamm* turned to face Emily. "That's nice of you to offer, Emily."

"I'll go ask Jacob to get the buggy ready."

Emily excused herself, found Jacob, and told him that he could either hitch up a buggy for her or stop by Martha's on his way to Beth Ann's. He quickly agreed to hitch up both buggies. Luckily they had two covered buggies, or Jacob would have complained about having to take his topless courting buggy in this weather. No snow so far today, and even with the frigid temperatures, the sun shone brightly, and it seemed warmer than thirty-eight degrees. A drive would be good, clear her head.

"Here. This is for Martha." *Mamm* handed Emily a bag when she walked back into the kitchen. She leaned closer to Emily and whispered, "I'm surprised you are offering to do this, Emily. It's cold, and Martha isn't the friendliest . . ." *Mamm* twisted her mouth to one side. "Surely you don't have other errands to run on Thanksgiving Day?"

"No. I just feel like going for a drive." Emily shrugged.

"I suppose we should be leaving too, Vera." Lillian stood and hugged Emily's mother. "*Danki* for having us. What a wonderful time we had." Lillian chuckled. "I can't imagine having to cook the Thanksgiving meal in our kitchen."

"Next year." *Mamm* eased out of the hug. "I'm sure that by next year we'll have your new home in tip-top shape."

"I hope so." Lillian grabbed a bag from the counter. "*Danki* also for sending home some leftovers." She turned toward the den. "Anna, Elizabeth, are you ready to go?" Both girls were sitting with Betsy in the middle of the floor putting together a puzzle.

Katie Ann offered *Mamm* her thanks for the meal as David crossed through the den to the kitchen.

"We leaving?" David addressed the question to Lillian, but quickly glanced in Emily's direction.

"*Ya*. I reckon so." Lillian called to her daughters one more time, then refocused on David. "It's almost two thirty, and I know the girls are tired." She smiled. "I'm a bit tired too. Can you go round up your father?"

David's eyes once again shifted to Emily, but when she didn't say anything, he looked back to Lillian. "Sure." He turned to walk out the door, but then hesitated and swung back around. "Emily, Jacob said you're going for a drive, that you need to drop some food off for a neighbor." He stuffed his hands inside his overcoat. "Think maybe I could get a ride, if it's not too much trouble? Otherwise I'll have Anna or Elizabeth in my lap, and *Onkel* Ivan said the backseat of his buggy is filled with empty boxes."

"I'm sorry, David," Katie Ann said. "I wasn't thinking yesterday afternoon when I piled those in the buggy for Ivan to haul off."

Emily's chest grew tight. "*Ach*, uh, Martha's house isn't really in that direction, and—"

"Emily . . ." *Mamm* said. "I'm sure it's no trouble at all for you to take David home, no? Mighty cramped, I'm sure, with his sisters in the backseat." *Mamm* narrowed her brows at Emily.

"That's all right. Don't make Emily go out of her way." Lillian smiled. "I made David ride with us, instead of in his own buggy, since it was Thanksgiving. I wanted us all to be together. He can squeeze in the back for the short ride home."

David didn't say anything, but he had a smirk on his face, like he knew Emily would end up taking him home.

Mamm scowled at Emily.

"No, it's all right, Lillian. I can take him home after I stop at Martha's. I'm sure David won't mind making a quick stop to drop the food off before I make the circle back home." She shot him a calculated smile, then grabbed her hat and bonnet from the rack and together they walked out the door. *He'll love Martha.*

VERA, LILLIAN, AND Katie Ann were in the kitchen while Anna and Elizabeth helped Betsy clean up the puzzle and other toys in the den.

The three women stood beside the window and watched David crawl into the driver's side of the buggy. "Guess Emily is letting him drive," Lillian said.

Vera watched her daughter climb into the passenger side. "I see that."

David turned the buggy and headed down the driveway.

Lillian turned to face Vera as her brows drew together with concern. "David has never had much interest in dating. He seems to avoid getting close to anyone. It worries Samuel and me." Then a smile eased across her face. "But I'm glad to see that he seems to have taken an interest in Emily."

"Emily seems like such a lovely girl," Katie Ann added.

Vera wished she could tell them about everything her family had been through, everything Emily had been through. Sometimes the pain overwhelmed her, and pushing forward as if nothing had happened was the only way she could survive. She liked these women, but she didn't know them very well. How would Lillian react when she found out that Emily had been attacked and taken by another man? Would she see Emily as unworthy for her stepson?

Lillian touched her on the arm. "Are you all right?"

"*Ya, ya.*" Vera tried to clear her thoughts of all that haunted her. "I was just thinking about how Emily hasn't been interested in dating anyone since we moved here. She mostly stays to herself."

They all glanced out the window again just as David pulled onto the main road.

"Well, as Katie Ann said, Emily is lovely, and I can see why David would want to spend time with her." Lillian glanced briefly toward Vera; then she looked back out the window. "I hope they have a *gut* time."

Vera nodded. "So do I." She forced a smile, then said a silent prayer for Emily. *Help her to feel joy again, Lord.*

THE SUN SHONE brightly as they headed toward Martha's house.

"*Danki* for letting me drive." David turned toward her and grinned. "Nothing worse than a woman driver."

Emily glanced briefly in his direction and cut her eyes, then focused on the snow-capped mountains ahead of her. "I can't wait to climb one of those some day."

"Why do you want to do that?" David gave her a sidelong glance.

She paused as she thought about how distant she was from God. "So I'll be closer to heaven."

David was quiet for a moment, then said, "Maybe I better climb up there with you."

Emily didn't respond, but by David's tone, she could tell he was troubled. She wasn't ready to dive into anyone else's problems, so she stayed quiet the rest of the short drive to Martha's.

When David turned down the driveway of the large home, Emily finally spoke. "Martha is not a very friendly *Englisch* woman." She reached into the backseat to retrieve the bag of food her mother had sent with them.

Martha lived alone. *Mamm* met her one day while dropping off some jams at Abby's bakery. Martha hadn't said much, but she loaded up on *Mamm's* rhubarb jam. She'd said it was the best she'd ever had. Guess that's all it took for *Mamm* to befriend her, although Martha didn't seem to need or want friends. The older woman was cranky to the point of being rude almost every time Emily was around her. She shook her head as she recalled that the whole point of this trip was to have some time alone, get away from David, and clear her head.

"Why are you shaking your head?" David eased the buggy to a stop next to an old car covered in snow.

Emily shrugged. "Just hoping Martha is in a better mood than she usually is."

"If she's so cranky, why does your *mamm* do things like this, send food for her?"

"I guess because she is alone." Emily thought briefly about how she'd been treating her mother lately. Poorly, she knew. And despite *Mamm's* bubbly attitude, despite the circumstances, Emily knew her mother to be a good woman, always helping others. *Then why can't she help me?*

Emily climbed out of the buggy. She was about to close the door when David spoke.

"Guess I'll just stay here." He grimaced. "No need for both of us to take the food to her."

Emily glared at him. "Oh no. You come with me. It would be rude of you to stay out here, and I'd hate for you not to meet Martha." She shot him a snide grin and waited until he had stepped out of the buggy before she closed her own door.

Together they trudged through the snow to Martha's front door.

"This place is huge." David glanced around Martha's spacious yard, then upward at her two story house, much larger than most of the homes in the area.

"*Ya*. She doesn't really do much with it. I mean, take care of it."

They climbed the steps to Martha's front door, and Emily knocked, softly at first, then harder when Martha didn't answer.

"Maybe we can just leave the food on the front porch

and run," David whispered, but his eyes were openly amused, and Emily was forced to stifle a giggle before she reprimanded him.

"Stop it. We can't do that." Emily repositioned the plastic bag across her arm just as David reached for it.

"Here, let me take that for you."

Emily jerked away from him. "*Ach*, no. I've got it." She narrowed her eyes playfully. "You'll just drop it and run."

He stared at her for a moment, then burst out laughing. "Do you really think I would do that?"

Emily tapped her shoe against the snow-covered porch step and raised her chin. "I think you just might."

His gentle laugh rippled through the air, and Emily laughed infectiously back at him, unsure why and not really caring. It felt good to laugh. "Why are you laughing?" she finally asked.

"Why are you laughing?"

Emily bent slightly at the waist as her free arm covered her abdomen. "I don't know."

The massive wooden door swung open in front of them, and they both choked back their amusement. Emily straightened. "Hello, Martha."

"What's so funny?" Dark, snappy eyes looked out from a wrinkled face topped with a mass of curly dark brown hair. Red lipstick lined thin lips pinched together into a scowl. Martha walked onto the porch and glanced back and forth between Emily and David. "Emily, who is this man?"

Emily cleared her throat. "Martha, this is David Stoltzfus. He and his family just moved here from—"

"What's in the bag?" Martha leaned toward Emily a bit and raised one brow.

"*Mamm* sent you some turkey and Thanksgiving side dishes." Emily pulled the bag from her arm and pushed it in Martha's direction.

Martha latched on, then peered inside as if poison were inside. "I don't see any cranberry."

"No, it's there." Emily leaned forward and pulled back the edge of the plastic bag, then pointed to a small plastic container. "The one with the green lid."

Martha's expression softened. But only a little. Emily stepped back. "Hope you enjoy it. It was nice to see you again."

"And nice to meet you," David added with much more sincerity than Martha surely deserved.

Emily turned to leave, David on her heels.

"Do you want to come in?" Martha's voice was loud and raspy, and Emily tried to hide her shock when she spun around to face her. Several times she had delivered food to Martha, and never once had she been invited inside. *And I'm not fond of the idea right now.*

"Uh, we don't want to bother you." She glanced at David, whose eyes seemed to be begging Emily to decline.

Martha turned around, pulled the door wide, and held it open. "No bother. Come in."

Her voice left little room for argument as she held the door until Emily and David moved slowly across the threshold and into a large den with no more light than at their own houses. She wondered briefly if Martha had electricity, but rays from a small lamp in the corner caught Emily's eye. Still, Emily's home, void of modern electricity, was much brighter and more inviting than this giant, but depressing, space that smelled like something Emily couldn't quite identify. Almost like—like the homemade ointment *Mamm* used on Levi's cut leg one time.

Wood creaked beneath Emily as she scanned Martha's den. A red and gold couch rested against a tan wall, and it looked like it was real fancy at one time, but it was worn now, the colors faded. There was a picture of an owl in flight above it. In front of the couch was a coffee table, presumably. You couldn't see it for all the magazines and newspapers strewn across it, and four cups were balanced unevenly on top of all that. To Emily's right was a large cage in the corner. Emily moved closer.

"That's Elvis." Martha slammed the wooden door and joined Emily. "He'll talk to you." She gingerly reached her finger into the cage and stroked the long snout on the big bird with every color in the rainbow nestled amidst its feathers.

"A parrot?" David moved closer to the women.

Martha nodded, and Emily was surprised at the tenderness the woman showed the bird. Elvis almost sounded as if he was purring like a cat as Martha continued to rub his hooked mouth. "Who is Elvis?" Martha leaned her head down closer to the cage.

"The king."

Emily jumped when the bird spoke. She turned to David, whose mouth tipped at one corner.

"Did he say 'the king'?" Emily didn't understand. There was only one King she knew of—Christ.

"Yeah, he's something, my Elvis." Martha smiled, something Emily had never seen her do. Then Martha bolted upright. "Anyway, sit down." She pointed to the couch. The only other piece of furniture in the room was a brown recliner with long tears down one side, exposing the white foam beneath it. The lamp on the end table wobbled when Martha sat down in the recliner, and Martha didn't even look when she reached over to steady it.

Emily and David took a seat on the small couch. Too small. Emily felt her knee brush against David's leg. She eased over as much as she could, but he was still uncomfortably close to her.

"You two make a nice couple." Martha made the statement, frowning as she spoke.

"Thank you." David turned to Emily and grinned, and Emily was sure that if there were more light in the room, Martha would have commented on the shade of red brightening Emily's cheeks. Emily twisted to face David, and she spoke directly to him.

"We are not a couple." She sat taller and held her chin high. David grinned, but Emily quickly pulled her attention from him and turned to Martha when the older woman cackled with laughter.

"Sure ya are. Might not know it yet, but the two of you definitely got a thing for each other."

I am never coming here again. Emily opened her mouth to speak but was clearly unable to say what was on her mind.

"That's what I keep telling her," David said, shaking his head. "But she just won't listen."

Emily faced David again, dropped her jaw. "What are you talking about?"

Before David could answer, the bird squawked, then sang, "Love me tender, love me sweet . . ."

Emily glared at the bird, then turned to David, who looked equally horrified, which made her laugh.

"Gotta love my Elvis. He tells it like he sees it." Martha choked the words out in her raspy voice, followed up with chopped laughter. Then she grew completely solemn and stared at Emily.

Emily waited and kept her eyes on Martha. To look at David would be too much right now. Silly bird needed to keep its mouth shut.

"Your mother got any of that rhubarb jam of hers? I'll gladly pay."

Emily didn't think she'd ever felt so relieved to have a change in subject. "I'm sure she does. I can ask her."

"Maybe you could, uh, come back and bring me some?"

"Sure." It was the last thing Emily wanted to commit to—coming back to this dreary place that smelled funny with a smarty pants bird as an occupant, but she nodded as she spoke.

Mamm had said once that Martha was in her sixties, but Emily thought she looked much older. Several deep lines ran parallel along Martha's forehead, and tiny wrinkles feathered from the corners of her eyes and around her mouth. She had dark circles under large brown eyes that were heavily made up. A few sprigs of gray were interspersed within her mass of brown curls, but not enough to notice too much. Some of the *Englisch* women Emily knew used boxes of hair color. Maybe Martha did too. Emily thought Martha must have been an attractive *Englisch* woman at one time. Now she seemed rather run down, and not in the way that comes from years of hard work, but maybe from a hard life. Martha never spoke of a husband, children, or any other family. *Mamm* told Emily once that Martha didn't have any family.

Emily took a deep breath and thought for a moment about

her own future. Even if she didn't have a husband or children, at least she would have her family.

"We should probably be going." David smiled briefly in Emily's direction, which she could see out of the corner of her eye.

"*Ya*, I reckon so." Emily stood up. "I'll bring you some rhubarb jam soon."

Martha stood up at the same time David rose from the couch. "When?"

"Uh, maybe later in the week?" Emily offered her a slight smile.

Martha folded her arms across her chest. "Hmm." Then she turned to leave the room. "Wait right here. I'll be back."

Emily stood quietly beside David, still too embarrassed to look at him. Martha returned quickly.

"Here." Martha pushed a piece of paper in Emily's direction. "My old car is on the fritz, and I can't get to the market. Can you pick up these things for me tomorrow and bring them by? You can bring the rhubarb jam then too."

Emily knew her eyes were as large as saucers. "Uh, Martha, I don't have my own buggy, but maybe *Mamm* can shop for you soon, or—"

"He can take you." She pointed to David. "I bet *you* have your own buggy." She raised her brows.

Before either one of them could answer, Martha handed Emily a wad of cash. "That's plenty for the groceries and a hundred dollars for your time."

Emily's mind was racing about what she could do with a hundred dollars. She could use it to buy a wedding gift for Jacob and Beth Ann. "Martha, we will figure out a way to get your groceries, but I can't take that much money."

"Fine." Martha snatched the money back, counted it and removed a few bills, then handed Emily the rest. She pushed the rest of the bills toward David. "You take fifty for carting her to town and because I need some firewood cut. Otherwise I'll freeze to death in this house, and I'm sure you wouldn't want that on your conscience, now would you?"

Emily turned to David, brought her hand to her mouth to stifle a grin, and waited to see how he would handle the request.

When David didn't reach for the money, Martha pushed it closer to him and raised her chin as her brows frowned along with her bright red lips.

David took the money as he hesitantly said, "Okay." Martha looked so scary, he was probably afraid not to.

"I eat supper at five. I'll need time to heat something up." Martha tapped her finger to her chin. "Can you both be here at four tomorrow?"

"Uh, I don't know if . . ." Emily glanced toward David, hoping he'd offer up some help, but he just stared wordlessly back at her. She turned back to Martha. "I have to work at the dry goods store, but I could probably leave a little early. But we'd need time to shop."

"I guess I could do the shopping, then pick you up at the store," David said with a shrug.

"No, no, no." Martha shook her head so hard half her hair fell from atop her head. She pulled a clip from her hair, bit down on it, then stuffed the curls back and pinned them. "Men can't shop. You take Emily shopping and then just show up here after that." She sighed. "There's a light in the backyard. Should be enough for you to cut me some wood." Another sigh. "I'll just eat late."

Emily and David headed toward the door, still clothed in their heavy coats. "I guess we will see you tomorrow, Martha." She thought about another trip with David tomorrow. Grocery shopping. David pulled the door open, and Emily walked onto the porch as David followed. "Bye, Martha." Emily waved, as did David.

"See you tomorrow." Martha waved, and Emily thought she caught a brief smile.

David opened the driver's side of the buggy. "Guess you can drive, since you have to drop me off." He waited until Emily got in, then closed the door behind her before he wound around to the passenger side and climbed in. "I'm not sure how we got pulled into this, but I can use fifty dollars." David chuckled. "And what about that bird of hers?"

"Weird." Emily shook her head as she flicked the horse into action. "I'm saving up to buy something special as a wedding gift for Jacob and Beth Ann, so the money will come in handy for me too."

David didn't look at her as he stared out of the window on his side. "I'm saving up so I can get out of here and move back to Lancaster County."

Maybe his words shouldn't have stung, but they did. They rode quietly until Emily turned into David's driveway and wound between the piles of debris in the yard.

"I'll be glad when the weather clears some so we can get this place cleaned up." David waited until she came to a complete stop, then turned to face her. "What time should I pick you up? I'm planning to help *mei daed* around here all day, so I guess I'll ask Lillian to hold my supper for me while we help out your friend."

For the first time, Emily was reading Martha's grocery list. "Uh, what?"

"I asked what time I should pick you up tomorrow?"

"I guess four, although we'll probably be traveling in the dark part of the way." Emily cocked her head to one side as she continued to stare at Martha's list. "I can't believe she pushed us into doing this, but . . ." She took a deep breath. "This list bothers me." She handed it to David. "Look at this food."

Eight

Katie Ann poured eggs into a skillet while Ivan read the newspaper at the kitchen table. It was a repeat of almost every morning since they'd moved to Canaan. Katie Ann fought the bitterness that threatened to seep into her heart and ruin the day. Today she was not going to wear her feelings on her shoulder, and she was going to be chipper and happy around her husband. Even if he seemed more interested in that newspaper than anything Katie Ann might have to say.

"Thanksgiving was nice yesterday, no?" She glanced over her shoulder briefly, then returned to stirring the eggs. "I like Vera and her family."

"Seem like fine folks." Ivan continued to peer down through his reading glasses at the newspaper.

"When we get things unpacked and the house readied for company, maybe we can have them over for supper one night." She adjusted the flame under the eggs when they started to stick. "And of course, Lillian, Samuel, David, and the girls too."

Ivan looked up. "Where would we put all those people?" He glanced around the kitchen table, only large enough to seat six.

"Sounds like a *gut* excuse to buy a larger table and chairs. This *haus* is bigger than our home in Lancaster County. It might need work, but there's surely room in this kitchen for a bigger table and more chairs."

Ivan didn't say anything and went back to reading. She kept stirring the eggs. "I sliced a little ham for breakfast this morning, to go with the eggs. I'll need to get some bacon at the market next time I go." She twisted to face him. "I hope we have our own pigs soon."

Ivan kept his face buried in the paper and nodded.

She finished the eggs, then spooned some on a plate for Ivan, along with two slices of ham. "Do you want some toast?" Katie Ann put the plate in front of him.

"No. This is enough." He closed the newspaper as Katie Ann joined him at the table. They both bowed in prayer.

"I'm planning to help Samuel and David with the yard today. There's lots of junk that the girls can get hurt on." Ivan took a bite of eggs but didn't look at her when he spoke.

"I'll see if there's anything I can help Lillian with. That *haus* needs much more work than this one."

They ate quietly, and Katie Ann was sure she could hear her heart cracking as loneliness settled in, despite her best intentions. She took a deep breath, refusing to be defeated.

"I think David has taken a fancy to the Detweiler girl." She wiped her mouth with her napkin, then kept her gaze on Ivan until his eyes met hers. "Remember when we were that age? When we were young and in *lieb*?"

Ivan smiled. Not a lot. But hope surged through her. "*Ya*, I remember," he said. Then his eyebrows narrowed, and he kept his eyes on his plate as he spoke. "Seems like such a long time ago."

Katie Ann's heart sank. There was no mistaking the sadness and regret in Ivan's voice.

They were quiet again for a while.

"I was thinking that I would like to get a dog," she said after she finished her breakfast.

"What kind of dog?"

She shrugged. "I don't know. We haven't had a dog in a long while. Not since Bear died." Katie Ann tapped her finger to her chin as she remembered their German shepherd who was hit by a car.

"Get whatever you want." Ivan stood up from the table, then pulled his hat from the rack. "Guess I'll go round up Samuel and David and see where they want to start."

Katie Ann nodded.

She watched Ivan close the door behind him.

Then she just sat and cried.

DAVID WAS WORN out by the afternoon. He'd spent all day helping his father and Ivan haul junk to the barn, things that were lying around the yard that Anna and Elizabeth could get hurt on. He had two cuts on his finger from a piece of jagged tin as proof. After bandaging them, he would get ready for his trip with Emily, which he had mixed feelings about.

First there would be shopping, which seemed odd. He'd never done grocery shopping except to pick up a few things here and there for Lillian, plus he'd be doing it with Emily. Martha had a long list of things she wanted, and her list was as strange as the woman herself.

After a quick bath, he told Lillian where he was going.

"That's nice of you and Emily to get her groceries for her since she can't get out." Lillian opened the door of the oven and peered inside. "This roast will be ready before you get home, and you know how your *daed* likes to eat right at five." She closed the door and turned to face him. "But there will be plenty left for you to have when you get home."

David reached for his heavy coat on the rack. "I like to eat at five too."

"*Ya*, I know. Like father, like son." Lillian smiled. "Is the woman as cranky as Emily and Vera said?"

"Uh, *ya*. I would have to say so." David pulled his hat from the rack, put it on, and was almost out the door when he turned around. "She's paying me and Emily to go to town for her and for me to chop some firewood for her." He paused. "Do you think that's wrong, for us to take money for helping her?"

Lillian folded her arms across her chest. "What do you think?"

David shrugged. "I guess it's all right. No different than other chores I've done for the *Englisch* in the past in Lancaster County."

"As long as you feel *gut* about it."

He was trying to feel good about it because he needed the money, but something didn't feel quite right about taking money from an elderly woman whose car wasn't running. He gave Lillian a quick wave and was glad to see it wasn't snowing. Hopefully, he and Emily could get to Monte Vista and back to Martha's before the sun set and the temperatures dropped. Doubtful, though.

Emily was on her front porch when he pulled up.

"We have to hurry," she said as she climbed into the buggy. "It's going to be dark before we get back to Martha's. And cold." Emily pulled the door closed and reached to the floorboard to turn on the portable heater. David grabbed a blanket he had in the backseat and handed it to her. "*Danki*. I forgot to grab one before I left the house."

He put the horse into a quick trot and waited until they had crossed the main highway before he said what was on his mind. "How do you feel about taking money from Martha?" He shrugged. "If she needs our help, maybe it ain't right."

"I was thinking the same thing." She turned toward him. "As much as I want to save my money for Jacob and Beth Ann's wedding present, to take money from an older woman whose car won't run . . . it just doesn't seem right." Emily pulled the brown blanket tighter around her. "I have an idea, though. A way we can help Martha, not keep the money, but not give it back either."

"This is about her list of groceries she wants us to get, no?"

Emily nodded. "It made me so sad. Every single thing on that list was something frozen or unhealthy. There were no fresh vegetables, no fruit, no flour or sugar for baking, and no meat."

"I reckon I don't know much about shopping, but I wouldn't want to eat that stuff."

"I'm going to get everything on Martha's list, but add my fifty dollars and get her some extra things. Some fruit, vegetables . . . healthier foods."

"Why don't we just skip the stuff on her list and get some meat, fruits, and vegetables?" *I really don't want to give up my fifty dollars*. He looked over at Emily and saw her scowling.

"Do you really want to return to Martha's and tell her we didn't get anything on her list?" she asked. "Somehow I think she would be angry."

David groaned slightly. "I guess I better throw in my fifty dollars too."

Emily twisted in the seat to face him. "You sound like it would kill you. Maybe you should keep your money."

"Nah. I wasn't feeling right about it anyway." He picked up the pace, which caused Emily to bounce in her seat. "Sorry," he said with a grin.

She didn't say anything, but faced forward until they reached the market in Monte Vista about twenty minutes later. But his eyes kept drifting in her direction.

EMILY LET DAVID load the grocery bags into the backseat of the buggy. Between them, they had fourteen dollars left out of the hundred they were supposed to keep. Martha had given them a hundred dollars for the items on her list, plus they'd picked up all kinds of fresh fruit, vegetables, and meat. David had mostly trailed behind her as she walked down the aisles, as if he'd never been to market before. It was an uncomfortable experience and one Emily didn't want to repeat.

"She might be mad we did this," David said as he loaded the last bag, then raised himself onto the seat.

Emily pulled the brown blanket around her. "Can she be any worse than she already is?"

"I guess we'll find out soon enough." With a flick of the reins, they were back on the road. Nightfall settled around them. He cut his eyes toward her, his teeth chattering. "Maybe you could share that blanket?"

She turned her head toward him. "Here, you can have it." She started to pull the cover from around her shoulders.

"You're being silly. Just scoot over here and share it with me before I freeze."

"I'm not that cold." She wadded the blanket up and pushed it toward him.

David grunted. "That's *dumm*. And I ain't the kind of man to warm myself under that blanket while you sit there with your teeth chattering. There ain't nothing to be scared of."

Emily held her breath and closed her eyes for a moment as thoughts of James raced through her mind. *David isn't James.* But the thought of being that close to David made her more uncomfortable than she knew how to explain. "I'm not scared," she squeaked out.

"You keep the blanket." He pushed it back toward her.

"I don't need it."

"Fine." David threw the blanket in the backseat on top of the bags of groceries, and they didn't say anything to each other the rest of the trip. Emily tried to control her chattering teeth and thought about how stubborn he was being. *Or is it me?*

It was completely dark by the time they pulled into Martha's driveway. They each grabbed two bags and eased their way up the porch steps. The door swung open before they had a chance to knock.

"Did you get everything on my list?" Martha stepped aside so David and Emily could enter with the bags.

"*Ya.* I think so." Emily waited for Martha to give them instructions.

"Kitchen is that way. You can just put the bags on the table." Martha pointed to her right, then followed behind them.

Emily walked into the spacious kitchen with enough counter space to line up a hundred shoofly pies for a Sunday gathering.

Unlike the den area where Martha must spend most of her time, the kitchen was spotless. Emily scanned the countertops. No fancy gadgets like the *Englisch* usually had. No toaster, electric can opener, or microwave. Not even a coffee pot.

"I'll go get the rest of the bags." David put his two bags on the table and quickly left the room.

"Emily Detweiler. What is this?" Martha held up a bag of fresh broccoli, then set it on the table and pulled out a bag of apples. She raised her dark brows. "I don't recall any of this on my list. Did you confuse these apples with my frozen apple turnovers?" She grunted as she picked up the broccoli again. "And I can't imagine what you confused this with?"

"We got everything on your list, Martha. We just—just thought you might enjoy some other foods too." Emily stood perfectly still as Martha began to pull the offerings out of the bags.

"Flour? What do I need flour for?"

Emily stepped forward and forced a smile. "For baking. You know, to make bread. Or cookies." Martha scowled as Emily hesitantly kept going. "And you can fry chicken using flour. Look, we got you some chicken." She pulled out a package of chicken breasts.

"And the hundred dollars I gave you for groceries bought all this?" Martha let out a heavy sigh and shook her head before Emily would have been forced to lie. "All right, Emily. The kitchen is all yours."

"What?" Emily swallowed hard.

David walked in with four more bags and placed them on the counter. "Three more left."

After he was gone, Martha continued the inspection. "Finally, here we go." She pulled out a single serving of frozen lasagna, a bag of French fries, a box of corndogs, a box of apple turnovers, and the last item in the bag was a box of frozen fish sticks. "These are the things on my list." She shook her head. "I had no idea you would get all these other things." She put her hands on her hips. "Whatever you decide to cook is fine with me."

And for the first time, Martha smiled.

Emily stood with her mouth hanging open. "I—you—you want me to cook for you?"

Martha's smiled faded as her brows narrowed. "Isn't that what you intended by buying all this food? I don't *cook*, Emily. Never have. Wouldn't know the first thing about it."

"Here's the rest." David plopped down the last three bags on the floor near the kitchen table. "I'll go start on the firewood."

"Good. Emily is going to cook us supper. Then we will all sit down to eat together." Martha's tone made Emily hesitant to argue, but this was not part of the agreement.

"Martha, I'll be glad to cook for you on another night, but tonight I—"

"Ohhh!" Martha bent at the waist as she cried out. Then she cried out again.

Emily ran to her side and put a hand on her arm. "What is it, Martha? What's wrong?" She'd never heard anyone moan like that before. "What can I do?"

David wasn't out of the room yet, and he walked to Martha, then pulled a chair away from the table. "Sit down, Martha."

"Thank you, David. Thank you both." She eased onto the chair. "It's just my back. It goes out like this from time to time." As she shook her head, her face scrunched together, which seemed to make all her wrinkles connect. "You kids go on now. I'm sure I can manage. I'll just heat up my frozen lasagna." She glanced up at David and batted long black lashes. "Like I always do."

"I reckon it's gonna take me awhile to chop up some firewood. I'm sure Emily can make us all some supper, if that's what you want."

Emily glared at David, who only shrugged innocently.

"I don't want to trouble anyone." Martha moaned again, and Emily started thinking about what she would prepare.

An hour later Emily placed a meatloaf, corn on the cob, and some creamed celery on the table as David stacked firewood outside Martha's back door. Martha's back didn't seem to be bothering her as much. She was placing gold-rimmed china plates on three white cloth placemats she'd set out. Fanciest plates Emily had ever seen, and it seemed they should be saved for special occasions. When Emily mentioned that, Martha said this was a special occasion, and Emily was touched enough to drop the subject.

"I'm sorry we don't have any homemade bread, and I didn't buy any at the store." Emily stood in the kitchen holding a jar of rhubarb jam she'd brought from home before realizing there was no bread. "Guess we won't be needing this."

"Nonsense." Martha took the jar from Emily and placed it on the table. "This stuff is good on anything."

David walked into the kitchen and pulled off his black gloves. "It smells *gut* in here." He smiled at Emily, and it suddenly seemed intimate to be cooking like this, then all of them sitting down for a meal together. She barely knew Martha or David.

"The girl can cook, that's for sure." Martha put her hands on her hips and lifted her chin toward Emily. "Bet you'll make a good wife someday."

Emily felt her cheeks heat, and she didn't dare look at David. Martha didn't know how untrue her comment was, but Emily tried to focus on her accomplishments in Martha's kitchen on such short notice. "Everything is ready." She put a glass of milk in front of each placemat.

Martha sat down at the head of the table, then shook her head. "I don't drink milk, Emily."

David sat down to Martha's right as Emily slid into a chair on Martha's left. "Why?"

"Because it's the foulest tasting thing I've ever put in my mouth, that's why." She sat taller as she turned toward Emily, frowning.

Emily got up and took the glass of milk from in front of Martha. "What would you like?" *How did I ever get talked into this?* She put the glass of milk on the counter, then turned and waited. But before Martha could answer, Emily asked, "Do you have any chocolate syrup, like you put on ice cream?" Levi didn't like the taste of milk either, and Emily's mother had been adding a squirt of chocolate syrup to it for as long as Emily could remember.

"No, Emily. I'm not adding chocolate syrup to my milk. I don't like milk, with or without chocolate in it." Martha sighed. "There's a cola in the fridge I can drink."

Emily picked up the milk and put it back in front of Martha. "Cola is bad for you. Milk makes you have strong bones." Emily folded her arms across her chest and pressed her lips together.

"I—I don't . . ." Martha sighed. "Fine, Emily. I will drink the milk."

Emily sat back down.

"Even though I can't stand it." Martha reached for the spoon Emily had put in the creamed celery. "I love the way your people make celery."

"My *people* also pray before a meal." Emily folded her hands in front of her on the table, then bowed her head. Out of the corner of her eye, she saw Martha ease the spoon back down, then bow her head. After she was done silently thanking the Lord for the food before them, she lifted her head to see Martha's head still firmly down, her eyes squeezed shut.

Emily waited. And waited. She looked across the table at David, who shrugged lightly. "Martha?"

Martha's eyes bolted open. "What?"

"Are you done praying?" Emily unfolded the cloth napkin and put it in her lap.

"Done? I was waiting on you to get started."

"We pray silently before and after a meal." Emily fought a grin. "I thought you knew that."

Martha let out a heavy sigh. "No, Emily, I didn't know that. For the sake of us who don't have a direct connection to God, maybe you could say a little something out loud instead of making me guess."

Emily looked across the table at David and noticed he had covered his mouth with his hand, though Emily could see him stifling a grin. She took a deep breath as she lowered her head and thought about her lack of connection with God for the past three months. Then she recited a generic prayer that she'd been silently saying before meals for months. "Dear Lord, bless this food before us, bless the days ahead of us, and bless all who cross in front of us or behind us, as we all make our way to You. *Aamen.*"

She knew she was just going through the motions. But she also knew that she hadn't really sought out true communion with God since her attack. She loved God, but her trust in His will had left her the day James forced himself on her.

Seek Me with all your heart, Emily . . .

Emily heard Martha and David both say Amen, and out of the corner of her eye, she saw them start to load their plates, but she sat quiet and still for a moment. She wondered if it was the inner voice that she hadn't heard in such a long time, but she was unsure how to seek out what she'd come to doubt. For the first time in her life, Emily found her faith tested, and she couldn't seem to find her way back to the peacefulness that she'd evidently taken for granted.

"I need to talk to you both about something." Martha scooped another spoonful of creamed celery onto her plate. Emily and David waited for Martha to take a bite, then swallow, before she went on. "I'm not a well woman, as you can see by my back trouble." She reached around with one hand and rubbed the middle of her back. "I could use some help around here, and I'll gladly pay both of you to come help me clean this place up, and"—she cut her eyes in Emily's direction—"maybe even prepare a couple of meals like this every week."

Emily halted her fork, filled with meatloaf, halfway to her mouth. "Martha, I'm sure there are lots of folks that you could pay to help you, but I have a job at the country store."

David didn't say anything, but instead pushed some food around on his plate.

Martha shrugged. "Suit yourself, but I was thinking along the lines of about fifty dollars per day, just a couple of hours each evening to help me clean, cook a meal, and . . ." She grinned at David. "I got all kinds of work you can do. Home repair type stuff." She paused with a sigh. "But if you aren't interested, then . . ."

"I'm interested." David put his fork down and repeated himself. "I'm interested."

Emily thought about all the things she could do with that much money, but spending that much time with Martha—and David—was out of the question. Plus, she already had a job, and she was expected to help with chores at home and with supper at night. "I'm sorry I can't accept your kind offer."

"Me too." Martha put her fork down, then grimaced as she reached around and grabbed her back. "It's just so hard for me to take care of this place."

Emily lowered her head. "I'm so sorry. I will ask others I know if they might be interested."

Martha shook her head as she eased out of her chair. "No. Only you." She turned to David. "And you. I'm not having any strangers in my house. No ma'am. No strangers. No cranky people underfoot."

Emily glanced across the table at David and tried not to grin.

"Well, uh, I can help my dad fix up the house during the day, then come do any handyman chores here and chop wood in the evenings." David wrapped his mouth around a cob of corn and took a hearty bite.

Martha straightened up, moaning. She frowned as she looked down on David who had a mouthful. "You cook?"

David swallowed. "No, but—"

"Then no. It's a package deal. The both of ya. Talk about it while I go to the bathroom."

Emily watched Martha shuffling to the bathroom, walking slowly as she held the small of her back with one hand.

"I am not coming over here several times a week. I can't, David." She shook her head. "Nor do I want to."

"What about three times a week? That's a hundred and fifty dollars each per week, Emily, on top of whatever you might make at the dry goods store." David put the corn down, then wiped his mouth with his napkin. "Couldn't you use that money for something?"

Emily thought again about the gift she wanted to buy, but shook her head. "I can't. I have to help *Mamm* make supper at night."

David shifted his weight in the chair. "Well, I don't know why she won't let me work for her without you." He tipped his head to one side. "That doesn't make any sense."

"I'm sorry if I'm holding you back, David, but I can't do it." Emily laid her napkin across her half-eaten plate of food. "Sorry."

"What about twice a week? I can pick you up and take you home. You wouldn't have to worry about using one of the family buggies or traveling in the dark. I can't do it forever, just until it's time to ready the fields for planting. Think your folks would agree to that?"

"Even if they did, I don't." Emily glared across the table at David, then looked toward the den when she heard footsteps coming across the wooden floors—floors badly in need of waxing.

"Emily, you take this to your momma when you go." Martha pushed two large bolts of colorful fabric in Emily's direction. "She can use them to make quilts."

"Thank you, Martha." Emily accepted the bolts, then set them down on the floor beside her. "How much does my mother owe for these?"

Martha waved her hand at Emily. "Nothing. I like to do for others." She leaned forward a bit and put her hand on her back again. Emily looked across the table at David, and he was glowering at her as if she was the worst person on the planet.

"Maybe—maybe we could come help you twice a week?" Emily took a deep breath. *I can't believe I'm doing this.* "Martha, you would be paying David and me too much money, though. You'd be paying us each a hundred dollars per week, and that seems like a lot."

"You'll earn it." Martha straightened up. "Believe you me."

Emily blew out a slow breath, fearing Martha's words to be true.

Nine

EMILY HELPED HER MOTHER FOLD THE LAST LOAD OF clothes they'd piled on the couch in the den. Her father and Levi were still at work, installing a solar panel for a nearby *Englisch* family, and Jacob was at the store. He had agreed to watch the store so Emily could get off early twice a week but only in exchange for baking him a chocolate shoofly pie once a week.

David would be arriving any minute, and her stomach rolled with anticipation about this entire venture. She tried to stay focused on the money she would be saving, but part of her was glad to be spending time with David, even though she was trying to push that thought from her mind.

"This is a nice thing you are doing, helping Martha." *Mamm* smiled as she laid a folded towel atop a stack of other towels on the coffee table.

"She's paying us, *Mamm*. It's a job." Emily brought two corners of a towel together and folded.

"*Ya*. She's paying you well."

"Do you think it's wrong? Maybe we shouldn't be doing it."

"I reckon Martha wouldn't have offered if she couldn't afford it and didn't need the help. If it wasn't you and David, it would be someone else."

Emily didn't say that Martha refused to have anyone but her and David. She reached for the last towel in the pile.

"And it's nice that you and David will be spending time together. He seems like such a nice young man."

"*Mamm*, please don't start this afternoon about David."

"What? I just made a comment, Emily." Her mother shrugged, then picked up the laundry basket.

Emily turned to get her coat and bonnet from the rack. "I hear David coming up the drive."

"Be safe. What are you cooking for Martha?"

"I don't know." Emily grinned. "But I'm sure she'll let me know what she wants."

Her mother chuckled. "*Ya*. I'm sure she will."

Emily tied the strings on her black bonnet under her chin, then buttoned her coat.

"Well, don't forget to make your brother's pie." *Mamm* raised her brows and grinned. "You do remember what he did last time you promised him a pie and didn't make him one, don't you?"

"*Ya*, I remember." Emily scowled as she recalled the way Jacob put a frog in her bed every night until he got his pie. Frogs were God's creatures, but Emily didn't care for them. Particularly in her bed. She and Jacob were much younger then, but she wasn't sure Jacob wouldn't repeat himself. "I won't forget."

Betsy rounded the corner with a book tucked under her arm. "Are you going to marry David Stoltzfus?"

"No, Betsy!" Emily pulled the wooden door open and saw

David exiting the buggy. That's all she needed was for David to overhear Betsy's comments. "I have to go."

Betsy set her book on the kitchen table. "*Gut*. I don't want you to marry him." Then she turned to *Mamm*. "Can I play with Anna and Elizabeth later today?"

Emily didn't hear her mother's response. She closed the door behind her, darted down the porch steps, and climbed into the buggy.

"This sunshine makes it feel not nearly as cold." David closed the door behind her and walked around and got inside. "It wasn't too bad a drive over here, but that blanket is still in the back. You'll probably need that." David pointed behind them, then maneuvered the horse until they were heading back down the driveway.

Emily reached for the folded blanket and laid it on her lap.

After a few minutes, David turned toward her. "Feel like sharing that?" He grinned, even though his body shivered.

"I thought you said it wasn't that cold?" Emily started to spread out the blanket.

"The sun is shining; that's what I said. It doesn't seem *as* cold, but it's still cold." David eyed her with a critical squint. "Plenty of blanket for both of us, I'd say."

Emily recalled their last squabble about the blanket, so she tossed part of the blanket onto his leg, careful not to touch him.

"*Danki.*" David pulled the brown wool across his lap.

They were quiet for a few moments, and Emily watched David eyeing their surroundings. "It seems so barren here," he said after a while. "And you hardly ever see another buggy on the road. At home, you couldn't drive a half mile without passing other Amish folks you knew."

Emily heard the regret in his voice and decided this would be an opportunity to learn more about David, especially since they would be spending so much time together.

"So, why exactly did your family move here?" Emily twisted slightly to face him, hoping he wouldn't throw the question back at her.

David shrugged. "I honestly don't know. I told you that my grandpa left us the land after he died, but the rest of our family is in Paradise, Pennsylvania, and *Daed* had plenty of land." He shook his head. "I'm going to help *Daed* get these fields ready when the weather clears, and with the money I've saved, I'll be making my way back to Lancaster County."

His words stung more than the first time she'd heard him mention this, but she certainly understood. "It is a lot different here."

David nodded. "*Daed* said even our planting schedule, what we plant, and everything will be different here. It's pretty—the view of the mountains and everything—but in Paradise everything was really well-kept and sharp looking. There were houses all along the rolling hills, but here, the homes are so few and scattered. It seems . . . lonely, I guess."

"I know what you mean. Except for the mountains around us, it's very flat here. And you're right . . . since the community is so new, there's a long way to go before it's like what we're used to."

"I won't be around that long." David stared straight ahead, his voice firm. He turned toward her. "What about you? You planning to get married and settle down around here?"

"No." The word escaped her lips before she thought it through. David would want her to explain. "I mean, I plan to stay here, I guess."

David smiled warmly. "And you'll get married."

Emily shrugged.

David's blue eyes searched her face, as if trying to reach into her thoughts. "You don't have much interest in dating, marriage, or any of it, do you?"

She raised her shoulders again, then dropped them slowly.

"That's odd. A pretty *maedel* like you."

Emily locked eyes with him as her heart fluttered. *Why can't things be different?* She pulled her gaze from his and stared straight ahead for a moment, then she turned toward him. "You said you don't have any interest in dating either. Why is that?"

David shifted his weight in the seat, and Emily suspected he was about to tell her a partial version of the truth. He had everything in the world going for him. She'd thought he was sparing her feelings when he'd told her before that he didn't want to date anyone, but he sure sent mixed signals. Like his playful flirting at Martha's house.

"Just not in my plan." He didn't look at her when he spoke. Emily kept her eyes on him for a few moments, but he didn't elaborate.

"Well, I guess we chose each other wisely then." His head turned toward Emily as she spoke. "We both needed a friend, and neither of us longs for anything more." Emily knew it was now her who was giving a partial version of the truth. She longed for nothing more than to be loved. Loved by a good man, someone she could trust and raise a family with. But unworthiness filled the space around her, the air she breathed, and everything she touched. She fought the buildup of anger as she thought about everything James had stolen from her. She felt David's eyes on her, and she slowly turned her head toward him.

"I'm glad we're friends." David smiled, and Emily's heart pattered against her chest so hard she could barely breathe.

"Me too."

"And, Emily . . ." David faced forward, his expression serious. "I know something happened to you, and I'm sorry. If you ever want to talk about it, or—"

"No." She shook her head hard. "No."

David held up a palm. "Okay, it's okay. I was just offering."

She took a deep breath, then watched the cold air cloud in front of her as she exhaled. "Maybe someday." She heard herself say the words, but she couldn't believe she'd said them. She could never tell David what happened. Never. *Then why did I say that?*

"The thought of anyone hurting you makes me feel like I could breathe fire and . . ." David scowled as he stopped midsentence, and Emily felt warm from head to toe, almost tempted to tell him. But then he'd see her as the ruined woman she was, and she'd prefer that he not look at her with pity.

She touched his arm, a spontaneous gesture that caught her off guard. "I'm fine now, David. Really."

His eyes landed where her hand rested, then she quickly pulled it away.

DAVID WANTED TO reach over and latch onto Emily's hand, for reasons that confused him. He had no plans to stay here, to ever marry, and certainly he didn't want anything more than friendship from Emily. But her gentle touch sent his heart racing, and he would need to keep reminding himself that friendship was all he had to offer her. Growing close to Emily would only hurt them both in the long run. And from the looks of things, Emily had been hurt enough.

They rode silently for a while, just the clippety-clop of hooves against the asphalt. Snow banks several feet high lined both sides of the road like tiny replicas of the mountains that surrounded them, each small peak glistening from the sun's bright rays. David was wishing he'd brought his sunglasses.

"So, which mountain are you going to climb?" he asked after the silence grew awkward. He looked her way, happy to see his question brought a smile to her face.

"I don't know." She frowned, folded her arms across her chest. "Levi said I can't climb any of these mountains, but I reckon there has to be one suitable for climbing. In the spring I will find my mountain, and when I do, I'm going to climb it." She nodded her head once, then turned toward him and smiled.

"You're so pretty." David silently blasted himself for voicing the thought, which just seemed to spill out, but it was so true.

She pulled her gaze from him, and it was cute the way she pinched her lips together as her cheeks turned a bright shade of pink. She didn't look at him when she finally spoke. "*Danki.*"

Then, as if programmed, she reached up and touched the scar above her brow, which again invoked anger that David tried to squelch. The scar did nothing to take away from Emily's looks, but she was so self-conscious about it. David fought the urge to yell out, *Who did that to you?* He knew that would only upset her, so instead, he took a deep breath and reminded himself that it was not their way to harbor such anger. Instead, he should be trying to forgive whoever hurt Emily.

But as he looked at her again, he realized that he felt a strong desire to protect her, and forgiveness would not come easily.

Emily had offered to clean up Martha's den and any other rooms in the spacious house, but Martha said everything was fine just the way it was. A quick glimpse into the formal dining room told another tale. Magazines, boxes, and other odds and ends were piled on top of a long table with eight high back chairs. In the dim light, Emily couldn't see more than the clutter, but she figured it was probably dirty.

"I don't use that room," Martha said. "So it doesn't need to be cleaned."

"What about the other rooms down here or upstairs?"

Martha reached out the palm of her hand to Elvis and offered him some nuts. "Nope. Just supper. I already have the table set."

"Do you need more firewood, or what chores would you like me to start on?" David removed his black felt hat and waited for instructions.

"Huh?" Martha looked up at him after the bird finished his snack. She brushed her hands together, and Emily cringed as tiny nut crumbs breezed to the floor. "Oh. Chores for you. Uh, yeah. The light bulb in my hall closet needs changing. That's also where I keep the spare light bulbs." She motioned down the hallway behind her.

David stood there, obviously waiting for something else to do besides change a light bulb.

"Then chop more wood, I guess." Martha shrugged before turning to Emily. "Let's go into the kitchen, Emily. I have something to ask you." She headed to the kitchen and Emily followed, turning once to see David walking out the back door toward the wood pile.

Martha pointed to a book lying open on the kitchen table. "Can you make this for supper?"

Emily leaned down to look at the recipe Martha was pointing to. "Chicken lasagna?"

"Yes. We have everything for you to make it, and that's what I'd like to have for supper." She nodded her head firmly.

Emily untied her bonnet and pulled it off. She secured loose strands of hair into her *kapp* as she read the recipe. "This calls for a can of cream of mushroom soup, cream of chicken soup, mozzarella cheese, and things you don't have. Maybe next time I shop for you—"

"No. I have all those things." Martha walked to the pantry and pulled the door open. "See?"

Emily didn't remember seeing any cans of soup the day before, but now there were at least six various soup cans. "I don't remember seeing these before . . ."

Martha waved a hand in the air. "They were there, probably in the back somewhere. And we have mozzarella cheese too." She closed the pantry and walked to the refrigerator, pulling out a package of white cheese. Emily didn't remember seeing that the day before either.

"I guess we can make it then." Emily walked to the refrigerator and pulled out the chicken breasts she had bought. "I need to get this chicken started to boil."

"Good. I found that in an Amish recipe book that I bought in town a long time ago." Martha frowned. "Although, I must say, Emily . . . I'm surprised your people cook with canned soups."

Emily pulled a pot from the cabinet, then placed it on top of the stove. "It's not our first choice, but sometimes we do." She turned to face Martha. "Why did you buy a cookbook if you don't cook?"

"I thought I might try to cook someday." Martha opened the refrigerator and reached for a soda, but she didn't pop the tab when Emily scowled. "I'm not drinking milk for pleasure, and I'm thirsty."

"I'm not going to tell you what to drink in your own *haus*, Martha." She put the chicken in water, then turned on the electric burner. "But water is *gut* for you."

"Fine, Emily." She put the soda back in the refrigerator, then turned on the tap and filled a glass with water.

"Do you want to learn how to cook?" Emily wondered how someone her age didn't cook.

"Why?"

Emily folded her arms across her chest. "Well, because. That's what women do. We cook. And we all need to eat."

Martha grinned as she eased into a kitchen chair. "That's why I have you now."

"But I won't be able to come here forever. I reckon it would be *gut* for you to learn." She started gathering up all the items to make the chicken lasagna. "How do you not know how to cook, someone your . . ."

"My age?" Martha cackled. "I don't know, Emily. I certainly like food, though."

Martha was about Emily's height, but her midsection was

considerably larger than Emily's. *She* definitely *likes food*, Emily thought and smiled. *Maybe a little too much.*

Footsteps drew their attention to the den, then David walked in, his teeth chattering. "The light bulb is changed, and, Martha, you have enough wood chopped for at least a couple of weeks. What else?"

"This boy needs something hot to drink, Emily." Martha pulled out the chair next to her. "Sit down, and Emily will make you some cocoa." She paused. "And yes, Emily, I have packages of cocoa in the pantry."

Emily smiled to herself. The cocoa wasn't there two days ago.

David didn't sit down but pushed his coat back and looped gloved thumbs beneath his suspenders. "I reckon I don't feel right about sitting down on the job. You're paying me to work, Martha."

Martha raised one brow until it arched way up on her forehead. Emily had never seen anyone do that. "I'm paying you to do what I tell you." Martha pulled the chair out farther. "Now, have some cocoa."

David finally did as he was told, and Emily began heating some water on the stove for his cocoa. Once it was done, David sipped it, but he was restless, and Emily knew he felt uncomfortable. "You can chop up an onion if you want," she said as she found a knife in one of the drawers.

"Sure. Okay." He stood up and walked toward her. Emily put the onion on a plate nearby. "I couldn't find a cutting board." She handed him the knife.

"I'm going to freshen up before dinner." Martha stood from the table. "I won't be long."

Emily started mixing the soups and other ingredients in a large bowl.

"This ain't right." David sliced into the onion. "This is women's work, and I should be earning my fifty dollars."

"Maybe she'll have more for you to do next time." Emily watched David butchering the onion. "What are you doing?"

"Chopping the onion."

"Give me that." She eased the knife from his hand. "Like this."

David's hand brushed across hers as he took the knife back, and it caused her heart to flutter a bit. And he was standing much too close to her. She went to the refrigerator and found the sour cream, another item that had mysteriously showed up. "I don't remember a lot of this stuff being here when we were here," she whispered. "I'm sure some of it wasn't here."

"Maybe we're her Tuesday and Thursday shoppers and she has someone else the rest of the time." David chuckled, but then sniffled.

"I doubt that." Emily picked up her bowl and moved farther down the counter so she wasn't so close to him. But she heard him sniffle again. "Are you crying?"

David wouldn't look up, but he swiped at his eye with one hand. "No."

"Rubbing your eyes with the hand you're holding the onion with will only make it worse." Emily bit her bottom lip as a smile threatened to form. David was rubbing one eye hard now, and Emily saw a tear roll down his cheek.

"Can't you give me some other job? I reckon I ain't too good at this one." He looked up at her, eyes filled with tears. She laughed. "Is this funny?"

"David Stoltzfus, have you never cut an onion before? You're supposed to breathe through your mouth and not wipe your eyes like that." She laughed again, and although he couldn't seem to control his tears, he laughed too.

"What is it with you two?" Martha walked back into the room. "Second time I've heard ya both laughing like this. What's so funny?"

Emily laughed harder, and it felt good to be a part of this moment. "Look at him." She pointed to David.

"Good grief. I've never seen a grown man spill that many tears." Martha walked to the refrigerator and pulled out the jar of rhubarb jam, then put it on the table.

David walked away from the half-cut onion, but he couldn't seem to get a grip on the tears. "I'm not cutting any more onions. This is real embarrassing." He pinched his eyes closed, and Emily laughed again.

"Go run water over your eyes and flush out the onion oils." Emily pointed to the sink, and David took her advice.

Emily finished preparing the lasagna and put it in the oven. While it cooked, they all sat around the kitchen table, and David told joke after joke until both Martha and Emily were the ones crying from laughing so hard.

"Here's one more. It's just short and sweet." David leaned forward. "The bishop asked a group of *kinner*—" He glanced at Martha. "I mean *kids*—why is it important to be quiet during worship service?" He paused and grinned. "Little Betsy answered, 'Because people are sleeping.'"

"That sounds exactly like something Betsy would say!" Emily laughed as she pictured her sister making a comment like that. "Back home there was a woman named Naomi, and she always fell asleep during worship service."

She couldn't remember having this much fun, at least not in a long time, and she couldn't take her eyes from David. Charming. Handsome. A hard worker. And now she could add funny to the list.

He was everything she'd ever wanted in a husband.

And she couldn't have him.

When the timer on the oven dinged, Emily excused herself and pulled out the lasagna. She put the lasagna, a salad, and some garlic bread that had mysteriously showed up on the table. Emily once again offered a prayer aloud, and Martha let out a boisterous "Amen."

"This is really *gut*, Emily," David said after he swallowed his first bite.

"Yeah. It is." Martha sat up taller. "I told you she'd make a fine wife, David."

Emily avoided David's eyes as she felt her cheeks warm.

"*Ya*. She will make a fine wife." David smiled. As he spoke, Emily's eyes took on a life of their own and melded with his.

Maybe it was the sweet tone of his voice or his gentle smile, but Emily had never felt more regret than she did at this moment. *I wouldn't be good for you.* She pulled her eyes away and took her first bite of the lasagna, surprised at how good it actually was. She'd never used processed foods like cream of chicken or cream of mushroom soup, even though she knew some Amish women who did. Her mother didn't, but maybe *Mamm* would warm up to the idea since the recipe did come from an Amish cookbook.

"I can't wait to see what Emily comes up with tomorrow." Martha shook her head. "Gonna be tough to top this."

"Uh, Martha. We won't be back until day after tomorrow." Emily brushed a hair away from her face as she spoke.

Martha swallowed, then let out a heavy sigh. "Oh. That's right."

David shifted his weight in the chair and put his fork down. "Martha, I reckon it ain't right to take money from you if you don't have enough work for me to do. Like tonight, all I did was change a light bulb and chop a little wood."

"Those jokes you told were worth a million." Martha slapped her hand on the table, but David was shaking his head.

"No. I can't take any money for tonight."

Martha narrowed her brows at him. "Stop that talk. Of course you'll take the money." She paused, lifted her chin. "Now let's enjoy our family time."

And now Emily knew what this was all about.

Martha wanted a family.

KATIE ANN WAITED for Ivan to finish bathing and come out of the bathroom. Dressed in her white nightgown, she sat on the edge of their bed, the cell phone lying in her lap. *Why does Ivan have a cell phone?* She flipped the phone open, realized she had no idea how to use it, then quickly closed it when she heard the bathroom door open.

Ivan walked into their bedroom with a towel draped around his waist, his dark hair still damp. He stopped in the middle of the room when he saw the phone in Katie Ann's lap.

She put the phone in the palm of her hand and lifted it up. "Why do you have this?"

Her husband raked a hand through his wet hair, then sighed. "So we can call our family back home."

Katie Ann bit her bottom lip and eyed him for a moment. "You know phones aren't allowed, especially ones you carry in your pocket."

Ivan dropped his towel and slipped into his night clothes, keeping his back to her. "Some bishops allow cell phones."

"For business. Besides, why do you need a cell phone when there is a phone in the barn?"

Ivan turned to face her. "Katie Ann . . ." He let out another sigh. "I'll get rid of the phone if it will make you happy."

She stood up, walked toward him, and handed him the phone. "*Ya*. I would like for you to get rid of it. We don't need a phone inside our home. It's intrusive and not necessary."

Ivan snatched the phone from her, then laid it down roughly on the nightstand. He crawled into bed and stayed far on his side as he pulled the covers to his neck.

"Does this make you angry, giving up the phone?" Katie Ann sat down on the edge of the bed, pulled a brush from her nightstand, and in the dim light of the lantern, ran the brush the length of her long hair and waited for Ivan to answer. When he didn't, she turned around to face him. His back was to her. "Ivan?"

"*Ya?*"

"I just don't see why we need a cell phone." She crawled into bed as he rolled over to face her.

"I will get rid of the phone tomorrow."

Katie Ann rolled the knob on the lantern until it extinguished. Tiny rays of moonlight shone through the window, and she turned on her side toward Ivan. His eyes were closed, and she stared at him for a few moments. "*Danki.*"

She kept her eyes on Ivan, and twice he opened his eyes. The second time he said, "Why are you staring at me like that?"

Katie Ann reached over and touched his arm. She felt him twitch. *Did he flinch?* She eased her hand away. "I was just watching you fall asleep."

"You should sleep too." Ivan closed his eyes again, then rolled over to face the window.

Katie Ann tucked her hands between her face and the pillow. Sleep seemed far away, and she wondered how long Ivan had been toting a cell phone around. Where was he keeping it? This evening it had fallen from his pants pocket, but she'd picked up Ivan's clothes plenty of times before and had never found a phone.

Ivan was snoring when the question popped into her mind. *Is Ivan using the phone to call Lucy Turner?*

Ten

THE LAST FEW TIMES THEY'D BEEN TO MARTHA'S, SHE'D found things for David to do, but not much. He felt guilty for not doing more, but every time he pushed Martha for more chores, it seemed a bother to her. She'd mumble as she walked around the house until she found enough odd jobs to keep him busy for about an hour, then she'd insist they spend the rest of the night eating, listening to his jokes, telling stories, then going to the den to play a game.

Little by little, Emily had convinced Martha to let her clean the house—the den anyway—and David always made a *gut* fire in the fireplace. The whole thing was odd but strangely pleasant. The best part—his time with Emily. He was experiencing a dream he couldn't have. Maybe that should have made him sad, but instead, he allowed himself to live in the moment each night, pretending that he could take care of Emily for the rest of her life, laugh with her, grow old with her.

As Martha cackled about winning a card game for the fourth straight time, Emily walked into the den carrying pieces of shoofly pie she'd made at home the night before. *She would make an excellent wife.* He knew he wasn't the right man for her, but watching her, being around her, and getting to know her were the highlights of his week. He'd even helped in the kitchen, something unheard of in most Amish households, and he'd learned to chop an onion without crying like a baby.

"Here you go." Emily smiled as she handed him a piece of pie. "I see Martha won again after I folded my hand."

"*Ya.*" David wanted to spend some time alone with Emily, but Martha was always right in the middle of everything. He laughed to himself. *Of course she's in the middle of everything; we're all at* her *house.* They were all together because of her, and he had to admit, she was a funny woman. Set in her ways, but David knew she had a good heart. There had to be more that he could do to earn the money she was giving them. "Martha, I noticed that your living room needs painting. Why don't you let me paint it for you?"

"No."

"But—"

Martha held up a crooked finger. "You can clean Elvis's cage next time, since you're itching to do more."

Emily giggled, and David glared at her for a moment, but it was impossible not to grin along with her.

"You got a problem with cleaning my Elvis's cage, David?" Martha walked to the bird and reached her hand in the cage. "Did you hear that, Elvis? Our David doesn't want to clean your cage. Precious boy."

"No. It's fine." At least he wouldn't feel as guilty about the money. Martha was paying them to be her part-time family, and that just wasn't right. It was bothering him more and more. He finished his pie, then said, "Emily, we best be getting on the road."

Emily stood up and reached for all of their empty plates. "*Ya*. You're right."

A few minutes later they said their good-byes. There was never any hugging or anything like that, and David was glad—'course, he wouldn't have minded hugging Emily.

As tired as he was, he wasn't ready to say good night to Emily. "Do you want to go get a cup of *kaffi* somewhere?"

Her luminous eyes widened. "Where would we go this time of night?"

He'd been worried she wouldn't want to go, but he was at least prepared this time if she said yes. "That small diner on the way to Monte Vista. It's only about four miles."

"I don't know, David . . ." As she tapped her finger to her chin, he waited, hoping. "Maybe just a quick cup. Is there something you want to talk about? Martha or our arrangement?"

That wasn't it, but if that would get him some extra time alone with her, he figured he better agree. "*Ya*. I'm feeling badly about her paying us to be her family."

Even in the darkness, he could see her serious expression. "Me too. And that is just what she's doing." She turned slightly in her seat. "But I think it would sadden Martha to no end if we didn't come see her twice a week. Maybe we should just refuse the money."

David thought about the money he'd been tucking away to get back to Lancaster County. "Maybe. But I don't think she'd hear of that."

They rode quietly the rest of the way, with the clippety-clop of hooves, chattering teeth, and a full moon overhead.

The diner was empty, except for an elderly couple eating pie in a corner booth and a young mother with her baby seated near the entrance. The waitress led them to a booth opposite the older couple.

David watched Emily sip her coffee and thought about how far they'd come. "Do you still miss Ohio, or do you feel better about being here in Canaan?"

"I still miss it." She ran her finger around the rim of her cup as she spoke. "But I guess it's getting better." Then she looked up at him and smiled in a way that plagued his heart with regret. *I wish I could take care of you forever.* "*Ach*, I was thinking . . ." She paused, grinning. "When the weather clears, maybe you could till a garden for Martha, and I'll plant vegetables for her, maybe get her involved and show her how *wunderbaar* it feels to tend the land."

"*Ya*, that's a *gut* idea. I'll have to ready the fields with *mei daed*, but I'm sure I can find time to till Martha a small garden."

"I plan to have a garden at home, and I have the dry goods store to tend, but I think it's important that we help Martha have her own too."

Emily's face glowed as she detailed how big she would like the garden to be, how she wondered if she could grow watermelons like she did back home, and how maybe they could even build a picket fence around Martha's garden. It was almost as if—as if they were talking about their own home. David thought about how they'd cooked together, played games together, taken care of Martha and her house together—all the time they'd spent together.

"And I'm going to get that living room of hers painted, one of these days." David took a sip of his coffee and wondered briefly if the caffeine would keep him up tonight.

"With hard work, that house of hers could be so pretty,

especially the outside. She has a big yard with flowerbeds that just haven't been tended to. You'll see when the snow clears what I'm talking about."

"We'll help her get it in shape."

They were quiet for a few minutes, and David wondered how much of all this he could actually do. His plans didn't include staying in Canaan.

For the first time since he'd arrived in Colorado, he wondered if maybe he could make a life here. But no sooner did he have the thought, than he was reminded that he wouldn't be good for Emily. She deserved someone who would be around for a long time, someone to raise a family with.

When the waitress returned, they opted for two pieces of apple pie.

EMILY WAS CERTAIN that she'd never been as cold as she was on this night. They'd barely gotten back on the main road, and her cheeks were numb. Even with the portable heater, the blanket, and the window protectors, she couldn't stop shaking. She rubbed her gloved hands together beneath the heavy blanket.

"Emily . . ." David said in a shaky voice. "If you will scoot over here next to me and wrap that blanket around the both of us, we will be a little warmer. Maybe even hold that heater in front of us." She could hear David's teeth chattering. "Please," he added.

Emily slowly moved toward him. She draped the blanket around both their shoulders. David pulled his arm free of the blanket and draped it across her shoulders, then pulled her close. He rubbed her arm, and she could feel him shivering.

"Put your arm back under the blanket so you'll stay warm."

"It's okay. I'm just worried about you. I can't believe we stayed as long as we did, and the temperatures sure have dropped."

Emily snuggled close to him, welcoming the warmth. "I'm okay, David." She tipped her head up, but the motion put her face entirely too close to his, so she quickly turned it away.

She tried not to focus on David's tender touch as he rubbed her arm atop the blanket. She felt comforted, yet leery at the same time. He was so sweet, so safe. And that frightened her. Was she falling for him? What a disaster that would be. But for now, she was so cold, and he felt so good next to her.

"It's starting to snow." Emily leaned forward and gazed into the night as white flecks of powder pelted the windshield of the buggy. "*Mamm* is going to be frantic."

"I'll talk to her when we get there and tell her this is my fault."

"No, no. You don't have to do that." Emily felt him pull her closer, and she felt warm inside, if not on the outside. "It's not your fault, any more so than mine."

She slowly rested her head against the crook of his arm and all her worries of the past began to fade . . . only to have new ones come into view.

DAVID COULDN'T DENY how good it felt to have Emily snuggle up next to him. He was glad that she now felt comfortable around him. They'd formed a bond over the past few weeks, and it was a welcome change from the frightened woman he'd first met. But he could tell by his growing feelings that he would need to put some distance between them. Emily had been hurt enough. Falling for her would only hurt them both in the long run.

"David?"

Her head shifted from against his chest, putting her face almost close enough that he could have easily leaned down and kissed her, and the sweet sound of her voice only made him want to do so even more. He took a deep breath. "*Ya?*"

"I'm glad . . ." She paused, and even in the moonlight he could see a twinkle in her big brown eyes. "I'm glad we're friends."

She smiled up at him, then lowered her face and once again nuzzled against him. He pulled her closer, knowing he shouldn't, but as the warmth of her body comforted his, something about Emily Detweiler warmed his soul as well. She made him want to be a whole man, someone with a long life ahead of him.

VERA WHIPPED THE buggy into the Stoltzfuses' driveway, against Elam's wishes. "Vera, I'm sure everything is fine," he'd said earlier. "And it's too cold for you to be traveling."

But she'd already called Martha from the phone in the barn. David and Emily had left over two hours ago, Martha had said, and Vera's heart had begun to race. The last time Emily had been late coming home, it was dark outside, as it was now, and the unthinkable had happened. She tried to ignore her upset stomach as she tethered the horse and marched across the snow to the porch steps. She grabbed the wobbly railing and carefully pulled herself up to the front door.

Even though David seemed like a nice young man, Vera

couldn't shake her worry. They could have been in an accident. She rapped hard on the wooden door, and as she stood in the cold, she noticed light coming from a window to her left. Only a few moments later, she heard footsteps.

"Vera!" Lillian swung the door wide. "Come in, come in. What are you doing out here in this weather?"

"I'm wondering why Emily isn't home yet. David never brings her home from Martha's this late, and I'm worried, and . . ." She shook her head as a knot formed in her throat.

"I'm sure Emily is fine. She's with David. He won't let anything happen to her." Lillian smiled, but Vera didn't reciprocate.

Vera glanced around the room and nodded at Samuel. "David should know not to have her out this late." She tilted her chin up and continued to fight the lump in her throat.

Samuel stood up, and while his eyes were sharp and assessing, Vera just wanted her daughter home. "Vera, I'm sure that the *kinner* are fine. If there had been an accident, I reckon we would have heard. They're young. Maybe they went for *kaffi*." He reached his hand out to her. "Can I take your coat?"

Vera knew she was dripping snow on the floor, but she held her position. "Emily knows how I feel about her being late, and David should—" She stopped herself and took a deep breath when she saw a distinct hardening of Samuel's eyes.

"Vera, let me get you something hot to drink." Lillian stepped closer. "Goodness, your teeth are chattering." She pulled Vera toward the fire. "Here, warm yourself. Not much in this old house works, but the fireplace is huge, and we've been enjoying a nice fire this evening."

Vera moved toward the fire with Lillian, pulled her gloves

off, and warmed her hands above the flames. "I'm sorry. I just worry. I shouldn't have come."

Lillian smiled. "You're welcome here any time. And I really am sure that everything is fine. Those two spend a lot of time together. Maybe more than a friendship is forming, no?"

Images of that night over three months ago raced through Vera's mind. She put her face in her hands. How well did she really know these people? Worry began to overtake her. "Maybe I should go look for them."

Samuel stepped forward. "Vera, I don't think that's a *gut* idea. I'm sure they're fine."

She turned around to face Samuel. "You don't know that. I don't even know David, and . . ."

Samuel frowned and opened his mouth to speak, but Lillian spoke up.

"Vera, honey. I was just getting ready to go check on Elizabeth and Anna. Why don't you take off your coat and bonnet and come with me?" Lillian gently touched Vera's arm. "Please. We can talk upstairs."

Vera drew in a deep breath and blew it out slowly. Then she unbuttoned her coat and removed it along with her bonnet. Lillian draped the garments on the back of the couch. "I really should be going home, since I reckon David will drop Emily off before coming here. I don't know why I came. I just . . ."

A tear rolled down Vera's cheek, and she quickly wiped it away. Her emotions about what had happened to Emily were catching up to her, and it was embarrassing. She saw Lillian and Samuel exchange looks before Lillian coaxed Vera toward the stairs.

Vera watched as Lillian checked on both her girls, then

motioned for Vera to follow her down the hall. They walked into what Vera presumed was Lillian and Samuel's bedroom. A large bed was on the far wall, a dresser in the corner, and boxes were stacked everywhere. Light brown paint was peeling from the walls. It was a mess, and Vera silently reprimanded herself for not making more time to come help Lillian work on this house.

"Please don't judge us by this house," Lillian said as her eyes scanned the room. "Someday it will be beautiful." She chuckled. "I hope."

"I would never judge, Lillian."

Lillian sat down on the bed and patted the spot next to her. Vera took a seat beside her.

"Now, what's going on?" Lillian leaned her head to one side. "It's not that late, Vera, and you know David is a *gut* young man. He'll get Emily home safely."

Vera pushed back several strands of dark hair that had fallen forward. She sat taller. "I know." She paused. "I shouldn't have come. It's just that I get so scared, and I don't think Elam understands." She turned to Lillian and grabbed her hand. "It's a sin to worry, Lillian. I know this, and yet I'm consumed with worry when it comes to Emily. I try not to show it in front of her. But sometimes it just overtakes me, and her being late tonight just seems to have pushed my emotions right over the top. I'm so sorry for my rude behavior. Please apologize to Samuel for me." She let go of Lillian's hand and stood up, ready to leave, but Lillian grabbed her by the elbow and pulled her back down.

"*Ach*, no ya don't." Lillian raised her brows. "Our kids being home a little late is not what this is all about. Not completely anyway. What's going on, Vera? Let me be a *gut* friend to you. You're the only friend I have here. Let me help."

Vera sniffled a bit. "No, really. I'm sure everything is fine." She shrugged nonchalantly. "I'm sure there is no problem." She spoke the words with conviction, but a tear still rolled down her cheek. It was as if every emotion she'd felt since Emily's attack was surfacing, and now she wasn't sure how to keep from telling Lillian what ailed her so. If she were honest with herself, she'd realize she needed a friend, another female to talk to about what happened to Emily. She'd never spoken of the incident to family or friends in Middlefield, and she and Elam had offered a partial version of the truth about their relocation to Canaan—cheaper land prices, more room to expand for future generations, and a better environment for Levi's asthma. And even though she and Elam had discussed what happened to Emily over the past few months, she'd never really allowed herself to show much emotion in front of her husband.

Emily had begged her family not to tell anyone what happened to her. Vera explained to her daughter repeatedly that she didn't have anything to be ashamed of, but Vera also knew that folks can be cruel sometimes. She knew in her heart that most of the community in Middlefield would have showered them with love and comfort, but there would have been a few who would have shunned Emily in their own way, not wanting their own sons to pursue Emily as a wife. At the time, it seemed like moving away from Middlefield was the right thing to do—for all of them.

In Colorado, Levi still had to use his inhaler, but not nearly as often as he did in Middlefield, the land truly was less expensive, and Elam was able to establish a new business. She and

Elam thought that a new place and new surroundings would help them all to heal, especially Emily. But there was no place far enough to run from the pain that still gripped them.

Vera buried her face in her hands and began to cry. When the tears turned to sobs, Vera couldn't stop them.

"Vera, oh Vera. Please talk to me. What is the matter?"

Lillian's voice was so tender, and as Lillian put her arm around her, Vera knew that she couldn't stay silent any longer. She lifted her head and, in a most unladylike gesture, swiped at her tears and nose with the sleeve of her dress. She took a couple of deep breaths, trying to control herself before she spoke.

"I know that everything is God's will, Lillian. I've been taught that my entire life, but . . ." She looked into Lillian's kind eyes. "Something—something happened to Emily before we left Middlefield, something horrible." She shook her head as the images came racing forward again. Emily's bloody forehead, the police, the ambulance, all the bright lights. Another tear rolled down her cheek. "Emily was—was . . ." Lillian dropped her arm from around Vera, then clasped both of Vera's hands in hers.

"Vera, God will see us through anything, and—"

"Then where was God when Emily was raped? Where was He then, Lillian? Please tell me, so that I can forgive, so that I can heal, so that I can somehow help Emily." She looked at her new friend and pleaded, "Tell me, Lillian! Where was God?"

Shame took over every inch of Vera's being as she realized that she had voiced her most secret feelings, yelled them in fact, to a woman she barely knew. She lowered her head as new tears spilled onto her dark green dress. "Forgive me, Lillian."

Lillian pulled Vera into a hug, then patted her on the

back while Vera sobbed. "Oh, Vera. Oh, my dear Vera. Poor Emily. That is horrible, for sure. But it's all right to feel like this, Vera. We're human. Something tragic happened to your baby girl, and I think God understands these emotions at a time like this."

Vera pulled away and wiped her eyes. "I love my God, Lillian. I love God." She felt desperate to convey that to her friend after her verbal lashing.

"Of course you do." Lillian shook her head. "And it's hard to understand how something so terrible could be of His will, but, Vera . . ."

Vera sniffled and locked eyes with Lillian, whose eyes held a pensive shimmer. "*Ya?*"

"As you know, I wasn't always Amish. And before I converted, I didn't know God or have a personal relationship with Him during times of trouble, which often made things unbearable. But Emily has a strong faith, and that is what will see her through this, help her to heal."

Vera nodded and wiped her face with the sleeve of her dress again.

"How long ago did this happen?"

"Right before we moved here, which would be about four months ago."

They sat quietly for a moment.

"How is Emily? I mean, has she been able to move forward? Is she starting to heal?"

Vera sighed. "I don't know, Lillian. Emily didn't want us to talk to anyone about what happened to her, and looking back, I'm not sure if agreeing to Emily's wishes was the right thing to do. But it was hard for all of us to face friends and other family members without saying anything to them. We weren't exactly lying, but we certainly weren't being truthful either." Vera closed her eyes for a moment, sniffed, then looked back at Lillian. "I try to always be upbeat around her, never let my feelings show in front of her. I try to make things as normal as possible, and sometimes I do extra for her, more than for Jacob, Levi, or even Betsy. Even if it's just to make her favorite foods, or give her a little extra spending money to go to market, little things like that. But she doesn't seem to have an interest in much, and she's . . ." Vera straightened and shifted on the bed. "She's very ugly to me sometimes. And that's all right, I reckon. She has a right to be mad at the world, I suppose. I do wonder if her faith is strong enough to see her through this." Vera swallowed hard. "Because my faith has certainly slipped, at a time when I need it most."

Lillian spoke more softly than before. "Maybe just realizing that, Vera, is a step in the right direction. I believe you and your family to be grounded in your faith, and we all slip. It doesn't mean we aren't *gut* Christians. Pray about it, Vera, and I will be praying daily for you and Emily both."

"You know . . ." Vera thought about her recent conversations with Emily. "Emily seems angry with me about what happened. And, Lillian, I've gone over it in my mind a thousand times, how I could have prevented it from happening. She went for a walk while we weren't home." Vera shook her head as she recalled Emily's statements the night of the rape. "I think she knows who her attacker is, but she won't tell a soul, and that worries me too. But what kind of man does such a thing, Lillian?" Vera shuddered slightly. "And Emily turned away from all the young men her age after this happened, refused to be friends with any of them. Then when we moved here, she wouldn't even work in the store by herself. She's afraid, and I hate that."

Lillian rubbed her back with one hand. "Emily doesn't seem afraid of David. And I'm sure they are fine. But, Vera, I can see why you would fly into a tailspin and worry about her."

"It's not about David, Lillian. I just got scared. The last time Emily was late, after dark, she came home with blood on her head, crying, and . . ." Vera started to cry again. "Please forgive me if I made out like David might do some horrible act like that, because that's not what I meant, and . . ."

Lillian continued to rub Vera's back. "I know that, Vera. I know."

"I've never talked to anyone about this, Lillian. Elam and I had been considering a move for a while—a place that would be better for Levi, and somewhere that would provide more opportunities for all of us. Then, after this happened to Emily, we knew it was time." Vera took a deep breath before going on. "But I know that my faith has been affected . . . and I wonder how much Emily's faith has been affected too."

"Time and prayer heal. And I know you know that." Lillian smiled. "Just a gentle reminder, my friend."

Vera smiled. "*Danki*, Lillian. For letting me release all this pent up emotion I've been carrying around, hiding from everyone. Even my husband. I'm so glad it was with you, and not with Emily. I wouldn't want her to ever see me like this. I try to be strong for her."

Lillian folded her hands in her lap and sighed. "Motherhood is the most rewarding job on the planet, but often the most challenging."

Vera nodded as she considered whether or not this was the right time to question Lillian about their move from Lancaster County. Perhaps Lillian needed a friend to open up to. "Lillian, please forgive me if I'm being too nosey, but I get a strong sense that your family moved here for reasons other than you mentioned. I hope and pray that something bad didn't happen to your family to drive you away from those you love, like us. And if you'd rather not say, I understand, and—"

"No, it's all right." Lillian cleared her throat, then seemed to force a smile. "We didn't have a tragedy, nothing like what happened to your family. Our reasons for coming here are a bit embarrassing."

Vera shook her head. "Oh, Lillian, please don't tell me if it will make you uncomfortable. I shouldn't have asked."

"Actually, it would do me *gut* to talk about it." Lillian pulled her eyes from Vera's, tapped her feet against the wooden floor for a moment, then took a deep breath. "We were having terrible financial problems, and I didn't know my husband had mortgaged our farm." Lillian stirred uneasily on the bed next to Vera. "I should have known, though. I should have realized that the cost of David's medications was—"

"Medication? Is David sick?" He didn't look sick to Vera.

"Not anymore, but David had a kidney transplant five years ago, and the medication he has to take daily is very expensive." Lillian let out a tiny gasp. "But, Vera, David doesn't know about this. We didn't lie to him, but we also didn't tell him about the financial problems. We didn't want him to have any kind of guilt. And Samuel and I know that David will be going off on his own someday. He'll have to know what the medications cost, but we just didn't want him to know that played a part in our falling behind on everything." Lillian locked eyes with Vera and chewed on her bottom lip for a moment before she went on. "But honestly, Vera . . . I'm not sure we did the right thing either. We told a few family members about our financial troubles, but I'm not convinced that we shouldn't have been more truthful with David."

Vera sighed. "I can understand why you did what you did. You just wanted to protect David. It sounds like he's been through a lot." She shook her head. "As mothers, we try to protect our children, but sometimes it's hard to know where to draw the line and let God take over."

Lillian nodded. "By selling our farm and owning this house free and clear, we can save for the future and help David to have a *gut* financial foundation when he starts a family of his own." She shrugged, then smiled. "Right or wrong, we're here now, and all we can do is make the best of it and pray that we've made good decisions." Then she chuckled lightheartedly. "Although, getting this place somewhat livable will take some of that savings."

"Lillian, I am committed to help you get this place in order. And I know Elam will be too."

"*Danki*, Vera. But don't pity us. We're more blessed than most. David's uncle gave him a kidney, and he'll go on to live a healthy, full life. And our girls are healthy, so that is the most important thing."

Vera reached out and hugged Lillian. "Lillian, I'm so glad we talked."

"Me too."

"I guess I better get home and wait for Emily. And even

though I probably shouldn't have made the trip in this weather, we would have never had this chat if I hadn't."

"Everything that happens is His will."

"*Ya*. It is."

EMILY COULDN'T BELIEVE how safe she felt nestled under David's arm, especially when she'd never thought she would feel safe again. Her head was filled with what-ifs. What if I allowed myself to really care for David? What if he cared for me? Instinctively, she reached up and touched the scar above her brow.

"You worry too much about that."

She jerked her hand down. "What?"

His arm was still around her shoulder, but over the course of the cold ride home, he'd put it under the blanket, which remained draped around both of them. He gave her a squeeze, which sent a warm sensation throughout her shivering body.

"You touch that scar above your forehead a lot. I wouldn't even notice it if you didn't do that."

"I don't do that." She knew she did. Every time a thought about what happened surfaced, her hand seemed to jump to the reminder above her brow.

As they neared a stop sign, David coaxed the horse to a stop and waited for a car to pass. A nearby streetlight dimly lit up the inside of the buggy. Emily tilted her face toward David. "Maybe I do touch it a lot. It reminds me . . ." She pulled her eyes from his and faced forward again, but David gently cupped her chin and turned her back to face him.

His blue eyes shone with tenderness as he pressed his lips above her brow, lingering on her scar long after all the cars had passed. Emily was speechless.

He slowly pulled his lips from her forehead and cupped her cheek in his hand and gazed into her eyes. "Maybe now you will think of me, of this moment, instead of something bad."

Emily swallowed hard, certain he could see the lump in her throat. He leaned down and his lips were almost on hers when a car eased up to the stop sign, then honked, waiting for them to go.

David smiled. "Oops." He put the horse into motion, and they crossed through the four-way stop. Once they were on the other side, Emily laid her head back in the crook of his arm. They rode quietly for a while down the back roads toward home. She leaned up to look at him, wondering if he might think about kissing her. But it was starting to snow hard, and he was focused on the road in front of him.

He pulled his arm from around her and used both hands to hold the reins. He leaned forward. "It's getting hard to see."

"At least we're on the back roads and off the main highway." Emily was disappointed that he was no longer holding her close, though she understood why.

After a few minutes, the snow let up a little and he eased back against the seat, but he didn't put his arm back around her. They were passing by Martha's house, which meant they were close to home. Emily didn't want this time to end. She glanced to her left when she saw movement in Martha's front yard.

Is Martha getting in her car?

Emily jerked when David pulled back hard on the reins and yelled, "Whoa!"

She leaned forward. "Oh no! What happened?"

A toppled buggy lay on the side of the road. As David pulled up to it, car headlights illuminated the inside of their buggy from behind. The car screeched as it came to a stop behind them.

David jumped out of the buggy, and Emily followed. Martha came running toward them, lifting her legs high in tall boots as she trudged through the snow.

"I saw it happen out my window!" Martha yelled. "That car sped by my house and ran that buggy right off the road. Looked like the animal got spooked, and the buggy went over!"

Martha caught up to Emily and David.

"Emily Detweiler, is that you?" Martha scowled as she glanced toward David. "What in the world are the two of you doing out in this weather? You should have been home hours ago." Emily could see Martha glaring at her as the car headlights continued to light their way.

"We're running a little late getting home."

"I'll say. Your momma is worried sick."

"I thought your car didn't run?" Emily picked up the pace but David was ahead of both women and made it to the buggy first.

"Uh, it's fixed now," Martha said as she huffed to keep up with Emily.

David crawled onto the side of the snow-covered buggy, pulled back the winter protectors, then leaned into the passenger window. "There's a woman in here."

"Is she okay?" Emily asked as she and Martha finally made it to the toppled buggy.

Emily heard David faintly say, "Oh no."

"What? How bad is it?" Emily moved closer, until she was leaning against the buggy.

"I already called 9-1-1," Martha said as she edged closer. "Help should be on the way."

David shoved the upper half of his body down into the buggy, and his next words sucked the breath out of Emily.

"Vera, hang on. Help is on the way."

Eleven

Emily didn't remember scaling the side of the buggy, or pulling David by his coat until he made room for her to see inside. He told her at the hospital that he'd never seen a person move that fast before.

A visit to the emergency room, and Emily and her mother were home, accompanied by David and Martha. When they arrived, Emily filled in her father and brothers about what had happened. Thank goodness Betsy was in bed asleep. Emily could feel her father's eyes blazing down on her, and she suspected he was angry with her for being late, which ultimately had caused her mother to travel in this weather.

"I told you there was no reason to go to the hospital." *Mamm* frowned as she glanced around the room. "I was knocked around a bit, that's all." She glared at Martha. "There was no need to make such a fuss and call an ambulance."

"That knot on your noggin was reason enough," Martha said as she raised her chin. "Looked like a big ol' golf ball on your forehead. It could have been a concussion, and it's better safe than sorry."

Vera waved off the comment. "A waste of community funds, I'd say." She touched the knot on her head, and Emily did see her flinch briefly. "See, it's almost gone anyway." But *Mamm* wasted no time resuming her role as cheerful hostess. "Can I get anyone some coffee or cocoa?"

Just for once, Emily wished her mother would feel something, like a normal human being. Surely the accident had scared her.

"I'm leaving." Martha, still dressed in a heavy gray coat with a purple scarf around her neck, moved from the fireplace.

"Thank you for everything, Martha." *Mamm* smiled warmly at Martha, who just shrugged.

There was a knock at the door. Jacob was closest, and he pulled the door open. "Can I help you, sir?"

"I'm Arnold Becker. Is your father at home?"

Emily's father moved toward the door. He eased Jacob out of the way.

"Arnold, come in. What brings you out in this weather?"

Emily glanced at the clock on the mantel. Nearly eleven o'clock.

"Just checking on you folks." The gray-headed man walked into the den dressed in a long black coat with a black felt hat. If he'd had the traditional beard, Emily could have easily mistaken him for an Amish man. "I was on my way home, and I saw the lights on. The fella at the gas station said there was a buggy accident and that he thought it was one of the Detweilers."

"It was my wife, but she's doing fine." *Daed* shook Mr. Becker's hand, then glanced around at everyone else. "You've heard me mention Arnold before, how he is going to head up the schoolhouse project. We met recently at the hardware store in Monte Vista. He overheard some of us talking about the construction, some of the things we weren't quite sure of, and he offered to help us." Her father introduced Arnold to everyone, then turned back to him. "It's nice of you to stop by and check on us."

The elderly man had kind gray eyes, and a gentle smile tipped at the corner of his mouth when Emily's father thanked him.

"As long as I'm here, Elam, I want to share some good news. I have all the permits for the new schoolhouse. As soon as the weather clears, we can get started." Mr. Becker pushed back the rim of his hat. "Might be a couple of months, though."

"We will all be ready when the time comes." Emily's father smiled as he pointed to David. "David and his father have offered to help too."

"*Ya*," David said.

"David, have you been in contact with Lillian and your father?" Emily's mother walked into the room after excusing herself earlier, and she was carting a tray filled with cups of hot cocoa.

"*Ya*," David said as he reached for one of the cups. "While you were in the ambulance on the way to the hospital, Martha followed me to *mei haus* so I could put Buster, my horse, in the barn. I ran in and told Lillian what happened. She wanted to ride with us to the hospital, but I told her I thought you were going to be all right. They know where I am." He turned to Martha. "So I guess I'm leaving now, too, with Martha. She said she'd drop me at home." David paused with a grin. "Now that her car works." He took another sip of his cocoa, then set it on the table.

"I'm not leaving yet," Martha announced as she walked over to the tray of cups and helped herself to one. She carried it over to where Mr. Becker was standing and smiled at the elderly man . . . *Did she just bat her eyes at him?* Emily held back a grin.

As usual, Levi didn't say much, and he excused himself and went upstairs. *Mamm* commented about the weather; then Jacob reminded everyone about his upcoming nuptials in two weeks.

"David, you and your family will attend, no?" David nodded. "And Mr. Becker, I hope you and your family can attend as well." Emily knew her mother had already invited Martha, although they'd all assumed she wouldn't be there.

Martha's eyes widened as she waited for Mr. Becker to answer.

"I'd be honored to attend, Jacob. But it's just me. I don't have any family."

Martha grinned up at him, and Emily covered her mouth with her hand. She'd gotten to know Martha over the past few weeks, but this Martha was new. Emily found it amusing, and she glanced at David to see if he did too. A smile hovered at the corner of his mouth. Instantly, she thought about the way he'd tenderly kissed her forehead and how he'd almost kissed her on the lips.

"The wedding is right before Christmas." *Mamm* smiled as she addressed the group. "It was the only weekend that worked for everyone during December." She turned to Mr. Becker. "In Ohio, Mr. Becker, we have weddings in November or December, after the fall harvest." *Mamm* shrugged. "So we're keeping things traditional."

"Vera, don't you think you should go on up to bed? I don't like the looks of that knot on your head, and I know that topple must have left you sore." Emily's father cut his eyes at Emily, then looked back at her mother. "You shouldn't have been out in this weather, and I told you that."

"Elam, I'm fine. And I'm enjoying visiting." *Mamm* took a sip of her cocoa, then she glanced around the room. "Now, who needs more cocoa?"

Mr. Becker placed his cup on the tray. "I'm going to head on home. It's late, and I know it's been a rough night for you all. I just wanted to make sure everyone was all right, and I must admit that I was excited to tell Elam that we got all the permits for the new schoolhouse for the children."

"We will build a fine school," Emily's father said as he extended his hand to Mr. Becker. "Thank you for stopping by."

Mr. Becker tipped his hat as he glanced around the room. "A pleasure meeting all of you."

Martha scowled, but quickly shifted her expression when Mr. Becker's eyes met with hers. "Lovely to meet you too, Mr. Becker." She extended her hand to him.

"Just call me Arnold."

"All right . . . Arnold." Martha flashed a full smile at him.

Mr. Becker was barely out the door when Martha's expression turned gruff. She looked at David and barked, "Let's go."

David jumped up from where he was sitting on the couch next to Jacob. He put his cup on the tray in front of him. "Okay."

"Say good-bye to your girlfriend, and meet me out front." Emily's heart thudded in her chest as Martha turned to Emily's mother. "Glad you're okay." Emily couldn't bring herself to look at anyone for a moment, then she lifted her eyes to meet David's. He was grinning, and she couldn't help but smile back at him.

Emily risked a glance in her mother's direction and saw her sporting a cool smile. The last thing Emily needed was for *Mamm* to think that she and David were courting. *Mamm* would never ease up about it now.

"*Danki* for the cocoa, Vera," David said. He was still dressed in his long black coat, so he grabbed his hat and headed toward the door. "Bye everyone."

Mamm walked him to the door. "See you soon, David,"

After her mother closed the door, she turned to Emily. "Girlfriend?"

"That's not the case, *Mamm*. I don't know why Martha said that." She gave a shrug. "I'm going to bed." She quickly kissed her mother on the cheek and ran up the stairs before her mother had a chance to question her further.

TWO DAYS LATER Martha fired Emily and David. She handed them each a hundred dollars when they showed up at her house, said she didn't need their help anymore, and didn't even invite them in. But a strange car was in the driveway, so Emily and David just smiled at each other, then went and had coffee and pie at the diner.

But it had been over two weeks since Emily had last seen David. One of those weeks, a blizzard kept everyone hunkered down inside. They didn't even have their scheduled worship service, which was to be held at the Huyards' down the road, because no one could get out. Emily and her family had worshiped privately in their home, as she assumed David's family and the other families in their small district had done.

She'd worked a bit at their country store, and from Jacob she'd learned that David had started a job at a furniture store in Monte Vista. But, if she was honest with herself, much of her time was spent daydreaming about David. His gentle lips on her forehead played through her mind over and over again. Maybe he did care for her. But every time she allowed herself to think like that, she was reminded that she wasn't a worthy bride. Despite that belief, in her heart she knew she was smitten with David, and she couldn't wait to see him today.

Today was Jacob and Beth Ann's wedding, and the sun was shining, with no snow in the forecast for at least a few days. Everyone in the Detweiler household had been up early, preparing for the event. By mutual agreement, the two families had decided the wedding would take place at the Detweilers' instead of at Beth Ann's home. The blizzard had caused a pipe to burst in the King household, and Beth Ann's father didn't think he could get the house ready in time. *Mamm* to the rescue.

Emily was looking forward to giving Jacob and Beth Ann the wringer washing machine she'd been able to purchase for them with the money she'd earned from Martha. It was a bit extravagant, but Emily felt badly about the way she'd avoided her future sister-in-law because she didn't want to hear about their wedding plans.

"*Mamm*, Jacob needs you upstairs!" Betsy yelled as she pounced down the stairs in her normal fashion.

"Betsy, what have I told you about that yelling?" *Mamm* closed the oven door. "Emily, please check on the turkey roast in fifteen minutes if I'm not back." She shook her head. "I think your *bruder* is actually nervous about his wedding day. And that's all he's talked about for months."

Emily still couldn't believe that Jacob was getting married. He'd met Beth Ann right after they moved here, and they were dating within a week. Their whirlwind courtship was a surprise to everyone, but Jacob said he didn't want to wait. He was ready to start his life with Beth Ann, and she had readily accepted his proposal. Jacob had been saving his money for as long as Emily could remember, and with the money he'd saved and some help from their parents, he'd purchased a small farmhouse with fifteen acres about five miles down the road.

Levi walked in from outside, carrying two more chairs that had been stored in the barn for when they held worship service at their house. *Mamm* said about sixty folks would be attending the wedding. All of Beth Ann's family lived here in Canaan, and when you combined them with Emily's family, the Stoltzfuses, Martha, Mr. Becker, and a few others, it would be a houseful. Emily wished their extended family from Middlefield would be coming, but the weather conditions kept them away. Even though they could have taken a bus, then hired a driver, it was a long way, and the weather was too unpredictable this time of year.

"Aren't you gonna help?" Levi slid past her, cutting his eyes at her.

"I am helping. I'm keeping an eye on the turkey roast." She dipped a spoon into a bowl of cabbage casserole, blew on it, and took a bite.

"I'm tellin'." Betsy skipped into the kitchen. Then she giggled. "Unless you give me a bite."

Emily smiled. "Okay, but just one." She got a clean spoon and scooped up a bite for Betsy.

"Anna and Elizabeth will be here today."

"*Ya*, I know. You haven't seen your friends in a while because of the weather. Are you excited to see them?" Emily leaned against the kitchen counter and faced Betsy, who wore a new emerald green dress Emily had made for her the week before.

"*Ya.*" Betsy tapped her finger to her chin. "I hope they studied the Bible lesson that I gave them last time they were here."

Emily shook her head, but smiled. "Betsy, I don't think today is the day to quiz them about Bible study. Just try to have fun."

Cold air from outside rushed in as their father came into the kitchen, carrying more chairs. "This is the last of them." He walked past them and into the den where he placed the chairs in a row behind the others. "There's a line of buggies coming up the drive. Probably Beth Ann's family."

Emily walked to the window and rolled up the green shade. She counted nine buggies, all black, except for two gray ones. David and his family, she presumed, since Beth Ann's family was also originally from Ohio. She quickly tucked loose strands of hair underneath her *kapp*, then wiped her hands on her apron.

Emily walked into the den and waited inside the door while the guests tethered their horses and slowly made their way up the steps that Levi had cleared of snow earlier. When she opened the door, Beth Ann's parents entered, followed by Beth Ann's three sisters, two of whom were married. Her oldest sister, Moriah, held her baby daughter.

"Come in. Let me take your coats." She peered around

Beth Ann to try to see David, but the two gray buggies were still making their way up the driveway. Bishop Esh came in behind Beth Ann's family. Emily's family had only met the bishop once since their arrival, when he stopped by to welcome them to the community. Because of bad weather, they hadn't yet attended a regular worship service.

"*Guder mariye*, Bishop Esh."

"*Guder mariye*, Emily." The bishop moved into the room to speak to the others. Emily stayed by the door, greeting the rest of Beth Ann's extended family. Her heart skipped a beat when she saw David leading his family up the walkway, toting Elizabeth on his hip.

"Hello." She smiled at David, already plotting how she could spend some time alone with him today, something she wouldn't have even considered a few weeks ago.

"Hi, Emily." David set Elizabeth down on the floor. "She can hardly wait to see Betsy."

Elizabeth tugged on Emily's dress.

"*Ya*, sweetheart, what is it?" Emily leaned down in front of little Elizabeth.

"I know all the answers to the Bible study questions that Betsy gave us."

Elizabeth was so proud that Emily didn't have the heart to say anything except, "I'm sure that will make Betsy very happy." Then Emily jumped. "Oh no! I promised *Mamm* I'd check the turkey roast. Talk to you later."

David could hardly take his eyes off Emily, and as she headed to the kitchen, he thought about how much she'd changed since he first met her over a month ago. He'd thought about her constantly since the last time he saw her, which filled him with anticipation and worry, all rolled into one big desire to do right by her. He could tell when they were together the last time that Emily was starting to care for him. The way she nuzzled against him during the ride, the way her eyes twinkled when she spoke to him—all things that would have pleased him a lot under different circumstances. He just hoped he had the self-discipline not to encourage anything more than friendship. Kissing her forehead and almost kissing her on the lips had been a mistake. Now he constantly thought about how much he wanted to hold her in his arms, kiss her, tell her that he was drawn to her in a way that scared him.

He'd prayed constantly, asked God to give him the strength to walk away from her before they both got hurt. David knew he would be going back to Lancaster County to live out the rest of his life, however long that might be. He recalled again how he overheard his father and Lillian talking after his kidney transplant. Lillian had been crying when she'd said, "But if his kidney only lasts five to ten years, he'll only be twenty or twenty-five." He took a deep breath and prayed for strength.

After Emily scurried off, David walked around the room, saying hello to everyone, introducing himself to most of them. He turned his attention toward the door and wasn't surprised to see Mr. Becker walk in—with Martha on his arm.

He hadn't seen Mr. Becker since the night of Vera's accident, but he'd figured it was his car in front of Martha's house until about eight o'clock a couple of evenings a week. David was happy for Martha. On the outside, a cranky old woman, but inside, she just wanted to love and be loved. He could certainly understand that, and neither he nor Emily were upset about Martha abruptly firing them. He'd felt guilty for taking Martha's money anyway. Now, with his new job at the furniture store, he could continue saving money to get back to Lancaster County.

"Hello, Mr. Becker." David shook Mr. Becker's hand, then turned to Martha. "Hello, Martha."

She nodded, still holding Mr. Becker's elbow. "Hello, David."

David heard Martha whisper to Mr. Becker, asking if he'd ever been to one of these Amish weddings. David heard her gasp when Mr. Becker told her that he had, and that the ceremony lasts about three hours. He watched them go find a seat and didn't notice Levi walk up to him until it was too late.

"You and Emily don't work together anymore. I reckon there's no reason for you to spend time with her." Levi's stern tone made David look up.

David started to tell Levi that what he did with his time wasn't any of Levi's business, but instead, he stated the truth. "I haven't seen Emily in two weeks." Knowing he should leave it at that, he still added, "But I'm hoping to spend some time with her today."

Levi leaned forward, his brows pressed so tightly together that a knot had formed between his eyes. "Stay away from Emily."

David could understand that Emily's brother might be protective of her, but this response was so aggressive that it went against their Amish ways. Levi walked away before David could defend his intentions—intentions he wasn't even sure of.

Bishop Esh took his place in the middle of the room, so everyone followed his lead and took their seats.

Following the ceremony, Katie Ann wanted so badly to latch onto Ivan's hand, squeeze it, and whisper in his ear—ask him if he remembered their special day almost twenty years ago. Public affection was frowned upon, though, so she sat quiet and still, watching Jacob and Beth Ann at the wedding table, being served their meal first, as was customary. She swallowed hard, fighting the lump in her throat. Such a blessed day, a new beginning for Jacob and Beth Ann.

But worry about her own marriage almost overwhelmed her. It seemed to be deteriorating more and more every day. After her unsuccessful attempt at intimacy with Ivan, they both seemed to be going through the motions, in an awkward way, but Katie Ann had just enough pride not to set herself up for another rejection. She hadn't seen the cell phone anymore, nor had she approached Ivan about it. Part of her was afraid he would lie about it.

She knew she would need to go back in the kitchen to help soon, but she wanted to sit with Ivan just a moment longer. She discreetly looked at him from the corner of one eye. It broke her heart to see such sadness in his expression, and she couldn't help but fear that they would never find their way back to each other. But she prayed constantly, and she wasn't about to give up. Somehow she was going to heal this marriage. Ivan was all she had.

Right away she realized that her thought was not in line with what marriage was all about. She should want to be with Ivan because she loved him, because he was her husband—not because he was all she had. Even though it was true.

She'd never made much attempt to develop relationships with Ivan's family, even though they'd always been close by.

Without her own family near, Ivan's sisters—Mary Ellen and Rebecca, along with her sister-in-law, Lillian—had tried to create a closer friendship with her when they lived in Lancaster County, and Lillian was still trying while they were living in this foreign place. Katie Ann knew that the sin of jealousy had often kept her distant from them. They all had children, a family to care for. All she'd ever had to care for was Ivan, and now he was as distant as Lancaster County was, and he didn't seem to need, or want, her at all. Sadness crept over Katie Ann as she watched the way Jacob and Beth Ann gazed into each other's eyes.

She silently prayed for God to mend her marriage, to help Ivan see that while she was once in a faraway place, depressed and childless, she had grown to accept her fate, and wanted to be close to him again. Despite what was acceptable, she reached for his hand and squeezed.

Ivan returned Katie Ann's gesture of affection, then turned to her, the hint of a smile on his face. *What are you thinking, Ivan?*

EMILY DROPPED ONE of her mother's best platters while she was helping the other women clean the kitchen. "Sorry, *Mamm*," she said as she scooped the larger pieces up with her hand.

"You're in such a hurry, Emily." *Mamm* threw her hands on her hips and frowned, but then her lips turned upward. "Are you rushing around like this so you can go spend some time with David?"

"No!" Emily walked to the pantry and pulled out a broom and dustpan, scanning the room as she did, to see who else might have heard her mother's comment. Lillian must have. Even though Lillian kept her head down, Emily saw her grin. She wondered if David had said anything to her.

Emily squatted and swept the small pieces of glass into the dustpan, hoping her mother would let it go. She saw David ease his way through the kitchen, nodding with his head for her to follow him outside.

"Do you need any more help?" Emily faced her mother, bit her lip, and knew her mother had seen David's nod.

Mamm arched one brow as she grinned. "No, you go ahead, Emily."

Emily put on her heavy black coat and gloves, then tied her bonnet atop her prayer covering. She walked out the door and saw David heading toward the barn. She was unsure if he was joining some of the other men in there or expecting her to follow. She pulled her galoshes over her black tennis shoes and decided to take a chance.

When she reached the barn, she peeked in the door. He was alone, leaning against a workbench.

David just stared at her, so much so that she pulled her eyes from his and looked down at the ground. When she looked back up, he was still looking at her. "What? What are you looking at me like that for?"

He gave a quick shake of his head. "I—I don't know. Nothing."

She moved closer to him. "Are you sure?"

David pushed his coat to the side, then looped his thumbs underneath his suspenders. "Aw, you wouldn't be interested anyway." He shrugged, but with a grin.

"Stop playing with me, David Stoltzfus." Emily playfully stomped her foot. "Tell me."

"Or what?" He leaned back farther against the bench and crossed his ankles.

Emily moved even closer to him. "Or I will—I will . . . Oh, I don't know!" She slapped her hands to her side about the same time that David stood straight up, leaned forward, and pulled her to him. It caught her off guard, but the feel of his arms gently around her caused her to feel weak in the knees. She laid her head against his chest, unsure what else to do but enjoy the moment.

David eased her away, then cupped her chin in his hand. Ben Byler had kissed her on the cheek one time after a singing, but nothing like she suspected was on David's mind. He leaned down, and when his lips met hers, Emily was sure she'd floated a foot off the ground. But it didn't last. He pulled back, clutched her arms, then eased her back.

"Emily, I'm so sorry."

Sorry, why? She looked down at the ground. It wasn't a long enough kiss for her to be actually bad at it. She wasn't sure exactly what happened, but she was embarrassed.

"I shouldn't have done that." He paused and let out a heavy sigh. "It's just that it's all I've been thinking about since the last time I saw you."

"Me too," she said sheepishly as she looked up and locked eyes with him.

"Really?" David smiled for a split second before his expression soured. "Well, it won't be happening again. I'm sorry. I know we both agreed just to be friends, and I was out of line."

Did you not hear me? She bit her bottom lip, unsure how to mask her disappointment. Her heart ached. She'd finally learned to trust a man after everything that had happened with James. She seldom thought about her attack these days, and she didn't flinch when David touched her. Now he wants to tell her it will never happen again?

I guess it's for the best. Maybe she didn't think about her attack as much, but it had still happened. And the results were still the same. She was ruined for marriage, and the realization hurt worse than ever before. She felt cheated. A glimpse of what it felt like to be held by a man she trusted, that she cared for . . . only to have him pull back.

Maybe it's a good thing he has the strength to do that, because Emily knew she didn't. But why? Why did he kiss her if he only wants to be friends? And while Emily had her own reasons for not wanting to be courted, what were his? What was so wrong with her that David wouldn't even consider it? Besides the obvious—but as far as she knew, he didn't know anything about what had happened. Her mind was filled with questions as she tried to get him to make eye contact. Finally, he did.

"I—I thought the kiss was fine." She lowered her eyes, then looked back up at him, wondering still if she kissed poorly.

David unhooked his thumbs from his suspenders, pulled his hat from his head, then raked his hand through his dark, wavy hair. "Emily, I just can't be anything more than friends with you." His tone was firm, and he shoved his hands into his pockets.

Emily swallowed hard. "We are friends."

David took a deep breath. "*Ya.* And I shouldn't have kissed you, since we can't ever be more than that. I could never court you." He stopped when he saw her eyes clouding with tears.

"You're taking this the wrong way." He stepped forward, but she took two steps back.

"No, I'm not." She blinked back tears. "Friends. We're friends."

David stepped toward her and reached for her arms. She jerked away, but he stepped forward and latched onto her forearms. "We are friends, Emily. And I want to stay friends with you. But I can hardly be around you without wanting to kiss you."

She stopped and held her breath, waiting for him to go on.

"Can't you see that? I want to kiss you so bad right now, I can hardly stand it. But we can't be anything more than friends, and I'm not gonna lead you on and hurt you like that. I can't spend any more time alone with you."

He spun around and headed out of the barn. Emily stared after him, her mouth hanging open.

KATIE ANN WAS sure that Beth Ann and Jacob's wedding was the reason Ivan had reached out to her the night before. Following their intimacy, she'd dared to hope that everything would be all right. *What happened between last night and this morning?*

Now, barely daylight, she blocked the front door in an effort to keep Ivan from leaving. She couldn't stop the trail of tears pouring down her face, even when she thought she couldn't cry anymore. Disgrace, shame, and failure surged through her heart. Even though Ivan refused to admit it, Katie Ann knew that Lucy had something to do with this, and her heart was filled with anger toward this *Englisch* woman she barely knew.

"Ivan, please . . ." she tried one last time. "What about last night? I don't understand!" Katie Ann tried to make sense of what was unfolding before her.

Ivan buttoned his coat, put on his best black hat, then picked up his packed red suitcase, the one that was under the bed when they'd moved in. "I'm sorry, Katie Ann."

"That's all? I'm sorry." She buried her face in her hands and sobbed. "Please, Ivan . . ." She was begging, and more shame engulfed her.

"I'm sorry, Katie Ann. There is enough money in the bank to get you by for several months until you figure out what you would like to do, and of course . . . the house and property are paid for." His eyes filled with tears. "You can have everything, but I have to go."

"But I want *you*, Ivan."

Her husband hung his head for a moment, then turned and left.

When the door closed behind him, she dropped to her knees. "Why, Lord? What have I done that is so terrible that I must endure such pain? I can't have any children to love, and now I have no husband. Why, Lord? How can this be Your will for me?" She rolled onto her side in a fetal position and pulled her knees to her chest as loneliness and despair overtook her. "Please, God . . ."

She stayed in that position for a very long time, thankful that God was the only one who could see her in such a pitiful state. "I'm sorry, Lord," she said softly. "Sorry that I don't have more faith."

For I know the thoughts that I think toward you, saith the L*ORD*, *thoughts of peace, and not of evil, to give you an expected end.*

Katie Ann stopped crying for a moment, slowly rose until she was sitting up, and brushed a tear from her cheek. *Jeremiah 29:11*. She placed one hand on her heart and took a deep breath as she speculated about why that particular Bible verse came to mind at that very moment. *To give you an expected end.*

Nothing in her life was going as she expected. It was falling apart. She pulled herself up, then brushed the wrinkles from her dark blue dress and walked to the window. Ivan's taxi had rounded the corner long ago. He was gone. Her husband of twenty years had walked out on their marriage, given up. And Katie Ann could never remarry. That's how it was, according to the *Ordnung*, and Katie Ann tried to mentally prepare herself for a life even lonelier than she could have imagined possible.

She watched the sun set, leaving a misty glow atop the packed snow.

For I know the thoughts that I think toward you, saith the Lord, thoughts of peace and not of evil, to give you . . . an expected end.

The scripture kept echoing in Katie Ann's mind, and she sighed, knowing that the Lord wanted only the best for her. *But how can this be the best? I wish I knew what thoughts You think toward me, what plans You have for me.*

She knew that God only had thoughts of peace for her, but she couldn't even begin to think how she would ever feel peace when such loneliness threatened to suffocate her to death. As she stood at the window watching an orange glow peek above the mountains, she realized . . . she'd been lonely for a very long time.

Katie Ann sat there for a few minutes until she understood that she knew her expected end. To be with the Lord in heaven for all eternity. How she gets there is in God's hands, in

His time, even if it isn't the path she's chosen for herself. But knowing it to be true was one thing; accepting it right now, on this day, at this moment was almost impossible. She could still breathe in Ivan's freshly bathed scent, the homemade soap he'd bathed with for all the years they'd been together.

"Help me, Lord, to trust Your plan for me. Give me strength." She buried her face in her hands again after saying the words aloud, knowing it was going to be a long night as she slept in her bed alone for the first time in twenty years.

Twelve

Time dragged by after Jacob and Beth Ann's wedding. A couple of good weather days preceded an onslaught of heavy snow that kept folks indoors for several days, and once again they'd missed community worship. But today was a much better day, with no snow in the forecast.

Emily clasped the thick brown blanket tightly around her, holding both ends close to her chest with one hand and the reins with the other. She hadn't seen Martha since the wedding, and *Mamm* said that since it was Christmas Eve, Emily needed to take Martha a hearty supply of rhubarb jam and invite her and Mr. Becker to their family's Second Christmas.

She hadn't seen David or any of his family since the wedding either, but her mother said they would be coming for Second Christmas. All of them, that is, except Ivan. Emily had been shocked to hear that Katie Ann's husband had left her. She'd enjoyed meeting David's aunt and uncle at the wedding, but even though she didn't know the couple, she sensed a problem between them. Still, she would have never guessed that it was a problem large enough for Ivan to leave his wife. That just didn't happen among the Amish.

Emily's thoughts turned to David, as they always did, but she scowled as she remembered his last words to her. She liked it better when she could focus on the kiss they'd shared, but that sweet moment was now followed by bitterness. Thankfully, Emily kept busy at the dry goods store. She felt more comfortable tending the store by herself these days, which freed Jacob up to get his own home in order, though he still spent five or six hours at the store each day. But when it came time for Jacob to ready his fields for planting, the plan was for Beth Ann to start working at the store. *Daed* said this first year would be a learning experience as they planted crops that could endure colder temperatures for much longer than in Ohio and Pennsylvania. Emily had heard Samuel Stoltzfus agree with her father at Jacob's wedding that it was going to be a learning year for all of them.

Emily parked the buggy in front of Martha's house and noticed right away that things looked different. For starters, the snow was cleared from the walkway, and she didn't remember seeing the small sign on a stick that said WELCOME FRIENDS before either. She smiled as she recalled Martha meeting Mr. Becker and then accompanying him to Jacob and Beth Ann's wedding.

She knocked on the door and waited, holding a gift bag with a Christmas tree on the front and six jars of rhubarb jam inside. Emily wasn't sure why her mother had purchased decorative bags with Christmas trees on the front, since putting up a tree was not Amish tradition, but *Mamm* couldn't resist a sale at the store. Once, she'd purchased Levi a pair of boxer briefs because they were half price—boxer briefs with red hearts all over them. "No one will see them," *Mamm* had said with a shrug. Emily couldn't recall ever seeing the boxers in the wash basket.

Mamm had grilled her repeatedly about David, to the point that Emily had yelled at her just yesterday. *If Daed had heard . . .* She grimaced when she thought about what her father's reaction would have been. Emily knew better than to be so disrespectful.

Emily heard the doorknob turn. When the door opened, Emily was speechless for a moment. This didn't look like the Martha she knew. Her hair was pulled up into a neat twist instead of heaped atop her head in a matted mess of curls loosely secured with a butterfly clip. The bright red lipstick she usually wore was gone. She was hardly wearing much makeup at all, and her red knee-length dress was lovely and conservative.

"Cat got your tongue?" Martha thrust her hands on both hips.

Emily smiled. *Definitely Martha.*

"Merry Christmas, Martha."

"I hope that's rhubarb jelly in that bag." Martha's eyes lit up as she pushed the door open and motioned Emily in.

"*Ya*, it is." She handed the bag to Martha. "Mmm. Smells like cookies in here." Emily glanced around Martha's den and saw festive Christmas decorations throughout, including a lighted tree in the corner. Everything was clean, and Martha had a cozy fire going.

"Hello, Elvis." Emily walked to the cage.

"Hello," the bird replied. "Merry Christmas."

Emily laughed out loud. "You too, Elvis."

Martha walked to Elvis's cage. "I taught him that just this morning," Martha said proudly as she reached in to pet the bird. Then Martha leaned down and put her lips on the bird's snout just inside the rails of the cage. "You are so smart, Elvis. Do you know how much I love you?"

"I love you, Martha," the bird said back. Emily watched Martha's eyes haze over, but she quickly blinked back any tears.

Martha stood up straight, patted the cage, and the hint of a smile crossed her face. "I've had that bird for nineteen years."

"What? You never told us that." Emily's jaw dropped. "That's amazing!"

Martha smiled proudly. "Yep. Elvis is amazing. Bet ya didn't know that he'll outlive me. Parrots live eighty to a hundred years if they are properly cared for." She leaned down to Elvis again and stroked his nose. "And my Elvis is very well taken care of."

Emily turned toward Martha's Christmas tree, which was covered with varying sizes of red and gold balls, and saw a few presents underneath.

"Mostly for Elvis," Martha said when she saw Emily eyeing the gifts. Then she walked toward the tree and retrieved a shoe-sized box wrapped in blue paper with snowmen. "This is for you folks."

Emily raised a brow. "Thank you, Martha." Then she snapped her finger. "*Ach*, I almost forgot. *Mamm* wanted me to invite you for Second Christmas on Wednesday."

"Huh?" Martha twisted her mouth from side to side. "How many Christmases do you people have?"

Emily giggled. "We celebrate Christmas with our immediate family on Christmas Day, but Second Christmas, the day after, we visit with extended family and friends. *Mamm* will make a big dinner at noon, but instead of turkey—since we just had it on Christmas Day—she'll make a pot roast and several different casseroles." She paused, remembering her mother's instructions. "Mr. Becker is invited too."

"You tell your mother I appreciate the offer." Martha stood tall, then reached up and patted the twist on top of her head. "And I love a good pot roast, so I'm sure Arnold and I will be there."

"That's great." Emily grinned. "Sure looks fancy and pretty in here. You got plans for Christmas Eve tonight?"

Martha raised her chin. "Not that it's any of your business . . ." She grinned. "But yes. Arnold and I are spending the evening together."

"That's nice." Emily folded her gloved hands in front of her, realizing that she hadn't exactly been invited to stay. "I heard Mr. Becker say he doesn't have any family. Has he always lived here?"

"You might as well sit down. I see you're full of questions." Martha looked at her watch. "He won't be here for another hour." She sat down in her rocker, which was still so near the table she jostled it when she took her seat, causing the lamp to teeter. She reached out and steadied it without looking at it.

Emily took off her coat and bonnet, sat down on the couch, and folded the garments in her lap. She waited for Martha to go on.

"Arnold said he's never been married." She paused. "Isn't that something?"

Emily nodded.

"I was married once," Martha said after a few moments.

"Really? I didn't know that. You never mentioned that to me or David. Do you have *kinner*?"

"Huh?"

"Sorry. Children. *Kinner* means children in Pennsylvania Dutch."

"No. My Herbert and I never had any kids. We always wanted some, but it just didn't happen." She looked to her left. "Instead, we had Elvis, who did indeed outlive Herbert." Martha sighed. "Herbert just dropped dead one day. Heart attack."

"I'm sorry."

"It was a few years ago." Martha gazed at the Christmas tree, seeming far away, and the flickering lights shone on her face.

After a few moments, Emily said, "Your cookies smell *gut*."

Martha chuckled. "I didn't learn much about cooking while you were here, Emily, but I figure even I should be able to make some cookies."

"I'm sure they'll be wonderful."

Martha bit her lip as she rubbed her chin. "Your people have a strong faith in the Lord, don't you?"

"*Ya*. We do."

Martha let out a deep breath. "So does Arnold." She frowned as she spoke.

Emily wasn't sure what to say. It wasn't her place to minister to anyone, so she just nodded.

"So, what makes a good Christian, Emily? Gotta go to church every Sunday?" Martha crossed one leg over the other and shifted her weight.

"I—I think a *gut* Christian tries to be the best person they can. They give unselfishly to others, worship God, believe Jesus to be our Savior, and, for us—we believe that everything that happens is God's will. Even the bad things."

Emily heard herself say the words, and guilt flooded over her for all the times she'd questioned God's will the past few months.

Martha folded her arms across her chest and stared at the fire for a few moments. "I think Arnold is a good Christian."

Emily nodded again. "He seems like a nice man."

Martha chuckled. "Doesn't he, though?" She shook her head. "Can't for the life of me figure out why that silly old carpenter wants to spend time with me." Her mouth twisted wryly. "You probably haven't noticed, but I ain't always real cheerful."

Emily bit her bottom lip, then took a deep breath. "I've always thought you were just fine, Martha."

"Well, you better go before my cookies burn." Martha stood up.

Emily jumped up and put on her coat and bonnet. "Thank you for the gift, Martha." She picked it up from the coffee table.

"Send my thanks to your mother for the rhubarb jelly."

"I will." Emily walked toward the door, then turned and smiled. "Have a nice time with Mr. Becker."

"Yeah, yeah." Martha rolled her eyes, scowled a bit, then mumbled, "Merry Christmas to you folks."

"Merry Christmas." Emily opened the door and left.

She was almost to her buggy when she heard the door open. She turned around.

Martha stood on the porch. "Emily?"

"*Ya?*"

"Is it too late for me to be one of 'em?" Martha took a step forward and rubbed her hands along her arms. "You know, a good Christian?"

Emily smiled. "It's never too late, Martha."

MARTHA PULLED HER cookies from the oven. "Argh!" She eyed the blackened edges as she set the pan on top of the oven. "Can't even seem to make a simple batch of chocolate chip cookies."

She lifted one of the cookies with the spatula, blew on it, then flipped it over. Too burnt to serve to Arnold. He'd think she had never baked cookies, which would be the complete and total truth.

Oh well. All wasn't lost. She eyed the pan of lasagna in front of her, the one she'd pried from the frozen container and put in her own casserole dish. The way the cheese melded to the edge of the pan made it look almost like she'd prepared it herself. And anyone could toss a salad, which Martha figured she'd done quite well. Boy, how she missed Emily in the kitchen.

Not my fault I never learned to cook. She didn't remember her mother ever teaching her. And when she'd married Herbert, they'd had a live-in housekeeper and a cook, so Martha had never pursued the craft.

But after Herbert died, Martha had traded their estate in Monte Vista for this much smaller home in Canaan, and she'd parted ways with the help, giving them enough money to either retire or take a lot of vacations. She missed the lavish meals from time to time, but it was easier to be alone. Or so she'd thought. She smiled to herself as she looked over her surroundings. It had been a long time since she'd cared what her place looked like. After Herbert died, she'd fallen into some sort of funk she hadn't been able to shake. Until now.

She jumped a bit when she heard a knock at the door and felt silly. She was going to have to do something to harness all the giddiness she'd felt since the day she laid eyes on

Arnold Becker. The man seemed to radiate kindness, and he was bringing a few things out in Martha that had been stuck beneath a lonely heart for several years.

She took a deep breath and pulled the door wide. He stood on the porch shivering, but then a smile spread across his face, and Martha couldn't recall ever feeling as warm as she did at this moment or as dizzy with happiness. *Maybe I'll learn to live with giddy.*

"You look beautiful," he said as he crossed the threshold.

"Get yourself in here out of the cold." Martha closed the door behind him. She tried to control the blush filling her cheeks, but be blasted if she just couldn't. "Warm yourself by the fire."

Arnold smiled as he walked to the fireplace. He pulled off his gloves and a black felt hat that looked similar to the ones the Amish folks wore.

"Here, let me take your coat." Martha waited while he shed the long black overcoat, then she laid it across the back of the couch.

"Hello, Elvis," he said as he made his way to Elvis's cage. Martha followed, anxious for Arnold to hear how she'd taught Elvis to say Merry Christmas.

"You'll love this. Listen to what my Elvis learned just today. Such a smart bird, my Elvis."

Elvis squealed before he spoke, then loudly said, "I think I love that Arnold. I think I love that Arnold. I think I love that—"

"Elvis! Shut your mouth! Good grief!" Martha was afraid to even look at Arnold, and any previous blush in her cheeks was now fire-red embarrassment. *Elvis, you are in big trouble.*

Martha slowly turned to Arnold, raised her brows, and flashed him a stiff smile. "Dumb bird. He was supposed to say Merry Christmas."

Arnold's mouth was curved into a smile, but his eyes were open wide. Luckily, he didn't comment on Elvis's new saying, though his cheeks were turning as red as Martha knew hers were. *No sunflower seeds for you today, Elvis. You're grounded.*

"Something smells real good, Martha."

She smiled. "I hope you like lasagna."

"I do."

Even the frozen kind? "Why don't you give the fire a poke while I go set the table?"

Arnold nodded, and Martha headed to the kitchen. Once everything was ready, she went to get him, and they sat down to eat.

"Shall I say the blessing?" Arnold folded his hands together and bowed his head.

Martha did the same. "Sure."

Arnold thanked the Lord for the food, for Martha, for his home, for his life, for his friends, and about near everything else. Martha was grateful for all those things he mentioned, and she'd grown accustomed to praying before meals. Occasionally, she'd try to talk to God on her own, but it felt awkward because she didn't really know much about Him. Her family didn't attend church when she was a child, at least not that she could recall, and Herbert hadn't been a church person when she met him either, so it wasn't something they ever did.

Over the years, Martha had watched the Amish. They were kind, generous, loving, and every last one of them seemed to have a strong faith. There was something comforting about being around them, but their sense of peacefulness wasn't easy for her. She wasn't unhappy. A bit lonely, perhaps. But her and Elvis had gotten along mighty fine. Just the same, maybe she should lift up her heart in prayer more, let God know she appreciates Him. Arnold sure seemed to have a rapport with Him. He talked about the Lord a lot. Martha was uncomfortable talking about her faith—or lack thereof—but she enjoyed hearing Arnold talk about his relationship with God and the peace it gave him. It made Martha want to buddy up with God too.

I'm an old woman. It's probably too late. Emily's words rang in her head. "*It's never too late, Martha.*"

Then as clear as the cute little pug nose on Arnold's face, she heard a voice in her head.

Seek Me with all your heart.

She said, "Huh?" about the same time Arnold said, "Amen."

Arnold grinned. "What?"

"Oh, nothing." She sat taller. "Amen. That's what I meant to say."

Arnold dove into his salad, and Martha spooned a large helping of lasagna onto his plate. Then she served herself some. All the while, she reflected on what she'd heard.

Seek who?

They ate quietly for a minute or two. Then it came to her. She knew who.

"Arnold, it's Christmas Eve. You going to church tonight?"

Her dinner partner looked surprised. "Yes. Midnight Mass."

"Think they'd let me in, if I was to want to go to church tonight?"

Arnold shook his head. "I don't know, Martha. You'd have

to talk to the priest, then confess your sins, then they would need to bathe you in holy water, and you'd have to address the congregation as to your intentions, and—"

"Forget it! I was just asking." Her eyes were large as she shook her head.

Arnold burst out laughing. "Martha, I'm teasing you. Of course you can go. Anyone is welcome in the Lord's home. I'd love for you to attend with me . . . if you would like."

Martha felt her face reddening again. Who would have thought Arnold had a sense of humor? "Okay," she said shrugging. Midnight was way past her bedtime, but something in her heart was driving her in this new direction.

Thirteen

MARTHA KNELT DOWN FOR THE UMPTEENTH TIME, HER knees crackling with every squat as she clutched the pew in front of her. It had been a long time since she'd attended a Catholic Mass, or any church service for that matter, but now she remembered that the Catholics were the ones who exercised while they worshiped.

She followed along best she could, and even found herself singing along to the Christmas songs led by a full choir. Their white gowns reminded her of the carolers that used to come by her house years ago, dressed similarly and carrying song books. Herbert had loved that part of Christmas, especially the children singing. But no one caroled anymore, and Martha suddenly found herself wondering why. Or maybe they did . . . but just never came to her house.

Thoughts about the way she'd lived the past few years bounced around in her head. She didn't have anything to be particularly angry about. Losing Herbert when he was a young man of fifty-eight had been a blow, and that had taken some time to get over, but she knew she didn't have a lot of the worries that some folks had—money issues, health issues, and other things that can drag a person down. Herbert was a good man, and memories of him always brought a smile to her face. They'd shared fifteen wonderful years together late in life. Even though Martha never did care for the fancy life that he'd introduced her to, she'd sure loved her husband.

Martha could clearly recall the day Herbert walked into her family's pet store to browse around. She'd heard a rumor that a rich man from Boston had purchased an estate not far from her family's farm. A huge house with nine bedrooms, a customer at the store had told her. Much of what Martha learned about their small town came from customers at the store. Her parents believed in hard work, and they didn't encourage outside interests or friendships, even when Martha was young. Martha had spent most of her time alone—or at the pet store—well into adulthood. So when Herbert had said he wanted to buy a parrot—the store's only parrot, her beloved Elvis—she'd been just about ready to tell the stranger that the bird wasn't for sale. But then her mother walked in from the back room and happily accepted a large sum of money for the bird. Then Herbert walked out of the store with the best friend Martha had ever had. She befriended Herbert in an effort to make sure Elvis was well cared for. But Herbert turned out to be a good guy and someone who tolerated Martha's unique disposition. They were married a year later.

Not hearing a word the priest said, she thought about why she hadn't made any other friends, not real friends anyway. If anything, she'd discouraged it. Seemed like a lot of work sometimes, to make friends. Although . . . she'd taken a liking to Emily and David.

She peeked at Arnold out of the corner of her eye. Martha knew she wasn't up on the styles like she had been in her younger days, but it didn't take a fashion model to figure out that Arnold's suit looked like it was from the days when young people wore peace signs on their shirts and drove around with flowers on their vans. Arnold had probably never had any material wealth. Herbert had it—tons of money. And he'd dragged her willingly into his life, but once he was gone, Martha realized that a smaller space in the world for her and Elvis was really all she needed.

She stood up when she saw those around her doing so, feeling a bit guilty that she'd missed out on the prayers being offered. She just wasn't sure about all this church stuff. Something about being in a big room where God seemed to be closer than usual made her feel unworthy. What had she really done in her life that was good enough to please God?

Maybe agreeing to go to church with Arnold had been a mistake, but after the service was over—after paying attention to the last half—she felt rejuvenated. What had been rejuvenated, she didn't know. But she just felt good in general. During the final prayer, she thanked God for having her in His home. *Wish I knew You better.*

Seek Me with all your heart.

Martha stopped abruptly as they were slowly following the crowd down the aisle toward the exit. "Did you hear that?" She turned to Arnold and frowned.

"Hear what?"

Martha looked toward the front of the church. Poinsettias lined the area, and the lights from the nearby Christmas trees twinkled atop the white surface of the altar, reflections bouncing in every direction like tiny little beings dancing in celebration. "O Holy Night" piped through the organ on the second floor, and Martha began walking against the crowd. Arnold called for her, but for reasons she couldn't explain, she gently elbowed her way down the aisle until she stood a few feet from the altar. She looked up at Jesus hanging on the cross and studied the pained expression on his face. She couldn't have explained her emotions at that moment to anyone. Except maybe to God. And she had a hunch He already knew how she was feeling.

She took a deep breath, stood taller, then turned around and headed back down the aisle with the others. Arnold was standing in one of the pews toward the back of the church, waiting for her.

"What were you doing?" Arnold stepped out of the pew and joined her. Together they walked several steps to the door.

"I don't know." Martha heard the voice in her head again. *Seek Me with all your heart.* "Maybe I'm going nuts."

Arnold smiled. "I think you're just fine."

Here we go again. Martha felt her cheeks turning red. It wasn't so much what Arnold said, but how he said it sometimes—so warm, in such a tender tone. Her old, wobbly knees felt weaker than usual. She let him latch onto her hand as they walked to his old Ford pickup truck, which probably had traveled alongside the vans with the flowers at some time in the past. Martha could remember fantasizing about being a flower child when she was younger, but work on the farm and at the pet store kept her away from that legacy. Probably just as well.

Tonight she'd offered to take her car. It wasn't new. No need for a new one since hers worked just fine. But it was at least twenty years newer than Arnold's. No matter. Arnold was happy carting her around. And as of late . . . when Arnold was happy, Martha felt happy.

Emily missed having Jacob at home on Christmas morning. She knew it had to be especially upsetting to her mother, but as usual, *Mamm* carried on with a smile on her face. Jacob was spending his first Christmas morning with Beth Ann and her family.

Emily thanked her mother for the black sweater *Mamm* had made for her, and she was about to thank her father for the cedar trinket box he'd made when Betsy squealed.

"Betsy, please don't scream." *Mamm's* scolding was less severe this Christmas morning, and it was hard not to smile as Betsy held up her present, a large backpack filled with books.

"Look, Emily!" Betsy flopped down beside Emily on the couch and began to dump the books on both their laps. "These are all the books I've been wanting!" Betsy covered her mouth with her hands and bounced up and down for a moment. "I can't wait to show Anna and Elizabeth!"

"They will be here tomorrow," *Mamm* said as she picked up the present from Martha. "So nice of Martha to send us a gift."

Levi grunted. "Probably a dead critter."

"Levi," their father warned. "It is Christmas Day." He pulled down his glasses and glared at Levi. "None of that today."

Levi was sitting on the floor near the fireplace. "Isn't she coming here tomorrow?"

"*Ya*, she is. And she is bringing Arnold Becker." *Mamm* was peeling the wrapping from Martha's present. "And Martha might not always be the friendliest of folks, but I expect you all to treat her with courtesy and respect." She narrowed her eyes at Levi.

"I know," Levi mumbled.

Daed stood up from the rocker, went to the wood stacked by the fireplace, and tossed another log on the fire, orange sparks shimmying up. Emily helped Betsy stuff her books back into the backpack, and when she was done, she glanced at her mother. *Mamm* held Martha's opened box on her lap and was just staring inside, her jaw dropped.

"*Mamm*, what is it?"

Her father gave the fire a final poke, then edged toward their mother. "Vera, what is it?" He leaned down and looked in the box. His eyes widened.

Mamm grabbed the lid, slammed it on top of the box, and jumped from the chair. She faced their father. "I will return this the minute I see Martha tomorrow!"

Emily stood up. Whatever was in the box, *Mamm* was not even trying to mask her anger like she normally did. "What is it, *Mamm*?"

"Don't worry about it. We are returning it." *Mamm* stomped to the kitchen.

DAVID BREATHED IN the smell of bacon cooking from downstairs. Lillian always got up extra early on Christmas morning to cook a big breakfast before everyone got up. She wanted them to have their own family traditions, and this had been the first one she'd incorporated when she married his father.

He grinned when he thought about how fast Anna and

Elizabeth would shovel their food, anxious to open their presents. Gifts were never fancy, but each year David made the girls and Lillian a special wooden trinket, and usually he made his father a little something too. But this year, with the move and lack of time, he'd purchased them all a little something with the money he'd made working at the furniture store in town. He'd even bought a new kitchen clock for *Onkel* Ivan and *Aenti* Katie Ann, since theirs got broken during the move.

His *daed* said they wouldn't discuss Ivan's departure, mostly for Anna and Elizabeth's sake, but a dark cloud hung over the family. Katie Ann refused to leave the house, even for Christmas. All of them were worried about her. Lillian checked on her daily to make sure she was eating well, and Katie Ann insisted she was, though the family suspected otherwise. Lillian said she would go see about Katie Ann later, but she wanted Anna and Elizabeth to enjoy their day. David's father turned red in the face every time Ivan's name was mentioned, and David shared his father's sentiments. He couldn't understand how Ivan could do this to Katie Ann. Unless Ivan changed his mind, returned, and confessed his wrongdoings, he would be shunned, and the family would have nothing to do with him.

David's other uncle, Noah, had been shunned years ago, but over time, the family overlooked it. His uncle chose to pursue an education past the eighth grade, which is unacceptable within the Amish community. Noah went on to become a doctor, a calling he said was too strong to ignore. He admitted that he should have never been baptized into the community. If he'd only recognized his calling sooner and not sought baptism, he wouldn't have been banned by the community.

Noah ended up returning home, and he built a clinic for

the Amish community. Even Bishop Ebersol recognized the good that Noah was doing, and he also eventually eased up on the shunning. For David, Noah would always be special. His uncle had saved his life when he unselfishly gave David one of his kidneys five years ago. They shared a bond that couldn't be broken.

As he made his way downstairs, he thought about Emily and the harsh way he'd spoken to her the last time he saw her. Tomorrow they would be spending Second Christmas with her family, and maybe David should tell her why he didn't want to get close to her. Did he owe her that, since she seemed to have feelings for him?

No, he decided. Then Emily would just feel sorry for him, and the last thing he needed was pity. That was one thing he enjoyed about living in Canaan. No one knew his medical history or felt sorry for him.

Anna, Elizabeth, and his father were already eating when David walked into the kitchen. David laughed when he saw Anna's cheeks filled like a chipmunk.

"You girls know you can't open presents until everyone eats." David grinned as he squeezed in beside Anna.

His sister swallowed, then said, "Hurry, David! Hurry!"

Lillian placed a basket full of homemade biscuits on the table, then thrust her hands on her hips. "Anna, let your brother eat. There is plenty of time for opening gifts." Lillian scurried around the kitchen, and David smiled to himself. Lillian was just like a kid when it came to opening presents, and he often wondered if she regretted this Christmas tradition she started because she—like the girls—seemed to do everything hurriedly in an effort to go open presents.

David estimated they finished in about five minutes, and they headed into the den. All of the boxes from the move were either unpacked or upstairs in the extra bedroom waiting to be unpacked. Lillian had done her best to make the old place a home, and David figured that once the floors were replaced and the walls painted, the house would start to perk up. He wondered if he would be around to help with all that. *How can I leave* Daed *with all this work?* He was also enjoying his job at the furniture store.

He thought about Emily again and sighed.

Anna ran to the far side of the room where several presents were wrapped and decorated. She began to eye the tags, looking for one with her name on it. Christmas trees were not a part of Amish decorations, but Lillian had poinsettias, candles, and wreaths about the house, and the presents were another decorative touch around the den.

David kicked back and watched his sisters open their presents. When they finally got to his, he smiled. "Do you like it?"

Anna and Elizabeth ran to him and jumped in his lap. "You are the best *bruder* in the entire world!" Anna said. Elizabeth kissed him on the cheek. "I love you so much, David."

David hugged the girls tightly, thinking that this would be the last Christmas he would have with them. Next year at this time, he'd be back in Lancaster County. For some reason, the thought of leaving didn't seem as appealing as it did a month ago.

Lillian called the girls' names. "Let me see what your brother got you," she said.

Anna and Elizabeth jumped from his lap to show their mother the small telescopes he'd bought for them.

Lillian handled them with care, commenting about what great gifts they were. "Now you can see the stars. They're so beautiful to see in the mountains."

He hadn't spent a lot on the telescopes, but he knew the girls would enjoy taking them out and looking at the sky on clear nights.

David swallowed hard. It was going to be tough. But he needed to stick to his plan, leaving after he helped his father ready the fields for planting in the spring. By then, he should have enough money to get back to Lancaster County.

DAVID WAS LAYING on the couch, dozing after their devotions earlier in the afternoon, when Lillian came running into the room. She slapped him playfully on the leg.

"Wake up, sleepyhead! It's almost three o'clock. It's time!" Lillian jumped up and down, and David grinned. "Go find Anna and Elizabeth. I think they're upstairs. Your *daed* is already in the barn. Hurry!"

"Okay, *ya, ya*. I'm getting up." David swung his legs off the couch, rubbed his eyes for a moment, then stood up.

"Anna! Elizabeth!" Lillian yelled, instead of waiting for David. "Come downstairs!"

David had been anxious for three o'clock to arrive, too, but Lillian was the most excited.

A few minutes later everyone had bundled up, and they met their father in the barn.

"Ready?" *Daed* smiled, holding the phone in his hand that he'd had installed just the week before. In Lancaster County, the Amish in their district had been allowed to have a phone in the barn for emergencies or business. It had been that way for several years, although Bishop Ebersol had been one of the last bishops in the area to allow it. David could remember, as a child, having to hike to the Lapp shanty, even in below-freezing temperatures. The boxlike structure that housed the phone on Ruben Lapp's farm was shared by six families in the area.

Here in this remote area of Colorado, the bishop didn't come around too much, and when they did see him, he was much more relaxed than Bishop Ebersol had been. When David's father had asked their new bishop about putting a phone in the barn for emergencies and business, Bishop Esh had responded, "And I'm sure you want to keep in touch with your family back home in Lancaster County."

So this Christmas morning, they had no guilt or feelings of wrongdoing, and everyone waited for *Daed* to dial the number. Lillian was bouncing on her toes. "Hurry, Samuel! Put it on speaker. Press that button right there. See, right there."

David's father gently pushed her hand away and chuckled. "I got it, Lillian."

A few moments later David heard Sarah Jane's voice.

Lillian cupped both hands to her chest. "*Mamm*, is that you? I miss you so much." David saw tears come to her eyes as she said, "*Frehlicher Grischtdaag!* Is everyone there?"

"*Ya, ya*. We're all here." Sarah Jane sounded just as excited as Lillian. "*Esther* is here too."

"Hi, *Mammi*," David said to his grandmother, his father's mother.

Lillian leaned closer to the phone. "Lizzie, are you there?" *Daadi* Jonas had married Lizzie after his first wife passed, and Lizzie was as special to the family as Jonas had been. After

Lizzie responded, Lillian, Samuel, David, and the girls individually addressed the rest of their family—David's Aunt Rebecca and her family; Uncle Noah, Carley, and their daughter Jenna; their good friends Sadie and Kade, along with their children, Tyler and Marie; and even their *Englisch* friend Barbie Beiler, who was there to wish them all holiday greetings.

"Is Katie Ann there?" Sarah Jane asked.

Lillian sighed. "No. She still won't leave the *haus*. I'll go check on her in a little while."

"We're so worried about her," Rebecca said. "How could *mei bruder* do this?"

"We are praying that Ivan will make the right choice and return home to his *fraa*." David's father shook his head as he spoke. But David doubted any of them believed Ivan would return.

The conversation lasted about thirty minutes, during which David and his family heard all the happenings with their family in Lancaster County. By the time they hung up, David was more confused than ever. Part of him wanted to go back to Lancaster County as soon as he could, but then every time he thought about it, he got an unsettled feeling in the pit of his stomach.

Fourteen

EMILY SAT ON THE SIDE OF HER BED, BOWED IN PRAYER. She thanked God for the many blessings He'd bestowed on her, and for most recently helping her to function as a normal human being without constantly being in fear and thinking about her attack. She still had flashbacks, but they weren't nearly as frequent, and she noticed that with each day, her fear lessened. The small inner voice that she knew to be God was louder and clearer now, and she tried to seek Him with all her heart every day.

But she struggled with the bitterness she felt toward David. She knew it was her own fault for allowing herself to get too close to him, but he should have never kissed her, never led her to believe that he cared about her. Every time her thoughts veered in this unhealthy direction, she firmly reminded herself that it was for the best, that David deserved a complete woman, untainted and pure. Something Emily was not.

She ended by praying for David's aunt, Katie Ann. Emily couldn't imagine how horrible it must be for Katie Ann. It was a sad situation, and she wondered if Katie Ann would be coming for Second Christmas today with the rest of David's family.

When she got downstairs, she slipped out the front door. She could see her father sitting on the porch, and she wanted to spend a little time with him before she went to help her mother in the kitchen.

"Emily, sit with me." Her father put down the newspaper he was reading and took off his glasses. "I've been meaning to tell you what a *gut* thing it was that you did for your *bruder* and Beth Ann, giving them the wringer. A fine wedding present."

There was nothing Emily liked more than pleasing her father. "I was happy to do it. Martha paid *gut* money." She smiled as she sat down in the other rocker.

They were quiet for a few moments as her father stroked his beard. "I've been thinking, Emily . . . I'm going to carve out some time to build you a cedar chest." He glanced in her direction. "One like your mother has."

Emily loved her mother's cedar chest. She knew her father had made it for her when they were first married. "I'd love that, *Daed*."

"Every *maedel* should have a special place to store things for her future, and I regret that I haven't made you one sooner." He angled his body slightly to face her. "I know your *mamm* has mentioned several things that she wants you to have."

Emily didn't know how to respond. Surely, he suspected that, after everything that had happened, she wouldn't be getting married. She forced a smile. "I better go help *Mamm* in the kitchen." She stood up and was walking to the door when her father called her name.

She turned to face him. "*Ya, Daed?*"

Her father stood up from the chair and walked toward her.

"You will make a fine *fraa* someday, and any young man who wins your heart will indeed be blessed by God."

Emily blinked back tears. It wasn't true, but what a wonderful thing for her father to say. "*Danki, Daed.*"

Then her father did the unexpected. He walked closer and embraced her. "I love you, *mei maedel*."

"I love you too, *Daed*."

Emily allowed herself a few extra moments in the safety and warmth of her father's arms, knowing that she would disappoint him again. Then she eased away and went into the kitchen to help her mother. She picked up a dishrag and started drying the plates in the rack, but her father's words lingered in her mind—and in her heart. As much as she wanted to believe him, she knew her dreams of becoming a wife and mother were gone. She thought of Katie Ann again and wondered how she was coping with her husband's abandonment of their life together.

"*Mamm*, do you think Katie Ann will be coming with the rest of the Stoltzfuses today?" She opened the cabinet to her right and stacked a plate on top of the others.

Her mother pulled a tub of butter from the refrigerator and began buttering slices of bread. "I don't know. I hope so." She shook her head. "Poor dear. I just can't imagine." *Mamm* went back to the bread, then said, "*Ach*, I forgot to tell you that the Kauffmans will be coming for the noon meal today also, so after you dry those plates, can you go ask Levi to put the fold-up table in the den for the little ones?"

Emily abruptly stopped drying the plate in her hand as she recalled the way Hannah had flirted with David at the singing a few weeks ago. It was as wrong as wrong could be, but if Emily couldn't have David, she didn't want Hannah to have him either.

"Emily, move along," *Mamm* said, cutting her eyes at Emily. "Finish those plates and go find Levi, please."

An hour later everything was ready, and everyone seemed to pull in the driveway at once. Hannah had three brothers, so they were arriving in two buggies. Emily could see David and his family also arriving in two buggies. David was carting one of the girls, although Emily couldn't tell which one from this distance.

"They're here! They're here!" Betsy jumped up and down.

"Betsy!" *Mamm* stomped her foot. "No screaming!"

Emily tried not to laugh, since her mother had actually just screamed much louder than Betsy.

Before everyone had tethered their horses, Emily saw Mr. Becker's old truck come up the driveway. He parked near the barn and slowly made his way across the yard until he met up with the others. Folks started heading to the house, and Emily greeted them as they came through the door.

"Emily, that's a lovely dress," Hannah said as she came into the den. David was behind her. Right behind her.

"*Danki*, Hannah." She paused while Hannah passed, then she raised her chin and folded her arms across her chest as David came in. "Hello, David."

"Hi, Emily."

Don't speak to me in that tone. His tenderness was what had put her in this state of mind in the first place. She liked him better when he was gruff, like the first day she'd met him. From now on, that's how she would think of David Stoltzfus—rude and gruff. She sighed, knowing that it would be a challenge to think of him in any way other than sweet, handsome, smart, and everything she'd ever wanted in a husband. She swallowed back a knot in her throat.

"Where's Martha?" Emily asked Mr. Becker as he came into the den.

Arnold lowered his head. "She won't be coming." He looked back up at Emily. "I don't know what's wrong. I called her to say I was on my way to pick her up, and she told me she didn't want to go anywhere." Arnold's lip almost looked like it quivered when he spoke. "Then she hung up on me."

"What? I thought the two of you were getting along so nicely." Emily touched Mr. Becker's arm.

Mr. Becker shrugged as his mouth turned down. "So did I."

THEY'D ONLY BEEN at the Detweilers' about an hour when David started to feel guilty about his behavior. He'd flirted with Hannah, and allowed her to flirt with him, since he'd arrived, and he could tell that Emily was fit to be tied, jealous as all get out, and nothing could have pleased him more.

I am a bad man. He'd made it perfectly clear to Emily that he didn't want to be anything more than friends, yet he was getting a thrill out of seeing her jealous. Maybe he just needed confirmation that she really cared about him . . . and her snippy behavior seemed confirmation enough.

"Here's the tea you asked for." Emily handed him a glass of tea, her cheeks red, her eyes filled with rage.

"*Danki*," he said with a smile. Then he turned back to Hannah, even though he wasn't hearing a thing she said. He saw Emily slip out the back door, swiping at her eyes as she went.

Did I make her cry? "I'll be back," he said to Hannah without even looking at her. He headed toward the back door.

It took him awhile to find Emily, out in the barn by herself crying.

"Emily?" He approached her slowly.

She quickly swiped at her eyes with both hands. "Leave me alone. Get out of here."

David kept moving toward her until he was only a few inches away. "Why are you crying?"

"I said, just leave me alone." She leaned forward, her face filled with anger . . . or hurt? Hurt that he had caused in his effort to affirm her feelings for him. He stood there, questioning his intentions. His original plan had been to not get close to her, so he wouldn't hurt her. Clearly, he'd done just that.

He reached for her arms and tried to pull her to him. "Emily, don't cry."

She pushed him away. "I said, leave me alone. Go back inside to Hannah. You two make a cute couple."

"I'm not interested in Hannah, if that's what has you so upset."

She snickered as she tossed her head back. "I don't care what you do, or who you're interested in, David Stoltzfus."

"Oh . . . but I think you do."

Emily held her position. "Well, you're wrong. We're friends, and I don't care who you choose to court."

"Is that what you think, that I'm going to court Hannah?" David pushed back the rim of his black hat.

Emily shrugged. "I don't care."

"Then why are you crying?"

She blew out a deep breath. "Did it ever occur to you that I might be crying about something that has nothing to do with you? My life and my emotions don't revolve around you. I'm upset about something else."

"What then? What are you upset about?"

"I—I . . . I don't have to tell you."

David grunted. "'Cause it's about me and Hannah."

"No, it's not!"

"You're yelling." David raised his brows and waited.

"It's—it's about Martha. I'm upset about Martha."

David cocked his head to one side, puzzled. "Martha? Why are you upset about Martha?"

"Well, because . . ." She folded her arms across her chest. "Because she hung up on Mr. Becker, and Mr. Becker is sad, and well . . . I figure there must be something wrong. And Martha seemed so happy lately. I just feel sad."

David's brows furrowed. "Enough to make you cry about it when you have all these people here?"

She edged past him and mumbled, "Just leave me alone."

"Let's go see her then!"

Emily spun around. "What?"

"When everyone leaves, let's go check on her."

Emily walked back up to him and glared at him. "Oh no. We can't be alone together. I will go check on Martha later. By myself!"

She stormed out of the barn and left David with his mouth hung open.

WHEN EVERYONE LEFT that afternoon, Emily knew she needed to go upstairs and bury herself in prayer for at least a couple of hours. She'd been rude to Hannah, yelled at David, and even barked at poor little Betsy for no reason. But she needed to see Martha first. She was sincerely concerned about her friend, and even her mother had pulled her aside and asked if Emily would go check on her.

As she eased into Martha's driveway, the sight in front of her made her want to spit nails. David stood beside his buggy right in front of Martha's house.

She climbed out of her buggy and walked directly to him. "What are you doing here?"

David smiled. "Waiting on you."

Emily pulled her coat tight around her and locked eyes with him. She thought about her dreadful behavior all day and took a deep breath. "What are you doing, David?"

"I'm here to check on Martha, just like you."

"No." Emily tucked her chin and spoke softly. "I mean, what are you *doing*?" She looked up at him, knowing her eyes were beginning to tear. "You tell me that you just want to be friends with me, but we can't spend any time alone together. David, you are sending me mixed signals. But I want to clear something up, so that maybe we *can* be friends, alone together or otherwise."

"Okay . . ."

She took another deep breath. "I can never be anything more than friends with you. Never. I care about you, and I think you are a wonderful person. But if you are worried about leading me on, there is nothing to worry about. I don't want to play games, though." She pulled her eyes from his. "I like you very much, but I'll never want to be anything more than your buddy. So you can stop trying to make me jealous with the likes of Hannah Kauffman. Because, honestly . . . I think you can do much better than her."

"Emily, you don't understand. If you understood, then maybe—"

Emily held her palm toward him. "I don't need to understand anything. I have my own reasons. Now, I'm going to check on Martha. You can come, or not come." She turned around and walked up the porch steps. She could hear David following her.

After several hard knocks and no answer, Emily turned to David. "Her car is here. Do you think she's okay?"

"Maybe she's napping." David reached forward and gave another hard knock on the door.

Emily turned the knob. "It's open. Should we go in and check on her?"

David shrugged. "I don't know, Emily. She might just be busy, or down with a cold, or something else that ain't none of our business."

Emily twisted the knob anyway and slowly pushed the door open. Martha was sitting in her chair, looking like the old Martha but a more disheveled version of her—hair unfixed, matted curls barely held on top of her head with the butterfly clip, a dingy pink housecoat and worn slippers as her wardrobe. She didn't even look Emily's way when the door opened. Emily stepped through the door, and David followed right behind.

"Martha?" Emily said softly. White lines ran from Martha's eyes down through her pink blush.

Emily looked from Martha's face to the blue blanket cradled in her arms. "Oh no," she whispered. Elvis's brightly-colored head lay tilted to one side, his eyes closed, his body unmoving under the blanket.

Emily was rooted in place, but David walked toward Martha. He slowly squatted down beside her, and with the familiar tenderness that Emily had grown to love, David lightly touched Martha's arm. After a moment, she turned to face him, then she spoke softly.

"I went to church," Martha said, sniffling. "I wanted to see what it was all about." She looked down at Elvis, and another tear rolled down her cheek. "I've even been praying." Then Martha looked hard into David's eyes and spoke in an even voice. "And this is how God rewards my good efforts? He takes my beloved Elvis. Why would He do that, David? Can you tell me that?" She smiled slightly as another tear rolled down her cheek.

Martha's calm demeanor was unnerving. Emily finally inched closer and squatted down beside David. But before either one of them could offer any words of comfort, Martha spoke again.

"Seek Me with all your heart." Martha paused. She looked down at Elvis and stroked his head, then looked back up at David. "I've been hearing that in my head, and I thought maybe it was God, so I've been trying to connect, I guess you'd say."

Emily didn't know what to say. She didn't know how to explain to an *Englisch* person that God's will is not to be questioned, even in the worst of times. James flashed before her, and she clenched her eyes shut. *Not now. Martha needs our help*. She wasn't sure how David's hand became intertwined with hers. She looked down, and he gave her hand a squeeze but kept his eyes on Martha. Emily was wondering how long Martha had been sitting there with Elvis in her lap. It was the most heartbreaking scene, and Emily fought her own tears.

David still had one hand on Martha's arm. "What can we do, Martha?"

The gentle way David spoke to Martha touched Emily so much that a tear did spill. She quickly wiped it away with her free hand, just as she felt David squeeze her hand again. She squeezed back.

"I suppose we need to bury him." Martha looked down at the bird and started to cry again. Then she turned to Emily. "I'll need a day or two to think about arrangements."

Arrangements? Emily had been nine years old when her hamster died, and they'd just buried it in a box in the backyard after saying a few brief prayers. Why a day or two to make arrangements? Wouldn't Elvis be rather . . . *unpleasant* by then? She crinkled her nose.

"Do you want us to fetch Mr. Becker for you?" Emily offered.

Martha immediately shook her head. "No. I don't want him to see me like this." She twisted her mouth to one side. "I think that old man has a big crush on me, and I don't want to ruin his fine image of me." She finally smiled without crying. Then she looked down again. "My poor, poor Elvis."

"Do you know what—what happened?" Emily bit her bottom lip.

"No. My Elvis has had the best of everything." Martha stared down at the bird for a moment, then looked up at Emily. "Can you help me plan Elvis's funeral?"

"Funeral?" Emily tried to hide her shock. "I mean, sure. Do you want me to find a cardboard box?"

Martha glared at Emily in a way that almost frightened her. "Would you bury a member of your family in a cardboard box?" She rolled her eyes. "Never mind. I've been to an Amish funeral, and I don't recall it doing justice to the dead."

David smiled. "We keep things simple, but I'm sure Emily will help you with Elvis's arrangements, whatever that might be."

Emily shot David a look, then smiled at Martha. "Of course I will."

"No. I owe it to Elvis to do it myself. You can just put together the list of people who will attend, and I'd like everyone to bring food to my home, as is customary." She opened her eyes wide. "I've been to plenty of funerals and brought plenty of food, and Elvis deserves the same courtesies."

"Okay." Emily was thinking about who she was supposed to invite to a bird's funeral.

Martha sighed. "I guess I should probably call Arnold. I should have never hung up on him. But I'm in shock."

"Of course you are." David patted her arm. "Martha, I was wondering . . ." He took a deep breath. "What are you going to do with Elvis? I mean, until the funeral."

Good question, Emily thought.

"I reckon I'll put him in the deep freeze."

Emily let go of David's hand as she stood. She took a step backward and covered her mouth with her hand.

"You got a better idea, Miss Emily?"

Emily was startled by Martha's sharp tone. "No, I suppose not."

Martha ran a hand through her tangled curls. "I'd like to be alone with Elvis now. Emily, let's plan to have the funeral at eleven o'clock on Thursday morning. And I'm not happy with God right now, but it seems fitting to have a member of the clergy recite. So get your bishop here as well."

Emily's jaw dropped. "What?"

"I'm sure we'll figure something out, Martha," David interjected before Emily could tell Martha how ridiculous that was, and how no bishop she knew of would recite final rites over a bird. "We'll go ahead and leave you alone now."

They said good-bye, and Emily marched ahead of David, down the porch steps, and to her buggy. She heard David close the door behind her.

"Emily, wait!"

She spun around as David walked toward her. "This is crazy." She lifted her hands in the air. "How are we going to gather people together for a funeral for a bird? And there is no way I'm asking Bishop Esh! Why in the world would she want me to help her with the arrangements? Shouldn't her new boyfriend be helping her?" Emily pulled the door of her buggy open, only to have David slam it shut.

"What are you—"

He pulled her toward him, then cupped her cheeks in his hands. His lips met hers with more tenderness than any words could have offered. Their kiss seemed to go on forever.

Emily's mind could only focus on one thing. *I love you, David. I wish you could love me back.*

VERA PACED BACK and forth across the bedroom, staring at the box she'd put on the middle of their bed so that the children wouldn't open it and see what's inside.

"Why didn't you just send it with Emily when she went to check on Martha?" Elam asked as he dropped his towel and winked at her.

Vera kept pacing and rolled her eyes. "Get dressed, Elam. I'm too upset to think about what you're thinking about right now."

Elam chuckled, ran a hand through his wet hair, then pulled a drawer open and took out some underwear. "Have you counted it?"

Vera gasped. "Well, of course not. The amount is not important. The fact that Martha would give us a box full of money is inappropriate. The minute I saw all those hundred dollar bills, I slammed the lid closed. I will return it to her tomorrow myself."

Elam tiptoed to the bed and playfully tapped on the box. "Maybe we should just have a little look-see."

Vera slapped his hand. "We will not." She unpinned her *kapp* from her head and let her hair fall to her waist over her white nightgown. "Stay away from the box."

"Will it permanently be residing in the middle of our bed?" Elam grinned.

"I just haven't decided what to do with it yet." Vera put her hands on her hips and stared at Martha's gift. "Does she think we are poor? Why would she give us this, Elam? That box is stuffed full of money!"

Elam sat down on the bed and raised his brows repeatedly, grinning like a silly boy. "I don't know."

Vera grabbed the box from the bed and clutched it to her chest. "It really doesn't matter, does it? I mean, we're going to return it anyway."

"Of course we are." Elam leaned back on one elbow in just his underwear. "So it doesn't matter if we see just how generous Martha is." He sat up. "Oh, come on, Vera. Let's just see how much is in there."

Vera pressed her lips together and thought for a minute. "Let's don't tell a living, breathing soul we did this."

Elam clapped his hands together. "Dump it out. Let's have a look!"

Vera sat down on the bed beside her husband and slowly pulled the lid off the box. Then she dumped the cash on the bed between her and Elam.

Elam's eyes grew as big as saucers.

So did Vera's.

Fifteen

If there was a wrong side of the bed, Emily had woken up on it the day after Second Christmas. David hadn't said anything after kissing her. He'd just gotten into his buggy, waved, and left. It confused Emily, but now she had to focus on planning a funeral for a bird—or at least contributing to the funeral by creating the guest list. She'd already spent the morning trying to train Beth Ann to work in the store, but Beth Ann was scatterbrained. Emily wasn't sure Beth Ann was keen on working in the family's dry goods store while Jacob tended the land. Not much to do this time of year, but Jacob was making some repairs on the outside of the house today, before planting season took up all of his time.

Her mother was humming in the kitchen, louder than usual, and it was grinding on Emily's nerves—more than usual. Everything was building, and she was resentful about everything in her life. She wanted to lash out at someone. And her mother was the only one at home. Since school didn't start back until tomorrow, Betsy had gone with their father and Levi to install a solar panel.

"Why don't we ever talk about what happened to me?" Emily

put her hands on her hips and challenged her mother to a conversation they'd avoided up to now. "About my—my . . ." She couldn't bring herself to say the word.

Mamm turned her back to Emily and started drying dishes that were in the drain. "I didn't think you wanted to talk about it."

"Why do you always have to be so happy when my life is ruined?" Emily walked to the window and peered out into the sunshine, snow still piled high in every direction, and she set her gaze on the snow-capped mountains. She wondered what the view from the top would look like when she climbed one of the mountains and left all her worries behind. *Will that day ever come?* She kept her back to her mother as she went on. "You pretend that nothing happened to me. I would think that each time you look at me and see the scar on my forehead, that maybe you would be reminded about what I went through. But, no . . . you just carry on with your own perfect life, in your own perfect world." She grunted to herself. "Lucky you."

When there was no response, she swirled around. *Mamm* was still drying dishes with her back to Emily. "I'm sorry you feel that way," her mother said without turning around.

Emily faced the window again. She raised the green blind all the way up so she could see the tops of the highest mountains. "You don't even care what happened to me."

A dish went smashing to the floor, and Emily turned around in time to see her mother pick up a second dish and throw it to the floor. Emily thought her heart might stop. "*Mamm!* What are you doing?" She took a step forward, but her mother held out her hand and motioned for her to stay back.

"Is that what you think, Emily? Is it? Is that really what you think, that I don't care?" Her mother bent at the waist, hugging herself with one arm. "Do you not think for one minute that I wouldn't trade places with you? Do you not think that every time I look at you I realize what a bad mother I am? I wasn't able to protect you from that animal." *Mamm* began to sob, and Emily took a step forward. Her mother again held out an outstretched hand for Emily to stay back. Emily stood perfectly still.

"I wanted to find him and hurt him!" *Mamm* cried harder. "My thoughts were, and often continue to be, in a direction God would never approve of, and I have to pray daily for Him to cleanse me of these thoughts." She placed both hands flat on her chest. "Do I care, Emily? Do I care?" She hung her head, and Emily couldn't move. "More than you could ever possibly know until you have a child of your own, and someone wrongs that child in a way that is unimaginable. I pray you never know how that feels." *Mamm* could hardly catch her breath. "If I've handled it badly, Emily, I'm sorry. I thought that if I made things as cheery as possible around here, that if we didn't talk about it, that maybe you would heal. Not forget, but be able to move forward." *Mamm* took a few deep breaths. "I'm sorry. I'm so sorry, Emily."

Emily ran to her mother's arms, sobbing as she sidestepped broken dishes. "I'm sorry, *Mamm*. I'm sorry for the way I've treated you. I just didn't think you understood or cared, and I needed to talk about it. I can never get married and have children, and my whole life changed on that one night, and—"

Her mother pushed her from her arms. "Emily, is that what you think? That you can never get married and have children? The doctors said there is no reason why you shouldn't be able to have all the *kinner* you want. Why would you say such a thing?"

Emily hung her head and cried. "I'm not pure anymore, or worthy of a husband."

Mamm clutched tightly to Emily's arms. "Look at me," she said sternly. "Emily Detweiler, you listen to me. You are worthy of any man's love, and any man would be blessed to have you as his *fraa*. Do you hear me? What happened to you was not your fault, and no man worthy of your affections will think any less of you." She pulled Emily into her arms. "My dear baby girl, I'm so sorry we didn't talk sooner. I'm so sorry you've had these thoughts."

Emily clung tightly to her mother and cried, and she stayed in her mother's arms until both of them could contain their sobbing.

When they finally separated, *Mamm* pushed back a strand of Emily's hair away from her face. Then she kissed her forehead. "I love you so much."

"I love you too, *Mamm*."

"I guess instead of spilling all my emotions to Lillian and trying to hide them from you, I should have just talked with you, been there for you, and listened to you, and—"

Emily tensed up. "What do you mean . . . talked to Lillian?"

"When I told Lillian about what happened to you, it—"

Emily jumped back, pieces of china crushing beneath her black tennis shoes. "You told Lillian?"

"She was very understanding, Emily, and at the time, I thought it was better to vent my emotions to her, instead of you. It was *gut* to have a friend, and I thought I was sparing you." *Mamm* shook her head, but it was all coming together for Emily. "I know better now."

"Does Lillian know about—about the . . ." Emily's heart was thumping against her chest.

"*Ya*, and I know—"

Emily backed away. "*Mamm*, how could you? How could you tell Lillian about this?"

No wonder David keeps pulling away from me. He knows. He knows what happened. He does *think I am unworthy! Why else would he kiss me, then apologize . . . more than once?*

"Emily, Lillian has become a *gut* friend to me. I didn't think you would mind me telling her."

Emily dried her eyes with her sleeve. She'd upset her mother enough for one day, but there was something she needed to know. "Can I use the buggy?"

"Emily, are you all right? I'm sorry if I betrayed a confidence. That wasn't my intention."

Mamm looked so frail that Emily just shook her head. "No, it's okay."

"Where do you need to go?" *Mamm* reached for a tissue from the box on the counter. She handed one to Emily, then dabbed one on her eyes.

"I just want to go for a drive. Some time by myself. Or . . ." Emily paused. "Do you need me to help start supper?"

Mamm shook her head as she eyed the broken china on the floor. "No, you go ahead."

Emily hugged her mother. "Do you want me to help you clean this up first?"

Mamm grinned. "No. I'm the one who threw dishes on the floor like a crazy person. I'll clean it up."

"I won't be late. It might be after dark, but I won't go far."

Mamm nodded.

Emily didn't know Lillian all that well, but she had to know if Lillian had talked to David. If Lillian had told him what happened to her. That seemed the only logical explanation for why David was treating her this way. As if he really cared about her one minute, then didn't want anything to do with her the next. Emily knew David worked at the furniture store until six in the evening, and it had been almost six when she'd left her house.

After securing the horse and buggy outside the Stoltzfuses', she hurried to the door and knocked. When no one answered, she started to knock again but stopped when she thought she heard a woman crying. She leaned closer to the door. *It is a woman crying.*

Emily wasn't sure whether to knock again and maybe offer her help, or mind her own business and head back down the stairs. While she was debating, the door opened.

Lillian gave her a small smile. "Hi, Emily." Though she didn't look like she'd been crying, she wasn't her normal bubbly self either. "Come on in."

She opened the screen door, then pushed the front door wide. "You know Katie Ann, right?"

Emily nodded and knew right away that she'd come at a bad time. It was obvious that Katie Ann had rubbed her eyes raw in an effort to clear the tears. "Hello, Katie Ann." She turned to Lillian. "I can come back another time. I—I just wanted to talk to you."

Katie Ann stood up from where she was sitting on the couch. "No, I was just leaving."

Lillian walked over and hugged her sister-in-law, then whispered something in her ear. When Katie Ann eased away,

Emily could see the tears building in her eyes. "I love you too," she heard Katie Ann say.

After Katie Ann closed the door behind her, Emily took a deep breath. "I'm sorry, Lillian. It looks like I came at a bad time."

Lillian waved off the comment. "Katie Ann will be okay. She is stronger than she thinks, and the love of family will get her through this." Lillian scowled. "But I'm so upset with Ivan, I'd like to just kick him in both his shins." She paused and let out a breath. "I was about to start supper. Do you mind if we talk in the kitchen?"

"Lillian, this is a bad time. We can talk another day."

"Nonsense. All I'm going to do is thaw some soup on the stove, so once I get it out of the freezer and warming in the pot, I'm all ears. Samuel is bathing, and Anna and Elizabeth are busy upstairs playing. I had just checked on them before you arrived. Come on."

Emily followed Lillian into the kitchen. "Can I do anything to help?"

"Nope. Just have a seat at the table, and I'm going to make my family think I worked all day on this." Lillian giggled as she pulled a plastic container from the freezer, then retrieved a pot from one of the blue cabinets that lined the kitchen. "Don't you love these cabinets? A successful day is when one of them doesn't fall off the hinges." She turned to Emily and grinned. "So what do you need to talk to me about?" Lillian ran warm water over the container until the contents started to loosen, and Emily began to question why she was even here—how she was going to get past her own embarrassment to find out if Lillian had said anything to David about what happened to her.

Emily opened her mouth to speak, but just blew out a heavy sigh.

Lillian turned her head and looked at her for moment, then turned to the stove and lit the burner under her soup. A moment later she took a seat across from Emily and asked, "What's bothering you, Emily?"

"I want to ask you something, but I don't know how." She hung her head and avoided Lillian's eyes.

Lillian reached over and put her hand on top of Emily's, which were folded on the table. "Honey, not much shocks me. Remember, I was *Englisch* many years ago. Has something happened? I know you're in your *rumschpringe*."

"No, no. It's nothing like that. I've already made up my mind to be baptized in the spring."

Lillian raised her brows and waited.

Emily pulled her hands out from under Lillian's, rested her elbows on the table, then cupped her face with her hands. She took a few deep breaths, then folded her hands on the table again. "*Mamm* said she told you about—about what happened to me." She kept her head down.

Once again, Lillian put a hand over Emily's. "*Ya*. And I am so sorry, Emily. My heart breaks for you."

"I never should have lied to my parents." She shook her head as she spoke. "I should have just gone to my *onkel's* party and never gone out with James."

Lillian pulled back her hand and sat up taller. "James? You knew your attacker? I got the impression from your mother that you didn't know who assaulted you."

Emily's heart began to thud against her chest. She'd made a horrible mistake. "Oh no." She blinked back tears. "I shouldn't have said that. Oh no." She shook her head. "*Mamm* doesn't know that I know. Please don't tell, Lillian. Please don't tell. That's not what I came here to talk to you about. Are you going to tell? I don't want anyone to know." Emily knew she was rambling. She finally locked eyes with Lillian.

"Honey, this James person deserves to be punished. Do you want him doing this to someone else?"

Emily shook her head.

"Someone who can dish out that kind of abuse will do it again and again." Lillian paused. "I know about this first-hand, Emily. Before I was married to Samuel, before I found the Lord, I lived with a man who was . . . abusive." She looked away for a moment, then back at Emily. "I'm not saying that he did anything as severe as what happened to you, but it was clear to me that he wasn't going to change."

"Please don't tell *mei mamm* that I know who did this. I'd snuck out of the house, and I was somewhere I shouldn't have been. Maybe it was my fault that—"

Lillian waved her finger in front of Emily's face. "No. Don't say that. It was not your fault. As women, we have the right to say no at any time, and I'm sure this *Englisch* boy was probably a smooth talker, and you are in your *rumschpringe*, and—"

"He wasn't *Englisch*." Emily looked away as shame overtook her.

"What?" Lillian tapped the table with her hand a couple of times until Emily looked at her. "Are you telling me the person who raped you is Amish? Was it someone in your community?"

Emily nodded.

Lillian spouted out a word Emily had never heard before, an *Englisch* word Emily suspected the bishop wouldn't approve of. "Sorry. I should know better than to say that. I'm just shocked."

"See? It would have been an upset for everyone if I'd told."

Lillian pointed a finger at Emily again. "Emily, there are good seeds and bad seeds in every walk of life. Even Amish. You need to prosecute that boy." She sucked in a breath.

"Lillian . . ." Emily cringed. "Can we please forget I mentioned this? It's not even what I came to talk to you about. It just slipped out, about James. There was something else I wanted to talk to you about."

Lillian covered her face with her hands, shook her head, and made an odd groaning sound. When she looked up, she frowned. "You are putting me in a very bad predicament with your mother. Over the past few weeks, we've become close. *Gut* friends. I don't like knowing this information and keeping it from her. I'm going to pray, Emily, that you will do the right thing and have this boy face his punishment for what he did to you. Maybe, just maybe, he will get some help, and this won't happen to someone else." Lillian jumped up when her soup started to sizzle in the pot. She stirred it, then adjusted the fire underneath it.

When she sat back down, her eyes met Emily's. "Just think about it, Emily." They sat quietly for a moment. "So, what did you want to talk to me about?"

"I guess it's kind of about this same thing." Emily bit her bottom lip. "Did you tell David about what happened to me?"

"No. I didn't. Why?"

"We—we've gotten close. I mean, as friends and all, and I was just wondering . . ."

Lillian smiled. "He talks about you all the time. He doesn't realize it, but he does. I think he has fallen for you over the past few weeks."

Emily's heart skipped a beat. "I like him a lot too."

"I think the two of you make a darling couple. I really do. David is a *gut* person, a wonderful person. I'm blessed to be his stepmother."

"Oh no. We're not a couple." Emily shook her head, then shrugged. "I don't think I'm worthy to be a *fraa*, after what happened and all."

"Oh, that's rubbish." Lillian slammed a hand down on the table. "Don't you think like that, Emily Detweiler."

"That's what *Mamm* said." Emily felt comforted knowing that Lillian agreed with her mother. "But then . . ."

"What is it, Emily?"

"Every time David and I start to get closer, as more than just friends, he pulls away. He's kissed me a couple of times, and . . ."

Lillian gasped as a smile filled her face. "Really! That's great, Emily. David didn't really date when we were in Lancaster County. We always wondered why, but maybe he was just waiting for the right girl." She winked at Emily.

"But, Lillian, David has made it very clear to me that he doesn't want anything more than friendship. In the beginning, that's all I wanted, and all I felt I deserved. But things started to change, and I began to hope for more."

"Of course you would hope for more." Lillian grinned. "David is a great guy."

"Then I wonder why he keeps pushing me away if you didn't tell him about what happened to me. I thought maybe he was attracted to me and liked me, but then he didn't want to get too close to me because I am not fit for marriage, which I completely understand."

Lillian leaned toward Emily and spoke in a low, soft voice. "Emily. You have got to stop thinking like that. You are perfectly fit for marriage. So stop those thoughts. Now as for David . . ." She leaned back against her chair. "First of all, he is not the kind of person who would think like that. David loves deeply and he doesn't judge. As for him getting close to you, then pushing you away . . . well, that is confusing." Lillian tapped her finger to her chin. "But I'm gonna find out why."

"Lillian, no. Maybe you better not say anything."

Lillian arched her brows high. "Look here, missy. I can only keep so many secrets for you. I won't tell your mother that you know your attacker, because I'm going to trust that you will do the right thing. However, David's standoffish behavior bothers me. Of course his father and I want him to marry and have a family of his own. If something is bothering him, I want to know."

"I understand. But he'll know we talked."

"Might as well find out what's going on in that boy's head." Lillian got up and stirred her soup again.

Emily felt sick to her stomach. This entire visit had been one big mistake. First, she'd blurted out about James, and even though Lillian's advice made sense, she didn't see how she'd ever face that situation. And now David would think she's a whiny schoolgirl, crying to his stepmother and asking why he doesn't like her.

"Emily, I can see the wheels in your head spinning at full speed. Don't worry, okay?"

Emily nodded, but she was consumed with worry.

DAVID WAITED UNTIL the buggy pulled out of his driveway. He strained to see who it was. *Emily?* It was dark, but as she passed by him, it sure looked like her.

He hurried to stable his horse and get into the house. "Was that Emily?"

"*Ya.*" Lillian pointed upstairs. "When you go wash up, can you round up Anna and Elizabeth . . . and your father? He should be through bathing. I told him he was too filthy to sit down to supper without a bath first." Lillian smiled as she carried a pot to the middle of the table. "He's working very hard to make this a nice home for us. He spent all day outside making repairs to the *haus*."

"What was Emily doing here?"

"She came to talk to me."

David stood still in the kitchen and waited for more, but Lillian just swooshed her hand in his direction. "Go, go. Wash up and bring the crew down with you before this soup gets cold."

David frowned, but he did as she asked.

After supper, his father retired to the den to read the Bible to the girls, and David did the unexpected. He helped Lillian clean up in the kitchen.

"So, what did Emily want?" He started to clear the plates from the table.

"I figured there was some reason you were helping me in the kitchen." Lillian turned to face him, a grin on her face as she filled the sink with soapy water.

"Was it anything about—about me?"

"As a matter of fact, it was."

David placed a stack of plates on the counter beside Lillian. "Are you going to make me beg?"

Lillian tapped a finger to her chin. "Hmm . . . maybe." She lifted the plates and put them in the water. "I'll wash. You dry."

David grabbed a rag from the drawer. "Deal."

"Seems the two of you are really *gut* friends."

"*Ya*. I guess so."

"You talk about her a lot too."

David reached for a plate in the drain. "No, I don't."

"*Ach*, but you do." Lillian turned to him and smiled. "I like Emily a lot. If you are dating her, or wanted to date her, your father and I would be thrilled about that. We've become close with their family since we moved here, mostly Vera and me, but your father seems to like Elam, too, even though he's only been around him a few times." Lillian paused, handed him a plate. "And Anna and Elizabeth love playing with Betsy."

"We're not dating." David was getting irritated that Emily would talk to Lillian about them.

"Why? She's lovely, and she really seems to like you. A lot."

His irritation eased up. "Really? What did she say?"

Lillian shrugged. "Not that much, really. Just that the two of you are friends. But . . ." Lillian grinned. "She said that you've kissed her. More than once."

David could feel his face reddening with a combination of embarrassment and mild anger.

"Oh, don't be mad that she told me. She's just confused. Emily said that every time the two of you start to get close, you pull back. And David, you did the same thing in Lancaster County every time a girl showed interest in you." Lillian lifted her shoulders, dropped them slowly. "I can't help but be curious why."

"If Emily wants to know how I feel, maybe she should just ask me, and not run to my stepmother."

"David, don't be mad. If I was Emily, I would be confused too. If you are attracted to her, kissing her, spending time with her, then why don't you want to move forward?"

David stowed a dry plate in the cabinet, set the dish towel down, and put his hands on his hips. "I can't believe you have to ask me that."

Lillian frowned. "What are you talking about?"

"You, of all people, should know why I don't plan on getting close to any woman. Actually, *mei daed* would have a better understanding about this."

"I'm lost." Lillian turned toward the den. "Samuel! Can you come in here, please?"

"Lillian, I really don't want to talk about this now."

His father walked into the kitchen. "How many people does it take to clean this kitchen?" He smiled, but his smile faded when he saw the scowl on David's face. "What's going on?"

"David seems to think that we, or mostly you, should know why he doesn't want to get close to a woman. Do you want to enlighten me?" Lillian went back to scrubbing another plate.

David's father shrugged. "Maybe he hasn't found the right one." He paused. "Is this about the Detweiler girl? The two of you sure have been spending a lot of time together."

"Just because we spend time together and we're friends, that doesn't mean that I have to date her. I have no interest in dating her!" David walked away from his dish-drying duties and stared out the window into the darkness. "I don't even know why we're talking about this."

"You said your father would understand." Lillian turned off the water and turned around about the same time David did.

David took a step closer to his father and Lillian. "I remember real well how upset *Daed* was when *Mamm* died. I didn't think he would ever get over it." He saw Lillian look down. "But then he was blessed to find you, Lillian." Lillian looked back up at him and smiled slightly. "Why, knowing what I know, would I ever marry someone, possibly even have *kinner*, only to leave them in a few years?"

Lillian stepped forward, her eyes clouded with confusion. "Why would you leave them? If you're talking about Ivan, David, you are nothing like your *onkel*. We know you would never do anything like that."

David shook his head in frustration. "I'm not talking about Ivan!" He cut his eyes back and forth between his father and Lillian. "I heard you talking five years ago. I heard you say that I'll be doing *gut* to live five or ten years."

"What?" Lillian glanced at Samuel.

David rolled his eyes and huffed. "Don't pretend you don't know what I'm talking about. After I had my kidney transplant, I overheard you and *Daed* talking. You were crying and said I'd only be twenty-five in ten years when my kidney could give out. Why would I marry someone, father *kinner*, then drop dead and leave them all to fend for themselves? I wouldn't do that to anyone. I saw you, *Daed*!" David faced off with his father. "You were destroyed when *Mamm* died. I'm never doing that to anyone! Especially Emily, because I think she has been hurt enough."

Lillian touched his arm. "David, you need to listen to us. Whatever you heard, you misunderstood."

David jerked away from her. "No. I don't think so. You said that my kidney might only last five to ten years, and then you started crying and said I'd only be twenty-five in ten years. I heard you, Lillian."

"You watch the way you speak to Lillian, David." His father stepped forward. "You watch your tone. I will explain this to you."

David stood there, looking at the floor and shaking his head.

"What you heard was that a kidney *can* last only five to ten years. Sometimes they fail. But even if that happens, you can have another transplant. And sometimes a kidney can last for much longer than that. You haven't been handed a death sentence, David, but a gift . . . a chance to live a full life. You've never had any problem with the kidney Uncle Noah gave you. Every time you go to the doctor for a checkup, he's impressed with how well you are doing."

David shuffled his feet, unable to look at either of them and embarrassed that perhaps he had misunderstood part of his diagnosis for all these years. He lifted his eyes to his father. "But it *could* fail."

"*Ya*, it could." His *daed* stepped closer and put a hand on David's shoulder. "But you can't live your life in fear of that, David. Trust in the Lord to keep you healthy. Why do you think we invest in all these medications? That's what keeps your kidney functioning the way it's supposed to."

David's stomach rolled. The word *invest* caused an instant speculation. "What do you mean, *invest*?"

His father pulled his hand from David's shoulder, then waved it in the air. "That was a poor choice of words."

"Exactly how much do all those pills I take cost?"

Lillian dried her hands on her apron. "It doesn't matter, David. They are necessary, and your father is right. Your kidney is doing great. There's no reason for you not to live a perfectly normal, happy life. I'm so, so sorry if you misunderstood when you heard us talking."

"You were crying." David turned to Lillian.

"*Ya*, I was." Lillian let out a heavy breath. "Even the thought of losing you at a young age is upsetting, David, but in your case, it is highly unlikely. You are doing great!"

"I'm going to go take a bath." David turned to leave.

"David."

He swung around at the sound of his father's sharp tone. "*Ya?*"

"Life is just risky. You never know what might happen. We can't live in fear of the unknown, and we must trust that God's will shall be done."

"I do trust God's will. And if it's His will that my kidney shouldn't last, I won't put anyone through that. I'm not getting married. Ever."

As David marched up the stairs, he thought about all the medications he was taking and what it must be costing.

Is that why we moved?

His heart sank at the thought.

Sixteen

Emily glanced at David, who stood on the other side of Martha several feet away. Ever since she'd spoken to Lillian, Emily was clear in her mind that David just didn't care enough about her to pursue anything more than friendship. He didn't know about her attack, so that wasn't his reason. Emily figured he liked her, cared for her . . . just not *enough*.

"I cannot believe we are having a funeral for a bird," Jacob whispered in Emily's ear.

"Be quiet. This is important to Martha." Emily straightened as she waited for the funeral to begin. A lovely spot beneath a large oak tree in Martha's backyard had been chosen as the final resting place. Arnold had arrived early, like Emily, and he had already dug the grave and cleared the snow in an area large enough for everyone to gather. The temperature was unseasonably warm, almost forty degrees, and the sun shone bright.

Jacob leaned closer to Emily again as more people gathered around. "Why is there a nun here?"

"She's a friend of Mr. Becker's. Her name is Sister Catherine from the Catholic church in Alamosa. It was either her or Bishop

Esh, and I wasn't about to ask Bishop Esh to offer prayers for a bird's memorial service. We haven't lived here that long. He'd think I was crazy, no?"

The elderly nun walked over to where Emily was standing, her face solemn but a hint of amusement showed in the wrinkles around her eyes. "When Arnold asked me to do this, I was certainly willing. But I must tell you, I've never led prayer for a deceased bird. I'm not even sure what to say."

"Just say Elvis was nineteen years old," Emily told her. "He has been Martha's companion—don't say *pet*—for nineteen years. He was a wonderful friend." Emily shrugged. "I don't know, Sister Catherine. Something like that, I guess. *Danki* for doing this."

Sister Catherine returned to her place next to Martha, who was dressed in all black: knee-length dress, a long overcoat, gloves, and a hat with a chest-length veil in front. Both hands were filled with tissues, and she alternated blowing her nose and dabbing her eyes. Arnold was at her side.

Emily glanced around at all those present. Both her parents, Jacob and Beth Ann, Levi, Betsy, all of the Stoltzfuses except Katie Ann, and Arnold. It was the best Emily could do, and Martha seemed pleased.

Emily's father stood on Emily's right. "What exactly are they burying that bird in?" *Daed* had cupped his hand around his mouth to keep his voice from carrying.

"It's a gold-plated casket that Martha picked out for Elvis."

"I'm not surprised. She can afford it," her father said with a light chuckle, although Emily didn't understand why he would say that. Martha's home was larger than most in the community, but she seemed to live a fairly modest life. She drove an old automobile, and her clothes weren't all that fancy. Of course, Emily had certainly been surprised when she saw the bird's casket, complete with a purple, velveteen lining.

Jacob leaned close to her other ear. "I think Martha should have chosen a closed casket. That bird is looking a little rough."

"Be quiet, Jacob." Emily stomped her foot lightly. "Have some respect."

"It's a *bird*, Emily."

Emily ignored him. She could feel David's eyes on her, but she was afraid to look his way. She was wondering if Lillian told him about their conversation, as she'd said she would. She'd probably told David everything Emily had said—how much she liked him, how she didn't understand why he was so standoffish. The thought just embarrassed Emily to death. She also couldn't help but wonder if Lillian explained Emily's true intentions to David, how the only reason she'd asked is because she felt unworthy after her attack. Now she wondered again, did David know about what had happened to her?

She sighed and reckoned none of it mattered anyway. David hadn't known about her attack before Emily talked to Lillian, so that part of the equation never played a part in him not wanting to be more than friends. But every time she recalled the kisses they'd shared, her heart filled with regret. She glanced his way, and he discreetly pointed a finger at her.

"I need to talk to you later," he mouthed.

She nodded as her heart filled with dread. He was upset with her for talking to Lillian about their personal business. She didn't really blame him.

Sister Catherine cleared her throat. "We are all gathered

here to pay our final respects to Elvis." She glanced at Emily, as if needing some encouragement. Emily nodded in her direction. "Elvis was Martha's favorite pet."

Emily cringed. *I told you not to say* pet. She looked at Martha, who'd abruptly stopped crying. The scowl on her face was frightening.

"Elvis was much more than a pet, though. He was Martha's friend, her companion, for nineteen years."

Emily breathed a sigh of relief and was glad to see Martha's expression soften a little bit beneath the thin black veil. Martha shoved the tissues from one hand to the other, then she reached for Arnold's hand. It was sweet the way they seemed to have found each other in the second half of their lives. Emily glanced at David again. He was staring at her, and it made her very uncomfortable.

"Elvis was—was loved by all, and—and I know we will all miss him."

Emily elbowed Jacob when he started to chuckle.

"Who got all these flowers?" Emily's father whispered in her ear as he nodded to the dozen or so arrangements surrounding the small hole where Elvis would be put to rest.

"I know it's not our way, the flowers, but it's the *Englisch* way. I guess Martha and Arnold got the flowers. I really don't know," Emily answered in a whisper.

Martha plucked two red roses from a nearby floral arrangement and placed them on top of Elvis's body. She narrowed her eyes at Arnold, who quickly did the same. Then her eyes shot directly to Emily. When Emily didn't respond right away, Martha flipped her veil up, a frown on her face. Emily closed the gap between her and Martha, plucked two roses from a nearby vase, and walked toward the casket. She nodded at her mother, who was standing on the other side of her father. With much hesitancy, the entire crowd slowly retrieved flowers and placed them on top of Elvis until you couldn't even see him, which Emily thought was a good thing.

Martha watched as Arnold closed Elvis's casket, then lowered the bird into his grave. Everyone stayed until the casket was covered with dirt and Martha faced the crowd and said, "Now, let's eat!"

Emily grinned. Some things about Martha were exactly the same. As it should be.

Martha walked over to Emily and pointed a painted fingernail in her direction. "I hope you had one of your people bring creamed celery, like I asked you to."

Emily nodded. "*Ya, Mamm* made it fresh this morning."

After the meal and clean up, people began to disburse to their buggies, and Emily took a peek out the window to see if David had come in a separate buggy from his family. Yep. She rounded the corner from the kitchen to the den to ask her mother if they were ready to go, and as fate would have it, she bumped right into David.

"You ready?"

"Where are we going?"

"To have a talk."

Emily couldn't read his expression. "Are you going to yell at me about something?"

He grinned. "Why, have you done something bad?"

She shrugged. "I didn't think so at the time, but now I'm not sure."

"Tell your folks you're going for a ride with me." David

reached for his coat, which was laid across the back of the couch.

Emily leaned closer and whispered, "Are you sure? Someone might think we're dating, and we don't want that."

He scowled, then headed out the door.

Emily found her mother, begged her not to make a big deal out of the ride with David, then found her own coat and bonnet. She walked outside and was still buttoning her coat when David opened the door for her to crawl into the buggy.

He didn't say anything until they were on the main road. "That was a first for me. A bird funeral."

Emily smiled, but her insides churned. "Me too."

"Don't look so scared, Emily. I'm not going to scold you about anything."

Emily didn't look at him. "You're mad because I talked to Lillian, aren't you?"

"No. I'm not mad. I'm just wondering why you didn't talk to me instead."

She bit her bottom lip and didn't say anything.

David took the next right, then pulled into the driveway of what appeared to be an abandoned home. "No one lives here, so this will be a *gut* place to talk." He parked the buggy, then turned to face her. "Emily . . . I like you." He waited a few moments, then added, "A lot."

Emily looked down at her lap, knowing her cheeks were bright red, and her heart was thumping much too fast.

David cupped her chin and gently raised her head until their eyes were locked. "And, *ya*, Lillian did tell me that you are wondering why I can't move forward, even though I care about you. A lot. It wouldn't be fair to you, and I don't want to hurt you any more than you've already been hurt." He glanced at her scar, and she reached for it. He grabbed her hand in midair, then intertwined his fingers with hers. As he'd done in the past, he leaned over and kissed her forehead. "I do care about you. Very much."

Emily's mind was alive with thoughts and speculations. If Lillian hadn't told David about her attack, then someone must have. It was the only thing that made sense. She was good enough to be friends with, to sneak kisses with here and there, but not good enough to date or pursue for possible marriage. She pushed him away, then opened the door and got out of the buggy.

She walked briskly across the packed snow, knowing she was about to cry, the sunlight blinding her on the way. There was an abandoned home to her right and two barns to her left. She just kept walking, not sure which way to turn, where to look, what to do. It wasn't long before she felt David wrap an arm around her waist. He spun her around to face him. "Are you going to let me finish?"

She pushed him away. "I don't need you to finish! I already know what you're going to say. I'm *gut* enough to be your friend, David! And you like me . . ." Tears began to stream down her face, and she covered her face with her hands. "But I'm not *gut* enough to date. I'm not *gut* enough to ever consider a future with because I'm ruined for marriage." She dropped to her knees in the snow. "That man robbed from me everything that a husband should expect to have in a *fraa*. He stole from me! I knew you'd find out, so you see . . ." She looked up at David but saw only a watery image of his face. "I already know, David." She sat back on her heels and hung her head. "I know why you don't want to be with me." Her shoulders drooped. "So let's both stop pretending you don't know."

David knelt down beside her, then reached one arm under her legs and wrapped his other arm around her waist. He lifted her up with ease, and she buried her head in his chest and sobbed. Tears blinded her eyes and choked her voice. He carried her all the way to one of the old barns, kicked open the door, and bent over to set her on an old bench against the wall. Kneeling in front of her, he reached over and brushed away her tears with his thumbs. Then he kissed her, more tenderly than he ever had in the past, cupping the back of her neck.

"You don't know anything, Emily Detweiler." He brushed away loose strands of hair from her face as she tried to catch her breath. "I fell for you a long time ago. And it didn't take me long at all to figure out what must have happened to you." He kissed her on the tip of her nose. "And your thoughts are all wrong." David stopped touching her and dropped his hands to his sides. He looked down, his fists clenched. "I've prayed to keep away the thoughts I have about whoever did this to you." He looked up at her. "But Emily, I don't think any less of you. I just hate that someone hurt you. And I don't want to hurt you."

Emily sniffled. "Then why don't you want to date me?" It was bold, but she wanted to know. *Am I not pretty enough? Not smart enough?*

"I don't want to date anyone." He took a deep breath. "But you are making it very hard for me to stick to that."

"Please talk to me, David. Please." This time it was Emily who reached up and cupped his cheek. "Please."

He grabbed her hand and pushed it closer to his face, then he closed his eyes. When he opened them, she felt hopeful that she would finally know what was going on inside his head, but when she saw his eyes glaze with tears, she wasn't sure. She pulled him into a hug, and for what seemed like forever, they just held each other.

"Five years ago I had a kidney transplant."

Emily eased away from him, looked into his eyes, and waited. The smell of old hay filled her nostrils and sunrays shone through a small window to her left. Aside from the bench, some scrap wood, and a few rusty tools, the barn was empty. "Do you want to tell me about it?"

David spent the next hour explaining his operation to her, how his shunned uncle had given him a kidney and had been welcomed back into the family, and how he'd feared he wouldn't live a full life.

"It wasn't until yesterday, when I talked to *Daed* and Lillian, that I realized that maybe I misunderstood some things."

"So . . . there's no reason why you won't live to be an old man." Emily smiled.

"I prayed about it a lot last night, and I've decided that I must accept whatever is God's will." He paused, frowned. "But someone else shouldn't have to take the risk that my kidney might fail in five or ten years."

Emily looked down and whispered, "I would give you one of mine." She looked up in time to see David blink back a tear.

"There's one other problem, though."

Emily waited, thinking that they had already covered quite a bit of ground in the land of troubles. What else could there possibly be?

"I have a feeling that my medications are putting a hardship on my family. I'm even wondering if maybe that's why we moved. It's the only thing that makes sense to me now. We all loved Lancaster County." He paused. "I was planning to go back there as soon as I saved enough money, but the sacrifices my family made for me . . . well, it makes me want to stay here and help my family build that old place into something really nice. Lillian and the girls deserve that. I even thought about not taking the medicines—"

Emily grabbed his arms. "You can't do that! You said you need the medicines to live!"

"I know. I know. And it would be like suicide, wrong in the eyes of God. So, instead, I'm going to work extra hours at the furniture store and help my father as much as I can to ready our home. This is where I belong."

Emily bit her bottom lip. "And we'll continue to be friends?"

David smiled. "Unless you're willing to take a chance on me being around for a long time?"

She threw her arms around him. "I am."

When he eased out of the hug, he said, "Emily, I won't have a lot of time for dating, though. I want to help my father. I said I'd help build the schoolhouse, and some day . . . well, I'd like to be able to have a place of my own. I'm going to have to work really hard."

"I understand."

"But I'd be honored to date you, if you'd be interested in doing that."

Emily smiled. "I think I'd like that."

VERA WAITED UNTIL everyone had left Martha's before she walked into the den with the shoebox under her arm. Levi and Betsy had caught a ride home with Jacob and Beth Ann, Arnold had taken Sister Catherine back to the convent, and Elam was sitting on the front porch waiting for Vera to "do the dirty deed," as he called it.

"Martha?" Vera approached Martha, who sat very still in her chair. She was still dressed in her mourning clothes, but she did have her black lace veil pushed back over the top of her hat. "I need to give this back to you." She pushed the box toward Martha. "We cannot accept something like this."

Martha rolled her eyes, which Vera thought was very rude.

"Why would you give us a box of money for Christmas?"

Martha scratched her nose, then sniffed. "You folks have everything I don't have. Faith. Hope. Love. Family." She raised her brows. "And I have something you don't have. More money than I'll ever need in the lifetime I got left." She shrugged. "I thought it might help build your schoolhouse."

Vera gasped, then leaned closer to Martha. "Martha, there's two hundred and fifty thousand dollars in this box! Exactly how much do you think a one-room schoolhouse for ten children costs?"

Martha sighed. "You don't want the money?"

Vera stood, indignant. "Of course not. We cannot accept something like that."

Martha stood up, grabbed the box from her hand, and walked through the kitchen and out onto the porch. Vera followed.

"Hello, Elam," Martha said as she tossed the box into a blue trash can on the side of the porch. "You can take your wife home now. I need to mourn my loss."

Martha marched back into the house, Vera on her heels. "*Ach*, now Martha, you are being ridiculous. You don't throw away money like that when there are people starving in the world! There are people who can use that money! You're being ridiculous."

Martha continued into the den. "Who is being ridiculous?"

Vera stomped her foot. "You are."

"I gave you the money. You're the one who couldn't find a use for it."

"It's not an appropriate Christmas gift."

Martha sat down in her chair, then put her hand to her forehead. "Vera, I'm tired. I buried my best friend today. Go home."

"Are you going to go get that money out of the trash can?"

"No."

"Why?"

"Because I don't feel like it."

"Martha!"

"Vera!"

"Argh!" Vera stormed out of the house, slamming the door on the way out, only to find Elam with his head buried in the garbage can. "What are you doing?"

He stood up, his eyes wide. "Nothing, dear."

"Let's go." Vera moved toward the buggy.

Elam didn't move. "Is Martha gonna leave two hundred and fifty thousand dollars for the trash man?"

"I reckon so."

Elam grabbed the box and tucked it under his arm.

"Put that back, Elam."

"I will not." He stood tall, raised his chin. "We might not

need this money, but someone can put it to good use. We just have to find that person."

Vera thought about what Martha said. "*I gave you the money. You're the one who couldn't find a use for it.*"

Then Vera knew what to do with the money.

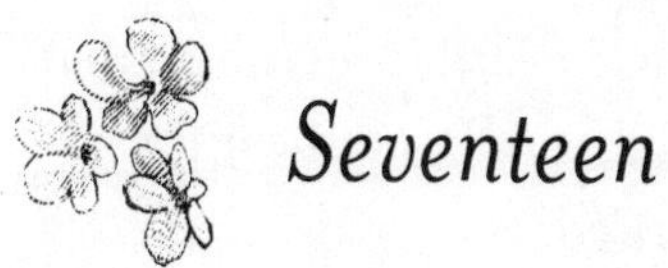

Seventeen

KATIE ANN SPENT THE MORNING CLEANING HER HOUSE. It wasn't dirty, but that's the way Amish women started their day, and somehow she needed to feel like a normal Amish woman. Even if everything was far from normal. She tried to ignore the stomach virus that had plagued her lately. If she was feeling all right when she was done cleaning, she'd go see if Lillian needed help at her house. During the three months since Christmas, Katie Ann had spent a lot of time helping Lillian work on their farmhouse, and it was starting to take shape. Samuel and David had put in new wooden floors, whitewashed the walls, and replaced the cabinets. For Katie Ann, the work kept her busy and her mind off her misery.

She'd also gotten to know her sister-in-law much better, and she babysat Anna and Elizabeth regularly, which she'd enjoyed. Despite what was happening in her marriage, she liked seeing David and Emily's relationship blossom. David spent the little bit of free time he had with Emily, and Emily often ate meals with them. Prayer combined with time heals, and Katie Ann was getting used to being alone. She'd heard from Ivan twice. She supposed he felt obligated to check on her after so many years of marriage, but he wasn't the same man she married, and it was a struggle to hide her resentment when she spoke to him. He was in Lancaster County, and she'd heard from others that he was with Lucy, even though he didn't offer up the information on the phone. She wasn't surprised.

Then there was the money. It would certainly enable her to open a business, fix up her house, and live out her life here in Canaan. She hadn't touched one dollar of the money for herself since the box showed up on her doorstep three months ago, not long after Christmas. Lillian and Samuel had also received a mysterious box of money, and like Katie Ann, they had no idea where it came from. Lillian planned to use some of the money to help with David's prior medical bills and medications, and they'd save the rest for when David started a family of his own, giving him a jump on the medical expenses he'd face for the rest of his life.

She'd tried to give Arnold Becker some of the money for the new schoolhouse, but he refused, saying all the materials had been donated.

Katie Ann thought about the note that was inside the box along with the money. *With God's blessing, start a new life for yourself.* She just didn't know what that life was. But her own money, the little bit Ivan left her, was running out, so she knew she would need to decide soon. For weeks, she'd lost sleep about who would offer her such a generous gift, but she never found out. So she just kept the shoebox under her bed until she could sort things out.

She stowed her broom in the pantry, then stopped to close the window in the kitchen. She'd opened it earlier to air out the room, glad to feel the beginnings of spring, but the air still had a cool edge during the day and near-freezing temperatures at night. Someone knocked on the door, and she walked into the den and opened it to see Martha. She'd gotten to know the *Englisch* woman over the past few months, and although she was an odd woman, Katie Ann liked her, as did the rest of her family.

"I was sent to let you know that the men are starting on the schoolhouse Saturday. I told Arnold I'd stop by and let you know . . . even though I haven't heard from Arnold in a couple of days." Martha scowled before she turned toward Lillian and Samuel's house. "I knocked on the door over there, but no one is at home. Can you let your kinfolks know too?"

"Of course." Katie Ann grabbed at her stomach.

Martha folded her arms across her chest and frowned. "What's wrong with you?"

"*Ach*, I'm fine. I just seem to have a stomach bug that won't go away." Katie Ann grimaced as the nauseated feeling settled in the pit of her stomach.

Martha stared at her for a moment before she said, "Anyway, we're all going to be there, and we're planning it like your people do a barn raising—frame it all in one day, put the roof on that evening, then spend the next few Saturdays working on the inside." Martha took a breath. "All the womenfolk are going to bring food and tea at noon. Even me." She cackled. "Though history dictates that I should leave the cooking to the others. I'll just bring the tea."

"That sounds nice. And *ya*, I'll be happy to bring something." She grimaced again. "I'm sorry, Martha. I hope I'm not being rude, but my stomach is getting worse. I think I best excuse myself."

Katie Ann didn't even have time to close the door; she just

turned and darted to the bathroom. She barely made it this time, and when she was done, she wiped her mouth, took a deep breath, and promised herself she would make an appointment with the doctor the following day if the nausea didn't stop by then. When she walked out of the bathroom, Martha was standing in the den with her arms still folded across her chest and a frown on her face.

"Well, that didn't sound good at all." Martha walked closer to Katie Ann. "You got fever?"

Katie Ann jumped a bit when Martha roughly slapped her hand to Katie Ann's forehead. "I don't think so," she said. "Just feeling sick to my stomach. Not all the time. Just in the mornings, and sometimes after I eat supper."

A grin spread across Martha's face. "Honey, that ain't no virus." Martha tipped her head at an angle, then squinted one eye. "How long since your husband's been gone, and how long since you've had your womanly visit?"

"What?"

Martha slapped her hands to her hips. "You know . . . how long since—"

"*Ach*, that." Katie Ann stopped Martha before the woman embarrassed her further. "No, I'm not pregnant. Ivan and I tried for many years to have a baby." She shook her head. "It never happened."

"You didn't answer my question." Martha tilted her head to the side and looked up at the ceiling. "He's been gone about three or four months, that husband of yours." She scowled at Katie Ann. "Who I think needs a good lashing for what he did to you." Martha waved a hand in the air. "Anyway, how long has it been since—"

"I don't know. But I'm sure I'm not pregnant." Katie Ann tried to recall the last time she'd had a menstrual period. She couldn't. She'd stopped keeping track of it a long time ago, when she'd reconciled the fact that children were not in her future.

Martha pressed her lips together for a moment. "You're a bit young to be going through the change."

This conversation was inappropriate, and Katie Ann felt her cheeks blushing. "I'm sure I'll be fine, Martha. Tomorrow I'll go to the doctor, and—" She gasped as she bent at the waist. A sharp pain jabbed at her abdomen. This felt different than the nausea, and it frightened her.

"Let's go," Martha barked. "Whatever is wrong with you, pregnant or otherwise, I'm hauling you to a doctor. So get what you need and let's go."

Katie Ann didn't argue as another pain stabbed at her stomach. *Dear Lord, haven't I been through enough?*

It was two hours later when the doctor was finally able to see Katie Ann. He gave her a complete examination, drew some blood, and asked her to urinate in a cup. As she waited for someone to return to the small room she was in, the clock ticked loudly on the wall and the sterile surroundings and smell of ammonia made her anxious. But at least her stomach wasn't cramping any more.

Martha was waiting in the reception area down the hall. Katie Ann was grateful to Martha for bringing her to the doctor, but she felt badly that the woman was spending her afternoon this way. Martha didn't seem to mind, though.

"When else can I catch up on my reading?" she'd said, holding up a magazine.

Katie Ann took a deep breath, blew it out slowly, then folded her hands in her lap. She wasn't sure whether to go sit in the chair nearby or stay seated at the end of the long examining table. She decided to stay where she was and hoped the doctor would be back soon. Normally, she would seek out a natural doctor, hoping for herbs or a homemade treatment to cure what ailed her, but Martha was insistent that Katie Ann go to an *Englisch* doctor. And Katie Ann suspected Martha was right in this case. Whatever was going on was more than a common cold or virus.

She heard shuffling outside the closed door and looked up when the doctor walked into the room. He was an older man with gray hair and small green eyes, but when he smiled, his kind features put Katie Ann's mind at ease.

"Katie Ann, you're about three and a half or four months pregnant." His smile grew broader, then he sat down on a small stool and began writing something on a pad of paper. "I want you to take these vitamins I'm prescribing, something a little better than what you can get over the counter."

He kept writing, but Katie Ann couldn't breathe. She unfolded her hands and pressed them against her belly. Dr. Morgan raised his brows to her.

"This is your first baby, right? You must be very excited."

Katie Ann opened her mouth to speak, but no words came out for a few seconds. "Are you sure?" she finally asked.

"Absolutely. And that cramping was due to the stretching of the ligaments in your pelvis. It's something that happens sometimes—usually during the first trimester—but you're not too far past that. We're going to keep a close eye on you, though."

A baby? She couldn't wait to tell Ivan as soon as—

Her heart sank, knowing that she'd dreamed of this moment her entire life and fantasized about the look on Ivan's face when he heard her speak the words, *Ivan, we're going to have a baby*.

But no one would be home to hear the news. And her husband was sharing his life with another woman.

"I want you to come back next week." The doctor handed her the slip of paper. "Just to make sure everything is all right, and we'll do an ultrasound at that time." He paused. "Do you know what that is?"

Katie Ann nodded. She was with Lillian when the doctor suggested her sister-in-law have an ultrasound during her second pregnancy.

"Do you have any questions?" Dr. Morgan stood up from the stool and walked closer.

Ya, I have a million questions. "No," she answered.

The doctor congratulated her before he left the room. Katie Ann sat there for a few moments, fighting the urge to question God's timing. She touched her stomach again with both hands and wondered how she was going to do this alone, at her age.

THAT EVENING MARTHA kicked her shoes off and poured herself into her recliner. She was relieved that Katie Ann was going to be all right, but the poor woman was a mess—thrilled to be pregnant a little late in life and scared to death to be raising a child on her own. Martha was hesitant to leave Katie Ann, but when Lillian showed up, she headed back to her house. Martha recalled her own desire to have children, but she'd lost one in miscarriage and was never able to conceive again. And she'd had Herbert back then. Poor Katie Ann was all by herself. Martha folded her arms across her chest as she thought about her own life.

She was more than a little peeved that she hadn't heard from Arnold for the past two days. They always ate dinner together on Wednesday nights. She'd slap something frozen in one of her own casserole dishes, heat it up, and Arnold would go on and on about how great it was, even though they both knew it originated from a box in the freezer section of the grocery store. She'd called him several times, and each time she'd gotten his answering machine. And today was Wednesday.

She glanced over at Elvis's cage, knowing she needed to move it out of the living room, but sometimes she could almost see and hear her precious Elvis singing and talking to her, and she just wasn't quite ready yet. She settled into the chair, crossed her legs, and thought about the money she'd given Vera. It had been impulsive, and she really hadn't a clue if Vera and her family needed any money, but Martha sure didn't need it. She was at a loss that day about what to give the Detweilers for Christmas, so she figured a quarter million bucks oughta do it. She'd about fallen over when Herbert died and the attorney said they had millions in the bank.

Martha had given away a lot of it over the years, but she'd about run out of good causes in the area, so she thought maybe the Amish might put some to good use. She smiled, knowing she'd been right. Katie Ann told Martha about a mysterious box of money showing up at her front door.

"Who would do such a thing?" Katie Ann had asked on the way home from the doctor's office.

Martha had merely shrugged. A true gift is one that comes from the heart, one you don't need credit for. She'd learned that from going to church with Arnold. "*Matthew 6:3–4 (NIV), But when you give to the needy, do not let your left hand know what your right hand is doing, so that your giving may be in secret. Then your Father, who sees what is done in secret, will reward you.*"

She sure hoped nothing had happened to Arnold. That old man made her want to be a better person. And while Wednesday was frozen food night, Mondays had been the nights that Arnold talked to her about God and His Son, Jesus.

"Jesus listens to us, Martha," he said over and over again. "Just talk to Him like you would a friend."

It frightened her at first, these conversations she seemed to be having with herself. But when she started to really listen, she could hear a voice in her head. She was pretty sure that's how she knew to give Vera the box of money, that she'd do the right thing.

Seek Me with all your heart.

She'd been hearing that in her head for months, and with each day, she felt like she was growing in the Lord's love, gaining faith. "I want to spend the rest of my life living the way You want me to live, God," she'd recently said to Him. "Give me a chance, and I'll make You proud."

Her thoughts were interrupted by the phone ringing.

She rose from the recliner and walked to the phone a few feet away. "This better be Arnold Becker calling to explain to me where he's been and why he isn't at my house tonight for supper," she said before she picked up the receiver and said hello, noticing that there was no number on her caller ID.

"Martha, Martha. I'm so sorry."

Relief flooded over her at the sound of Arnold's voice. "Where in the world are you? I've tried calling, but your machine picks up."

"I'm in Georgia."

Martha was quiet for a few moments. "Arnold . . . are you in another state when you are supposed to be in Canaan, Colorado, having lasagna with me tonight?" She kept her voice as calm as a windless sea with enough turbulence hidden below the surface to erupt into a tidal wave if he wasn't real careful about what he said next.

"I'm sorry, Martha. I hate missing our dinner night."

Martha scratched her head so hard she knocked her butterfly clip to the floor. "You gonna tell me what you're doing in Georgia?"

"I'm with my son."

Martha folded herself back into her recliner. "What son? I thought you didn't have any children."

She heard a heavy sigh on the other end of the line. "No, I do. Just one son. Benny."

"I heard you say that you didn't have any family to speak of that first day I met you."

"Right—to speak of. I haven't spoken to Benny for years, since he was a boy. But his wife called me, Martha." She heard only silence for a few moments; then Arnold spoke. "Benny is sick, and I need to be here right now."

"Oh. Of course you do." She thought for a moment. "What's wrong with him?"

"Pancreatic cancer."

Martha was quiet. "I'm sorry, Arnold. Is there anything I can do?"

"No. But thank you." He paused. "I've enjoyed our time together, Martha, but I feel a strong calling to stay here and help take care of my son, and to try to make things right between us while I still can."

There was such sadness in Arnold's voice that Martha hesitated to ask a question she already knew the answer to. "How long will you be there?"

"I've been invited to stay indefinitely, for better or worse. I won't be coming back. I couldn't tell you in person. I just couldn't."

Martha fought the bitterness rising to the surface, but how could she fault the man for wanting to be with his sick child? "I hope that things go well for you and your son, Arnold."

"Thank you, Martha."

They chatted for a few more minutes, and Arnold said he was going to speak with David about completely taking over the schoolhouse project, and he'd already made arrangements to have his things shipped to Georgia. They had just said goodbye when Martha quickly spoke into the receiver.

"Arnold? Are you still there?"

But he'd already hung up. "I'll be praying for you and your boy," she whispered to herself as she hung up the phone.

"Lord, I'm trying. I really am," she said as she walked to the kitchen, then pulled out an almost-burnt container filled with store-bought lasagna. "You said, 'Seek Me,' and I did. I've opened my heart, and I've given money to those in need, like I heard you're supposed to do. I've tried to clean up my act and not be so cranky all the time." She looked toward the ceiling. "But You took Herbert. Elvis is gone. And now my friend, Arnold." A tear rolled down her cheek. "I don't understand what it is You want from me." She sat down at the kitchen table and stared at the pan of food. It seemed fine eating it with Arnold, but right now, it was the most unappealing thing she'd ever laid eyes on.

MARTHA WASN'T FEELING much better the next night. She wiped tears from her eyes when she heard a knock on the door. She knew it wasn't Arnold, so she didn't rush to open it.

"Katie Ann. You sick? You all right?" Martha opened the door and stepped aside so Katie Ann could step inside. "Whatcha got there?"

"It's chicken lasagna. Emily told me it's your favorite, and I wanted to do something for you, for taking me to the doctor yesterday." Katie Ann smiled as her eyes watered up. "I might not have a husband, but I'm going to have a baby, and I thank our heavenly Father for that."

Martha closed the door, then accepted the lasagna from Katie Ann, noticing how much better it smelled than the frozen meal she'd ended up tossing in the trash last night.

"Come on in here, honey. I'll make us some tea to go with this lasagna."

Katie Ann shuffled into the kitchen. "Thank you, Martha, but I can't stay. I'm not hungry and I have much to think about." The poor woman sniffled, and Martha could tell her mind was on overload. "And *danki* again for spending so much time with me at the doctor's office."

Martha thought for a moment. Maybe they could both use a little company.

And the girl needs to eat. She's with child.

KATIE ANN SAW Martha bend at the waist and grab her back. "Martha, what's wrong? Can I do anything for you?"

"No, no, honey. You go on." Martha eased into a chair as she frowned. "I'm sure I'll be better soon. It's just my back."

"Can I do anything for you before I go? Can I get you a plate from the cabinet or pour you something drink?" Katie Ann sat down in the chair next to Martha and waited. It wasn't like she had anything to do at home, but she could feel a knot in her throat, and it was exhausting to keep holding back tears. She'd had a good cry the day before, but she was trying to keep her emotions in check. God had blessed her with the miracle of a child after all these years, but she worried how she would manage as a single mother in this unknown place called Canaan.

Martha grimaced again. "That would be nice if you could get me a plate. Might as well get yourself one, too, since you're staying to tend to me."

Katie Ann got up and went to the cabinet Martha was pointing to, not realizing she had committed to staying past getting Martha a plate. But if Martha needed tending to, that was the least Katie Ann could do for her since she'd spent hours with her at the doctor.

Martha bowed her head in prayer before Katie Ann did and offered a prayer of thanks. Katie Ann dished them each out a small helping of lasagna.

"Arnold's gone." Martha stuffed a bite into her mouth, but Katie Ann could see the tears in her eyes.

"What do you mean . . . gone?"

Martha swallowed, then said, "Gone to live with his son in Georgia." She shook her head. "I didn't even know he had a son. And now his son is sick, and Arnold wants to be with him."

"I'm sorry, Martha. I know that you and Mr. Becker had grown to be *gut* friends. I hope everything will be all right for his son."

"Yeah. Me too."

Martha seemed far away, and Katie Ann wasn't sure what to say, so she ate quietly, thinking about her own situation. A baby. The blessing was still sinking in.

"You tell your husband that you're with child?" Martha scooped up another load of lasagna.

"No."

"Are you going to?"

That was something Katie Ann had been thinking about since she'd received the news. She wondered if Ivan would feel obligated to come home and be with her and the baby, even though his heart belonged to someone else. She knew she couldn't live like that. But she felt cheated, that she could never marry again. Lillian and her family, along with the friends she'd made here, would help her with whatever she needed, but it certainly wasn't the same as having a husband.

"No. I'm not going to tell him," she finally said. She blinked back tears at the thought. "I don't want him to be with me just because I'm pregnant."

"I don't blame you. Dirty scoundrel." Martha shook her head.

"I'm just—just worried about taking care of a baby on my own." She paused as she looked at her plate and picked at her food. "And there's much for me to do before the baby comes. There's clothes to be sewn, blankets to be made, and a baby's room to prepare." She paused. "I mean, I know folks will help me, but I'm not . . . not young like most women having their first child."

"Arnold told me that all things happen in God's time frame." Martha swallowed, then let out a heavy sigh. "Although . . . I can't figure out why God would send me Arnold, only to take him away."

"We don't always understand His will for us." Katie Ann knew she didn't. They were quiet for a few moments as Martha finished her helping of lasagna.

"So, what are you hoping for, a boy or a girl?" Martha took hold of the spatula and piled more lasagna on her plate.

Katie picked at the remainder of her food with one hand. She reached for her belly with the other hand, still hardly able to believe a life was growing inside her. "I always thought that if I had a girl, that I would name her Anna Marie, after my grandmother who died when I was young."

"And if it's a boy?" Martha asked with a mouthful.

"Jonas. I would name the baby Jonas, after a very special man that I knew in Lancaster County who died not too long ago."

Martha swallowed, then stared long and hard at her. "You can't get married again, can you? Did I hear that somewhere, that Amish folks can't divorce or remarry?"

Katie Ann put her fork down and took a deep breath. "*Ya*. That's right."

"Well, at my age, I figure Arnold was probably my last

shot at another chance." Martha leaned back in her chair and folded her arms across her chest. Katie Ann couldn't help but notice that her back seemed fine now. "Guess your kinfolk will help you get a baby's room ready, huh?"

Katie Ann shrugged. "*Ya*. I'm sure they will help me ready up the room."

Martha leaned forward a bit and lifted her chin. "But they got their own families to take care of. And at your age—no offense, honey—but you're going to have to take it easy during this pregnancy." She paused. "You done eating? I'd like to show you something."

Katie Ann nodded and stood up when Martha did. "Is your back better now?"

Martha bent slightly and moaned. "Not really, honey. But if you can help me up the stairs, there's something I'd like for you to see."

Katie Ann latched onto Martha's elbow, and slowly they made their way up the stairs.

"I ain't been up here in a long time. My bedroom is downstairs, and I don't even use this part of the house." They eased down the hallway, and Martha pointed to a closed door on the right at the end of the hallway. She stopped, and Katie Ann let go of her elbow. Martha just stood there quietly. "This is a storage room." She paused. "I never could figure out why I kept some of this stuff. But . . ." She smiled warmly at Katie Ann. "I think I held on to it until I felt it would be in the hands of the right person." She pushed the door open, then fumbled for the light switch and turned it on.

Katie Ann's eyes went directly to the vintage cradle in the far corner of the room, a beautiful piece of mahogany furniture with a simple design. Inside was a pastel quilt with yellow, pink, and blue bunnies on it, and a fluffy pillow to match. "Why do you have all of this?"

Martha eased her way around an old suitcase, then stepped over two blue hat boxes. She walked closer and fingered the quilt. "I was pregnant once. Lost the baby."

"I'm so sorry, Martha." She searched Martha's eyes from across the room, but her friend just shrugged.

"It was a long time ago." Martha picked up the small quilt. "It all needs washing, of course. And I'm sure that cradle could use a new coat of finish, but this was my mother's cradle, and my cradle, and I thought someday . . ." She looked at Katie Ann. "I'd be honored for you to have it."

Tears welled in Katie Ann's eyes. She'd always assumed Ivan would build a cradle for their little one. "*Ach*, Martha. I couldn't." She shook her head.

Martha scowled. "Why? You don't like it?"

"No, no. I think it's the most beautiful piece of furniture I've ever seen." Katie Ann went to where Martha was standing, then ran her finger delicately along the frame of the cradle. "But don't you want to save this for—"

"For what? My children or grandchildren?" She cackled. "Honey, that ain't looking good for me." She pulled a sheet off of a nearby piece of furniture. "And here's the dresser to match." She paused, lifted her brows. "And ya know what? Herbert had this furniture handmade by an Amish man when I was—was pregnant. It's perfect for you."

"Oh, Martha. It is so beautiful," she said again as she eyed the six-drawer chest with a matching mahogany finish. "Are you sure you are willing to part with it?"

Martha grimaced. "Well, not to just anyone." She gave her head a taut nod. "But . . . to you. Yes. I'm sure."

"I will pay you for it, of course."

"No. It's a gift."

Katie Ann smiled. "Martha, I have money."

Martha chuckled. "So I've heard." She waved her hand in the air. "You keep your money. From what I hear, kids are expensive. Even Amish ones." Then she walked over to a stack of boxes pushed up against the wall. She pried the flap up on the top one and pulled out a diaper carrier and held it up. "In these boxes is everything you'll ever need for a baby. Now, I imagine that some of it will be a bit fancy for your taste, but you can pick and choose whatever you'd like."

Katie Ann watched as Martha pulled out tiny baby gowns, bottles, and everything else necessary for a baby.

"Some of this stuff might be outdated, but you can go through it to see what's safe and suitable, then we'll have David come over and haul whatever you want to your place." Martha crinkled her nose. "These clothes smell a bit musty, so we might want to toss these."

"I don't know what to say, Martha." Katie Ann blinked back tears. "This is so kind of you."

"We're going to need to go shopping." Martha cut her eyes at Katie Ann. "And you shouldn't be riding in a buggy in your condition. Remember, I said you're going to need to take it easy. So, on Tuesdays, I'll take you to town in my car. We'll load up on those days with everything that I might not have in here." She waved her arm around the room, and Katie Ann felt a tear roll down her cheek.

"What's wrong?" Martha put her hands on her hips and frowned.

"I'm going to have a baby." She jumped as the realization literally kicked. "The baby moved." Katie Ann laughed aloud. "Martha, I felt the baby move."

Martha smiled in a way that Katie Ann had never seen her do before. "That must be a wonderful feeling."

Katie Ann reached for Martha's hand and placed it against her stomach. They waited, then Martha laughed. "How about that? I felt the little one give a kick." Martha pulled her hand back, then smiled. "All things happen in God's time frame." She paused, twisted her mouth to one side. "I'm starting to understand that."

Then Martha grabbed Katie Ann and pulled her to the floor with her, and they sat cross-legged as Martha slid boxes toward them. Again, Katie Ann noticed that Martha's back didn't seem to be ailing her anymore. "Now, we will go through all of these things, then make a list of what you need. I was wondering what I was going to do without Arnold around." She looked at Katie Ann and smiled. "Now I know."

Katie Ann sat quiet for a moment. Her husband was gone. Her parents were far away. Her relatives had family of their own. She wanted someone by her side who would share in this joyous journey with her. She smiled. *Sometimes God puts people in our path so unexpectedly, in His time frame.*

"Martha, thank you for all you're doing. For the first time, I'm forgetting about my troubles and looking forward to getting things ready for the baby." She sat up tall, took a deep breath, and blew it out slowly. "I can do this!"

"Yes, we can!" Martha pulled out a tiny blue gown. "Here's one for Jonas, if it's a boy." She handed it to Katie Ann and kept digging, but Katie Ann reached over and threw her arms around Martha.

"*Danki*, Martha." She held tight, and while Martha was stiff as a board, as if she'd never been hugged, she slowly let her hands relax around Katie Ann.

"You're welcome," she said softly. Then she quickly pulled away, shrugged, and started digging back through the boxes. "Who knows. Maybe the kid will even call me grandma one day."

Katie Ann smiled. "I think you can count on it."

Eighteen

RUMORS WERE ALL OVER THE PLACE THAT DAVID WAS going to propose to Emily soon, and while that kept her spirits high, she knew she must close one chapter in her life before she could truly move forward. Facing James in court and telling her story would be the hardest thing she would ever do, but in two days, she would leave with her parents for Middlefield to do just that.

Three weeks after Christmas she'd confessed to her family that she knew who her attacker was. Both *Mamm* and *Daed* had been deeply hurt that it was James, an Amish man from their community, but they insisted he be held accountable for his actions. "We can't have him do this to anyone else," her mother had said. Her father used language that she'd never heard before. His fury had been mixed with tears, just like her mother's.

But on this night, she tried not to focus on the upcoming trial. Tomorrow was the schoolhouse raising, as it had been fondly referred to over the past few months, and members of the community would join together for hard work and fellowship. Mr. Becker had left David in charge of the project, and she was looking forward to watching him in action. David was a hard worker and balanced his job at the furniture store with helping his father make repairs on their farmhouse. On top of that, he and his father were readying their land for the first planting. David didn't have a lot of time for Emily, and she understood. But the time they did have together was always special, even if it was just holding hands while going for a short walk under a moonlit, starry sky.

During several of their walks, David explained his plans for the schoolhouse. Though Mr. Becker had left him detailed instructions, David had made some changes, even adding a small storage room where the children could store their books, lunch pails, and winter clothing. He was excited about erecting a fine schoolhouse, and Emily was just excited in general—about a future filled with hope and a sense of peace . . . hopefully as David's *fraa*.

Emily closed her Bible when her father nodded his head to indicate that devotion time was over. Betsy asked to be excused to her room, and Emily suspected that her younger sister wanted to bury her head in a book for a while before bath time.

It was so much quieter without Jacob around. Emily missed his fun-loving ways, but she could see how happy her brother and new sister-in-law were. Levi was still sulky and withdrawn, and tonight was no different.

"I don't think your boyfriend ordered enough lumber." Levi kicked his rocking chair into motion and folded his arms across his chest. Emily glanced his way from the other rocker, as did their parents from their place on the couch. "I reckon he probably don't know what he's doing."

"Mr. Becker ordered the lumber," Emily said as she cut her eyes at her brother. "And I'm sure he knows what he's doing."

Levi grunted and rolled his eyes. Emily waited for one of

her parents to say something, but when no one did, she considered speaking up. She was tired of walking on tiptoes for fear of upsetting Levi about whatever it was that ailed him. Levi had never been as talkative and friendly as Jacob, but Emily could recall a time when he was pleasant to be around. Emily figured that Levi was still unhappy about the move from Middlefield.

Mamm stood from the couch and yawned. "Coming, Elam?"

"*Ya, ya.*" *Daed* stretched his arms as he stood, and a few minutes later both her parents were upstairs and out of earshot.

"Why don't you like him?" Emily stopped rocking and turned to face Levi.

Levi got up from the rocker he was in, then shuffled across the floor and plopped on the couch. "I never said I didn't like him." He reached for a gardening magazine that was on the coffee table, something Emily had recently picked up in town. Levi flipped nervously through the pages. She was sure the magazine didn't interest him. She'd only bought it because there was an article inside detailing how to grow the best watermelons in a difficult climate.

"He's a wonderful man, Levi. Maybe if you would just get to know him . . . but all you ever do is avoid him. He tries to be nice to you, Levi." Emily crossed one leg over the other and shook her head. "But you are always very rude to him."

Levi shrugged and kept turning the pages.

"I like him, Levi. I like him a lot, and I wish that you could—"

Levi threw the magazine on the table. "*Ya*, well, you liked James, too, didn't you?"

Emily grabbed her chest as tears instantly welled in her

eyes. "Don't compare them," she whispered as she lowered her head. Then she looked up at her brother, whose brows were drawn into a frown. "That's mean of you, Levi."

Levi bolted from the couch, then marched across the den. But before he got to the stairs, he stopped. He didn't turn around to face her, and he whispered something Emily didn't understand.

"What?" she asked.

"It's my fault."

"What's your fault?" Emily uncrossed her legs and stood from the chair. "What are you talking about?"

Levi slowly turned around and faced Emily, and she was shocked to see his eyes filled with tears. "I knew you were with James." He took a deep breath. "I knew he was the one who hurt you that night, and I didn't speak up."

Emily eased closer to her brother. "Levi, I didn't speak up either. I don't fault you for not telling. I probably would have been very upset with you if you had told. I needed to come to terms with everything in my own time."

"We hung out together, a group of us." Levi paused as a tear rolled down his cheek. "Emily, I didn't know he was like that. He asked about you, and I told him what a great girl you were."

Emily smiled. "You did?"

"*Ya*. Stop smiling. Don't you see?"

She supposed she didn't. It warmed her heart that Levi would tell someone she was a great girl. She was letting that soak in for a moment. Then she shook her head. "I guess I don't see."

"I told him you'd go out with him. I should have seen

through him, seen what kind of person he was, and told him to stay away from my sister. The whole thing is my fault, and I wanted to hurt him the way he hurt you. I failed you! I failed God!" Levi's voice rose, then quickly fell in volume as he glanced upstairs. "It's all my fault, and I can't live with it."

Emily walked closer to her brother, then threw her arms around him. To her surprise, he buried his head on her shoulder. "Levi. My dear, sweet Levi. This is not your fault."

"I don't want anyone to hurt you again, Emily. I don't want anyone around you. I don't want you to date anyone, or—"

"Levi." Emily eased him away. "I love you, *mei bruder*." She waited for his eyes to meet hers. "But what happened with James was not your fault. I had been waiting for James to ask me out for months. I was smitten with him for a long time." She paused. "Levi, you need to talk to Bishop Esh about this. He will help you to realize that this was not your fault. Levi, you know that everything that happens is by the will of God."

Emily heard herself say the words, and she realized she meant them. Despite everything that had happened to her, she was exactly where she was supposed to be, according to God's plan.

"I wish I could make it up to you." Levi stepped back, wiped his nose, and looked away from her.

"There's nothing that you have to make up to me, Levi." She stepped closer. "But . . ." She smiled as she waited for him to lock eyes with her. "It would make me very happy if you would get to know David. You will trust him the way I do, Levi. He's a *gut* man."

Levi ran a hand through his hair and stared at the floor.

He lifted his eyes to her. "I'm sorry, Emily. I don't know if I can do that."

Then he headed up the stairs.

"Please, Levi," she said as he padded up the stairs.

But her brother kept going and didn't turn around.

When Saturday rolled around, David counted thirty-six people on hand to help with the schoolhouse, and for his small community, that was a big success.

His community.

He smiled at the thought. To his surprise, Canaan had turned out to be his Promised Land, just the way his father said it would. He worked hard at the furniture store, on the farmhouse, and preparing the land for the first harvest. But hardly anyone here knew about his past medical problems, so no one worried about his abilities, which he found freeing. Well, then there was Lillian. Every now and then she would ask him if he'd taken on too much. But David was sure that the heavy load kept both his body and mind healthy.

Free time was scarce, but the little he had was spent with Emily. His heart swelled with feelings he'd never had before. She made him feel whole. Emily saw him as strong, protective, and wise—all the things a man wants to be in the eyes of the woman he loves. If she only knew how the sight of her made him weak in the knees sometimes.

He glanced around to make sure everyone had a job. His father and Emily's father were busy nailing down the flooring, and Jacob and several other men were working to frame the perimeter. Even the young boys, no older than Anna and

Elizabeth, were busy helping—standing nearby with bags of nails, fetching requested supplies, and making sure the horses were given an occasional drink of water. The women kept a steady supply of tea and snacks coming.

"You haven't eaten anything." David turned to see Emily, a pretzel in her hand.

"*Danki.*" He took the snack, but what he really wanted was to pull her into his arms and kiss her. Her cheeks turned a rosy shade of pink, as if she could read his mind, then she walked away, but she turned around once and smiled.

She'd only been gone a few seconds when Levi approached. David tensed. Levi would most likely criticize his efforts.

"What would you like for me to do?" Levi looped his thumbs under his suspenders.

The only thing left to do was to unload the rest of the wood from the trailer that had arrived earlier that morning. "I need help unloading that trailer." David nodded to his right.

"*Ya*, all right." Levi waited for David to take the lead, which he did. As they walked side by side, Levi kept turning briefly to face David, but then he would look away.

"Something on your mind?" David finally asked, not sure if he wanted to hear what it was.

When they reached the trailer, both men stopped. Levi faced David, folding his arms across his chest. "I love Emily. I will do anything to protect her."

Under any other circumstances, he would have found Levi's comment to be completely out of place. "I love her too," he finally said, keeping his eyes locked with Levi's. "And I will never hurt her."

Levi took a deep breath, then slowly extended his hand

to David. "See that you don't." His voice was firm, but a smile tipped at the corner of Levi's mouth. David felt relief that things were changing between them.

EMILY BASKED IN the feel of David's arms around her the next morning at the bus station. He told her how proud of her he was and then kissed her on the forehead—right in front of her parents. He assured her that he would be there to pick her up when she returned, and she prayed that his words, along with God, would get her through the next few days.

Emily was filled with hope for the future and fear over the present. She would be face-to-face with James in a big courtroom the following day. She liked the attorney her parents had hired, and she knew her parents would be there with her, but she honestly wasn't sure how she was going to get through it.

"Everything is going to be okay, Emily," David whispered in her ear as he eased out of the hug. "And I'll be here waiting for you when you get back in a week."

She forced a smile, sad to be leaving him, and unhappy about her destination, but she knew it was the right thing to do. The lawyer had talked to her parents about what would happen in court. A bunch of legal talk that Emily didn't understand. But her parents explained that James had admitted he had hurt her, so the case would go before a judge, not a jury. Either way, Emily had forgiven him a long time ago, and even though it had been hard to accept what happened as God's will, with each day it became easier.

Emily glanced at her parents who were standing far enough away not to hear their conversation. "I'll miss you."

David pulled her into another hug. "I'll miss you too." He eased away and cupped her cheek. "Wanna know why?"

Emily waited, her heart fluttering.

"Because I love you." Then David kissed her tenderly on the lips, and under any other circumstances, Emily would have pulled back, knowing her parents—especially her father—were nearby. But instead she kissed him back.

"I love you too, David."

A silly grin filled David's face. "I have a big surprise for you when you get back."

Emily gasped. "Tell me!"

"Then it wouldn't be a surprise, silly." He gazed into her eyes, and Emily could feel how much he loved her. "I hope knowing that will give you something to look forward to when you get home."

Emily heard her father calling her name. "I have to go."

She backed away from him, and knew she would count the hours until she was back in his arms.

EMILY HAD NEVER been on a bus, and the ride was over twenty hours—too long. She didn't care if she ever traveled again. She just wanted to get back home—to Canaan. To the place where she planned to spend the rest of her life. Her Promised Land, where new beginnings were blessed by God.

When they arrived at the hotel, Emily was sure her accommodations would be the only neat thing about the trip. She had her own room with a television, alarm clock, beautiful big bed, and roomy bathroom. She wouldn't have to worry about Levi using all the hot water before she bathed. But the fancy hotel room could only distract her for a short time.

She heard a knock on the door and opened it.

"Do you like the room?" *Mamm* walked in. "It's much like our room."

"*Ya*. It's very nice." Emily walked to the bed and sat down. Her mother took a seat beside her.

Mamm grinned. "Don't get used to it."

Emily forced a smile.

"Emily, the lawyer *Daed* hired called us awhile ago."

Emily's stomach churned, and she wished she could just run out of the room and catch a bus back home, no matter how long the ride. She waited for her mother to go on.

"James has made a full confession, but you're still going to have to briefly tell what happened to you so that the judge can decide on his punishment." *Mamm* took a deep breath. "Emily, what he did to you was such a bad thing, but we need to pray for his family. They are shamed beyond anything we can imagine, and they will be in the courtroom tomorrow as well. His lawyer will be asking that he not go to a regular jail, but instead go to a place where he can get help with this rage he has. What he did to you was terrible, and we don't want him doing this to anyone else." *Mamm* twisted to face her. "Mr. Webster, the lawyer, said that the judge will most likely ask you how you feel about having James not go to jail, but go somewhere else to get help. So I know we've discussed some of this before, but I want you to pray about this. And pray for James and his family."

"I will." Emily had already forgiven James, and she couldn't imagine what his family must be going through.

Mamm patted her on the leg. "All right. I'm going to go to bed. You should probably do the same." She smiled. "Don't spend too long soaking in that big bathtub."

THE NEXT MORNING Emily walked into the courtroom with her parents and Mr. Webster. They'd already been there an hour, and Mr. Webster had explained to Emily how the morning would go, but none of what he said eased her anxiety. She'd even thrown up earlier that morning, and her entire body was shaking as she entered the large room.

She kept her eyes straight ahead as she and her parents moved down the aisle toward a large bench. Emily knew that's where the judge would sit. A woman was sitting at a small desk to the right of the judge's desk, typing. There were long benches on either side of them, and Emily could see out of the corner of her eye that they were mostly empty.

Emily, her parents, and Mr. Webster took a seat at one of two tables facing the judge. Emily shivered in the air-conditioning, and her mother latched onto her hand.

"It's going to be all right, Emily."

Emily glanced at her father, surprised to see his face was incredibly pale. He'd said very little during their trip.

About ten minutes later, James and his family walked into the courtroom. Mr. Webster told her not to look at James, so Emily tried to keep her eyes from drifting in their direction. Her stomach roiled in such a way that she prayed she didn't vomit right there in the courtroom. *Mamm* squeezed her hand.

Everyone stood up when the judge walked into the room. The elderly, gray-haired man wore gold-rimmed glasses and a long black robe. If James hadn't been in the room, Emily would have thought he was the scariest person she'd ever seen. Her heart started to beat so fast, she put her hand to her chest.

Please, dear Lord, please help me to get through this and to say the right things. And please have mercy on James and help him to get the help he needs.

Emily continued to silently pray while the judge and lawyers talked about a lot of things she didn't understand. Then Mr. Webster said, "We call Emily Detweiler." She knew it was her time to come forward.

"God is with you, Emily," her mother whispered as she stood up.

But before she moved from the long desk to go up front, her father stood up. He turned to Emily, tears in his eyes. *Daed* opened his mouth like he wanted to say something, but instead, he embraced her. Then he whispered in her ear, "I love you, my precious *maedel*. May our Lord be with you."

"I love you, *Daed*." Emily eased out of the hug and moved past her father. She kept her eyes locked on the judge. His expression seemed to soften as she approached him. She sat down to his left in a big chair that faced everyone in the room. She locked eyes with James for the first time since her attack, and she couldn't find any sign of remorse in his stony glare. *Surely he is sorry for what he did.*

Emily's eyes filled with water, and she shifted her gaze to her mother. Then to her father. Then to the total strangers seated in front of her. She felt dizzy, and she was certain that there was no way she could talk about what happened in front of all these people. Mr. Webster approached her, and after asking her to place her hand on a Bible and promise to tell the truth, he said, "Emily, can you tell the court what happened to you on the evening of August twelfth?"

Her hands were clammy, her lip trembling, and the rest of her body wouldn't stop shaking. She opened her mouth, but nothing came out. She stared around the courtroom. Again, she focused on her mother, then her father.

Then the courtroom seemed to cloud in front of her, like the fogs that she remembered forming in their Middlefield yard. They started far off, then slowly moved toward the house and settled across their farmland. Her vision was hazy, and she could vaguely hear Mr. Webster's voice, as if he were a long way away. But then she heard another voice loud and clear.

Seek Me with all your heart, Emily.

She squeezed her eyes closed. *Help me, Lord.*

I am here, My child. You are your Father's child.

Slowly, the fog lifted and she saw everyone in the room waiting. She scanned the room, looking for the strength to push forward. As she locked eyes with her father—eyes filled with strength and determination—she knew that his love, and her heavenly Father's, would see her through this.

She took a deep breath as she recalled the events of August twelfth. She could feel James's eyes on her, but she stayed connected with her father, who gave her a nod.

"I had a date." She watched *Daed* to see if she would see disappointment in his eyes, but she didn't. "A date with James Miller."

"Can you point to whom you're referring?" Mr. Webster edged slightly closer to her, and Emily pulled her eyes from her father's. James looked straight ahead, not making eye contact with anyone, and forgiveness flooded over Emily as she pointed her finger at him. *I hope you get the help you need, James.*

Mr. Webster told everyone that Emily identified James Miller as her attacker, then he asked her to go on.

"I was supposed to have gone to my *Onkel* Abram's birthday party, but James had already asked me to have supper with him at the diner." She hung her head for a moment, then locked eyes with her father again. His expression hadn't changed. "I lied to my parents and said I was sick."

"And what happened, Emily, when you got to the diner?"

"We ordered baked chicken, potatoes, green beans, and a roll." She paused. "And shoofly pie for dessert."

A smile tipped at the corner of Mr. Webster's mouth. "That sounds good, Emily. Can you tell us what happened after your dinner with Mr. Miller? Did he have a car?"

"*Ya*. He's in his *rumschpringe*, and he had a car that he kept mostly hidden from his folks. But I think they knew he had it." Emily turned toward Sarah Miller, James's mother. Sarah's bottom lip was trembling, and Emily wished more than anything that she didn't have to continue. "We—we went to his car after we ate."

"Where was his car, Emily?"

"In the alley behind Raber's Diner."

Mr. Webster walked closer to where Emily was sitting. "Take your time, Emily. What do you remember happening next?"

"We were laughing as we sat in his car. We saw a man walk by the alley with a pink hat on his head, and he was dressed in green and white polka dots." Emily smiled slightly, glad for a momentary distraction. "He was in costume for something, I'm sure. But we thought it was very funny."

"And then what happened?"

Emily shifted her weight, then searched for her father's eyes, again fearful that at some point his expression would change, that she would see disappointment. She fixed her stare on his and recaptured the same comfort she'd felt earlier. "James kissed me. On the lips." She pulled her eyes from *Daed's*. As much as she longed for his strength, she couldn't face him. "And I let him," she added in a trembling voice. She swallowed back tears, unsure if she could go on.

"It's all right, Emily," Mr. Webster whispered as he drew near. "You're safe here."

She didn't feel like she wasn't safe. She just felt sad. Sad that she'd lied to her parents, sad that James was sick, sad that it happened—and embarrassed to talk about it. Mr. Webster asked her to go on. She still couldn't look at her father. Not now. Not during this part.

"James—he—he touched me places. I told him to stop." She blinked back tears that threatened to spill. "Then I *begged* him to stop." She brushed away a tear and took a deep breath. "But he wouldn't. He wouldn't stop." Emily hung her head as her shoulders began to rise and fall along with deep sobs she fought to muffle. "I can't talk about it anymore," she whispered without looking up at Mr. Webster or anyone else.

"I know it's hard, Emily. But we're going to need you to explain in detail as much as you can remember." Mr. Webster's voice was soft and kind, but Emily knew she couldn't go on. She shook her head.

"I'm sorry."

"Do we need a recess?" The deep voice came from Emily's right, and she knew the judge was talking to her. The thought of having to take a break, then come back and start over was even worse than continuing.

"No." Emily raised her head to face him. "I'm sorry. I'll go on." She bit her lip, swiped at her eyes, then took another deep breath. "He—James—he . . ." How could she speak the words? Tears began to trail down her cheeks. "James put his hands . . ."

"Stop!"

Emily looked up to see her father standing, and two police officers were moving in his direction. Her father faced Mr. Webster. "Please. Don't make her go on." He blinked back tears as he spoke. The uniformed men stood beside *Daed*, waiting for instructions from the judge. Emily couldn't breathe.

"Your honor, is this really necessary?" Mr. Webster asked. James's attorney joined Mr. Webster when the judge motioned for him to do so. As the two men drew closer to the judge, Emily couldn't hear what was said, but after a few moments, it was decided by everyone that Emily did not have to go on. And for that, she would be thanking God for a long time to come.

And her father.

EMILY COULDN'T GET off the bus soon enough. She was thrilled that her ordeal was over and that they had been able to return two days early. She could see David walking toward her, along with Lillian and Samuel.

Even her parents raised a brow when they saw them all approaching. They'd all thought David was coming alone with an *Englisch* driver to take them back to Canaan.

Lillian ran to Emily's mother and threw her arms around her, and Samuel shook her father's hand. And when David got near, Emily couldn't wait. She ran into his arms.

"I love you so much," she whispered in his ear.

"I love you, too, and I missed you." David pulled from the hug and looked toward the sky. "Look what a beautiful sunshiny day it is here in Denver." He grinned. "It's the perfect day for my surprise."

Emily pulled her sweater around her, but it truly was a blessed day. Blue skies overhead and a slight breeze, but the sun warmed her face. David warmed her heart.

"Levi is probably about to pull his hair out," Lillian said with a giggle. "We dropped Anna and Elizabeth off to play with Betsy."

"It'll be *gut* for Levi." *Mamm* smiled. "But why did you all come? Does the driver have a van? Will we all fit?" She glanced around, then turned back to Lillian. "Oh, *danki* for coming." She hugged Lillian again.

Samuel cleared his throat. "We came in two different cars, two drivers."

"What for?" *Daed* looped his thumbs in his suspenders and stood tall as two *Englisch* folks walked by them.

Samuel waited until the two women passed and were out of earshot. "David has a surprise for Emily, so they'll be riding in that blue car over there." Samuel pointed to his right. "And me and Lillian will be taking the two of you home in that green car parked next to it." Samuel shook his head and grinned. "And let me warn you, that driver has one speed. Fast!"

Daed was busy stowing their luggage on a cart, and when

he was done, they all headed to the cars. Once the luggage was stored, they parted ways. Emily climbed into the backseat and David sat beside her. After a few minutes, Emily looked at him.

"Are you going to tell me where we are going?"

"You'll see."

Emily thought she might burst with excitement. "How long will it take to get there?"

Before David could answer, the nice gentleman driver spoke up. "A little over an hour."

David rubbed his hands together. "You think you love me now, just you wait."

"I can hardly stand this! Can you give me a hint?"

"No way."

The hour's drive seemed to take forever, but then David turned to her. "You have to close your eyes."

"Are you serious?"

"*Ya.* Close your eyes. I had to get special permission to take you to this place, but I think you'll like it."

Emily squeezed her eyes closed and resisted the temptation to peek.

"No peeking."

"I'm not."

She felt the car slow down, then come to a stop.

"Do not open your eyes! I'll come around and lead you out of the car."

Emily waited until David had hold of her hand, then climbed out of the car.

"Have fun. I'll be here when you return," the driver said as David closed the car door.

"Keep your eyes closed, but step up." David guided her up several steps. She heard him take a deep breath. "You can open your eyes now."

Emily took in the view. "David . . ." She was speechless as she looked up the mountain before her, snow still capping the peaks in every direction.

"The mountains in our area are too hard to climb. We are in the heart of the Rocky Mountains here. Now you can climb your mountain. And there is a path leading up this mountain that leads . . . to Him." David pointed to the top of the mountain.

A tear rolled down Emily's cheek as she stared at the top of the mountain where a giant white statue of Jesus stood, his arms outstretched, as if waiting for her. "Where are we?"

David grabbed her hand and they began walking up the path, wispy green grass and early spring foliage on either side. "We're at a camp called Santa Maria. That fifty-five foot statue of Jesus was built in 1933 at what was then a Catholic charities camp for underprivileged children." He smiled. "Sister Catherine helped me with this plan."

"It's the most beautiful thing I've ever seen."

"They say that it's lit up at night, but I wanted us to be able to walk all the way to the base of the statue."

With each step, the statue of Jesus seemed to grow, the way her love for Jesus grew with each passing day. She left her past behind her as she trekked upward, embracing freedom.

Emily was breathless by the time they reached the base of the pure white statue, and she openly wept. "*Danki*, David. This is the happiest moment in my life." She gazed up at Jesus' outstretched arms.

"I hope the next moment will top that."

Emily gasped as David dropped to one knee. The sun seemed to shine even brighter as he spoke. "Will you marry me, Emily?"

Emily looked up at the statue of Jesus, standing tall and protectively above them. Then she looked down at David, the man she would spend the rest of her life loving.

"*Ya*. I will."

David stood up and wrapped his arms around her. "I will love you forever."

"And I will love you forever."

She glanced up toward heaven and smiled.

And ye shall seek Me, and find Me, when ye shall search for Me with all your heart.

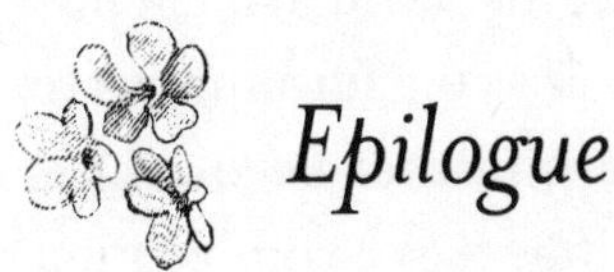

Epilogue

EMILY WALKED THE SITE OF HER FUTURE HOME, THE colorful wildflowers brushing against her legs. As light from the setting sun illuminates the Sangre de Cristos with a brilliant rose color, she scanned the area and tried to picture her home.

David's father gave him a large chunk of land the week after David proposed to Emily, and shortly thereafter, Emily and David had found the perfect spot to build their new home. In November, Emily would become Mrs. David Stoltzfus.

Her hands grazed the tips of the flowers as she breathed in the smells of summer. July was pleasant in Canaan with long days filled with sunshine. Emily came to this spot often, not only to visualize the home David would build, but also to commune with God. She knew that she was as close to God here as she would be on the top of any mountain.

She closed her eyes, the warm wind in her face, and thanked God for the many blessings He had bestowed on her. When she was done, she spun around, picturing her den, kitchen, four bedrooms, mudroom, and large walk-around porch spanning two sides of the clapboard house. And two bathrooms. One upstairs and one downstairs.

Her garden would be on the west side of the house, and a white picket fence would enclose the front yard. There would be two barns. One for animals, and one for David to build furniture in. In the beginning, David's job at the furniture store had been to assemble prefabricated furniture for *Englisch* customers to buy. The ready-made furniture was a combination of wood and particle board, but David offered to build some solid wood furniture for the owner to sell. And what started out as a hobby quickly blossomed into much more. David had orders for fourteen rocking chairs and two cradles.

Emily hoped that he would be building a cradle for their own little one soon after they were married.

She gathered some of the flowers in her hands and arranged them into a tight bouquet, careful to select a colorful variety. David's Aunt Katie Ann loved the flowers that grew wild in the fields, and Emily enjoyed collecting them for her when she came here. Her new baby would bless all their lives in September. It was unusual for an Amish woman to raise a child on her own, but Katie Ann had her friends and family, particularly Martha, who'd stepped in and made herself at home in Katie Ann's life.

Emily eyed her selection and decided it was perfect.

Yes, a new baby in September for Katie Ann, and a wedding in November. Her own wedding—to David Stoltzfus.

She closed her eyes and thanked God again for His divine blessings in her life.

Acknowledgments

NATALIE HANEMANN, it is an honor to dedicate this book to you. Our paths crossed for a reason, and I hope that we are always on this incredible journey together. Peace, prayers, and love to you my friend—and to the rest of my Thomas Nelson family.

Special thanks to Sherry and Tim Gregg for your friendship, hospitality, and research assistance. By the time this book hits the shelves, we will have shared another fun-filled adventure visiting the Amish folks in Colorado. Blessings to both of you always. Big hug to you, Sherry, for reading the manuscript prior to publication.

Thank you to an Old Order Amish friend in Monte Vista, Colorado, who spent time with me while I was there, and also to my Amish friends in Lancaster County, who answer questions and allow me to use their fabulous recipes.

Barbie Beiler, you rock! You're a Daughter of the Promise whose namesake will forever be a part of this series. Thank you for reading each book prior to publication to verify authenticity. AND for answering my many, many questions on a regular basis.

To my husband, Patrick. "Who do you love?" "You, baby." Always and forever.

Janet Murphy, you are the best assistant a girl could have. What a blessing you are. You wear many hats, and they all fit you perfectly. So glad to have you on this wonderful ride with me.

To my mother-in-law, Pat. I have yet to find one person whose mother-in-law cooks for them twice a week. You're the best!

Jenny Baumgartner, as a line editor, you go above and beyond to make my books the best they can be. And the fact that you are a super sweet, loving individual is a huge bonus. Blessings to you and your beautiful family.

To my agent, Mary Sue Seymour, thanks for all you do to strengthen my career and for being a super friend.

Eric and Cory, Seek Him with all your heart. Always.

Friends and family not mentioned here, please know how much you mean to me and how much I appreciate the day-to-day things you do for me.

Without You, God, I'd be a lost soul scribbling words that make no sense. Thank you for guiding my hand in an effort to draw folks closer to You.

Reading Group Guide

1. In the beginning of the story, Emily is fearful of men because of what happened to her in Middlefield. At what point do you see her beginning to heal and to trust again?
2. Samuel and Lillian aren't completely honest with David about the move to Colorado, choosing not to tell him about their financial hardships. Should Samuel and Lillian have told David about the cost of his medications, or were they right to shelter him?
3. There are two issues of miscommunication. One is between Emily and Vera. How might things have been different for Emily if she and her mother had talked openly early in the story? What about David? What misconception does he live with that affects his choices?
4. Which characters hear "Seek Me with all your heart"? Do you ever hear the small voice in your heard that they refer to, and do you believe this to be God?
5. Martha offers Vera a box full of money, and Vera ultimately shares the money with Lillian's family and Katie Ann. Neither Martha nor Vera ever seek credit for their generosity, but we hear Martha quote a scripture that she heard in church

relevant to this gift. Have you ever felt motivated by Scripture to give unselfishly, and did it change you in some way more than it aided the recipient?

6. Emily lives with fear of being unworthy because of her attack. David believes he shouldn't marry because he might not live a long and full life. What other person lives with a misconception that affects his life and those around him?
7. What is the difference between Amish prayer coverings for Amish women in Lancaster County, Pennsylvania, and Middlefield, Ohio? What about the color of their buggies?
8. Vera wears herself out trying to provide a perfect household for her family, despite a past that follows them. At what point in the story does everything finally catch up with Vera? How are things different after that?
9. Katie Ann chooses not to tell her husband that she is pregnant, fearing he will return to her out of a sense of obligation. Did she do the right thing? Do you think Ivan would have returned to her if he knew she was carrying their child? If so, would he have returned for the right reasons?
10. An unlikely friendship forms first between Emily, David, and Martha—then later between Katie Ann and Martha. Why is this?
11. Emily must forgive James before she can truly be free and move forward. In what part of the book do you see Emily starting to forgive? Who does her inability to forgive affect the most throughout the story?
12. During the court scene, there is a correlation between God the Father and Emily's father. Have you ever had a similar situation where you can see God working through someone for the good of all?

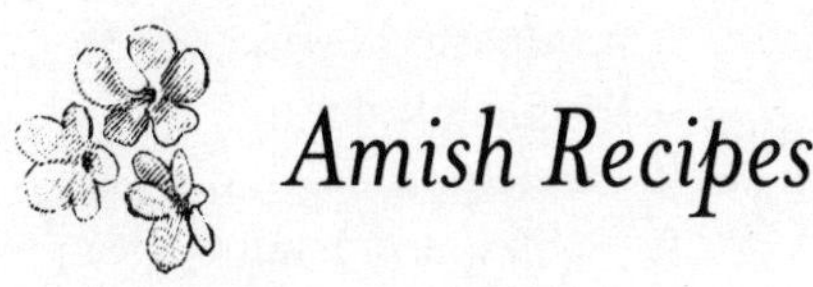

Amish Recipes

Chocolate Shoofly Pie

1	unbaked pie shell	1 1/3	cups unsifted all-purpose flour
1/4	tsp. baking soda	1/2	cup sugar
1 1/3	cups boiling water	1/4	tsp. baking soda
1 1/2	cups (16 oz. can) Hershey's syrup	1/4	tsp. salt
1	tsp. vanilla	1/3	cup butter
			cinnamon

Dissolve 1/4 teaspoon baking soda in boiling water; stir in chocolate syrup and vanilla. Set aside. Combine flour, sugar, baking soda, and salt. Cut in butter with pastry blender to form coarse crumbs.

Set aside 1 cup each of chocolate mixture and crumbs. Gently combine remaining chocolate and crumbs, stirring just until crumbs are moistened (mixture will be lumpy). Pour reserved cup of chocolate mixture into pastry shell.

Pour chocolate-crumb mixture evenly over liquid in shell. Top with remaining 1 cup of crumbs. Sprinkle with cinnamon. Bake at 375° for 50 to 60 minutes or until set. Cool completely.

—From Renee Klevenhagen, Slatedale, Pa.

Cabbage Casserole

- 3 cups fresh cabbage, shredded
- 1 pound hamburger, sautéed and drained
- 3/4 cup diced onion
- 1 teaspoon salt
- 1/2 teaspoon pepper
- 1/4 teaspoon garlic salt
- 10 1/2 oz. can of tomato soup
- 1 soup can of water
- 1 cup cooked rice
- 1 tablespoon brown sugar
- 1 tablespoon lemon juice
- 1 cup shredded cheddar cheese

Shred cabbage and place in a greased, 2-quart casserole. Mix in meat and onions. Then stir in remaining ingredients, except cheese. Stir the whole casserole well. Cover and bake at 350° for one hour. Top with cheese before serving.

Chicken Lasagna

- 1 can cream of mushroom soup
- 1 can cream of chicken soup
- 1 medium onion, diced
- ½ cup sour cream
- ¼ cup mayonnaise
- ¼ tsp. garlic salt
- ¼ tsp. pepper
- 4 cups cooked chicken, cut in bite-size pieces
- 1 cup shredded cheddar cheese
- 1 cup shredded mozzarella cheese
- 1 box lasagna noodles, cooked
- ½ cup parmesan cheese

Mix all the ingredients except the noodles and parmesan cheese. In a 9" x 13" baking pan, alternate one layer of chicken mixture and one layer of lasagna noodles. Repeat. Top with the parmesan cheese. Bake at 375° uncovered for 45 minutes.

The Wonder of Your Love

Beth Wiseman

THOMAS NELSON
Since 1798

NASHVILLE DALLAS MEXICO CITY RIO DE JANEIRO

To Sherry Gregg

One

Katie Ann reached into the drawer of the end table next to the couch and pulled out the letter she'd received two weeks ago. She knew it would upset her stomach to read it—as it had a dozen times already—but she unfolded it anyway. She couldn't imagine why her husband's mistress, Lucy Turner, was planning to travel all the way to Colorado to see her. She took a deep breath and read the letter again.

> Dear Katie Ann,
>
> I hope this letter finds you well. I heard from some of our mutual acquaintances here in Lancaster County that you had a healthy baby boy and named him Jonas. Congratulations to you. A baby is such a miracle from God.

Katie Ann rolled her eyes, the way she always did at Lucy's mention of God. *A good, godly woman wouldn't get involved with another woman's husband.* Although she knew good and well that it took two for such deception. She let out a heavy sigh and continued reading.

> I'm sure that I am the last person you want to hear from, and I'm sorry to bother you, but I need to meet with you. I know it is awkward, but I have something important to discuss, and it's too much to say in a letter, or even over the phone. As soon as I can arrange to be off work, I will be traveling to Colorado. I hope that you can find time to meet with me to discuss this urgent matter. I thought it might be easiest for you if you knew in advance that I'm coming.
>
> All the best to you and your new little one,
> Lucy Turner

Katie Ann folded the piece of paper and put it back in the drawer, determined not to let thoughts of Lucy ruin this day. But as she crossed through the living room toward the kitchen, she couldn't help but wonder exactly when Lucy was going to show up on her doorstep. And what she wanted.

Katie Ann poured a large bag of M&M's into a Tupperware bowl, then put the container next to the other food she would be carting to the Detweilers' house. Both the candy and container were a gift for the bride and groom. It was traditional to place a fun and edible gift on the *eck*, something that held special meaning between the giver and the recipient. Katie Ann guessed that lots of people would choose M&M's, though. It was no secret that the candy was Emily's favorite.

She couldn't believe that the wedding was tomorrow. It seemed like just yesterday her husband's nephew David was a young boy, but tomorrow he would marry Emily in front of a hundred friends and family. A small crowd for an Amish wedding. She recalled the nearly four hundred guests at her own wedding, but she quickly brushed the memory aside as she snapped the lid closed on the bowl.

"Martha! Are you ready? Is the baby ready?" She walked back through the living room, turned the corner, and strolled into little Jonas's bedroom. It was a beautiful room, painted in powder blue and trimmed with a lively, multicolored border of dancing ponies. Matching curtains covered the two windows facing the Sangre de Cristo Mountains. The fancy décor would be frowned upon by the bishop if he were to visit, but it was all Martha's doing, and Katie Ann didn't have the heart to change it. Martha was a widow and didn't have any children of her own.

"This little one needs a real nursery," her *Englisch* friend had said with a huff before Jonas was even born.

Martha would be upset if she knew that Katie Ann had heard from Lucy.

Katie Ann stood quietly in the doorway for a moment, savoring the view of her little miracle in Martha's arms and the contented expression on the older woman's face. Martha was as much a grandmother to Jonas as Katie Ann's own mother would have been if she were still living. Katie Ann smiled as Martha gently cradled Jonas in her arms, pushing the oak rocking chair into motion with her foot.

"Why don't you let me stay with the baby while you go on over to the Detweilers' house? No need to drag this young one into the cold, plus he's finally stopped crying and is sleeping soundly." Martha touched her finger to Jonas's cheek as her lips curved into a smile. After a moment, she looked back up at Katie Ann. "Unless it's too cold for you to take the buggy. We can bundle him up real good and take my car."

Katie Ann shook her head. "No, no, I don't mind the buggy ride. It's crisp outside, but sunny. It would be *gut* if you could stay with Jonas. Are you sure you don't mind?"

Katie Ann had been up more than usual during the night with Jonas. He just wouldn't stop crying, and nothing she did seemed to calm him.

Martha looked up at her and scowled. "Now where else on the planet do you think I'd rather be than with this baby?" She raised one hand out from under Jonas and tucked a piece of brownish-gray hair behind her ear, a strand that had fallen from beneath the butterfly clip on the top of her head.

Katie Ann pushed a loose tendril of her own hair beneath her *kapp* as she moved toward the rocker. "Just checking." She leaned down and kissed her precious bundle on the cheek. "See you soon, my darling."

Martha raised her chin as she spoke in a whisper. "You tell Vera Detweiler that I'm expecting creamed celery tomorrow. Lots of it."

Katie Ann nodded as she moved toward the door. "You know there's always lots of celery at weddings." She pulled her heavy black coat, gloves, and bonnet on. Once she was bundled up, she came back to the bedroom door and glanced in at Martha. "I'll be back soon. You'll check on him often, right?"

Martha nodded. "Yes, I will. Now, you go." She waved a hand at Katie Ann.

Martha hadn't missed a day since Jonas was born. Sometimes she stayed for hours, and she often spent the night. Katie Ann was grateful to have the older woman in her life. Being a single mother was challenging.

As she closed the door behind her, she thought about Ivan. Despite her husband's infidelity, she was sorry that he would never see his son. She still mourned Ivan's untimely death, but with each passing day, her sorrow became less as her anger grew stronger. She was thankful to God for blessing her with Jonas so late in life, but even her relationship with Him had suffered. Maybe it was all the sleepless nights she'd been up with Jonas, too tired even to pray. That's what she kept telling herself.

She climbed into the buggy and turned on the battery-operated heater on the seat next to her. The thermometer outside her window showed thirty-three degrees, but as was usually the case here in the San Luis Valley, the sun shone brightly, making it seem much warmer than it was. Clicking her tongue, she set the buggy in motion and breathed in the fresh country air, wondering if it would snow later. She'd read in the newspaper that morning that there might be a flurry, but no hard weather was forecast. She wondered if the Detweilers' relatives had arrived safely. Vera was doubtless beside herself, busy with preparations for her daughter's wedding. Katie Ann was disappointed that the weather back in Lancaster County would prevent Ivan's side of the family from attending. She'd always been close to her in-laws, and she was sure David must be disappointed as well.

Once again, recollections of her own wedding swirled in Katie Ann's head, and her eyes filled with tears as she thought about the good years she'd had with Ivan. And the bad. But she never could have predicted that Ivan would leave her—for the likes of Lucy Turner—and take up residence with the *Englisch* woman back in Lancaster County. She still struggled to forgive her dead husband's choices . . . and Lucy Turner.

ELI DETWEILER THANKED the cabdriver and whistled a tune as he walked across the snow to his cousin's house. He blocked the sun's glare with his hand; he'd never seen a more beautiful day. His spirits were high, and he felt like he had his entire life ahead of him—even though he'd already lived at least half of it. But at forty-three he had a new sense of freedom, the kind that comes from being a new empty-nester, as the *Englisch* called it. He'd married off the youngest of his *kinner* two weeks ago, and with Maureen out of the house, he was on his own. After Sarah died, he'd managed to raise six young children by himself, and he couldn't recall a moment's peace.

Five of the six were girls, and he never could have predicted the challenges of raising daughters. Thankfully, he had one ally in Jake, his only son and the oldest of the bunch. He grinned as he knocked on the door, knowing he wouldn't have changed anything about his children or his life—except for that one dreary day in November seventeen years ago, the day he lost his beloved Sarah. She'd been his one and only true love, and not a day went by that he didn't think about her. No woman had even sparked his interest since then, despite the many attempts by family and friends to fix him up. It was the Amish way to remarry quickly following the death of a spouse, and he had to admit he could have used the help. He'd had a few random dates, but there hadn't been anyone who could hold a candle to his Sarah.

"Eli! It's so *gut* to see you." His cousin's wife wrapped her arms around his neck.

"*Gut* to be here, Vera," he said as he returned her embrace. "Hard to believe it's been over a year."

Vera stepped aside so he could enter, and the warmth of a glowing fire met him as he stepped into their living room. His eyes scanned the room. He saw his cousin Elam and two of their four children, Betsy and Levi. He knew Elam and Vera's third child, Jacob, had married last fall and was living in his own home with his wife, Beth Ann. Eli regretted not being able to attend the boy's wedding, but the weather had kept his family away last year. After he said his hellos to all of them, they all turned their attention to the stairs and watched Emily come down. A year had made quite a difference. Elam and Vera's daughter looked . . . happy. And as her face lit up, Eli recalled everything that the girl had been through. It was a true blessing to be here for her wedding.

"You look so *schee*, Emily," he said as he hugged her.

"*Danki* so much for coming, *Onkel* Eli."

Elam's *kinner* had always called him uncle, even though he was really their cousin.

"I wouldn't have missed it, *mei maedel*." He eased away and found Vera. "Now, Vera, don't let me be in the way. I remember with *mei dochders*' weddings, it's a busy time. So you just put me to work wherever I'm needed."

Vera dismissed his comment with a wave of her hand. "You must be tired from your travels, and really, I think everything is about ready. We've had people helping us all day. We'll be up early in the morning to start warming food and to finish setting up the chairs. You can help then."

She sat down in one of the rocking chairs facing a tan couch on the opposite wall, motioning for him to sit as well. "Everyone else from Middlefield is staying at the local bed-and-breakfasts since this house isn't nearly as big as we were used to back home. They were all here earlier helping, but you probably won't see them all until *mariyefrieh*."

Tomorrow morning was fine by Eli. He was weary from travel, and just chatting with his cousin's family would be plenty for this evening. He nodded, and a moment later Betsy walked up to him, toting a book under her arm. "Hello, Betsy. You've turned eight years old since moving here, haven't you?"

A strand of curly blond hair fell from beneath her *kapp* as she nodded. "*Ya*." She cocked her head to one side and stared at him.

Eli knew from past experience that there was no telling what might come out of Betsy's mouth. He braced himself.

"*Mamm* doesn't understand why a handsome man like you doesn't have a *fraa*."

"Betsy!" Vera covered her eyes with her hand as a rosy blush filled her cheeks. "Excuse Betsy, Eli." Then she glared at her daughter, but Eli just grinned.

"Because I just haven't found anyone as pretty as you," he said. Then he tickled her, and she squealed until he released her.

When someone knocked at the door, Vera stood up and eased her way across the living room. Cousin Elam moseyed to the fireplace and stoked the dwindling fire until orange sparks shimmied upward, then he gave the logs a few more pokes until the flames stretched high.

Eli leaned back against the couch and crossed one ankle over his knee. He stroked his beard as he thought about how long he might stay in Colorado. This was his first trip, there'd be much to see, and he didn't have to rush home to tend to one single thing. *A vacation*. His daughters had all married fine men who took good care of them and the six grandchildren they'd given him, and his son's wife was expecting number seven, the second for the couple. Yes, all was well in Eli's world. Freedom to do as he pleased. He stroked his beard, feeling giddy as a young man in his *rumschpringe*. His musings were interrupted by the return of Vera and another woman.

"Eli, this is Katie Ann. She's soon to be Emily's *aenti*." Vera motioned toward the woman on her right. "She's David's *aenti* on his father's side."

Eli uncrossed his ankle from atop his knee, stood up, and extended his hand to the woman. "Nice to meet you."

She latched onto his hand, nodded, then followed Vera to the kitchen.

Elam waited until the ladies were out of the room before he spoke in a whisper. "Pretty, isn't she?"

Eli narrowed his brows, wondering why his cousin would make the comment about another man's wife, and not sure how to respond. "*Ya*, I suppose so." He tried to sound casual. "What's her name again?"

"Katie Ann." Elam told Betsy to go help in the kitchen, and his young cousin pouted a bit before padding out of the room. "And she is a widow." He kept his voice low. "But she hasn't been a widow for long. Her husband was killed only a few months ago in a car accident." Elam stepped closer and lowered his voice even more. "He'd left her before that, though, for an *Englisch* woman. He'd moved back to Lancaster County and was living with that woman when he died."

Eli glanced toward the kitchen for a moment before he looked back at Elam. "That's terrible."

"*Ya*." Elam shook his head. "A real shame."

Eli stroked his beard again, and the two men were quiet as the ladies reentered the room.

"It was nice to meet you, Eli." Katie Ann waved briefly in Eli's direction as she moved toward the door. "See you all tomorrow."

Eli returned the gesture, watching her as she crossed the threshold. As the door closed behind her, Eli scratched his chest. Not that it itched. He just wasn't sure why his heart was beating so fast.

Katie Ann drove home and tethered her buggy, then waved to Lillian as she walked toward her own house. She was blessed to have Ivan's brother and sister-in-law living right next door on the same property. The two households shared a barn and phone, and Samuel and Lillian were as much her family as they were before Ivan left her.

She slipped quietly into her living room, where Martha was sitting on the couch reading a magazine, bare feet propped up on the coffee table.

"Did Jonas sleep the whole time I was gone?"

"Yep. I kept checking on him, but the little fella is sleeping soundly." Martha didn't look up as she flipped a page.

"When did you last check on him?" Without waiting for an answer, Katie Ann hurried to Jonas's room. She stared down into his crib. As his tiny chest rose and fell, she breathed a sigh of relief.

After a few moments, she walked back into the living room. Martha's arms were folded across her chest, and Katie Ann quickly pulled her eyes from the older woman's glare.

"I told you that I have been checking on him. He's just fine, isn't he?"

Katie Ann fluffed a throw pillow on the couch beside Martha and slowly sat down. "*Ya*. He is." She crossed one leg over the other and nervously kicked her foot into motion. It had taken her a long time to leave Jonas with anyone, and the only ones she trusted with her baby were Martha and Lillian. And that hadn't come easily.

They were quiet for a few moments, and Martha resumed turning the pages of her magazine.

"I'm doing better," Katie Ann finally said as she fingered the string on her prayer covering. "You know, about checking on him."

Martha twisted her mouth to one side and grunted. "How many times did you get up to check on him last night?"

Katie Ann thought about all the nights she'd just watched Jonas sleeping. Martha would be shocked if she knew the real amount of sleep Katie Ann had lost hovering over the baby, fear consuming every inch of her being. "Not that many."

Martha faced her. "How many, Katie Ann? Once to feed him? Three times? A dozen times?"

The last was probably most accurate, but Katie Ann just shrugged. "I don't know. But he has been crying during the night, and I don't know what's wrong with him."

It was true. The past week she'd been up with him even more than usual. And not just to watch him breathe. He would wail, and Katie Ann wasn't sure what was wrong, which just added to the fear that he would die before he reached his first birthday. The way Annie did.

"You're a good mother, Katie Ann, and Jonas is a healthy little bundle." Martha patted Katie Ann on the knee and returned to her reading. "Babies cry sometimes."

Katie Ann had never told anyone but Ivan about Annie. It happened so long ago . . .

They were quiet again, and after a few moments Katie Ann glanced at Martha and frowned. "I don't know why you read that garbage. It has nothing to do with us or our community."

"I'm not Amish. It's allowed." Martha didn't look up this time.

Katie Ann gently elbowed her. "I think you should be baptized and become one of us." She'd had this conversation with Martha many times, and the answer was always the same. "You attend worship with us every other Sunday, you love the Lord, and you are always doing for folks in our community."

Katie Ann thought back almost a year, to when she'd become close to Martha. It was an unlikely friendship—a pregnant Amish woman whose husband had left her . . . and an older *Englisch* widow who was gruff, outspoken, and set in her ways. But it didn't take Katie Ann long to realize that beneath Martha's crotchety temperament was a woman who just wanted to love and be loved—to have a family. And that's what Katie Ann, Jonas, and Martha had become. Family.

Martha closed the magazine slowly, pressed her lips together, and squinted her eyes as she glared at Katie Ann. "I'll tell ya *again* . . . I'm not wearing those clothes of yours, and especially not those prayer coverings. Anything on my head makes my scalp itch. And I am not giving up my television." She tossed her head back, grunted, and went back to her magazine.

Katie Ann took note of Martha's red-and-white-striped pants outfit, her mismanaged curls beneath the butterfly clip, and her bright red fingernails, and grinned. Converting would indeed require a large makeover for Martha. But

Martha often visited the bishop, and Katie Ann wondered what they talked about.

All of a sudden Martha gasped, slammed the magazine closed, and twisted to face Katie Ann. Her eyes were round as saucers. "Did you meet *him*?"

"Who?" She leaned her head back against the couch as she yawned.

"Eli Detweiler, Elam's cousin."

Katie Ann uncrossed her legs and shifted her weight. "As a matter of fact, yes. Why do you ask?"

Martha pinched her face together until her wrinkles looked like they were all connected. "Is he as handsome as Vera says?"

"What?" Katie Ann turned her head to face her.

Martha cackled. "Vera's got good taste. That Elam of hers is quite a looker. If she says Eli is handsome, I bet he's a hunk."

Katie Ann shrugged. "I didn't notice."

"Did she tell you that he's a single man? Lost his wife seventeen years ago, and—"

Katie Ann bolted from the couch, slammed her hands to her hips, and glared at her friend. "I am in mourning, Martha. My husband has only been gone for a few months. How could you possibly think—"

"Oh, stop it." Martha stood up. "That scoundrel cheated on you and left you for another woman. I'd get to know that handsome Eli Detweiler while he's in town."

Katie Ann blinked back tears, determined that there would be no more crying where Ivan was concerned. "You are being inappropriate, Martha."

Martha placed her hands on Katie Ann's arms. "Katie Ann,

I couldn't love you any more if you were my own daughter. It's your people's way to marry soon after a spouse dies, and Vera said that Eli is a fine fellow."

"If he's such a fine fellow, then why has he been single for the past seventeen years?" She freed herself of Martha's hold and walked to the fireplace. She poked the glowing embers several times until a spark eased up between the logs.

"Apparently he's been raising six kids, and the last one just got married. Maybe he was dedicated to his family? An admirable quality, wouldn'tcha say?"

Katie Ann didn't look up as she gave the fire another poke. "Maybe."

Martha chuckled. "Or maybe he's just been waiting for *you* for the past seventeen years."

Katie Ann put the fire tool in its holder and faced off with Martha. "*Ya*. I'm sure that's it." She rolled her eyes.

Martha clomped across the wooden floor, grabbed her red purse from the couch, and slipped on her black slippers by the door. "I'm heading to my house. I need a nap."

Katie Ann followed and wondered if she'd have time for a little shut-eye before Jonas woke up. "Martha, why do you wear your slippers when there is snow on the ground?"

Martha raised her foot and flashed the sole of her shoe upward, giving it a pat. "These aren't regular slippers, dear. I ordered these on the Internet, and they weren't cheap. They're water resistant and easy on my corns." She put her foot down before she lost her balance. Her brows shifted upward. "Another thing I couldn't give up to join your people. My Internet!" She pulled Katie Ann into a hug. "You get some rest. Gonna be a long day tomorrow." Then she winked.

Katie Ann stepped onto the porch as Martha eased her way down the porch steps. "Martha?"

Martha looked over her shoulder. "What?"

Katie Ann wagged a finger in her direction, recalling the time Martha tried to fix her up with an Amish fellow at the hardware store barely a month after Ivan died. "No funny business tomorrow. No matchmaking. Do you hear me?"

Martha flashed a broad toothy smile. "Of course, dear."

Katie Ann closed the door and went to check on her precious baby. She tiptoed into his room, lightly touched his head, and spoke to him in a whisper. "You are all that I need, my little miracle."

She and Ivan had tried to have a baby for most of their twenty years of marriage. It was bittersweet the way it all turned out, and again she wished Ivan could have held his child. He died three months before Jonas arrived, and never even knew Katie Ann was pregnant. She wondered if she'd done right by Ivan not to tell him, but at the time she hadn't wanted him returning to her out of obligation, and she wasn't sure he even deserved to know.

It was quiet in the house. She considered taking a nap, but sure as she laid her head down, her baby boy would wake up. Instead, she let her mind drift to a place she often went during quiet times. As visions of her early years with Ivan danced in her head, she tried to stay focused on those happy memories, but as usual, it wasn't long before images of Ivan and Lucy bombarded her thoughts. She shook her head and anger wrapped around her heart in the familiar way.

In the beginning she'd blamed herself for not being a better wife. Later she'd faulted Lucy for seducing her husband away from her. Most recently she'd decided that Ivan was a weak, dishonest coward—and he was the one responsible for ruining her life.

How could Martha even suggest that she open her heart to another man? *Even good Amish men lie and leave their wives.*

Two

Eli slipped on his shoes, surprised at how well he'd slept in the extra bedroom upstairs. He couldn't remember the last time he'd awakened anywhere besides his own bed. After he pulled his suspenders up on his shoulders, he lifted his arms high above his head and stretched. It was five thirty, still completely dark outside. Only the light from his lantern flickered nearby. But he could hear folks bustling about downstairs. It was a fine day for a wedding, and he was looking forward to all that life had to offer him in this new stage.

He walked casually down the stairs, fighting the urge to whistle. When he reached the bottom of the stairs, he hugged several of his cousins who had arrived early to help. He spotted Katie Ann among the women scurrying around in the kitchen. She smiled, and he found himself holding her gaze for longer than he should have. She looked away and went back to buttering loaves of bread. Eli wondered if she knew that Elam was trying to play matchmaker.

Elam walked in then, followed by Jacob and Levi. They

were carting chairs, and Eli figured that was his job for the moment. "More chairs in the barn?"

Elam nodded. "*Ya. Danki*, Eli."

Eli recognized the tense lines running across Elam's forehead. It wasn't just a busy day for the father of the bride—in a way, he was losing his little girl, sending her off into adulthood, trusting that her husband would always take care of her. Eli had felt the rush of panic on the wedding day of each of his daughters.

After he retrieved four more chairs, he met up with Elam in the living room. "David seems like a *gut* man, from all I've heard."

Elam unfolded one of the metal chairs and placed it in a row with the others. "*Ya*. David is a fine fellow."

There was nothing he could say to alleviate his cousin's anxiety. Eli glanced up to see Katie Ann walking into the living room, and he nodded at her, knowing he was flirting, yet unable to take his gaze from her. Her deep brown eyes drew him in, but she looked away as she leaned down into a playpen and scooped up a baby.

He eased his way slowly toward her. "What a fine-looking *boppli*."

Katie Ann's face lit with pride. Her eyes softened and her cheeks glowed as she looked down on the little one. Nothing like a baby to warm a woman's heart—or a man's, for that matter. Every time someone commented about one of his grandchildren, Eli's heart swelled with pride. Even though it wasn't the Amish way, Eli was pretty sure God allowed it for grandparents.

"*Danki*. This is Jonas." She twisted so that Eli could see the child she was cradling in her arms. Eli leaned closer to the baby—and to her. His arm barely brushed against hers, causing her to step back a bit, but not before the sweet smell of lavender filled his nostrils. He wasn't sure if the scent came from her or the baby, but he drew in a deep breath as he gazed upon the child.

"He looks to be about two months, no?" Eli forced himself to stand tall and give the woman some space.

"*Ya*. He is two months old this week."

Eli remembered when his first grandchild was born. His daughter-in-law, Laura Jane, had gone into labor early. Scared them all to death, but little Leah fought her way into the world at four pounds, and today she was a healthy, beautiful four-year-old. "He has the same deep brown eyes as you," he said after a moment.

Katie Ann's cheeks took on a pink flush. "He's everything to me." She eased the baby up in her arms and kissed him on the forehead.

"Your first one?"

She lifted her head to face him. "*Mei only* one."

Eli nodded. "I have six . . . and one on the way."

Katie Ann narrowed her brows as she squinted, and Eli could almost feel the prick from her piercing eyes. "Did you say . . . one on the way?"

"*Ya*. Due next month."

She bit her lip. "I see."

Eli looped his thumbs beneath his suspenders, knowing he should be carting more chairs in. He chuckled. "I'm guessing I'll have a dozen or so more when it's all said and done."

Her eyes grew round as she stared at him. "*Really?*"

"Sure. Aren't you hoping for lots more?" He stroked his beard as he wondered how many children she had.

She raised her chin and gave him an icy stare. "I'm quite sure this will be my only one."

Eli scratched his forehead, unsure what to make of her comment. "*Ach*, you never know. We can't control how many grandchildren we'll end up with."

Katie Ann gasped as she took a step back from him. "*Grand*children?"

Oops. He'd made a big mistake. He took off his hat, pressed it against his chest, and cringed for a moment. "That's not your grandchild, is it?"

She shifted the baby in her arms and stiffened. "No. Jonas is *mei boppli*." Katie Ann's cheeks were red as her eyes avoided his.

Eli felt like a heel. "I'm sorry. I guess I just figured that—"

"—a woman *my* age would be a grandmother and not a new *mudder*?"

"*Nee, nee*." Eli's mind searched for a way to mend the situation. "Of course that's not what I thought. I know lots of Amish women who've had *kinner* into their forties, but Elam told me that you were a widow, so I guess I just assumed the child must be a grandchild."

She smiled politely, but the damage was done. Then Eli recalled the way the rest of the conversation had gone, and gave a laugh.

Katie Ann pulled the baby closer to her, cradling him with one arm as she cupped her free hand to her hip. "This is funny?"

"*Ya*. It is." He took a deep breath. "I must have sounded *ab im kopp* when I said I'd probably have a dozen or so more. Of course I meant grandchildren, not children, and . . ." Eli shrugged, hoping for a smile, but she brought the baby to her shoulder and frowned.

"I have to go now."

She hurried across the living room before Eli could get her to see the humor in the situation, and a moment later she headed up the stairs and drifted out of sight.

He put his hands on his hips and sighed. He had embarrassed her. He'd just assumed her children were grown, like his, and that maybe she'd be interested in getting to know him better as they both started the second half of their lives. But she was starting the second half of her life with a baby. *No way*.

Eli had raised all the *kinner* he was going to. There was no point in getting to know this woman, however attractive she might be.

Too bad.

Katie Ann had intrigued him for sure.

KATIE ANN FINISHED changing Jonas's diaper on Vera's bed atop a small blanket she'd brought with her. She picked up her baby and kissed him on the cheek. "Is that better?"

She packed her supplies back into the diaper bag, depositing the wet cloth diaper in a plastic bag. Martha thought she was crazy for not using disposable diapers, but she didn't mind washing the cottony linens for Jonas. They were softer on his behind and caused less chafing.

She walked to the mirror in Vera's room and almost gasped. Her eyes were puffy, with dark circles underneath. No wonder the man had thought she was a grandma. She leaned closer to the mirror and took a better look.

She'd gotten even less sleep the night before than usual. Jonas had cried on and off, and although she'd tried everything to make him happy, nothing had worked. She was thankful that he seemed content so far this morning.

So much for Martha thinking that perhaps a romance would develop—not that she would have considered such a thing. Even if she weren't recently widowed and hadn't lost all trust in men, Eli was a chatty fellow, not at all her type. And was it really necessary for him to get such a chuckle out of their misunderstanding?

She let out a huff before nuzzling her nose to Jonas's neck. "We don't need anyone else, do we?"

AN HOUR INTO the wedding ceremony, most of the congregation was focused on Katie Ann and her little one, who was wailing at the top of his lungs. Even from across the room, Eli could see her bottom lip trembling as she tried to comfort the child, rocking him back and forth. She'd already left the room twice, and both times when she returned, little Jonas was quiet for about a minute before he started up again. An older *Englisch* woman sitting next to her—dressed rather brightly in a pink and white dress—had tried to comfort the child as well, but ultimately handed him back to his mother, shaking her head.

Katie Ann had circles under her puffy eyes, and he sympathized with her. He remembered when Maureen was that age. She'd cried constantly. At first Eli had assumed it was because the poor child didn't have her mother and that he was failing miserably, but it turned out to be something entirely different. And there had been an easy fix.

He watched Katie Ann maneuver her way past a row of women, then slip out the back and into the mudroom. Eli tapped his foot as he tried to focus on what the bishop was saying. He glanced at the clock on the wall. It would be at least another hour before Emily and David actually said their wedding vows. And that poor child was still wailing. He shifted his weight, knowing that what he was about to do was irregular for an Amish man. Children were women's work.

Unless your spouse died and left you six of them to raise.

"Excuse me," he whispered to his nephew Jacob as he stood up and eased by him. He hoped everyone would think he was heading to the bathroom. His black dress shoes clicked against the wooden floor in the Detweilers' living room, and he was glad when he rounded the corner and the bishop's voice faded. His heart sank, though, when he saw Katie Ann sitting on a chair in the far corner of the mudroom crying right along with her child. She looked up at him with teary desperation as he walked toward her, but quickly swiped at her eyes.

"What are you doing back here?" she asked in a loud whisper.

"I thought I might be able to help."

She cut her eyes at him. "I assure you, I've tried everything."

Eli sighed, unsure what to say. Katie Ann started to cry again.

"I don't know what to do." She dabbed at her eyes with a tissue. "He just won't stop crying." She shook her head as she continued to rock Jonas. "He did this most of the night too, and I'm so"—she closed her eyes for a moment, then looked down at the screaming child—"tired."

Eli squatted down beside her. "May I?" He reached his hands out toward the baby, but Katie Ann stiffened and sat taller.

"No. I'm sure you won't be able to help." She sniffled as she shook her head.

Eli couldn't help but notice how pretty she was, even with her eyes swollen from little sleep and tiny lines that feathered from the corner of each eye.

He kept his arms out as he spoke, easing into a chair beside her. "I've raised six children on my own for the past seventeen years. I've learned a thing or two." He raised his brows, and Katie Ann reluctantly handed over the unhappy little fellow.

"There, there," Eli whispered, lowering the little one onto his lap, faceup . . . and still screaming. He slipped one hand under the baby's neck, and with his other hand, he took two fingers and traced them from below Jonas's breastbone all the way down his tummy, applying a small amount of pressure. When he could feel the top of the child's diaper beneath his blue onesie, he moved his hand in a circular motion back and forth across the child's abdomen. In less than a minute, Jonas had stopped crying.

Eli smiled at Katie Ann, whose jaw hung low.

"How did you know to do that?" Her eyes held a glint of wonder.

Eli was surprised at how nice it felt to hold a newborn. He thought about his son's wife, Laura Jane, who would be delivering next month. It would be nice to have another baby around. On a part-time basis, of course.

He handed Jonas to his mother, then shrugged. "A little something I learned when my daughter Maureen was that age. She struggled with a gassy tummy too." He swallowed, recalling the hardship of losing his wife while she was delivering Maureen.

Katie Ann cuddled her child in her arms, smiling down at the little one. After a few moments, she looked at Eli. Her eyes grew sharp and assessing, and with what seemed like resistance, she thanked him.

"You're welcome. Does he get fussy like that a lot?"

"*Ya*. He does."

Eli stood up and rubbed his hands together. "Rub some baby oil in your hands like this, until it gets warm. Then do what I just did with your palm against the baby's bare skin." He grinned. "Works every time."

Katie Ann stiffened. "I should have known that, I suppose." She pressed her lips together as she stood up, and Eli wished he hadn't boasted.

"You learn these things with experience." He smiled again, but she did not. Eli reprimanded himself for being prideful, but there was no denying that experience played a big hand when he'd raised his children, and sometimes he *was* proud of what he'd accomplished on his own. Jake and Hannah were already six- and five-years-old when Sarah died, but he still had a three-year-old, two-year-old, one-year-old, and baby Maureen to raise.

"I should get back to the wedding." She placed the baby up on her shoulder. "*Danki* again."

"You're welcome." He wasn't sure he was winning any points with this woman. No matter, he decided. He waited a minute, then rejoined the service.

KATIE ANN DABBED at her eyes when Emily and David took their vows. She couldn't think of a couple more deserving of such happiness, and she knew that everyone in the room was thinking the same. They might be young, but they had both lived through much. David had nearly died six years earlier, his life saved only through a kidney transplant. And before Emily's family moved from Middlefield to Canaan last year, Emily had suffered a rape and had to endure the trial of her assailant.

Katie Ann was glad that they had fallen in love and had each other to lean on. *Be good to each other*, she said silently.

Ivan's faced flashed in her mind's eye, and memories of their own wedding danced in her head. She never would have imagined that he would run off with another woman, leaving her to raise a baby on her own. A baby he didn't even know about. She dabbed at another tear before it made its way down her cheek. Again she wondered if she'd been fair to her husband by not telling him she was pregnant. As the bishop blessed the union, Katie Ann wondered if visions of her life with Ivan would ever stop haunting her. She had believed that her marriage was sacred, a union blessed by God. Where had it gone wrong?

She bowed her head along with the rest of the congregation, but her communion with God was as it had been for the past several months—limited. Something had gone amiss after Ivan left her, and she was struggling to get it back. She missed God. The way it used to be. And no matter what the circumstances of their separation, she missed Ivan.

"Amen!" Martha said loudly beside her.

Katie Ann gently elbowed her friend.

"Don't nudge me, Katie Ann." Martha raised her brows. "You know how these long services hurt my back. Thank goodness you people have added some chairs to your worship services. I don't know who started that whole backless bench thing, but it's ridiculous." She pointed a few rows in front of them. "Look at poor Lillian up there on the front row. She's half my age, but I watched the poor girl rubbing her back on and off throughout the service. I say you should ban all those backless benches."

Katie Ann sighed as she and Martha stood up. "Time to serve the bridal party." She glanced down at Jonas, who was sleeping soundly in his baby carrier.

"How'd you get him to stop screaming earlier?" Martha now nudged Katie Ann. "I saw the Detweiler fella follow you out of the room. What was that about?"

"Keep your voice down," Katie Ann whispered as she picked up the baby carrier. They followed some of the other women toward the kitchen. "As you pointed out, he's raised six children, so he was helping me with Jonas."

"Now that's a good man, I tell ya." Martha grinned. "You need to get to know him."

"We talked about this. I'm in mourning." Katie Ann frowned in Martha's direction. "Besides, the man is a bit . . . prideful."

"With his good looks, he's got plenty to be proud of." Martha cackled.

"That is not our way, Martha, and you know it." Katie Ann moved toward the stairs. "I'm going to go lay Jonas down in Vera's room."

"Did you bring the baby monitor?"

"*Ya*. Tell Vera I'll be back to help serve in just a minute."

Martha rubbed her hands together. "Can't wait to dig into that creamed celery."

Katie Ann wound her way around the others in the room and went upstairs. After she had Jonas settled in the playpen in Vera's room, she quietly made her way back down.

Martha was busily chatting with Eli in the living room. They both looked up at her, and Katie Ann could tell that Martha was up to no good.

Three

Martha quizzed Eli about his life back in Middlefield, and she listened intently as he told her about his children and grandchildren. He was certainly qualified to take care of little Jonas, so she mentally checked that off her list.

"And what kind of work did you say you do?" Martha batted her lashes at him. If only she were a little younger, she'd convert and snag this fine Amish man for herself.

"I worked construction for many years—and farmed, of course. But right now I'm just farming."

A hard worker. Good. Katie Ann stayed busy, and like most of her people, she believed in hard work and love of the land. "How long will you be staying in Canaan?"

"I'm not sure." He smiled, and Martha decided she was going to slap Katie Ann upside the head if she didn't latch onto this handsome fellow.

"I've never been here before," he added. "Since I was raising six children on my own, there was no time for travel. I guess you could say that this is like a vacation for me. Vera and Elam told me to stay as long as I like, but I don't want to wear out my welcome. And my son, Jake, is tending to my farm. I don't want to burden him for too long."

The wheels in Martha's head were spinning at full capacity when she saw Katie Ann heading her way. Katie Ann was so suspicious of men now, Martha feared she'd never give this nice man a chance. "Vera needs you, Katie Ann," she said quickly and waved her away.

Katie Ann hesitated but then headed toward the kitchen.

"She's like my daughter," Martha said as she raised her chin. "And that little one is like my grandson. I figure he'll call me Granny when he gets older." She sighed. "But I won't always be around to take care of Katie Ann and Jonas. I have my own life to lead, don'tcha know?"

He nodded, and Martha decided she'd better not travel along that road just yet. She didn't want the guy to feel pressured. He'd fall in love with Katie Ann on his own, and the rest would come together.

"I'm making chicken lasagna Saturday night at Katie Ann's house. You should come for supper." Martha grinned. "I'm not much of a cook, but Katie Ann has taught me how to whip up a few things, so every Saturday I cook for her. Easier for me to bring supper to her house so she doesn't have to get the baby out in the weather."

"I, uh . . . should you check with Katie Ann first?"

Has manners too. He's too good to be true. Martha waved her hand. "Nah, she'll be fine with it. Seven o'clock?" She raised one palm toward him. "I know your people normally eat at five o'clock, but my stomach isn't on that schedule." She lifted one brow and waited.

"*Ya*. Seven o'clock then."

"*Wunderbaar gut!*" Martha slapped him on the arm and went to help the ladies in the kitchen.

Eli watched the funny *Englisch* woman walk away, and grinned. Only tourists said *wunderbaar gut*. The Amish folks poked fun at it.

Martha was a character, though, and she was certainly playing the matchmaker. But Eli didn't mind playing along. Katie Ann was sure pretty, and he loved lasagna.

He stroked his beard as he walked out the door to join some of the men on the porch. He was already looking forward to Saturday night.

Katie Ann wrapped Jonas in an extra blanket before she eased him out of his car seat in the back of Martha's car. "I'm glad you wanted to come home early. I'm so tired."

"Bundle that little one up good." Martha looked over her shoulder from the driver's seat.

Katie Ann shut the back door, then leaned in the front window on the passenger side. "*Danki* again for driving. See you tomorrow?"

"No. I have a doctor's appointment in town."

Katie Ann's chest tightened. "What for?"

"Don't look so worried. Routine tests. But it's gonna take most of the day, so I won't see you until Saturday."

Katie Ann nodded.

"I'm bringing lasagna, a nice salad, and garlic bread."

Katie Ann grinned. "*Ach*, that sounds very fancy."

"That's 'cause company is coming."

Katie Ann squinted her eyes. "Who might that be?"

"That nice Eli Detweiler is coming for supper." Martha held up a crooked finger before Katie Ann could speak. "And don't you dare be mad. He is a fine man, and it wouldn't hurt you to get to know him."

"Martha! You shouldn't have done that. You know how I feel about dating. I'm still in mourning."

Martha rolled her eyes. "Well, I'll give you until Saturday night to get done with mourning that scoundrel husband of yours."

Katie Ann's eyes started to tear. She knew that Martha loved her, but she still couldn't stand it when Martha talked badly about Ivan. Only *she* could talk badly about him. "I've told you before how upsetting it is to me when you talk like that. I loved Ivan, and—"

"Okay," Martha said loudly. "I'll try to do better. Now get that baby out of this cool air."

Katie Ann narrowed her brows. "I know what you're doing, and you should not have invited Eli for supper. I can tell by our short interaction that we are nothing alike. He is . . . I don't know . . . so . . ."

"*Happy*, Katie Ann. That's the word you're looking for. The man smiles a lot. Something you should do more of."

Martha rolled up the window, and Katie Ann watched her pull away. She pulled Jonas closer to her and walked up the steps to her house. *Martha's wrong. I am happy.*

After she fed the baby and tucked him into his crib, she ran a bath and climbed into the tub. As she sat in the warm water, she leaned her head back and cried. She'd waited to have a baby and a real family her entire life. She only had half the equation. Even though she loved Martha, it wasn't the same. She missed Ivan with all her heart. *Why, Lord, did You take him from me? And why did Lucy Turner have him when You decided to call him home?*

She laid the warm washrag across her face as she thought about what Martha said. *I am happy*. She was happy about being a mother and thankful that the Lord had blessed her with Jonas. But she wasn't fulfilled. And it was no mystery to her as to why. Her relationship with the Lord had changed since Ivan's death. She just couldn't understand why everything had to happen the way it did, and through no rhyme or reason could she understand what God's plan for her might be. She'd been taught her entire life not to question the Lord's will, and the more she did so . . . the further away she felt from Him.

After allowing herself another fifteen minutes of self-pity, Katie Ann pulled herself from the tub, dressed in a clean blue dress, and went into the living room. It was too early to change into her nightclothes and go to bed. Jonas would be up for another feeding, plus she didn't want to get caught in her nightclothes if Lillian or Samuel came calling after the wedding.

She sat down on the couch, crossed her legs, and opened up a book she'd bought in town about being a new mother. *That is all I need to concentrate on . . . being the best mother I can to Jonas.*

Saturday morning, Katie Ann bundled up Jonas and herself and walked next door to her sister-in-law's house. She knew Lillian would be baking, and Katie Ann often visited with her this time on Saturdays.

She lifted her tall black boots and picked her way carefully across the snow as she toted Jonas in his carrier. She was thankful to have gotten more sleep the past two nights. Thursday night after the wedding she'd been exhausted, and both she and Jonas had slept much better. She'd only gotten up once to feed him and once to soothe his gassy tummy by using Eli's technique with the baby oil, which had worked—and twice she'd tiptoed into his room to make sure he was breathing. Friday she'd gone back to help Vera with cleanup, and again she and Jonas had gone to bed early and followed the same routine as the night before.

Martha had overstepped her bounds by inviting Eli to supper, but she'd worry about that later. This morning she needed to talk to Lillian about something else. As she eased up the porch steps to the old farmhouse, she marveled at all of Lillian and Samuel's hard work. In a year they'd taken this run-down old house with no bathroom, no insulation, in need of an entire overhaul, and turned it into a beautiful home. She knocked on the door.

"Hi, *Aenti* Katie Ann."

Katie Ann smiled at her youngest niece, Elizabeth. The five-year-old was Jonas's biggest fan and loved to keep him company while Katie Ann chatted with Lillian.

"Hello, Elizabeth." Katie Ann moved past the little girl and into the living room. "Is your *mamm* in the kitchen?"

"*Ya.* She's making peanut blossoms!" Elizabeth bounced on her toes.

Katie Ann let out an exaggerated gasp. "Really! That's special, Elizabeth. We usually make those only at Christmastime."

"I know, I know!"

Katie Ann followed Elizabeth across the living room and into the spacious kitchen. Katie Ann recalled the chipping blue paint on the cabinets when Lillian and Samuel had first moved in, now shimmering with shiny white paint and gold knobs that bordered on being fancy . . . but Lillian said she deserved the knobs after having to live in that house prior to the overhaul.

Lillian hadn't always been Amish. She'd married Ivan's brother, Samuel, eight years ago and converted. Most of the time, you'd never know that she hadn't been Amish her entire life, but occasionally she'd bend a certain rule based on her own way of thinking, and no one faulted her for it. Lillian was bubbly, happy, and kindhearted, and Katie Ann didn't know of a soul who didn't adore her.

"You are just in time for peanut blossoms," Lillian announced.

Lillian's older daughter, Anna, was sitting in a chair at the kitchen table mashing chocolate kisses on top of the warm peanut butter cookies. "*Guder mariye, Aenti* Katie Ann."

Katie Ann placed Jonas's carrier on the table. "*Guder mariye* to you, too, Anna."

She was glad to hear Anna using their native dialect this morning. She'd worried about the girls when they were younger, because they didn't know much Pennsylvania *Deitsch*. Normally, children didn't learn English until they started school, but since English was Lillian's native language, she'd raised the girls by speaking that to them. Samuel said it didn't matter what language they spoke, only the meaning behind the words they said. And Elizabeth and Anna were good girls. Lillian and Samuel were doing a fine job with them. Katie Ann hoped she would do as well with Jonas.

Lillian wiped her hands on her apron, approached the table, and leaned down to kiss Jonas on the forehead. "Hello, my precious Jonas."

Lillian looked up, and Katie Ann knew what she was going to say. She said it daily, and it had just become a "thing" between the women.

"Have I told you how glad I am that you named this baby Jonas?"

Anna spoke up before Katie Ann had a chance to. "*Mamm!* You say that all the time."

Lillian cupped her daughter's chin. "I know I do, and you'd know why if you had known your great-grandpa Jonas. The best man who ever lived, I believe."

"I thought *Daed* was the best man who ever lived," Elizabeth said.

Lillian smiled. "Well, besides your *daed*!"

Katie Ann sat down beside Anna. "So what's the occasion? Why are you making peanut blossoms today?"

Lillian walked to the stove and pulled out a fresh batch of cookies. Without turning around she said, "Whatever do you mean?"

Katie Ann heard the playfulness in Lillian's tone. "*Ach*, so there *is* a reason."

Elizabeth skipped to Katie Ann's side. "Martha asked *Mamm* to make them to have tonight for your date."

Katie Ann stiffened. She took a deep breath. "Elizabeth, I don't have a date tonight. Martha is just having a friend over to have supper with us."

"That's not what *Mamm* said. She said—"

"Elizabeth!" Lillian spun around. "Take your sister and go

play in your room for a while so I can visit with *Aenti* Katie Ann." She took a step forward. "Scoot now. After I chat with your *aenti*, you can both come back downstairs and have a double helping of cookies."

Both girls nodded, then scurried upstairs. Katie Ann waited until they were out of earshot before she spoke. "Lillian . . ."

"*Ya*, dear sister-in-law." Lillian grinned from ear to ear as she eased into a chair beside Katie Ann.

Katie Ann stifled a grin. She needed Lillian to understand that there was no chance of courtship with Eli Detweiler. "This is not a date tonight, but I am well aware that everyone is trying to play matchmaker between me and Eli." She shrugged. "I suppose in some ways that makes sense. We are both alone, without spouses. But . . ." She held up one finger. "That does not mean that we are anything alike. And besides, Lillian, I am still mourning Ivan."

Lillian reached over and patted Katie Ann's hand. "I know, sweetie." Lillian quickly sat taller and grinned. "But he sure is handsome, and Vera said Elam's cousin would be a great catch. Did you know his wife died seventeen years ago and he raised his six children alone since then?"

Katie Ann stiffened again. "*Ya*. I know. And he is very proud of his accomplishments."

Lillian put her elbows on the table and laid her chin in her hands. She spoke softly. "Don't you think he should be a tad bit proud?"

"I don't mean to sound harsh, Lillian. I'm sure he did a wonderful job, but I'm not ready to date anyone, and if I was, I don't think it would be Eli."

"I wouldn't rule him out so quickly, *mei* sister."

Katie Ann waved her hand in the air. "Never mind about Eli. I need to talk to you about something else."

Lillian's eyes widened. "What is it?"

Katie Ann took a deep breath. "It's about Lucy Turner."

Lillian grimaced. "What about her?"

"She sent me a letter a couple of weeks ago." Katie Ann watched Lillian's left eyebrow lift. "And she is coming to visit me."

"What *for*?" Lillian placed her palms flat on the table. "She doesn't need to come here for anything. I'd like to get my hands on that woman and—"

"Lillian!"

"I know, I know. It's not our way. But I'd still like to rough her up a bit." It was endearing the way Lillian had always been protective of Katie Ann, even if sometimes her old *Englisch* ways rose to the surface. "Did she say in the letter why she's coming?"

"To discuss an urgent matter." Katie Ann shrugged. "I have no idea what could be so pressing. And, Lillian . . . I haven't told anyone about the letter. Not even Martha."

"Can't blame you there. Martha would camp out at your house, and I wouldn't put it past her to follow through and take that—that *woman*—to the woodshed for a *gut* licking!"

They were both quiet for a moment as Jonas squirmed, but he quickly grew still, sleeping soundly.

"Anyway, it's just bothering me. I don't want Lucy coming here, but I'm so curious about why she'd even want to."

"It's bound to be driving you crazy."

Katie Ann sniffed. "Lillian, is something burning?"

"*Ach! Mei* cookies!" She jumped up, and Katie Ann waited while she pulled a fresh batch of cookies from the oven and set them on a cooling rack. "There, that was the last batch," she said as she sat back down. "Wow. You have a lot to think about. First the letter from Lucy, and now your *date* tonight."

"Lillian, what did I say?" Katie Ann shook her head. "I'm sorry to disappoint everyone, but nothing is going to develop between me and Eli."

"We shall see."

Katie Ann loved to be around Lillian. Her sister-in-law was always cheerful and happy. She recalled what Martha had said about Eli. *"He smiles a lot, Katie Ann. He's happy."*

Well, good for Eli Detweiler. I'm happy too.

"Do you think you could watch Jonas for a few minutes?" Katie Ann leaned over her baby, who was still sleeping soundly. "I want to carry a few logs to the *haus*."

Lillian put her hands on her hips. "I'm always ready to watch my little nephew, but you should let Samuel haul that wood for you."

Katie Ann waved a hand at Lillian. "*Nee*, I will do it. I can use the exercise, and besides, Samuel probably feels like he has two *fraas* half the time, the way he's always doing extra chores for me."

"He loves you, Katie Ann. He doesn't mind at all."

"He's a *gut* man, but I need to stretch my legs." She kissed Jonas on the forehead as she stood up. "I'll be back shortly. I just want to make sure we have plenty of logs tonight."

"*Ya*, for sure." Lillian winked. "For your *date*."

Katie Ann playfully swatted Lillian before she left the room through the door in the kitchen.

Pulling the barn door open, she was surprised to see that Samuel had split even more wood since the last time she was out here, and her brother-in-law made sure the logs were small enough that both she and Lillian could carry them inside. Katie Ann liked to keep several in her rack by the fireplace and a few more in her small mudroom at the back of the house. She lifted two logs, cradling them in front of her, and turned to leave, but was startled by a movement to her left. The three horses didn't seem bothered, nor did the laying hens or four pigs farther down the way. She stood perfectly still and silently prayed that it wasn't a skunk.

She was getting ready to head out when she heard a tiny cry from the far corner of the barn, back behind where the shovels leaned in the corner. She eased the logs onto Samuel's workbench, then headed toward the pitiful meow.

"Hello," she said softly as she reached her hand out toward a small black cat. The little fellow cowered back even farther against the wall, his fur standing on end and his ears pulled back as if taped to his head. "It's all right." She squatted down until she was at eye level with the animal. Poor thing was shivering.

She stood up, picked up her logs, and went toward the house. When she returned, she brought an old blanket. She laid it in the far corner on the other side of the workbench atop a pile of hay. "There. You have your own bed now."

Ivan had never liked cats, said all they were good for was keeping mice away. Barn cats, he called them. So Katie Ann had never had one for a pet. But Ivan wasn't here anymore.

Katie Ann jumped when the cat dashed out from behind the shovel, then ran across the barn like its tail was on fire. She'd barely focused on the animal when it took off again down the aisle, horses on one side, pigs on the other. One of the hogs let out a snort, but otherwise, the cat went unnoticed. Katie Ann tiptoed down the aisle, but the cat had either gone out a stall window or was hiding. Either way, she decided, she was going to name her cat Dash.

IT WAS SIX thirty when Eli readied his cousin's buggy to travel to Katie Ann's for supper. He'd spent most of the previous day helping with cleanup after the wedding. Katie Ann had come to help, too, but the woman seemed to steer clear of him all day. But tonight there would be no avoiding each other. He'd thought about canceling, but he hadn't been able to come up with a good excuse, plus Vera would have been awfully disappointed. She'd made reference to his supper plans several times throughout the day.

Everyone was playing matchmaker, but none of them knew that it was all in vain. Eli and Katie Ann were moving in different directions in life, and he wasn't about to step onto a different path.

By the time he arrived at her house, it was straight up seven o'clock.

Martha answered the door. "Come in, Eli."

Eli took note of her bright green britches, matching blouse, and big gold earrings. Her hair was bundled atop her head in a mass of brownish-gray curls, and bright red lipstick matched her fingernails. Clearly Katie Ann was close to this woman, but it seemed an unusual friendship.

"*Danki,*" Eli said as he moved into the living room, which he found instantly inviting. As with most Amish homes, the walls were white and there were no pictures hanging, but the focal point in Katie Ann's living room was a large bookcase that spanned one wall. In addition to books, she had several potted ivies on the shelves, two candles, a lantern, and a basket full of yarn and knitting needles. A light brown couch faced two finely crafted rocking chairs, and there was a small coffee table in front of the couch. A propane lamp lit the area, and Eli breathed in the aroma of what must be the chicken lasagna.

"Hello, Eli." Katie Ann stopped a few feet in front of him. "Can I get you some iced tea or *kaffi*?"

"Tea, please." He smiled, suddenly wondering what he was doing here. She was bound to know this was a setup, and he had no business leading her on.

"Let me take your coat." Martha held out a hand, and Eli removed his long black coat and black felt hat. She hung them on a rack by the door, then pointed to the couch. "You have yourself a seat, and I'll go see if Katie Ann has everything ready."

Martha disappeared around the corner too, but instead of sitting down, Eli found his way to the bookshelves and gingerly ran his hand along the titles. In addition to novels, she had a large collection of books on parenting. He turned when he heard footsteps.

Katie Ann handed him a glass of tea.

"*Danki*." He nodded toward his left. "You have a fine collection of books."

"I like to read when I have time."

A slow smile trembled over her lips, and Eli could tell that she was nervous. He stroked his beard, studying her.

Martha's voice broke the trance. "Supper's ready! Come and get it!"

Eli couldn't help but grin at the woman's loud voice booming from the other room. But Katie Ann laughed, and it was everything he could do not to tell her how pretty she was when she smiled.

"Forgive Martha." Katie Ann scratched her forehead, grinning. "She's the best friend I have, but we are working on her manners."

Eli just smiled, and Katie Ann motioned with her hand for him to follow her. Martha was already seated at the table.

After they were seated, and following silent prayer, Martha scooped a generous portion of lasagna onto Eli's plate first, then Katie Ann's.

"Help yourself to some salad and bread, Eli." Martha pushed the serving bowl closer to Eli from where she was seated across the table.

"Little Jonas in bed for the night?" Eli scooped some salad from the bowl.

Katie Ann sighed. "He doesn't sleep through the night, but his tummy troubles have been better."

Eli nodded but didn't say anything. He already felt he'd been a bit boastful.

"This lasagna is very *gut*, Martha," Eli said after he swallowed his first bite.

"Yeah, it's not bad." Martha grinned. "Our Katie Ann is the real cook around here."

Eli glanced to his right at Katie Ann, whose cheeks flushed slightly.

He'd almost cleaned his plate and was considering a second helping when someone knocked at the door.

Katie Ann excused herself.

After several long minutes of silence with Martha, the older woman finished her lasagna. "I'd better go see who's here and what's taking our girl so long." She flashed a toothy smile and pushed back her chair.

Our girl? Eli wondered again if this was a mistake. But the lasagna was excellent. He piled another helping on his plate but stopped cold when Martha bellowed from the next room.

"I don't care why you need to talk to Katie Ann. You have no business coming here!"

Four

"Stop it, Martha." Katie Ann clenched her hands into fists at her sides and wished Martha hadn't overheard her call her visitor by name. Even though Martha had never met the woman, she'd certainly heard a lot about her. Katie Ann wasn't sure what was worse—Lucy Turner on the doorstep, Martha yelling, or the fact that Eli Detweiler could hear everything from the kitchen.

"You got a lot of nerve showing up here unannounced." Martha leaned around Katie Ann, her face twisted, her voice loud.

Katie Ann, holding a lantern, could barely see Lucy's face by the dim light. But even in the darkness, she recognized the deceitful blue eyes of the woman who'd stolen her husband. "Now is not a *gut* time, Lucy."

Lucy pulled her black jacket snug. "Didn't you get my letter telling you I was coming?"

"What letter?" Martha glared at Katie Ann. "Did you get a letter from this tramp?"

"Martha! Stop it." Katie Ann heard footsteps and briefly wondered if this situation could get any worse.

"Everything all right in here?" Eli eased up to the door and peered through the screen.

"This woman was just leaving," Martha said with force as her hands landed on her hips.

Katie Ann gently pushed Martha back. "*Ya*, Lucy. I received your letter. Please come back Monday morning. As I said, now is not a *gut* time, and tomorrow is the Sabbath. Please come back on Monday."

Lucy nodded. "I'm sorry, Katie Ann. I wouldn't have come if—"

"You're sorry?" Martha huffed. "Little late for that, don'tcha think?"

Katie Ann took a deep breath as she recalled the way Martha often talked about Lucy. "*No excuse for infidelity,*" she always said. Katie Ann had reminded Martha several times that Ivan was not an innocent bystander.

"Again, I'm sorry." Lucy took a step backward. "Katie Ann, I'll see you on Monday morning."

Martha slammed the heavy wooden door before anyone could say another word. Katie Ann wished the floor would open up and swallow her. Her cheeks burned, and she wondered if Eli knew about her past—about Lucy.

"You're not really going to meet with her, are you?" Martha demanded. "And what's this about a letter?"

"Martha, let's finish our supper. We'll talk about this later." She finally looked at Eli. He was stroking his beard with one hand and glancing back and forth between Katie Ann and Martha.

"I'm not hungry anymore." Martha pulled a brown overcoat from the rack by the door. "I'm going home."

Again Katie Ann wondered which was worse—that Martha was mad at her for not telling her about the letter, or that she was about to be left alone with Eli.

"No, Martha. Don't go." She reached out to touch her arm, but her friend pulled away and put her coat on.

"I ate too much anyway." Martha buttoned her coat as she held her chin high. "You kids have fun."

"But—"

As the wooden door slammed for the second time, Katie Ann briefly wondered if Martha would go hunt Lucy down, and the thought touched her as much as it frightened her. She took a deep breath but couldn't look Eli in the eyes. "I'm so sorry."

Eli slowly walked closer and put a hand on her arm, which was unsettling. "Don't be."

Katie Ann pulled away and stepped back. "I'm—I'm just very embarrassed." She could feel Eli's eyes on her, and when she finally looked up at him, she could see the pity in his expression.

Don't you dare feel sorry for me.

She stood taller, folding her hands in front of her. "Should we finish eating?"

"Sure." He nodded, and Katie Ann didn't think this night could end soon enough.

Eli followed her back to the kitchen, and they both finished eating without conversation, except for an occasional comment from Eli about how much he was enjoying the meal. Katie Ann felt obliged to offer him coffee and some peanut blossoms.

"*Kaffi* would be *gut*." Eli stood from the table. "I saw you shivering. Should we have *kaffi* in the living room, in front of the fire? I can add a log."

For a moment Katie Ann reflected fondly about how nice it would be to have a man to take care of such things, no matter how small. "*Ya. Danki.*"

Eli went into the living room, and Katie Ann started the percolator on top of the stove, then set to clearing the table. She was sure Martha would be over first thing in the morning to find out about Lucy's letter, and then her friend would most likely camp out here on Monday, waiting for Lucy to arrive. She wondered how she would handle Lucy and Martha in the same room at the same time. She knew Martha's angry attitude was propelled by love, but her ranting and raving were only going to make things harder. She'd just finished cleaning the kitchen and pulled two coffee cups from the cupboard when Eli walked into the kitchen.

"I think I hear the *boppli* stirring."

Katie Ann wiped her hands on her apron. "He's probably hungry. I'm sorry, the *kaffi* is almost ready. I'll be right back."

Eli walked toward her and reached for the coffee cups. "I can ready our *kaffi* if you'd like."

His fingers brushed against hers as he took the mugs in his hands, and a tingle raced up her arms. It took her a few moments before she nodded.

When Katie Ann walked into the living room with Jonas a short while later, Eli was sitting on the couch and asked if he could hold the baby. She leaned down and eased Jonas into Eli's arms, then stepped back. It usually made her nervous for a stranger to hold Jonas, but the warmth of the freshly stoked fire hit her, and the sight of Jonas in Eli's arms caused a lump to swell in her throat. She could almost see Ivan sitting on the couch holding his son. She shook her head to clear the thought.

She sat down on the couch next to Eli and had to admit it was touching, the way he cradled Jonas and made funny little baby talk. She'd never seen a man do that, and she lifted her hand to her mouth as she stifled a grin.

"He is a beautiful child." Eli glanced over at Katie Ann. "Like his—"

"If you say *grossmammi*, I'll smack you." Katie Ann was shocked at her own playful comment, but Eli's face lit up, and a certain amount of tension between them seemed to melt away.

"I was going to say, like his *mudder*."

Katie Ann felt the flush filling her cheeks. His smooth, gentle voice sounded almost seductive, and she became very aware of how intimate this scene was. But as he returned his gaze to Jonas, Katie Ann let her eyes scan the stranger sitting next to her. He was handsome, no doubt. Even beneath his long-sleeved blue shirt, she could see the strength in his arms, and she'd already noticed the tall, confident way he carried himself. A trace of gray at his temple and speckled discreetly through his beard lent him a sophistication that was attractive. His hazel eyes were soft, and when he smiled, laugh lines filled his face. Martha's voice rang in her mind. *"He's happy, Katie Ann."*

"Danki," she finally managed to say. She watched as Eli lifted Jonas to his shoulder, patting him on the back. She wondered if Ivan would have been as involved with Jonas as this visitor in her living room. "Tell me about your *kinner*," she said.

Eli lowered Jonas, placed him faceup in his lap, and rubbed his tummy as though he'd done it a million times. "Jake is my oldest. He's twenty-three. Then there are all my girls—Hannah, Ida Mae, Karen, Frieda, and my youngest, Maureen." He leaned down, smiling at Jonas. "And I've been blessed with six grandchildren." He glanced up at Katie. "And one on the way. Laura Jane is expecting in a couple of weeks. She's Jake's *fraa*."

"When did your . . ." Katie Ann wondered if she was being too personal.

"When did *mei fraa* die?" Eli looked up, but his eyes drifted somewhere else as he spoke. "She died giving birth to Maureen. Seventeen years ago."

"I'm so sorry," Katie Ann said. "I can't imagine how hard that must have been on you. And the *kinner*."

Eli turned to face her, and a different kind of expression filled his face, one Katie Ann couldn't quite interpret. "I had lots of help in the beginning, but over time I realized that I was somehow going to have to be both parents, and be *gut* at it, if I wanted *mei kinner* to have a *gut* upbringing." He chuckled. "Everyone tried to match me up with women in our district, but no one could compare to my Sarah." Eli's face brightened as he mentioned his wife's name.

Katie Ann bit her bottom lip. *Why couldn't Ivan have loved me like that?* "I'm sure you did a wonderful job raising them all. Jonas has sure taken a fancy to you."

Eli gently lifted the baby and handed him to Katie Ann. "*Ach*, I don't know about that." He avoided meeting her eyes.

He took a deep breath, then let it out slowly. "I do feel like I've earned a bit of a vacation, so to speak. All *mei kinner* have made fine homes for themselves, and I plan to travel some." He raised his brows. "Of course, I'll still farm. My love of the land won't change. But I plan to enjoy some time to myself." He looked hard into Katie Ann's eyes. "Do you think that's selfish?"

She was surprised by the question. "*Nee*. I don't. I know how much time and energy it takes to take care of one small *boppli.* I can't imagine you raising six *kinner* on your own. Very admirable." She smiled. "I think you've earned some time to yourself. Where do you plan to travel?"

Eli stood up, walked to the fire, and gave it a poke. "*Ach*, I have a long list." He turned to her and smiled as he stowed the fireplace tool. "But I'm starting here in Colorado. Maybe you can tell me some nice spots to visit while I'm here?"

Katie Ann cradled Jonas in her arms and rocked him back and forth. "I'm probably not a *gut* person to ask. Since we've lived here, I've either been pregnant or with a newborn. I'm afraid I haven't had a chance to travel much farther than Monte Vista, the nearest town."

Eli sat down beside her, took a sip of his coffee, and stared at her for a moment. "You do know that several of the folks around here are trying to play matchmaker between us, no?"

Katie Ann pulled her eyes from his, again feeling a blush in her cheeks. "I—I, uh . . ."

"I'm sorry. I didn't mean to embarrass you. I just felt it was best to clear the air. I'm planning to stay for a short while to do some sightseeing, so I'm sure we will be seeing each other, but I don't want you to feel uncomfortable around me."

She lowered her head and rubbed her forehead. "I'm in mourning, and it would be inappropriate to . . . to . . ."

Eli ran a hand the length of his beard and shook his head. "No worries. I know you recently lost your husband, and we . . . well, we're in two different places in life." He shrugged.

"But we could sure give them all something to talk about." He grinned. "You said you haven't seen much of the area. Would you and Jonas like to spend the day doing some sightseeing with me?"

Katie Ann was shaking her head before he even finished his sentence. "*Nee, nee.* I'm not going to fuel gossip. And besides, it's much too cold for Jonas to take a buggy trip anywhere."

Eli chuckled. "It must be different here than where I come from. Gossip might be frowned upon, but it's plentiful just the same."

Katie Ann started to agree, but Eli went on. "And no buggy ride for me. I'm going to hire a driver. You should take advantage of my offer and see some sights while I'm here visiting." He grinned. "And providing a ride with a heater."

It was a tempting offer, but inappropriate. "*Danki.* But I think not."

"Why?"

Katie adjusted Jonas in her arms and stiffened. "Because I just can't shuck my chores around here and go on a frivolous outing with you."

"Why?"

She narrowed her brows. "Because I just can't."

Eli drank up the last of his coffee. "Okay. I just thought it might be nice for two friends to share a sightseeing trip together."

He stood up as if preparing to leave. *Finally*. She rose from the couch, too, and allowed herself a few moments to dream about seeing more of the San Luis Valley, maybe even the sand dunes. She'd heard about the massive mounds just an hour away. "Where are you planning to go?"

Eli chuckled. "Aha. You are interested, just a little?"

Katie Ann shrugged one shoulder. "Maybe." She had felt a bit claustrophobic as of late. And she'd never admit it, but it would be fun to see Vera, Lillian, and especially Martha's reaction to her spending time with Eli. And besides, Eli's plans for his future were so completely opposite of her own that he suddenly seemed *safe*. Maybe even someone she could be friends with.

"Tomorrow there isn't worship service, so I thought I would spend the day with Elam, Vera, and the *kinner*. Monday I was planning to travel to the Great Sand Dunes. Have you heard of them?"

Katie Ann's heart leaped as she considered the possibility. "*Ya*. I have. David took Emily there before they were married, and they said it is quite the sight."

"I can be here with a driver on Monday at nine o'clock. How does that sound? You, me, and Jonas can have a nice lunch somewhere and see some things neither of us has seen before." He raised a brow. "Always more fun to sightsee with a friend."

Suddenly she remembered Lucy. "I'm sorry. I forgot that, um . . . the woman you saw earlier . . . she'll be here Monday morning."

Eli walked toward the front door. Katie Ann followed, watching him pull his hat and coat from the rack.

"I'm wide open on Tuesday too."

She took a deep breath and wondered if spending time with Eli would be acceptable. It wasn't like they were teenagers. And Eli had made it clear that he sought nothing from her but friendship. Before she could answer, Eli spoke.

"I hope that you and the woman named Lucy have a nice conversation."

It was a strange thing to say, in light of what he had seen, and it was clearly an invitation for Katie Ann to share about Lucy, which was not going to happen. "*Danki*," she said smoothly.

He looked at her, waiting.

"I'm sorry about the display earlier. Lucy is someone I knew in Lancaster County, and as you could see, Martha is not fond of her."

Eli grinned. "I noticed that. I hope I don't ever get on Martha's bad side."

Katie Ann couldn't help but smile as she propped Jonas up on her shoulder. "It's not a *gut* place to be."

"See you on Tuesday?" Eli adjusted his hat.

Katie Ann bit her bottom lip for a moment. "I would like to see the sand dunes." Then she shook her head. "But I don't know, Eli—about Jonas. Maybe I shouldn't have him out in the weather."

Eli leaned close and touched Jonas on the cheek. "We will keep this little one bundled up well."

Jonas puckered with delight at Eli's touch, but Katie Ann went weak in the knees as Eli's hand brushed against hers. She wondered if she was making the right choice about going with him. But she just nodded.

ELI FOUGHT THE night chill all the way to his cousin's house, and by the time he got home everyone had retired for the evening. He went straight to bathe, then propped himself up on the bed. After he adjusted the lantern, he read from the Bible for a while, but eventually his thoughts about Katie Ann won over, and he closed the book. He sighed as he made a mental note to do a little extra reading from the Good Book in the morning. Right now he couldn't seem to shake the vision of Katie Ann playfully teasing with him about not calling her a grandmother. She didn't smile a lot, but when she did, it stirred things in Eli that had long been dormant. A thought that was both exhilarating and frightening.

He snuffed the lantern, lay back, and closed his eyes, wishing that things were different. Katie Ann was the first woman since Sarah who had lit a spark inside of him, but she was not anyone he'd ever pursue. Although she was lovely, and Jonas was a cute little *boppli*. He smiled, thinking about his time holding the child.

Rolling on his side, he knew those days were behind him. All he had to take care of was himself, and it had been a long time coming. But surely it was safe to spend time with Katie Ann. The woman was mourning her husband, and Eli had been deliberate in his use of the word *friend* in their conversations.

He rolled onto his back, then back onto his side.

So why am I having so much trouble falling asleep?

KATIE ANN FINISHED nursing Jonas, laid him back down, and watched him until he fell asleep. Normally she'd eat a bowl of homemade granola for breakfast, but this morning she'd made herself some scrambled eggs. She couldn't wait until Jonas was old enough to sit at the table. Lillian often invited her to take dinner with her family, since they lived right next door, and Martha came for most suppers, but breakfast time was lonely.

After checking on Jonas, she carried her leftover eggs

out to the barn. Maybe Dash would eat scrambled eggs. She opened the barn door and was pleased to see that the cat was using the blanket she'd laid out for him. "I have a treat for you," she said softly as she walked across the barn. She hadn't taken three steps when the cat dashed around the corner and out of sight. "I'll leave this for you anyway."

She set the plate down, then headed back up to the house. A few minutes later there was a knock at the door. She looked at the clock on the wall. As Katie Ann predicted, Martha had arrived early.

"*Guder mariye*, Martha."

Martha squirmed out of a black jacket and stocking cap and hung them on the rack by the door. She grunted before she asked if Katie Ann had coffee ready.

"*Ya*. A fresh pot in the kitchen. I knew you'd be here early." She grinned as she closed the front door.

Martha didn't say anything as she padded across the room in a black velour sweatsuit, her brownish-gray hair matted in the back of her head as it rested in a crumpled mess above her shoulders.

"Yes, I know. My hair is a mess." Martha glanced over her shoulder and frowned. "But that wool head covering is warm, and I don't care."

Katie Ann followed her friend to the kitchen, where Martha was already helping herself to a cup from the cabinet.

"I didn't say a thing about your hair." Katie Ann found her own cup that she'd used earlier for coffee, and she poured herself some after Martha was done.

Martha sat down at the kitchen table, crossed her legs, and leaned back in the chair. "Now I want to hear about your time with that handsome Eli, but first things first. Tell me about this letter from Lucy."

Katie Ann pulled out a chair across the table and sat down. "She sent me a letter a couple of weeks ago, saying she needed to talk to me about an urgent matter."

Martha uncrossed her legs, leaned forward, and placed her palms on the table. "What urgent matter could that woman possibly need to talk to you about?"

"I don't know." Katie Ann shrugged. "But you don't need to be here when she comes tomorrow."

Martha folded her arms across her chest. Scowling, she said, "I thought I was your best friend. But you didn't even tell me about this letter."

"Martha . . ." Katie Ann spoke gently. "You are my best friend, but I knew you would react like this."

Martha snapped her fingers. "A woman like that only wants one thing. Money! I bet that tramp is coming to ask for money."

"I am not going to have you use such language in my house. Do you hear me?" Katie Ann cut her eyes at Martha across the table.

"Fine. But I'm sure she must be trying to get some money out of you. That's got to be it."

Katie Ann searched her heart and soul for a moment. "Maybe she's coming to say she's sorry?"

Martha grunted. "I doubt it." She pointed a crooked finger at Katie Ann. "And I know it's your people's way to forgive and forget, but the woman had an affair with your husband."

"I don't need to be reminded, Martha, and yes . . . we do try hard to forgive." She sighed. "Forgetting is not always so easy. Don't you think I'm nervous about Lucy coming here tomorrow? But she's traveled a very long way to talk to me."

"I don't care if she took a rocket from the moon. She's got no business here."

Katie Ann stood up, one arm folded across her churning stomach and her coffee cup in her other hand. She paced the kitchen. "I don't want you here tomorrow morning, Martha. It will be hard enough just having Lucy here."

"Don't worry. I won't be here."

Katie Ann breathed a sigh of relief. She had expected resistance. "*Gut,*" she said as she smoothed wrinkles from her apron. "It will be best that way."

Martha scratched her nose, then pulled a handkerchief from her pocket and blew her nose. Then she blew it again, and again, and again.

"Are you sick?" Katie Ann sat back down across from Martha.

"Yes, I'm sick. I'm not well at all." Martha squeezed her nose with the handkerchief and blew with force. "I feel like poop, but I'm forced to come over here in this weather this morning to find out about a letter from that . . ." She looked up at Katie Ann and huffed. "That *woman*."

"I was going to tell you. After my visit with Lucy."

Martha shook her head as her face shriveled into a frown. "I don't even like to hear her name."

"Well, it doesn't please me to say her name either." Katie Ann decided to try to change the subject. "You said you went to the doctor the other day. Did you have this cold then?"

"I don't have a cold. I'm much sicker." Martha pinched her lips together.

Katie Ann knew that Martha often exaggerated her aches, pains, and illnesses. Sometimes her friend even faked ill health for attention. When the women first became friends, Martha often complained of a backache. Katie Ann was never sure of the extent of the ailment, but Martha's backaches always manifested when she needed something from Katie Ann, even if it was just companionship. And when Martha showed the slightest sign of a cold, she was worse than a child. But Katie Ann always showered Martha with sympathy and affection—sick or not sick. Because the woman truly was her best friend.

However, Martha disliked doctors. For all her aches and pains, Katie Ann couldn't recall one single time Martha had visited a physician.

"I'm sorry you feel poorly. What's wrong with you?" Katie Ann tapped her finger to her chin. "And what type of routine tests did you have?"

Martha stood up from the table, straightening the collar of her black velour pullover. "Once a year I force myself to visit that idiot doctor in Alamosa, and I let him run all those stupid tests on me. And every year, I'm fine."

"Did you mention your cold?"

Martha slammed her hands to her hips. "Did you not hear me? I don't have a cold." She raised her chin. "I'm very ill." She lowered her gaze. "I have to go for more tests tomorrow."

Katie Ann eased closer to her friend. "What kind of tests?"

"Lung tests."

That sounded serious to Katie Ann, but she tried to speak as though she wasn't concerned. "I'm sure everything will be fine."

Martha sighed. "I doubt it. But we all gotta go sometime."

She didn't say anything more as she turned and walked toward the living room.

"Martha . . ." Katie Ann caught up to Martha by the front door. "Do you want me to go with you to the doctor?"

"And cancel that fine visit with Lucy you have scheduled?" She grunted, rolling her eyes. "I wouldn't dream of asking you to do that."

Katie Ann grinned as she stuffed her hands in the pockets of her apron. "Martha, now you stop it. You know I'll cancel with Lucy to be with you."

"Do you even know where she's staying?"

"Well, no . . . but . . ."

"Don't worry about it. I'll give you a full report tomorrow evening." Martha frowned. "Kiss Jonas for me. I don't think I should be too close to him until the doctor finds out what's wrong with me."

"I will. But please come over tomorrow evening and let me know what the doctor said."

Martha cut her eyes at Katie Ann. "Only if you tell me what that horrible Lucy had to say." She pulled on her gloves, then pointed a finger at Katie Ann. "I still say she's here for money."

Money was something Katie Ann had plenty of, thanks to a mysterious box of cash that had been left on her doorstep last year—money she suspected had originated from Martha, even though the woman denied it. But she couldn't imagine Lucy coming all the way to Colorado to ask for money from Katie Ann, the woman whose husband she'd stolen.

"I don't think she's coming to ask for money."

"No, you wouldn't think that. You see the good in everyone."

Katie Ann didn't say anything, but she certainly didn't see

the good in what Lucy Turner had done. Or her husband. And forgiveness was much farther out of reach than Martha might realize. It was something Katie Ann struggled with daily.

"I'll see you tomorrow night."

"Hey, wait." Martha lifted her chin. "You didn't tell me about Eli. How'd it go after I left?"

"Fine." Katie Ann grinned, intentionally fueling Martha's curiosity.

Martha cackled. "Really?" She leaned closer and whispered, "I think that man's got a thing for you."

"Well, you're wrong. We agreed to be friends, though. And that's all. We are at two very different places in life."

A full smile spread across Martha's face. "The fact that you are both trying to clarify the relationship this early on . . . well, that means something. When are you going to see him again?"

"What makes you think I'll see him again?" Katie Ann fought to hide her expression as she realized that she was looking forward to Tuesday.

Martha tried to snap her gloved fingers. "Aha! You are going to see him again. When?"

Katie Ann lifted one shoulder as she pulled her eyes from Martha's. "Tuesday."

Martha's eyes grew round. "Fabulous!"

"We're going to travel together to see the sand dunes, as *friends*. Eli is hiring a driver."

Martha crossed herself, which she often did, even though she wasn't Catholic. "Thank God. I've been praying for you to find someone." She let out a heavy sigh. "In case I kick the bucket, you'll have someone to take care of you."

Again Katie Ann felt sure Martha was exaggerating, but

the comment was disturbing nonetheless. "Don't say things like that, Martha."

Martha hugged Katie Ann. "Don't you worry about a thing." She kissed Katie Ann on the cheek and closed the door behind her.

And for the first time since she'd met Martha and nursed her through a host of ailments, some real, some not so real—Katie Ann felt truly worried about her friend.

Five

LUCY THANKED HER HOSTESS AT THE MANSION BED-and-Breakfast after a meal that should have been more than satisfying. Eggs Benedict were her favorite, and the fruit bowl and homemade granola also topped the list of her preferred breakfast items. But this morning her stomach roiled with anxiety, and she wondered if coming all this way to see Katie Ann was a mistake. Ivan's wife might be Amish, but she was still human, and Lucy had seen the loathing in Katie Ann's eyes on Saturday. She wished this trip hadn't been necessary, but after much deliberation, she didn't see any way around it.

She carted her red suitcase to her rental car, popped the trunk, and stored the luggage inside. It was only ten miles from the B&B in Monte Vista to Katie Ann's house, and she planned to drive as slowly as possible. She'd hoped to get this dreaded visit over with on Saturday and be back in Lancaster County by now, but she was certainly willing to work around Katie Ann's schedule. That was the least she could do.

As she pulled off the main highway, she touched her hand to her stomach and felt the baby kick. In the darkness of the other night, and with a heavy coat on, her pregnancy hadn't been noticeable to Katie Ann. The last thing she wanted to do was cause the woman more pain. But she didn't have a choice. Ivan was gone, and he'd been the only person who could explain the contents of the box he'd left behind. Lucy's future depended on Katie Ann being able to identify the picture.

She took a deep breath and tried to calm her rapid heartbeat. So many times she'd wanted to defend herself to Katie Ann and the members of her community. She knew that everyone in the Old Order district thought she'd seduced Ivan away from his wife, that surely no good Amish man would pursue an *Englisch* woman. If they only knew.

She thought back on Ivan's many advances and wished more than anything that she could go back in time, wished she had never agreed to have lunch with the handsome Amish man who was clearly unhappy at home. One lunch led to another, until eventually Ivan had kissed her. She ended it after that, but Ivan only tried harder. Every day he would wander into the café where she worked. He'd also call her from a cell phone he was hiding from Katie Ann. And when he said he never loved anyone the way he loved her, she had melted. All she'd ever wanted was to be loved, and she'd managed to go thirty-two years without true love. Until Ivan.

She pulled into the driveway that led up to Katie Ann's house. She glanced to her left at the house she knew to be Samuel and Lillian's. She hoped that neither of them would be at Katie Ann's when she arrived. Or the scary woman who had been there on Saturday night. It would be hard enough to talk to Katie Ann without an audience.

KATIE ANN PULLED the last of the clothes through the wringer washer, then began to hang the wet items in the mudroom. Temperatures had dropped during the night, and a blanket of frost still covered everything at nine o'clock this morning. She'd tried to stay busy for the past four hours, since she'd gotten up to nurse Jonas. After feeding her little one, he'd drifted back to sleep, and Katie Ann had busied herself cleaning and washing clothes. Anything to keep her mind off Lucy's impending visit.

She didn't know the woman well at all. She had worked at a café back in Lancaster County, and they'd only spoken a handful of times before Katie Ann caught Ivan kissing her one day. After that, her husband had promised her that he'd stopped seeing Lucy, that there'd never been more than a shared kiss and a few phone calls. Katie Ann knew now that Ivan had lied to her, and she couldn't help but wonder if there were other untruths built around his relationship with Lucy. Maybe he had tried to end it with Lucy, but Katie Ann could still remember the way she begged Ivan not to leave their marriage. She and Ivan had relocated to Colorado for a new beginning, but Ivan's heart had remained in Lancaster County. And even though Katie Ann had adjusted nicely to her life in Colorado, Lancaster County was where her own roots were. She wondered if she would ever move back there.

As she clipped a towel to a hanger, she recalled Ivan's funeral a few months ago. Lucy had been racked with grief, and Katie Ann almost felt sorry for the woman. Almost. But there was always enough bitterness in Katie Ann's heart to drown out any sympathy for Lucy. Perhaps she shouldn't have even agreed to this meeting. *An urgent matter?*

She thought about what Martha said. Could Lucy be coming to ask for money? When she heard a car pulling in, she left the rest of the wet clothes in the laundry basket. Her stomach clenched tight as she smoothed the wrinkles from her black apron and moved through the house. Her heart felt like it would beat out of her chest as she stood on the other side of the closed door, waiting for Lucy to knock. She listened to her heels click up the porch steps, then a soft tap against the door.

Katie Ann opened the front door, took one look at Lucy, and almost gasped. A knot formed in her throat, and she couldn't speak.

"Hello, Katie Ann." Lucy tried to pull her long beige coat tighter around her, but it didn't hide her enlarged belly.

Katie Ann managed to open the door and motion for Lucy to enter.

"Come in," she finally said after Lucy was already inside the living room and Katie Ann was shutting the door. She could hear the tremble in her voice, and she wondered if Lucy was half as nervous as she was.

"I guess you must have noticed . . ." Lucy's voice trailed off as she placed both hands on her stomach. "I'm six months pregnant."

"Ivan's?" Katie Ann asked.

Lucy looked down at her brown boots. "Yes."

Katie Ann moved as if she were a character in someone else's nightmare, unable to believe that this adulteress was in her home. Any earlier thoughts of polite small talk or an offer of coffee slipped from her mind. Still standing, she asked, "What do you want, Lucy?"

Lucy's bottom lip trembled as she avoided eye contact with Katie Ann. "First of all, I want to say how very sorry I am. For everything."

She looked up at Katie Ann as a tear rolled down her cheek, and Katie Ann stared at her, knowing she didn't have one ounce of forgiveness for the woman, despite what she'd said, thought, or prayed about in the past. And she had no plans to make this visit easy on her.

"What do you want?" she asked again.

Katie Ann was surprised at how plain Lucy looked. She didn't have on the heavy makeup she'd seen her wear before, and her clothes were conservative, not as if she'd selected them that morning with the intention of seducing someone's husband. Perhaps being pregnant had humbled the woman.

Still standing, Lucy reached into her oversized brown purse and pulled out a wooden box. "I found this after Ivan died." She held out a small cedar container for Katie Ann to see.

Katie Ann recognized the box right away. It was half the size of a shoe box, and Ivan's father had made it for him when he was a boy. He'd always kept it on their dresser.

"What about it?" Katie Ann couldn't imagine why Ivan's old keepsake would have brought Lucy all the way to Colorado.

Lucy leaned forward slightly and grimaced.

Instinctively, Katie Ann took a step toward her. "Are you all right?"

"Yes, just a hard kick from the little one."

Lucy smiled a bit, and Katie Ann stiffened. But despite her resentment of Lucy, she asked her if she would like to sit down.

"Thank you." Lucy kept her coat on, thankfully, and sat down on the couch.

Katie Ann sat in the rocking chair across from her. "Lucy, I'm sure you didn't come here to show me Ivan's box." She folded her hands in her lap, bit her bottom lip, and waited.

"Actually, it's what I found in the box." Lucy unlatched the tiny clasp and pulled out a photograph. She reached across the coffee table and handed it to Katie Ann, who took it hesitantly. It was a picture of a house, a beautiful white house with black shutters and a white picket fence.

Katie Ann handed the picture back to her. "Why are you showing me this?"

Lucy's voice wavered as she spoke, her eyes watering. "I was hoping you might know where this house is." She reached back into the box and pulled out two keys. "These keys were in the box also. I think Ivan bought us a house somewhere, and—"

Katie Ann blinked her eyes a few times. "What?"

"I'm sorry, Katie Ann. I'm so sorry. But our bank account is wiped out, and I think Ivan used the money that was in there to purchase this house. But I have no idea where it is. I know that sounds crazy, but I can't afford to keep making the mortgage on our current house. They've cut my hours at the café, and I'll need to stop working when the baby comes."

Katie Ann rubbed her forehead and tried to picture Ivan cleaning out their bank account. "That doesn't sound like Ivan."

"The money was his. I mean, I had very little when we moved in together. So it isn't like he stole my money or anything." Lucy stood up. "I think he was planning to surprise me with a new home."

Katie Ann thought about all the ways Ivan used to surprise her in the past, whether just a bouquet of flowers, or even once a new buggy. She thought for a moment. "That doesn't make any sense. Ivan would have put your house on the market to sell before he invested money to build a new one." Katie Ann shook her head. "I can't believe this is what you came here to talk to me about."

She wondered how much money Ivan had put in Lucy's bank account. He'd told her he left with very little, but Katie Ann had never been familiar with their finances . . . until she'd started to run out of money several months after Ivan left her. Then the mysterious box of money showed up on her doorstep.

"After Ivan was killed, I went to check our bank account," Lucy said. "His landscaping company had been doing very well, and the money he'd been saving was gone. I haven't made a mortgage payment since he died. We bought the house I'm in together, and I can't afford it on my own. I'm going to lose my home, and I'm pregnant. So if I don't find out if this is our house, I'm going to be homeless."

Katie Ann tried to absorb what Lucy was saying, but it still didn't make sense. "If Ivan bought a house, there would be some paperwork or something. How could you not know about it?"

Lucy raised her palms in the air. "Exactly. I was wondering if you knew anything about it."

"Why would I know? Ivan left me a year ago." Katie Ann reached down, picked up the picture from the box on the coffee table again, and stared at it, resentment filling every pore.

Lucy sat down and put her head in her hands. "I don't know. It was a long shot coming here. But I have no paperwork, nothing. Just money missing, a picture of a house, and two keys. It was the only thing I could think of, that Ivan used the money to buy us another house, then died before he had a chance to tell me about it." Lucy started to sob. "I'm going to have a baby, and I'm going to lose my house. I never even wanted . . ." She stopped and looked up at Katie Ann, and her face reddened.

"You didn't want a baby?" Katie Ann felt like this surreal conversation was choking her.

Lucy sniffled. "I don't see myself as a very good mother. I don't know the first thing about babies."

Katie Ann eased back into the rocking chair, feeling nauseous. All she'd ever wanted was a baby, and for her and Ivan to have a family together. Now his mistress was sitting on the couch crying. "Being a mother will come naturally to you."

Lucy swiped at a tear. "Do you think? Did it come naturally to you?"

Katie Ann didn't like being compared to Lucy, and she didn't want to share such an intimate detail with her. "It came naturally. And it will for you too."

Lucy lowered her head again. "I just don't know what I'm going to do. I took an advance from work to be able to make this trip." She stared up at Katie Ann. "Do you think Ivan bought this house for us? To surprise me?"

Katie Ann studied the woman's expression. "I don't know."

"It's the only thing that makes sense." She put a finger to her lips for a moment, then asked, "You haven't gotten any mail regarding this, have you?"

Katie Ann recalled a letter she received from Ivan's attorney awhile back, but there was no mention of any house. "No. I haven't."

Lucy started crying again.

"Can I get you something to drink?"

"Maybe just a glass of water." Lucy pulled a tissue from her coat pocket and blew her nose.

Katie Ann left her in the living room and returned a moment later. She handed the glass of water to her, then folded her arms across her chest. "How much do you need?"

Lucy swallowed a gulp of water. "What?"

"How much money do you need to keep your house from going into foreclosure?"

Lucy stood up and faced Katie Ann. "I didn't come here to ask you for money. I just came here to see if you recognized that house, or knew where it might be located."

Katie Ann gazed into Lucy's eyes, and for some reason . . . she believed her. She left the room, and a minute later she returned with her checkbook.

"Katie Ann, I will not take any money from you."

Katie Ann scribbled out what she thought would be enough to carry Lucy for several months. She tore the check out and handed it to Lucy. "Take it. You are going to give birth to Jonas's brother or sister."

Lucy stiffened her arms at her sides and shook her head. "I can't." Then she covered her face with her hands. "How could you even make this offer, after what I did to you?"

Tears poured down Lucy's face, and Katie Ann dabbed at her own eyes.

"I'm the most horrible person on the planet, and if I could go back, I would have never, never . . ." She sobbed harder. "Please forgive me, Katie Ann." She looked up at her. "Please. I need to be forgiven."

Katie Ann swallowed back a lump in her throat. She knew that she could ease Lucy's pain by telling her that she was forgiven, but the words just wouldn't come. The image of Ivan walking out the door, abandoning their life together, kept flashing before her.

She pushed the check toward Lucy. "Take the money, Lucy. If not for you, for the child."

Lucy slowly reached for the check. "Ivan should have stayed with you. You're a much better person than I am."

Katie Ann wanted to say, "Yes, he should have." Instead she moved toward the door, hoping Lucy would follow.

She did.

Lucy stepped out on the porch and then peered at Katie Ann through the screen, tears still streaming down her cheeks. "I loved him. And I miss him very much."

Katie Ann took a deep breath, rubbed her forehead, and thought about how much she missed Ivan too.

"Ivan and I had a fight the night he was killed." Lucy closed her eyes tightly for a moment before she looked back at Katie Ann. "We said ugly things to each other, then he left." She locked eyes with Katie Ann and tipped her head to one side. "I always wondered if he was going back to you."

A tear rolled down Katie Ann's cheek, and with Lucy's eyes still locked with hers, she closed the door. Katie Ann knew that she would spend the rest of her life wondering too now.

MARTHA SAT DOWN in her recliner, bumping the small table next to her chair for the thousandth time. Katie Ann asked her why she didn't move the table over, but once she was settled in her chair, the table was close enough to reach her hand lotion, the remote for the television, and the phone without even having to stretch a muscle.

She stared at the empty space a few feet away where Elvis's cage used to be. It had been almost a year, but she sure missed that bird. Sometimes she could still hear him saying her name. She tapped her fingernail on the hard surface of the table next to her. That parrot should have outlived Martha, but the Lord had seen fit to call her beloved Elvis home. She'd thought about getting another parrot, but it just didn't feel right.

Closing her eyes, she thought about Arnold. *Why did you take him too, Lord?* Her close friend and companion didn't go home to see the Lord, but instead went to Georgia to be with his dying son. How could Martha fault the man for that? But she sure missed him. They exchanged the occasional letter, and Martha had sent flowers when his son passed, but Arnold had decided to stay on in Georgia instead of returning to Canaan. He had kinfolk there, and he'd reestablished those relationships. Martha was glad for Arnold. He deserved to be happy.

She thought back a couple of months to when Arnold had asked if he could come for a visit. As much as she'd missed him, she made up an excuse for him not to come. She just wasn't sure her heart could take another good-bye. Easier to just leave the past in the past without stirring up old feelings. But after her appointment with the doctor today, she had the strongest urge to call Arnold. Part of her wanted to share her news with him, but she feared Arnold would feel obligated to hop a plane to see her. She didn't need his pity.

Laying her head back against the recliner, she thought about Katie Ann. She sure hoped that Eli Detweiler would fall madly in love with Katie Ann. Her friend needed someone to take care of her and Jonas, and clearly Martha wouldn't be around forever. She opened her eyes, placed her hand on the telephone, then tapped her finger on the table again.

She picked up the phone, and this time she managed to dial nine out of the ten numbers before she placed the telephone back in the carrier.

"Oh, why not," she said aloud as she picked up the phone again. She dialed the numbers quickly, knowing that once the phone rang once, there was no turning back. Arnold was a nonprogressive man—as anyone would know by looking at his outdated clothes and truck—but even he had caller ID.

Her heart raced as the phone rang a third time, then a fourth, and she was about to hang up when she heard the soft, gentle voice of a man she still loved.

"Hello, Martha."

"Hi, Arnold. How are you?"

"Still missing you."

Martha put a hand to her chest and closed her eyes as she pictured Arnold's kind face. The man made her want to be a better person, and he'd introduced her to the Lord, something she'd always be grateful for. "How's the weather there?"

"Chilly. But not as cold as in Colorado, I reckon."

There was silence for a moment, and Martha struggled to keep her voice in check as a tear rolled down her cheek. "Temperatures dropped last night. They say it will be mighty cold by Thanksgiving."

"What are your plans for the holiday?"

"Oh, I'll be with Katie Ann and Jonas. Probably at Lillian and Samuel's house. What about you?"

"My son's wife invited me to Thanksgiving at her folks' house, and a cousin of mine invited me, but . . ." He sighed. "I think I'll probably just stay home."

"Now, Arnold Becker, I've never known a man to love turkey as much as you do. It's not right for you not to have any on Thanksgiving." Martha realized that she was hinting toward an invitation and quickly backtracked. "But I guess it's your choice."

"How's your back?"

Arnold always asked about Martha's back, even though most of the time it was fine.

"Feeling pretty good." She dabbed at her eyes. "I have to go. I was just checking on you."

A long silence ensued, but Martha was choking back tears and afraid to speak. Finally Arnold did.

"I'm fine, Martha. As I said, I'm just missing you."

Well, if you cared about me half as much as I care about you, you wouldn't have stayed in Georgia. She'd wanted to say it a dozen times, but for reasons she wasn't sure of, she never did. "You take care, Arnold."

"You, too, Martha."

She hung up the phone as another tear rolled down her cheek. She clicked on the lamp on the table. Nightfall was settling in, and normally she would have been at Katie Ann's by now. She hated to miss a day with Katie Ann and Jonas, but Katie Ann would know something was wrong, and that girl had enough on her plate. She didn't need to be worrying about Martha.

And curiosity was nipping at her, making her wonder how Katie Ann's visit with that hussy Lucy had gone. Martha was still sure that Lucy had come calling for money.

KATIE ANN WATCHED Jonas sleep, her own eyelids growing heavy. She tucked his small quilt around him and made sure he was warm enough, then forced herself to leave his bedroom. She wondered if there would ever come a time when she wouldn't worry so much about him. God had taken Ivan away, and the thought of losing Jonas, too, was more than she could bear. All this fear and worry went against everything she'd been taught. She knew the only way to bring peace and calm was to believe in God's will, to pray about it. She was sure she couldn't trust another man the way she'd trusted Ivan, but had she stopped trusting the Lord as well?

In the living room, she lifted the lantern until a reflection lit the clock on the wall. Surely if there had been a problem at the doctor, Martha would have been at her house in an instant. Katie Ann would have showered her with sympathy, even though she suspected that Martha simply had a bad cold. Probably best that she didn't come over and expose Jonas. Martha went to bed early, so it was too late to call her, but Katie Ann decided to go out to the barn to see if she had left a message on the answering machine.

A light snow dusted her black coat as she walked across the yard. She pushed the barn door open, waking some of the residents. One of the pigs snorted as a chicken flapped across the space in front of her. But nestled in the corner on the quilt, Dash slept peacefully.

Katie Ann tiptoed to the workbench and shone the light from the lantern onto the answering machine. No messages. She leaned down, hoping to pet the sleek black cat. But as her hand drew near, the animal hissed, and within seconds he resembled a porcupine, every hair on his body standing straight up.

"It's okay, fellow. You can trust me." But the cat hissed again, cowered for a moment, then leapt underneath the workbench and around the corner where he'd retreated before. She reached into her pocket and pulled out some leftover scrapple she'd put in a plastic container, unsure if the cat would be interested in the cornmeal mush.

After giving each of the four horses a quick scratch on the nose, she made her way back to the house. She checked on Jonas, who was sleeping soundly. He was still having bouts with a gassy tummy, but Katie Ann had been practicing Eli's technique, which continued to work well. She carried the lantern back into the living room and placed it on the coffee table in front of her, then sat down on the couch with a book. It was so quiet, except for a coyote howling in the distance. After only a few minutes of reading, she felt fidgety, so she got up and put another log on the fire.

It was bizarre. Ivan always had a good business sense about him, and buying a new house before he sold the old one just didn't make any sense. She knew Martha would scold her for giving Lucy money, but someone had given Katie Ann money when she needed it the most, so it seemed the right thing to do. Or had she done it to ease her own conscience because she couldn't forgive Lucy, or Ivan? Was it her way of trying to get right with God? She wasn't sure, but she hoped that it was enough money to keep Lucy far away from Canaan.

LUCY SAT AT the airport, waiting for her flight to board. She kept thinking about Katie Ann's generosity, and she wondered whatever had made Ivan choose her over his wife. The woman seemed so unselfish and filled with goodness. Lucy, on the other hand, didn't think life could get any worse. She'd sunken lower than a snake by accepting Katie Ann's money, and the only man she'd ever loved was gone. Along with his money. It hadn't been a ton of money that he'd brought to the relationship, but it was substantially more than Lucy had ever had, and his contribution to their bank account had always given her a sense of security.

But Ivan had always loved to surprise her, like with the new car he'd bought her a few months ago. He had adapted well to his job in the outside world doing landscaping projects, saying it allowed him to keep a small part of his past, his love of the land. And the money had been good, but old habits die hard, and Lucy was always on edge about money.

She recalled the fight they'd had the night Ivan was killed in the accident. Lucy was concerned about their finances, and Ivan said that was all she cared about—money. The last thing he did when he left was to mumble something in Pennsylvania *Deitsch*, and Lucy had no idea what he'd said in his native dialect.

She rubbed her tired eyes for a moment as she wondered once again what Ivan's final words had been. She'd pushed him to get a divorce, but Ivan said he didn't believe in divorce, which Lucy found ironic since the man was sharing her bed.

Sometimes Ivan said one thing but did another. She knew he felt bad about their living arrangements, but he still insisted divorce from Katie Ann wasn't an option. He also said that he knew he'd failed in the eyes of God, that he missed his relationship with the Lord. Most of the time Lucy didn't understand his reasoning. She just knew she loved him.

Lucy stood up when people started to board the plane. She picked up her carry-on bag and edged toward them. A woman in front of her moved to the front of the line, since she was boarding with a small baby. Lucy touched her stomach with her free hand and wondered for the thousandth time what in the world she was going to do with a child.

Six

Eli asked the driver to wait while he went to get Katie Ann and Jonas. He was worried that Katie Ann would cancel because of the snow, but the driver had the car toasty warm, and Eli had an umbrella opened to protect them from the light flurries. Although he wasn't sure a trip to the sand dunes was the best plan. He'd wait until they were on the road to mention it and suggest an indoor outing instead.

Katie Ann opened the door a few seconds after he knocked, with Jonas bundled in her arms, a car seat at her feet, and a diaper bag over one shoulder. "We're ready," she said.

Eli was thrilled to hear excitement in her voice. And the woman looked absolutely beautiful. A faint alarm rang in his head, reminding him that they could be nothing more than friends, but he ignored it, picked up the car seat, and motioned Katie Ann ahead of him, holding the umbrella over her head.

"Careful down the steps," he said, latching onto her arm.

Once they had Jonas secure in the backseat, Eli offered to

sit there with him, but Katie Ann insisted on being close to the baby. So Eli sat in front with their driver, Wayne, an older man whom Vera had recommended. Vera said he was a regular driver for the few Amish in their small community.

The car hadn't even pulled out of the snow-covered driveway when Katie Ann spoke up. "Would you mind if we make a stop around the corner before we go to the sand dunes?"

Eli was surprised that she was still open to seeing the massive dunes with the weather as it was. He twisted his neck to face her. "*Ya*. Wayne can take you wherever you need to go."

"I want to check on my friend Martha." Katie Ann frowned. "She comes to see me and Jonas every day, and she didn't come last night." She hesitated. "And Martha had a doctor appointment yesterday."

Wayne reached the end of the driveway. "Which way to your friend's house?" The gray-haired man looked over his shoulder at Katie Ann.

Eli had liked the *Englisch* man right away. He was soft-spoken with a gentle smile.

"Turn right here," Katie Ann said. "Then it's the second right, and Martha's house is the third one on the left."

Wayne did as he was instructed, and in five minutes they pulled into Martha's driveway. It was snowing harder.

"If it's all right, I'll just leave Jonas in the car and run in to check on Martha." Katie Ann opened the car door after Eli nodded.

"What a beautiful woman," Wayne said as they watched Katie Ann walk up the sidewalk to Martha's front porch.

Eli cleared his throat. "*Ya*, she is." Stroking his beard, he kept his eyes on her.

KATIE ANN KNOCKED hard on the door until Martha finally answered in her pink housecoat and matching slippers. Her hair was atop her head in the butterfly clip.

"I'm just checking on you."

"Come in out of the cold." Martha grabbed her arm and pulled her across the threshold, then peered past her to the car in the driveway. "Who's that, and where's my baby?"

"Eli hired a driver. His name is Wayne, and Jonas is in the car. I only have a minute. I just wanted to hear what the doctor said. Do you just have a bad cold?"

Martha nodded. "Yes. Just a cold. I'm fine. Now you go play with that handsome Eli."

She grinned, but Katie Ann was not fooled. Martha was the first one to complain about the slightest ailment, and it was disturbing that she wasn't offering up much information.

"Did he give you some medicine? Is it the flu?"

Martha tugged Katie Ann toward the door. "Yeah, yeah. I've got medicine."

Katie Ann shook free of Martha's grip and squinted her eyes as she spoke. "Martha, are you not telling me something?"

"Oh, good grief. I'm fine, Katie Ann. Go and have fun today." Martha opened the door and pushed the screen wide as she stepped out on the porch in her robe. She cupped a hand above her brow and peered across the yard. "Although this weather isn't the best."

Katie Ann moved onto the covered porch, pulled her

black coat around her, and glanced up. "*Ya*. It's snowing even harder now."

Martha chuckled. "Good snuggling weather, I'd say."

Katie Ann narrowed her eyes at Martha. "What did I tell you? Eli and I agreed to be just friends."

"Whatever." Martha rolled her eyes, then her expression suddenly changed. "Hey, real quick. What did Lucy want? Money, huh?"

"I'll explain later."

"I knew it." Martha shook her head. "The tramp wanted money, and you probably gave her some."

"We'll talk about it later. I have to go." Katie Ann turned her back to Martha and eased down the porch steps. She glanced over her shoulder. "Stay out of the weather and get well."

"Katie Ann Stoltzfus!" Martha yelled, and Katie Ann cringed. "Did you give that woman money?"

Katie Ann raised her hand and waved Martha off as she neared the car.

"I knew it!" Martha yelled as Katie Ann opened the door and crawled back in.

She'd deal with Martha later. Today she was looking forward to seeing some sights in the San Luis Valley, although as it snowed harder she started to worry about having Jonas out in the cold.

"I'm afraid most of our sightseeing may have to be done from the car." Eli twisted in his seat and smiled.

He smiled a lot, and Katie Ann thought again about what Martha said, that the man was just happy. Katie Ann knew it couldn't hurt her to have a bright light in her world, and as Eli waited for her to answer, she wondered if she should have agreed to this outing. She reminded herself that a person can never have too many friends and that as long as she kept her relationship with Eli in perspective, all would be well.

"It's snowing harder," she said softly, wondering if he was going to cancel their outing.

"There's a diner about fifteen miles north of here," Wayne said. "If you folks are hungry, they have the best pancakes in the area. Maybe this snow will ease up while you're eating."

Katie Ann could see Wayne struggling to see through the flurries coming harder now. She waited for Eli to respond.

"I could go for some pancakes." Eli patted his stomach in the front seat before twisting around to face her. "Katie Ann, what about you?"

She'd eaten cereal that morning, but a cup of hot coffee sounded nice. "*Ya*. That's fine."

Jonas stretched in his seat, his eyes wide, but Katie Ann was glad that he appeared content. On the way to the diner, Eli questioned Wayne about the area . . . and about farming. Katie Ann had heard Samuel talk about the challenges of farming in Colorado, since the state only had a few months of frost-free weather. Wayne told Eli that he farmed a few acres just for his family.

"It's not so bad once you get used to the climate," the older man said.

Eli stroked his beard. "Lots of solar panels here, *ya*?"

Katie Ann nodded but quietly listened as Wayne answered.

"Yep. Since we have over three hundred days of sunshine on average per year, the solar panels make sense." He turned slightly to face Katie Ann and smiled. "And they are permissible for you folks."

Katie Ann had considered purchasing some of the solar panels for heating, but hadn't as of yet.

Wayne pulled into the diner. "I've got to go to the post office while we're near town, if that's all right with you. And I need to stop at the pharmacy to pick up something for the wife." He put the car in park. "So, okay if I'm back in about an hour? Maybe the snow will have eased up by then." He leaned his face closer to the windshield and looked up.

"That sounds fine." Eli opened his door, and before Katie Ann could climb out of the car, he already had Jonas's car seat out and was hurrying toward the diner entrance with the umbrella protectively shielding Jonas from the snow. Katie Ann hurried behind them.

Eli pushed the door open, got Jonas safely inside the warmth of the diner, and held the door for Katie Ann. "I'm sorry," he said softly. "I should have waited for you."

Katie Ann smiled. "No. I'm glad you didn't. You made sure my Jonas was warm and protected."

Eli's face reddened a bit as he pulled his eyes away from her. "Habit, I guess. Tending to the *kinner*."

A young waitress asked them to follow her to an empty booth toward the back of the diner. Eli got Jonas situated on one side of the booth, waited for Katie Ann to sit beside her son, and took a seat across from them.

After they scanned the menu, Eli ordered pancakes, and Katie Ann opted for coffee and a banana nut muffin. Then they slipped into a conversation with surprising ease, and Eli's infectious smile set the tone as he talked about his children and grandchildren.

"Did I tell you that Ida Mae has twin boys?" Eli raised a

brow. "Luke and Ben are almost a year old." He chuckled as he reached for his coffee. "Cutest little fellows in the world, but they're a handful, like most *kinner* that age. Luke is already walking, but Ben hasn't quite gotten there yet."

Katie Ann was mesmerized as she listened to him go on about his other grandchildren. It was so unusual for an Amish man to carry on this way, and she found it endearing. She felt so at ease with him, she even shared some of her fears about motherhood. Eli was polite and affirming, assuring her that she was a great mother.

"It's just wonderful the way you've raised your *kinner*." She paused, unintentionally locking eyes with him. "And very . . . touching, the way you talk about your grandchildren."

Eli kept his eyes fused with Katie Ann's. "The Lord saw fit to take Sarah, but He sure did bless me in other ways." He looked down for a moment and shook his head. "Believe me, there were many days when I didn't think I would make it. Days when I needed to work the fields, but two or three of the *kinner* would be sick and I couldn't leave them. Or there was the time when Jake toyed with the idea of leaving the community, and . . ." Eli took a deep breath. "I don't know what I would have done." Then he grinned. "Do you know what Frieda did when she was seven years old?" His hazel eyes grew round as his voice rose an octave.

Katie Ann smiled. "I'd love to hear."

"She cut her hair!"

Katie Ann brought a hand to her mouth in an unsuccessful attempt to stifle a laugh. If she hadn't felt the laughter all the way to the warm pit of her stomach, she might not have recognized it. It had been so long. "What did you do?"

Eli grunted. "What could I do? The damage was done." He chuckled. "She had a bob for a long time until her beautiful blond hair finally grew past her shoulders."

"Did she say why she did it?" Katie Ann leaned back a bit as the waitress arrived with their food.

Eli gave a nod of thanks as the young woman put his pancakes in front of him. "She said that it took too long to dry and that long hair was hot in the summertime."

"But surely she knew that it is not our way to cut our hair."

"*Ya*. She knew." He shook his head. "But that's my Frieda. Always thinking practical."

Katie Ann bit her bottom lip.

"Go ahead and laugh. I know it's a bit funny." Eli took a big bite of his pancakes. "Did I mention that she cut it about fifteen minutes before church service?"

Katie Ann put a hand to her chest, but a giggle escaped just the same. "Oh no."

"*Ach*, I've got about a thousand more stories I could share, but I don't want to bore you."

"I can't imagine getting bored hearing stories about your *kinner*." She glanced down at Jonas, who was sleeping soundly. "I'm sure Jonas will fill me with surprises. I can't wait."

"He will grow to be a fine boy."

Katie Ann circled the rim of her coffee cup with her finger. "I hope I'll be a *gut mudder*."

"You already are." Eli's voice was gentle, his eyes soft. "Jonas is blessed to have you."

As she added a pat of butter to her muffin, Katie Ann struggled to ignore the other thoughts fighting for space in her mind. Was it possible that Ivan had been coming back to her on the day he died, as Lucy thought? Would they have been a family again?

"You look a million miles away," Eli said after a few moments. "And I bet I know why."

Katie Ann picked at her muffin but didn't say anything. He reached across the table and put his hand on hers. She was too stunned to move.

"I know this isn't how you thought your life would unfold, but I know God has big plans for you. You're going to do just fine." He pulled back his hand, but Katie Ann could still feel his touch long afterward.

"I hope so," she finally whispered. Fearing the conversation was drifting to a place she didn't want to go, she decided to change the subject. "So tell me more about your plans to travel."

"I will still work hard. I won't be traveling all the time."

Katie Ann waited while he finished off his last bite of pancakes.

"I have cousins in Indiana, and I know folks who have traveled to Florida, so I think I'll start with those two places." He shrugged. "I haven't decided where else."

"Lots of folks in Lancaster County travel to Florida to vacation. They love spending time at the beach."

"Did you always live in Lancaster County before you moved here?" Eli laid his fork across his plate.

"*Ya*. But my folks aren't alive anymore. I don't really have family there, but I have Ivan's . . ." She glanced up at Eli. ". . . Ivan's family there. His sisters, Rebecca and Mary Ellen, live there with their families. And Ivan's brother Noah and his family live there."

"You don't have any *bruders* or sisters?"

She thought about Annie. "No."

"What made you move to Colorado?"

So many questions. She wasn't sure how much to share. "I guess you could say it was a fresh start for me and Ivan." She paused but avoided eye contact. "A fresh start that didn't work out." She finally looked up at him. "Did Vera or Elam tell you what happened?"

"*Ya.*" For the first time since they'd been at the diner, Eli frowned. "I can't imagine an Amish man shirking his duties."

She knew she should be embarrassed, but something about the warmth in his tone coaxed her to just accept the compliment. "*Danki* for saying that."

They were quiet for a few moments, then Katie Ann said, "The woman you saw at my house, Lucy, she is the one who . . ." She lowered her chin, surprised at how easily she revealed the information, but caught off guard by it too.

Eli folded his arms across the black coat he was still wearing. "Does she live here in Colorado?"

"No. She traveled from Paradise, Pennsylvania, to see me."

Eli's brows lifted, and Katie Ann surprised herself even more by telling Eli about most of her conversation with Lucy, except for the part about giving Lucy money.

"I see." Eli nodded. "And she's pregnant?"

"With Ivan's child."

"I think the woman had a lot of nerve to seek you out to ask about a *haus*." Eli accepted the bill when the waitress returned, and he quickly pulled cash from his pocket and placed it on the table. "Today it is my goal to make sure that your mind is not on anything to do with Ivan or Lucy. We are going to enjoy this day . . ." He strained to see out a nearby window. "Snow or no snow."

Katie Ann leaned to her left to see outside too. "Look, the sun is shining."

Eli nodded. "*Ya*. It will be a *gut* day."

Eli watched Katie Ann take Jonas with her to the ladies' room for a quick diaper change before they got back on the road. He couldn't believe how easy she was to talk to, or had he just gone so long without female companionship that he'd forgotten? She seemed like a good Amish woman, too, who deserved a husband and someone to take care of her and the *boppli*. Eli knew he'd need to tread carefully, always making it known that he only had friendship to offer her. It was dangerous territory for him because he was the type to nurture, no matter how uncharacteristic it was for an Amish man. He'd spent much of his life tending to the needs of others, and even at this point in his life it came naturally to him.

He sat a little taller, resolved that he had his life planned out and there was certainly no room for romance with a new mother, no matter how beautiful she was.

When Katie Ann returned, they glanced out the window and saw Wayne waiting in the car outside. The hour-long ride seemed to fly by as the three of them talked. Wayne shared the history of the Great Sand Dunes, and Eli was glad to see Katie Ann involved in the conversation, laughing and appearing to have a good time. He might not be able to take care of her the way she needed, but it gave him satisfaction to bring some joy into her life.

Before they reached the National Park and Preserve, they could see the majestic dunes nestled against the rugged Sangre de Cristo Mountains, and as Eli peeked over his shoulder, he saw the twinkle in Katie Ann's eyes as she peered through the window.

Wayne pulled into the entrance of the park. "Amazing, isn't it? These dunes are a landmark for travelers. Did you know they are the tallest dunes in North America? They cover nearly twenty thousand acres." He chuckled. "Just a little history for you."

Eli glanced at the massive dunes for as far as he could see, but his eyes kept veering back to Katie Ann. As her smile widened, her eyes glistened like the tiny specks of snow-covered sand that stretched before them, and Eli smiled along with her. She seemed so different from the first couple of times he was around her. She seemed happy, and her fulfillment sparked something inside of Eli that he hadn't felt in a long time.

He forced himself to look away from her and focus on the beauty of the mountains.

Then she leaned forward and touched his shoulder. "Look, Eli!" She pointed to her left, but Eli's eyes were on her hand on his shoulder. "There are two elk."

Eli glanced to where she was pointing. "*Big* elk," he said as his eyes drifted back to her hand. Her touch sent a thrill up his spine, and he was again reminded how long it had been since he'd been in the company of a beautiful woman. As his eyes trailed up to her lips, Eli pictured his mouth pressed tightly against hers, a vision that he suspected he would replay in his mind long after this day ended.

After about thirty minutes, they got back on the road.

Wayne explained more about the dunes. "You folks really should see them when the weather is better and they aren't covered in snow. Each time you climb over one of the dunes, there is another one waiting on the other side. They go on forever."

"They're beautiful, even covered in snow," Katie Ann said, keeping her eyes on the mountains as they pulled out of the park.

She was chatty all the way back to her house, talking about the garden she planned to have in the spring, the black bear she'd seen a couple of weeks ago out her window, and the repairs she needed to do on her house, most importantly a leak in her roof that Samuel had tried to repair twice without success. She mentioned several times how fortunate she was to have her brother-in-law and his wife living next door.

It was almost three o'clock when they pulled into her driveway, and little Jonas was beginning to fuss. Couldn't blame the poor fellow. He'd been cooped up for hours in the car, but he'd fared well, not even a whimper until now.

Eli opened the door, unhooked the car seat, and lifted Jonas out. He met Katie Ann on her front porch and waited for her to open her front door. Once she was inside, he handed the carrier to her, wanting more than anything to step inside. He waited, but she merely thanked him for a wonderful time.

"Why don't I have a look at that leak in your roof? I'm a pretty good carpenter."

Katie Ann peered over Eli's shoulder. "Wayne is waiting for you. Besides, I can't let you do that. I'm sure Samuel will have another look at it."

"Do you have any tools?"

She nodded. "*Ya*, a few, but . . ."

"If I send Wayne home, I can walk to Vera and Elam's *haus* from here." He pushed back the rim of his hat. "And I'm willing to have a look at your roof in exchange for a hot cup of *kaffi*."

She tapped her finger to her chin, grinning. "Hmm . . . I do need to get it repaired before the next storm." She nodded. "All right."

Eli shuffled down the porch steps to the car. He quickly paid Wayne, thanked the man, then started back to the house. He stopped and looked up at the roof, causing a burst of adrenaline to shoot through him. In truth, he preferred to keep his feet on solid ground.

Katie Ann had left the door cracked, so he walked in. She wasn't anywhere in sight, so he busied himself by starting a fire. She walked in a few minutes later.

"Jonas went back to sleep. Hasn't he been a *gut boppli* today?" She folded her hands in front of her, eyes glowing.

"*Ya*. He's like Maureen." He added another log to the fireplace. "Maureen was happiest when I had to hire a driver to take us somewhere."

As he built the fire and finally got it lit, he thought about Katie Ann having to do this by herself every day. "Why don't you invest in some solar panels for heat?"

"I've thought about it." She shrugged. "I guess I just haven't gotten around to it."

Eli blew underneath the logs until a small flame caught onto the wood. "What about in Jonas's room? Is he warm enough in there?"

"I have a small battery-operated heater that I keep in there, plus once the fire is going, it heats this small *haus* nicely."

After Eli got the fire going strong, he shed his coat and hat, and Katie Ann quickly took them from him and hung them on the rack by the door. He glanced at the clock and realized he'd better have a look at her leak and see if he could get it repaired before dark, or he'd be walking to his cousins' house in freezing temperatures.

"Where's your leak?"

Katie Ann motioned for him to follow, talking as she walked. "You really don't need to bother with this. I should have declined the offer . . ."

Eli pretended to be listening by giving her an occasional nod, but his eyes roamed around her bedroom. A queen-sized oak bed topped with a yellow and blue quilt took up most of the space in the small room, and there was a fragrance in the air teasing his senses, lavender perhaps. On the nightstand, several books were piled next to a lantern, along with a pair of gold-rimmed reading glasses and a box of tissues. It felt intimate, being in her bedroom.

He crossed the room to where she was standing, her arm stretched and pointing to the ceiling. Maybe it was the dim natural light coming through the window, the floral scent wafting through the room, or the way her mouth moved when she spoke, but Eli closed the space between them until he was standing a few inches from her. He touched her cheek with the back of his fingers, fully expecting her to step back. But she didn't. And as their eyes locked and held, Eli knew what was coming, and he was helpless to stop himself.

Seven

Katie Ann was paralyzed by the feel of Eli's touch, and any rational thoughts she had about how inappropriate this was left her when he leaned in and kissed her. As he cupped her cheek, his mouth lingered on hers with more intimacy than she could recall ever having with Ivan, but even as her body reacted to his touch, it was still Ivan's face that flashed before her, and she reminded herself that this man was not her husband. She eased away.

"I know I'm supposed to say I'm sorry, Katie Ann." Eli put his hands on his hips and stared at the floor for a moment, then looked back up at her. "But I'm not."

"I think you'd best leave." Katie Ann walked out of her bedroom, and Eli followed. She pulled his coat and hat from the rack and handed them to him. "*Danki* for a lovely time sightseeing, but I think I'll have Samuel look at the leak on another day."

Eli didn't take the items. "No, Katie Ann. Don't do this. I like you, and I want us to be friends, so let's talk about what just happened."

She could feel her cheeks reddening, embarrassed about

her own desires and wondering if he noticed how she trembled when his lips were pressed against hers. "I don't want to talk about it." She pushed the coat and hat forward until they hit his chest and he was forced to take them.

He locked eyes with her. "I guess I *am* sorry. If this is going to keep us from being friends, then I regret my actions."

Katie Ann put a hand to her forehead, not wanting to look at him, but not wanting him to leave either. He gently cupped her chin and raised her face.

"I'm sorry. I really would like to fix your leaky roof." He smiled. "But maybe you'd better stay in the living room."

The way he said it caused Katie Ann to smile.

"Okay, *gut*. A smile. All is not lost." He hung his hat and coat back on the rack, then pointed a finger at her. "Now you stay here. Don't even think about coming into the kissing room . . ." He let out an exaggerated gasp. "I mean bedroom."

He gave his head a quick shake as he walked across the living room and toward her bedroom, and she put a hand over her mouth to stifle a grin. He wasn't just handsome, caring, and nurturing . . . he was funny too. Strangely enough, she began to feel a bit more at ease.

"I'll make us some *kaffi*," she said as she walked toward the kitchen. She filled the percolator, the kiss playing over and over in her mind. But with each recollection, the image seemed to transform itself from Eli to Ivan, then back again. She should never have let it happen.

Eli walked into the kitchen. "I can see where Samuel repaired the area, but I'm going to need to get up on the roof to figure out why it's still leaking. When is a *gut* time for me to come back tomorrow?"

"I appreciate the offer, and if it had been something simple to repair today, I would have been grateful, but I can't let you come back and start on a project like this." She raised an eyebrow. "You have sightseeing to do, remember?"

Eli waved a hand. "Plenty of time for that. What if a storm comes?"

"I'll put a bucket under the leak, as I have done in the past."

Eli pointed to the living room. "*Kaffi* by the fire?"

Katie Ann noticed him shivering. He must be finding the Colorado weather awfully cold. "All right."

She followed him to the living room, thinking how inappropriate this would be if they were not grown adults. Then she found humor in that thought. As a teenager, she never would have kissed a boy in her bedroom, and yet as an adult, she'd let it happen. She sat in the rocking chair, and Eli sat on the couch across from her.

"So how long will you be staying in Colorado?" she asked.

"Until next Tuesday. Another week. I want to be home for Thanksgiving." He stroked his beard for a moment. "Who will you spend Thanksgiving with?"

"Lillian and Samuel are having Thanksgiving, and Vera, Elam, and all their children will be there, and of course the newlyweds, David and Emily. And Martha." She took a sip of coffee. "I'll be making sweet potatoes and bringing the butter bread."

"Sweet potatoes are my favorite food at Thanksgiving."

"Really? So will one of your daughters prepare them?"

"Hannah. My oldest *dochder*. She's made them every year for as long as I can remember." Eli paused, took a deep breath. "And I hope that Hannah will be making our family sweet potatoes for many, many more years to come."

Something about the way he made the comment left Katie Ann unsure what to say, so she waited.

"Hannah had breast cancer last year." Then he smiled. "But *mei* girl is a fighter, and she beat it. She's doing very *gut* now."

Eli's love for his children shone in everything he said.

"I will pray for Hannah," Katie Ann said. "I'll include her in my daily devotions and pray for continued *gut* health."

Thinking about illness made her think about Martha, and she wondered if her friend would be coming over this evening. Katie Ann hoped so. She didn't believe Martha had been entirely truthful with her about her doctor appointment.

"*Danki*, Katie Ann." Eli stood up, and so did Katie Ann. "I haven't had a lot of time over the years to have any really close friends. I mean, I've always had *mei kinner*, but now that I have some time, I'd like to have some adult relationships." He stepped closer to her but kept a safe distance. "Please don't let one kiss keep us from being friends. I haven't kissed another woman since my wife. I don't know what got into me . . ." He lowered his gaze and took a deep breath.

Katie Ann was equally as concerned about what had gotten into her. She'd not only allowed it—she'd kissed him back. She started toward the door, and Eli followed. "I think you're going to regret taking on this project. Samuel tried twice, and it still leaks."

Eli stroked his beard. "You're probably right."

Katie Ann's eyes rounded. She hadn't expected him to agree so easily.

"You should probably cook me supper, no?"

She crossed her arms across her chest. "Hmm . . . I might

be able to do that." She grinned. "Martha might be here. She's here most nights."

"*Gut.* A chaperone." He winked, then headed out the door.

Katie Ann watched him walk into a light flurry of snow, glad it wasn't a far walk to Vera and Elam's house. She closed the door, leaned her back against it, and couldn't help but smile. She was mourning her husband, and Eli had big plans for the second half of his life. But her new friend was a big distraction from everything else on her plate. And she was looking forward to cooking for him tomorrow night.

ELI FOUGHT THE chill in the air on the way back to his cousins' house. He stuffed his hands in the pockets of his long black coat and gazed to the east at the Sangre de Cristo Mountains, then to the west at the San Juan Mountains. He knew from his research about the area that Sangre de Cristo meant "blood of Christ," and as the sun eased below the horizon, he could see how the mountain range got its name, as an orange glow could be seen on the opposite horizon. The phenomenon was known as an alpenglow, he had read, and it was an amazing sight.

He replayed the kiss with Katie Ann over in his mind, leaving him feeling both elated and like a heel. A woman like Katie Ann needed a husband and father for Jonas, and Eli knew he was not that man. Kissing her was wrong on several levels, and he would make sure it never happened again. But there was no mistaking the fact that she had kissed him back . . . and that thought was going to keep him up at night.

"Whoso findeth a wife findeth a good thing, and obtaineth favour of the Lord."

The scripture had come into Eli's mind many times over the past seventeen years, and he often wondered if he was failing God by not remarrying. But it seemed like betrayal—to Sarah. Perhaps it was God he was betraying.

Once again he questioned the path he'd chosen for himself—one filled with travel and less responsibility.

As he rounded the corner to Elam's house, he knew he was going to face a lot of questions from his cousins about his outing. He could see Vera sweeping snow from the front porch as he grew closer.

"How was your day, Eli?" She sent him an all-knowing grin as she pushed the fluffy powder from the porch with her broom.

"It was a *gut* day. The sand dunes were a sight to see." He walked up the freshly swept steps.

Vera stopped sweeping and put her hand on her hip. "And Katie Ann? Did you enjoy her company?"

Eli thought about the kiss. "*Ya*. Very much."

Vera's face lit with a smile. "Wonderful!"

He could see where this was going, and as much as he'd like to please his cousins, it probably wasn't right not to be honest with them. "I suspect Katie Ann and I will be *gut* friends." He eased closer to his cousin's wife, lowered his gaze, and spoke firmly. "But nothing more."

Vera scowled. "You never know, Eli."

"*Ya*. I do know, Vera. Katie Ann is lovely, but she is a new *mudder*, and I've already done all that. I'm not going back there." He waited for her to absorb what he was saying. "It might sound selfish, but I have a plan for the rest of my life, things I want to see and do. So I don't want you to be thinking there will be a romance with me and Katie Ann."

Guilt pinched at Eli's heart as he wondered again if he was failing God.

Vera smiled. "Well, you just go ahead and make all the plans you want to. Sometimes God has His own plans in the works." Then she winked at him and moved into the house.

Eli shook his head. Katie Ann deserved someone committed to the idea of marriage, not a man committed to his own pursuits. Then he thought about fixing Katie Ann's leak tomorrow afternoon and having supper with her afterward. There was absolutely no reason why he and Katie Ann couldn't be friends.

MARTHA PARKED HER car in front of Katie Ann's house, then clopped across the snow, scowling. She was going to have to tell her friend about her surgery that was now scheduled for the week after Thanksgiving—in case she didn't survive. She tucked the envelope closer to her chest as she moved up the steps.

"I was hoping I'd see you tonight." Katie Ann was holding Jonas when she opened the door. Martha fought tears as she thought about not being able to see that little bundle grow into a man.

"I don't like to miss a meal. What are we having?" Martha dropped her coat on the rack, glad to see there was a good fire going.

"Meatloaf."

Martha sighed. It wasn't her favorite, but it was food. "I'm not contagious, so let me have my precious baby."

Katie Ann handed Jonas to her. "I made you some creamed celery. I'll just go finish up in the kitchen."

Creamed celery. Thank goodness. *The meal has been saved.* She sat on the couch with Jonas and leaned down and kissed him on the cheek. "I love you so much, my little man." She dabbed at one eye, determined not to cry in front of Katie Ann. Her friend was going to take the news hard. "You always take care of your mama, you hear?"

Martha leaned against the back of the couch and pulled Jonas up on her chest. She loved the way the baby smelled, a combination of powder and Katie Ann's homemade lavender soap. She held him close until Katie Ann walked back into the room.

"Supper's ready."

Martha did her best to eat Katie Ann's meal, but her stomach was a mess. She'd wait until a bit later to talk to her friend. "How was your day with Eli?"

"It was nice. We saw the sand dunes, and they were amazing."

Katie Ann's smile told Martha how much she liked this Eli Detweiler. Martha grinned as she swallowed a spoonful of creamed celery.

"Don't give me that look."

"What look?"

"The one on your face. There will be no romance between me and Eli."

"You are the one who is always telling me that God has His own plan, so don't go planning your future just yet." She pointed her fork at Katie Ann. "Now you tell me the truth, Katie Ann . . . Did you give Lucy Turner money?"

Katie Ann pulled her eyes from Martha's and sighed. "It is none of your concern."

Martha wanted to tell her that it was her business. She'd

given Vera a box of money last year and told the woman to find someone who could use it. That was before Martha knew Katie Ann very well. Martha was glad that the money ultimately ended up with Katie Ann, but she sure didn't want that trampy Lucy to have any of it.

"I knew you'd give her money," Martha said before taking another bite of celery. "How much?"

"It doesn't matter. Just enough for her to get by."

Martha shook her head, then listened as Katie Ann told her a bizarre story about a house that Lucy thought Ivan bought. On another day Martha would have voiced her opinion about all of this much louder, but today her thoughts were on something else. She waited until they were having coffee in the living room.

"What's wrong, Martha?" Katie Ann held Jonas on her lap, rubbing his tummy the way Eli had shown her. Martha knew that she'd be praying every day she had left that Eli would step up to the plate and take care of Katie Ann and Jonas.

"I'm sick."

Katie Ann looked up at her with fearful eyes. "What did the doctor say?"

"My cold was just a cold, but when they x-rayed my lungs, they found something else. I've got a tumor the size of a grapefruit in my belly." She rolled her eyes. "And all this time, I just thought I was fat."

Katie Ann put Jonas in his carrier, then edged closer to Martha with tears in her eyes.

Martha latched onto Katie Ann's hand. "Now don't you go falling apart." Martha swiped at a tear that rolled down her own cheek. "Argh! I was determined not to cry."

"Tell me what the doctor said." Katie Ann pinched her trembling lips together.

"Well, apparently, the thing has to come out. I'm a goner for sure if I don't have the operation. So that dumb doctor over in Alamosa referred me to a surgeon. That's who I met with yesterday, and I'm having the surgery the week after Thanksgiving." Now here was the hard part. "I likely won't survive."

Katie Ann pulled her hand from Martha's and slapped it over her mouth.

"It doesn't look good." Martha shook her head. "And I'm so sorry to have to tell you this." She reached for the envelope. "Here's everything you'll need to know about my business. I've left everything to you."

"I don't need that envelope," Katie Ann said as she blinked back tears. "Because you are going to be just fine."

Martha shrugged. "Maybe. But I doubt it." She dropped the large manila envelope in Katie Ann's lap. "So you just keep this." She patted Katie Ann on the leg. "Now, now . . . no tears. You and Arnold introduced me to the Lord, and I'm in pretty good standing with Him, so I know where I'm going."

"Don't talk like that." Katie Ann sniffled. "Have you told Arnold?"

Martha pointed a finger at her friend. "No, I haven't. And don't you tell him either. He'd feel obligated to come, and I don't want that. If the man loved me enough, he would have already moved here to be with me."

Katie Ann blew her nose, which was as red as Martha's fingernail polish. "That's not true. Arnold just said he wanted to get to know his relatives again. He's invited you there several times and asked if he could come here. You always say no."

"Because saying good-bye is just too hard." She raised her chin. "I don't want to talk about Arnold." She cut her eyes at Katie Ann. "But you'd better not tell him about my diagnosis or I will be very upset with you."

"I think he needs to know."

"Katie Ann, do you hear me?" Martha raised her voice.

"*Ya.*"

They were quiet for a few moments. Then Katie Ann reached for Martha's hand and squeezed. "I will be there with you for everything."

Martha returned the squeeze. "I wouldn't have it any other way."

They were quiet again, and Katie Ann fought tears. She knew she needed to be strong for Martha. In the past, Martha had been a hypochondriac, but Katie Ann always knew that her friend just sought attention and love. But this was different. If she was having surgery, her condition was serious, and the thought of anything happening to Martha terrified her.

"Eli is coming to fix my roof tomorrow night," she finally said.

Martha smiled as she leaned over and pulled Jonas from his carrier. "Is he now?"

"Don't presume anything, but I am making supper for him for his efforts."

Martha rocked Jonas as she spoke. "Well, I'm not coming for supper tomorrow night, so the two of you can have some time alone together."

Images of the kiss flashed through Katie Ann's mind. "No, Martha. You *must* come."

"No."

"But . . . I need you here. You're here most nights for supper, and especially tomorrow night—"

"No. I'm not coming. I'm sick, Katie Ann. I can't come over here every single night."

Katie Ann frowned. "Are you sure you're not just saying that so that I'll be forced to be alone with Eli?"

Martha handed Jonas to Katie Ann and shook her head. "It's not all about you right now, Katie Ann. It's about me. I'm sick."

"Of course, I know that." Katie Ann elbowed her gently. "But how do you know you'll feel bad tomorrow night?"

"Because I feel bad now." Martha let out a heavy sigh. "Meatloaf is not my favorite. Gives me gas." She turned to Katie Ann. "You know that, and I don't know why you still make it."

Katie Ann cradled Jonas as she followed Martha to the door. She waited until she pulled her coat on to give her a sideways hug so she didn't squash Jonas. "I love you, Martha. And I know everything is going to be fine."

"I love you too. I guess all we can do is pray."

Katie Ann watched Martha leave, knowing that praying wasn't all she would do. First thing in the morning, there was something else she was going to do. Whether Martha liked it or not.

Eight

KATIE ANN VISITED LILLIAN WEDNESDAY MORNING and told her the news about Martha.

"Can you watch Jonas for a few minutes while I go to the barn and make a phone call?" she asked. She felt inside her apron pocket to make sure she'd brought the number.

"Of course. And you're doing the right thing."

"I'll be right back." She buttoned her long black coat and stepped outside, expecting a burst of cool air, but just in the hour since she'd been at Lillian's, the sun had peeked over the mountains and tricked their part of the world into thinking it was warmer than it really was.

She traipsed across the snow to the barn, knowing Martha would be furious with her.

"Hello, Dash," she said quietly, pleased to see the cat curled atop the quilt. He opened his green eyes and squinted in her direction. She moved slowly, picking up the empty container she'd left on her prior visit. "You must like scrapple after all, no?" She stood up, surprised Dash hadn't held to his name and sprinted around the corner. She squatted down and eased a bit closer. The cat's ears went back, and his tail took the shape of a bottle brush. "It's all right, boy."

She leaned closer, earning a small hiss from her new friend, and noticed Dash's protruding belly. "Oh my. I guess I will have to call you *Mrs.* Dash." Katie Ann reached out her hand. "When are you due, little mama?"

Mrs. Dash made her escape faster than in the past, disappearing around the corner. Katie Ann suddenly wondered if there was a Mr. Dash anywhere.

It's hard to raise kinner *on your own, girl.*

She made her way to the phone on Samuel's workbench and dialed Arnold's number. He answered on the second ring.

"Hello, Arnold. This is Katie Ann Stoltzfus calling."

"Is Martha all right?" he asked at once.

Katie Ann could hear the concern in his voice. "*Ya*, she's fine, Arnold." She paused. "But . . . she's . . . well, she's going to be having some surgery soon, and I thought you would want to know."

"I'll come right now. Thank you, Katie Ann."

"Wait . . . I mean, maybe you should wait until the week after Thanksgiving."

Katie Ann smiled at Arnold's reaction. She'd prayed hard about whether or not to tell him, despite Martha's wishes, but she felt called to let him know. She knew he still loved Martha.

"She's having the surgery the week after Thanksgiving. I can call you when I know the details."

"What's wrong with my Martha, Katie Ann? How serious is it?"

Katie Ann took a deep breath and blinked back tears. "I think it's serious. She has a tumor in her stomach that has to be removed."

"Oh no. Oh no."

Katie Ann could hear the elderly man's voice breaking up.

"But let's don't worry too much just yet. You know Martha. She's as tough as they come, and I'm sure everything will be fine."

"Please call me the minute the surgery is scheduled. Are you sure I shouldn't come now to be with her?"

"No." Katie Ann brought a hand to her chest. "Actually, Martha doesn't even know I'm calling you. She would be very angry with me. I don't think she wants to worry you."

"I've begged her to let me come visit her, or for her to come here. Surely that woman knows how much I love her."

Katie Ann wasn't sure if it was her place to comment, but she'd been as curious as Martha about why Arnold hadn't moved back here. "I think, Arnold, that since you made a decision to stay in Georgia . . . well . . ."

"I had to stay. At least for a while. It's a long story. But I will be there as soon as you tell me to be."

Katie Ann smiled. "I know you will. Have a wonderful Thanksgiving next week, Arnold. And I will call you back as soon as I have the details."

After she hung up the phone, she peeked around the corner. No Mrs. Dash. She reached into her pocket and left some scraps of bacon in the container, then went back to Lillian's. She'd never wanted to tell anyone anything as badly as she wanted to tell Lillian about Eli's kiss, but she knew she couldn't. It was inappropriate, and she was much too embarrassed. But she did tell her that Eli was coming to repair her roof and that she was making supper for him.

Lillian stomped a foot before she went to the sink to wash her hands. "I told Samuel that he needed to go back and fix that roof correctly!" She joined Katie Ann at the kitchen table and grinned. "But I guess it's a *gut* thing he never got around to it."

"No matchmaking, Lillian."

Lillian pouted. "Why not? He's perfect for you."

"No. He's not. And I'm even less perfect for him. Eli has big plans to travel and do all the things he couldn't do while he was raising six *kinner* on his own." She picked up Jonas's carrier. "I'm heading home. I have much cleaning to do. *Danki* for watching Jonas."

"I love watching the *boppli*." Lillian snapped her finger. "*Ach*, I've been meaning to ask you—have you seen a big black cat in the barn lately? That thing scared the daylights out of me the other day when I went to collect eggs."

"You mean Mrs. Dash." Katie Ann grinned.

"Mrs. Dash?" Lillian frowned. "You've named that poor animal after a spice?"

Katie Ann shifted Jonas's carrier from one hand to the other. "A spice? What do you mean?"

Lillian walked to the kitchen cabinet, pulled out a yellow container, and pointed to the name. "Mrs. Dash is a combination of different spices."

Laughing, Katie Ann said, "Why do you buy those store-bought spices when you can get fresh herbs at the market in Alamosa?"

"This is easier."

"No matter. Next year I think we should have our own herb garden."

Ignoring the comment, Lillian cocked her head to one side. "That cat is solid black. Bad luck." She crinkled her nose as she shook her head. "Don't let it run across your path." She pointed to Jonas. "And don't let it near Jonas. I already told the girls not to go near it. It hisses and balls itself up like a porcupine! And he—or *she*—is big!"

Katie Ann knew most of her people were superstitious, a part of their upbringing that had clearly rubbed off on Lillian. "That's rubbish," she said. "Mrs. Dash isn't bad luck. And she's big because she's pregnant."

"Oh." Lillian twisted her mouth from one side to the other. "Hmm . . . maybe that's why she's so skittish."

"Maybe." Katie Ann walked toward the door as Lillian followed.

"What did Arnold say? How did he take the news about Martha?"

Katie Ann smiled. "He was ready to leave right this very minute to come and be with her. I told him to wait until the week of the surgery, after Thanksgiving." She cringed. "Martha is going to be so mad at me."

Lillian put her hand on Katie Ann's shoulder. "Martha gets mad about a lot of things, but you were right to call Arnold. I'm glad he's coming."

IT WAS TWO o'clock in the afternoon when Eli loaded up his cousin's buggy with tools and headed to Katie Ann's. When he pulled up the driveway, she was carrying firewood from the barn to the house.

Eli hurried from the buggy and tethered the horse. "Wait! Let me help you with that." He ran toward her and pulled three small logs from her arms. "You should have waited for me to get here."

"Eli Detweiler, I am perfectly capable of carrying a few logs." She turned his way and smiled. "But *danki*."

Once inside, Eli placed the logs in the carrier by the fireplace. Katie Ann already had a small fire going. "It smells *gut* in here," he said.

"I'm slow-cooking a stew."

"Well, I'd better get to work then. Elam sent along just about every tool he had, along with some extra shingles he had left over from when they reroofed their house last year, so I'm sure I can get your leak fixed. I just need a ladder."

"In the barn. Do you need anything else?"

He took a deep breath and lied. "No, I'm all set."

What he needed was a quick cure for fear of heights. Thankfully, his oldest son didn't suffer from the same affliction, and from the time Jake was ten years old, Eli had given him all the chores that required climbing, especially on the roof. Jake loved being the one to clean the gutters. It practically made Eli break out in hives.

But here he was. And up the ladder he would go. For Katie Ann.

"See you shortly."

Eli propped the ladder against the house and thanked the Lord that it was only a one-story home. He eased up the steps and prayed that he could make any repairs from the ladder, without actually crawling onto the roof. Two rungs from the top, and he could already feel his legs shaking. He scanned the area and saw the loose shingles. Shaking his head, he took one more step up and realized that he was going to have to climb up on top of the roof to be able to get to the problem area. Most of the snow had melted from the afternoon sun. He slung Elam's box full of tools onto the roof, along with a few shingles he had tucked under his arm.

As luck would have it, the shingles slid right off the roof. He started his descent back down the ladder, sighing. *This had better be the best stew I ever had.*

KATIE ANN TOOK a bite of stew, closed her eyes, and savored the taste of the seasoned beef, carrots, and potatoes. "I wish you were old enough to try this, Jonas." She took another sampling before putting the lid back on the pot.

She pulled a loaf of bread from the oven and began to set the table with chow-chow, butter, and several jars of jam. She couldn't stop thinking about Martha and wished her friend would join them for supper.

Sunshine poured through her window in the kitchen and bounced off her shiny wood floors that she'd cleaned earlier in the day. She could still smell a hint of ammonia, but mostly she smelled stew and burning cedar in the fireplace. Everything was ready, so she picked up Jonas and laid him in the playpen in the living room so she could keep an eye on him while she and Eli ate. She expected him to fall asleep soon since she'd just nursed him.

She could see the ladder propped up against the house from her window in the living room, and while she'd been cooking, she'd heard activity on the roof. As she walked closer to the window, she looked up and saw Eli working, so she went back to the kitchen. She'd just set the table with her best china and laid out napkins when she heard a thud. Followed by a groan. Gasping, she feared the worst as she ran through the living room and bolted out the door.

Sure enough, Eli was sprawled out on his back in the snow, and he wasn't moving. Katie Ann got to him as fast as she could and leaned down over him as her heart beat out of her chest. He crinkled his forehead and slowly opened his eyes.

"*Ach*, thank goodness you're not dead." Katie Ann cringed as she realized what she'd said.

"*Ya*. Thank goodness." Eli laughed but quickly moaned, closing his eyes again.

"Should I go call for help?" She touched his shoulder but pulled back when he clamped his eyes closed and groaned again. "How badly are you hurt?"

"I don't know yet. I'm afraid to move. I guess I lost my footing."

"I'm going to go get Samuel." Katie Ann started to stand up, but Eli opened his eyes and grabbed her arm. He eased her back down.

"Please don't. I'm embarrassed enough." He slowly sat up, and Katie Ann was horrified to see blood in the snow where his head had been.

"You're hurt." She reached up and gently twisted his head so she could try to inspect his wound. "I think we'd better get you to a hospital."

"Really? Because I'd rather not." He bent his legs, propped one arm against the ground, and tried to stand up, but lost his balance.

Katie Ann put an arm around him. "Here, let me help you."

"I should fall off the roof more often." Eli leaned into her and smiled.

"You will not be getting back on my roof."

"Don't need to. It's fixed." He glanced upward. "Although Elam's toolbox is still up there."

"We'll get it later. Let's get you into the *haus* so I can have a look at your head."

Katie Ann knew that she shouldn't be thinking about the way Eli's arm was draped around her shoulder, or the way that her arm was around his waist. She got him situated on the couch, checked on Jonas in his playpen, and hurried to the kitchen for a wet rag. When she got back, Eli was standing in the middle of the room.

"I was dripping blood on your couch." He lost his footing, and Katie Ann was afraid he was going to fall over.

"I don't care about that. Sit down." She helped him back to the couch and began dabbing at the back of his head. "You must have hit a small rock or something. There's a jagged little cut, and I really think you need some stitches."

"Can't you just put a butterfly bandage on it?"

Katie Ann smiled at his sad, puppy-dog eyes. "Eli Detweiler, are you afraid of a few stitches?"

"No. I'm *hungry*." He drew in a long deep breath. "I've been dreaming about that stew the whole time I was working."

"Well, all right. I'll be right back with my first aid kit, and I'll bandage you up as best I can."

"Maybe some aspirin too?"

Katie Ann nodded as she headed down the hall to the bathroom. She quickly found some bandages, antibiotic ointment, and aspirin in the medicine cabinet. After getting a glass of water, she gave him the aspirin and got to work doctoring his head. It seemed much too intimate to be running her hands in his hair to clear the area for the bandage.

"I still think you need to have a doctor look at it." Katie Ann stood up.

"*Danki*, Nurse Katie Ann. But I feel *gut* as new." He rose from the couch. Slowly. He grabbed his back as he straightened. "Okay, maybe not exactly *gut* as new." He grinned. "But still hungry."

"Come, come." She motioned with her hand for him to follow her to the kitchen.

After they both prayed silently, they ate with little conversation. Eli helped himself to some butter bread and finished three bowls of stew, commenting several times about how much he liked it. Katie Ann was pleased that he enjoyed her cooking. Ivan had rarely said anything about her meals, especially the last few years. It was nice to have a man enjoying her efforts.

Katie Ann brought coffee into the living room while Eli stoked the fire. As darkness set in, she lit the two lanterns in her living room and one by the front door. Jonas started to fuss in his playpen, but before she could go to him, Eli had picked up the baby and settled back on the couch with Jonas in his lap. Katie Ann sat down beside him.

Eli looked up at her. "How's his tummy been?"

"Much better. If he doesn't have a hearty burp after his feeding, I rub his tummy, and that seems to solve the problem. He's sleeping much better during the night." She smiled. "And so am I."

Eli let out a quiet moan.

"I bet *you* won't sleep well tonight, though. I'm so sorry that happened, Eli."

"Me too." He chuckled. "I'm feeling a little stiff. But . . . all worth it to have that stew. Katie Ann, that was mighty *gut*. Some of the best I've had."

Katie Ann tucked her chin, feeling her face heat up. "*Danki*. I was happy to cook it for you." She looked back up to see him gazing into her eyes, and a faint alarm went off, but she knew she wasn't going to ask him to leave. As much as she loved Martha's company in the evenings, it was nice to have a man in her home, sharing a meal and conversation.

For the next four hours Katie Ann sat on one end of the couch, facing Eli who was at the other end. Jonas was in between them, sleeping soundly on a blanket. As the fire crackled and lit the room, Katie Ann watched the shadows dance across Eli's face as he talked about his childhood, his teenage years, and how he met Sarah.

"I was with her when she took her last breath, and the last thing she said to me before she died was that I should find a new *mudder* for the *kinner* right away." Eli blinked several times and avoided Katie Ann's eyes. "I failed her." After a few moments, he looked back up at her. "I know it's our way to remarry as soon as a spouse passes, but I just couldn't. Sarah was my everything, and replacing her just seemed so . . . so wrong." He leaned back against the couch. "I didn't even really try. I mean, everyone in the community was trying to fix me up with someone, but I just wasn't interested. And not only that, I didn't have time for dating. I had six *kinner*."

"It must have been so hard for you." Katie Ann couldn't

remember having such a deep conversation with Ivan. Ever. This was nice.

"Looking back, I should have tried harder. I'm sure Sarah was right. It would have been better for the *kinner* to have had a *mudder*, and it was selfish of me not to have tried harder to find them one." He took a sip of his coffee. "There were babysitters and family members who helped, but I was young, and I thought I could do everything myself. Prove to Sarah that I didn't need anyone else." He put his coffee on the coffee table, then reached over and touched her hand. "I'm sorry. I've mostly been talking about me. Tell me about you."

Katie Ann told Eli about her childhood . . . and even told him about Annie. "*Mei* sister was only four months old when she just went to sleep and didn't wake up."

Eli's eyes never left hers as she spoke, and even though he didn't seem to have any words for her loss, his eyes blinked with sadness and compassion. She also told him how she and Ivan tried for years to have a baby, but she skimmed quickly over the part about Lucy and how Ivan eventually left her.

"That must have been so hard for you."

She wasn't sure if Eli meant when Ivan left or when he died. In some ways, it was as if he died the day he walked out the door.

It had been a surprisingly good evening. They'd taken turns getting coffee refills and even shared a piece of shoofly pie. But it was getting late. She glanced at the clock as she stifled a yawn.

"I saw that." Eli grinned. "I remember how it is to have a little one. You're probably already thinking about how many times you will be getting up with him during the night. I'm going to go. It's almost nine o'clock."

Katie Ann stood up, tired, but not anxious for him to leave. "I've enjoyed tonight."

"Me too."

She followed him to the door and waited as he got bundled up. "I'm sure Elam and Vera have a heavy blanket in the buggy. You'll need it." She handed him his hat. "How is your head? And your back?"

He grimaced a bit as he put his hat on. "I might be a little sore, but I'll think of you fondly." He laughed before he leaned down and hugged her. Then he kissed her on the cheek. "*Danki*. For everything."

"You're welcome. See you at church on Sunday?"

"If not sooner." He winked as he headed out the door.

Katie Ann picked up Jonas and carried him to his bedroom. As she dressed for bed, she realized that this had been the best night she'd had in years. And for the first time since she'd met Eli Detweiler, she regretted that all they would ever be is friends.

AS ELI DROVE home, he thought about the way Katie Ann always seemed to have one eye on Jonas, especially when the baby was in Eli's arms. But hearing her story about Annie explained why she might be unusually jumpy and protective about the child. He was glad that she'd shared some intimate details about her life and wondered when he would see her again. Then he remembered that he had left Elam's toolbox up on her roof and smiled to himself.

If only he'd met Katie Ann sixteen or seventeen years ago, right after Sarah had died. But no sooner had he had the thought than he wondered if he would have felt the same way about her. His grief for Sarah probably would have kept him from seeing Katie Ann. Not only that, but Eli knew that he was not the same person he was seventeen years ago. He tried to speculate what Katie Ann must have been like as a younger woman.

Why, Lord, is she in my path now? Eli was not going to veer from the plans he'd made, but he found himself caring about Katie Ann in a way he never anticipated. But he would be leaving on Tuesday, and once he was back in his surroundings, he'd work for a few weeks, then schedule one of the many short trips he'd planned to take. Maybe he would send her a postcard from his travels, check on her and Jonas occasionally.

Then that kiss flashed in his mind again and he shivered, only partly from the cold.

Nine

KATIE ANN DRESSED IN A NEW GREEN DRESS FOR worship service, one she'd just finished hemming a few days ago. She bundled Jonas in a thick blue jumpsuit, a handmade gift from Lillian. Sometime over the past three days the toolbox had slid off the roof, and she'd repacked all Elam's tools to take to him today. It was already loaded in her buggy, and she tried to shed the disappointment she felt that she hadn't heard from Eli since he left Wednesday night. She'd thought he would at least come by to pick up the tools. Or to say hello. Something. Maybe he hadn't enjoyed their time together as much as she had.

She'd treasured her time with Martha on Thursday and Friday evening. Thursday, Katie Ann cooked what she and her friends called Lazy Wife's Dinner, a casserole with noodles, cheese, potatoes, carrots, and beef. And she prepared a side dish of creamed celery for Martha. On Friday night Martha brought supper—a pizza she'd picked up in Monte Vista, and that was just fine by Katie Ann. Martha tried to grill her about Eli, but Katie Ann wiggled her way out of saying too much, especially since she hadn't heard from him since he left.

On Saturday, Martha had stopped by early in the afternoon, saying she wasn't feeling well and that she wouldn't be at church service the following day. "Everyone will probably think I croaked," she'd said.

Katie Ann's stomach churned.

Once Jonas was buckled in beside her, she clicked her tongue, setting the buggy in motion. Church service was being held at the home of Vera and Elam's oldest son, Jacob, and his wife, Beth Ann. It was their first time to host worship service since their wedding the year before.

She wondered how much more sightseeing Eli had done over the past three days. The weather had been unusually warm for mid-November, sunshine and mild temperatures. She fought the feeling of disappointment that he hadn't invited her to tag along.

It was almost eight o'clock when she pulled into Jacob and Beth Ann's driveway. In their small community, there were never more than about fifty people at worship service—a small crowd compared to the hundred and fifty or so back home in Lancaster County. With only thirty-two families in the Monte Vista area, they were split into two districts with one bishop serving both. Bishop Esh actually held worship service every Sunday, alternating between the two districts.

After she tethered her horse, she carried Jonas in his carrier toward the house. She knew she would be walking in right as the service started, and she quickly found a seat in the back next to Vera. As she got settled, she glanced across the room to where the men were sitting, but she didn't see Eli.

"I don't see Eli this morning." She tried to sound casual as she whispered in Vera's ear.

"Didn't you hear? I assumed that somehow word had gotten

to you. We had to get a driver to take him to the hospital on Thursday. I was concerned because he had such a bad headache." Vera leaned closer to whisper since the bishop was entering the room. "He had to have four stitches in his head, and he has a concussion. The doctor told him to rest for a few days."

Katie Ann gasped as she brought her hand to her mouth. "I knew he should have gone to the hospital after he fell off my roof. I tried to get him to go, Vera. Really I did."

"*Ach*, I'm sure you did. It took me forever to convince him to let us call a driver to take us all. None of us can figure out why he offered to fix your roof."

Katie Ann lowered her chin. "I know. I'm so sorry. It wasn't his place, and I shouldn't have let him."

"No, dear." Vera grinned. "That's not what I meant. Eli has been terrified of heights his whole life. Elam said he couldn't believe that he asked for tools to fix your roof." Her grin broadened. "He must have really wanted to make an impression."

"Afraid of heights?" Katie Ann bit her bottom lip and shook her head. "I didn't know."

As much as she tried to focus on worship, her mind kept drifting back to Eli and what she could do to make up for his fall at her house. *Off* her house. She mentally scanned her recipe box at home, trying to think of something she could make to take to him, but she knew Vera was an excellent cook. Most likely Eli had everything he could possibly want to eat already. Then she remembered something she had at home. Something that would be perfect for Eli.

She was glad when church service ended a little early, and as she helped the other women prepare the noon meal, she found Vera and pulled her aside. "I feel terrible about Eli.

Would it be all right if I come by this afternoon and bring him a small gift?"

Vera's face lit up. "That would be very nice. I think a visit from you will cheer him up."

"I don't know about that." Katie Ann felt her cheeks brighten as she lowered her chin. "But I do feel bad." She looked back at Vera. "I'll come by later."

ELI KICKED HIS feet up on the coffee table and looked at the clock. He estimated about another hour before everyone came home from church. Smiling, he flipped through a gardening magazine he'd found in the kitchen, and he shoved another handful of roasted pecans into his mouth.

Peace. Quiet. A magazine. And a snack.

He felt a little guilty that he hadn't gone to worship, especially when he was feeling one hundred percent better. But when Vera insisted he stay home and rest as the doctor said, well . . . who was he to argue? Although he did miss Katie Ann, and now that his head didn't throb as though it might fall off his shoulders, he couldn't wait to go see her. He still needed to pick up Elam's tools, so that would be his excuse. He couldn't recall having as much fun as he'd had with her Wednesday night. And it seemed like a lot more than four days since he'd seen her.

He closed the magazine when he heard the family buggy pulling up the drive.

Betsy was the first one to bolt through the door. She didn't take off her coat or bonnet before she started to talk, and Eli struggled to understand her as she tried to catch her breath.

"Katie Ann is coming to see you today! *Mamm* is very

happy about that!" She took another big breath. "But *Daed* says you will break Katie Ann's heart if you get too close to her . . . because you are leaving and all, and Levi said—"

"Betsy!" Vera gently grabbed her young daughter by the arm and helped her out of her coat. "Must you repeat everything you hear?" She glanced at Eli but quickly looked away.

Levi trailed in behind Vera. "I told you to be careful what you say in front of Betsy Big Ears." He grinned as he nodded at Eli and headed up the stairs.

Betsy slammed her hands to her sides as her mother struggled to untie a knot in her bonnet strings. "I don't understand why people say things if they don't want them repeated." She pulled from her mother and leaned her head toward the stairs. "I do not have big ears, Levi!"

"Be still, Betsy, so I can get this knot out." Vera finally pulled the bonnet from the child's head.

Eli had gotten used to the bedlam in his cousins' house. Most of the time. Occasionally, Betsy screamed at the top of her lungs when she was angry, and that had been a bit rough when he'd had his headache. But he'd lived through the chaos of family, and he figured himself to be somewhat immune.

He recalled what Betsy said. Katie Ann was coming to see him?

After Betsy marched upstairs, Vera sat down next to Eli. "I'm sorry about that." She tapped a finger to her cheek and took a deep breath. "How are you feeling?"

"*Gut* as new." He cringed a bit, knowing he'd need to put in some extra devotion time this evening to make up for playing hooky.

"No more headache?"

"No. I really do feel much better."

Vera frowned. "I'm sorry you had to hear all that."

"So . . ." He lifted one brow. "Katie Ann is coming to see me?"

"*Ya*. She feels bad that you fell off her roof." Vera grinned. "I still can't believe you were up there in the first place. Elam says you're terribly afraid of heights."

Eli chuckled. "I was hoping I was over it."

"I'm sorry you didn't get to do any more sightseeing. And you're leaving day after tomorrow. Maybe you'll come back for another visit? There's lots to see and do around here." She paused. "Maybe in the springtime, when it's warmer."

"I'd like that. Despite the fall, I've enjoyed my time here. I wouldn't have missed David and Emily's wedding, and I enjoyed seeing the sand dunes."

"And spending time with Katie Ann?" Vera bit her bottom lip. "Sorry, I couldn't help myself."

"Vera . . ." Eli sighed. "We talked about this. And I know you're still trying to play matchmaker."

She batted her lashes playfully. "Whatever do you mean?"

"Uh, if I didn't already know, I think Betsy just confirmed it." He chuckled. "But a reminder . . . Katie Ann and I are in two different places in our lives. She's just starting out with a new baby. And, Vera . . . I've done all that. Six times." He waited for a response, but Vera just lowered her head a bit. "But Katie Ann and I are friends, and I expect us to stay that way."

Vera stood up from the couch, put her hands on her hips, and stared down at him. "Well . . . as a reminder, you just never know what the Lord has planned for your future. 'For I know the thoughts that I think toward you, saith the Lord, thoughts of peace, and not of evil, to give you an expected end.'" She gave him a smug smile and headed toward the kitchen.

Eli knew exactly what the Lord had planned for his future, and it didn't include raising a new family. And he was starting to resent the butterflies that danced in his stomach at the very mention of Katie Ann's name. He sat taller, knowing he needed to keep his priorities intact. He'd be leaving in two days.

KATIE ANN KNOCKED on the Detweilers' door with Jonas cradled in one arm and a plastic bag in the other hand. She was glad she could remember where she stored the travel guide, the one she'd picked up years ago when she thought Ivan might take her to Florida or one of the other beach destinations described in the book. Her people didn't usually fly on a plane unless it was an emergency, but most of the places listed could be reached by bus. She certainly didn't have any use for the book anymore. Maybe Eli would enjoy it, possibly travel to one of the locations pictured within the covers. Perhaps even send her a postcard?

"Hello, Katie Ann." Elam stepped aside so that Katie Ann could enter, and she gave him a nod.

Eli stood up from the couch when he saw her. She walked toward him and held out the bag as Elam left the room.

"It's a gift for you because I feel so bad about what happened."

Eli smiled. "Katie Ann, you didn't have to do that. It was just an accident." He opened the bag and took a peek inside.

"I thought it might be helpful for your travels." She paused while he pulled out the guide and flipped through the pages. "Although it's mostly beach locations, so I don't know if—"

"It's wonderful. *Danki*." His eyes were fixated on a page for a moment, then he closed the book. "Where did you get this?"

"I've had it for a long time, and I don't see where I'll be needing it anytime soon." She repositioned Jonas in her arms, smiling. "*Ach*, and I sent your tools with Elam. Vera told me at worship that you have a concussion."

Eli grimaced. "Please tell me that you didn't climb up on the roof to get them?"

"No." She chuckled. "They slid off the roof at some point."

He sighed. "*Gut*."

"Because of your fall, you didn't get to do any more sightseeing as you'd planned. I'm so sorry about that."

"I have one day left. Tomorrow." He reached out his arms. "May I?"

Katie Ann handed Jonas to Eli, and Eli sat down on the couch. He laid Jonas faceup in his lap, and once again he talked to her son in baby talk. It was endearing, and she still couldn't recall seeing another Amish man carry on that way about a baby.

"Are you up for another day of sightseeing tomorrow?" Eli raised an eyebrow. "I was thinking about taking a trip to Alamosa, since it's only about twenty minutes from here by car. That would be easy on our boy here." He gently ran the back of his hand along Jonas's cheek, and Katie Ann felt a warm glow flow through her.

"I love Alamosa. I don't get there as often as I'd like since it's quite a haul by buggy, but I keep up with the Amish folks there by reading *The Budget*." Katie Ann sat down next to Eli on the couch.

"Then it's a date."

"*Gut.*" She smiled and pretended not to notice his choice of the word.

Eli lifted the heels of his feet up and down, bouncing Jonas slightly in his lap. She noticed he was without his shoes, and his left sock had a tiny hole near the toe.

Then Eli stood, smiled, and handed Jonas back to Katie Ann. "I'll go to the barn and call Wayne, see if he can take us tomorrow. But either way, I'll make arrangements. Eight o'clock all right?"

"Perfect." Katie Ann bundled Jonas in his blanket and tucked his wool cap tight around his ears. "Then I'll see you tomorrow."

Eli walked her to the door. "Looking forward to it."

She nodded as butterflies played in her stomach. She wished she were looking forward to it a little less.

THE NEXT MORNING Eli watched the sun rise above the mountains as he crossed the snow-covered yard to get in the car with Wayne.

"Glad you were free today," he said as he climbed into the front seat.

Wayne looked up through the windshield. "You've got a great day for travel. No snow predicted, and lots of sunshine . . . if not a bit chilly." The elderly man smiled. "Are we picking up Katie Ann and the child again?"

"*Ya*. She doesn't have an opportunity to go by car much, so . . ." Eli shrugged, wondering if Wayne could sense his excitement.

Wayne nodded, but he didn't say anything.

A few minutes later Eli walked up the path to Katie Ann's porch. By the time he climbed the stairs, she had opened the door and was ready and waiting, Jonas in a carrier at her side.

"*Guder mariye.*" He picked up the carrier and put a gentle hand on her arm as he carried Jonas down the steps. "Careful."

"*Guder mariye* to you too."

Eli tried to calm his racing heart as he helped her and Jonas into the backseat. He'd been like a kid the night before, barely able to sleep. Just the thought of spending the day with her sent his adrenaline pumping. And the thought of leaving them tomorrow caused him a bit of grief. But he wasn't going to think about that today. He was going to make sure she had another wonderful outing.

During the short drive to Alamosa, the three of them chatted, and Eli was surprised to learn that Katie Ann's favorite flower was an orchid. Like Maureen's. Katie Ann also shared a little about their move from Lancaster County to Colorado, and how difficult it was. In addition to the repairs that had to be done on the property and houses, she said she had missed Lancaster County for a long time, especially after her husband left to go back.

"Do you think you'll ever move back there?" Eli twisted in his seat to face her.

"I don't know. I have more friends and extended family there." She shrugged. "Sometimes I'd like to go back, but I've made a home here in Canaan, and I'd miss Lillian, Samuel, Emily, David, and of course Vera and Elam and their family." She paused with a sigh. "And then there's Martha. I don't know if I could ever leave Martha. At least not anytime soon. She's having surgery next week. She has a tumor in her stomach." Katie Ann's forehead creased as she bit her bottom lip.

"That sounds serious. I'll pray that she makes a full recovery."

"*Danki.*"

Wayne slowed the car as they stopped at a light. "This is it. Alamosa. What would you like to do first?"

Katie Ann's face lit up as she spotted an Amish furniture store to their right, so Eli suggested they have a look.

"I've been in this store, and it's very nice, run by Amish folks."

Eli couldn't take his eyes from her, and he really didn't care what they did today. Just being in her presence made him content. More alarms rang in his head, but he was leaving tomorrow.

Today was a day to spend with Katie Ann. And Eli planned to enjoy every minute.

Ten

Lucy sat down at her kitchen table with all of her bills in front of her. For the first time since Ivan's death, she wasn't afraid to sort through them, and she knew she would have enough money to pay them all. Thanks to Katie Ann.

She didn't recognize the envelope on the top of the pile addressed to Ivan, and she instantly wondered if it might have something to do with the mystery house. She ripped into it, but it was only an advertisement for landscaping supplies. Tossing it aside, she laid her head down on the table and wept. She wondered if the crying would ever stop. It had been months since Ivan's death, but she couldn't wrap her mind around the fact that he was never coming back. He was the only man she'd ever loved, and her life seemed pointless at the moment. She rubbed her belly, then cried even harder.

After a few minutes she forced herself to sit up and focus on the bills, reminding herself that things could be much worse. If it hadn't been for Katie Ann's generosity, Lucy wasn't sure what she would have done. She still couldn't get over the fact that Ivan's wife had given her money—a substantial amount of money that would enable her to stay afloat until she found the house that she hoped existed. She was sure there had to be a house somewhere. Nothing pleased Ivan more than to surprise her, and that was the only explanation for why his money was gone from their account and there was a picture of a house and two keys in his cedar box.

She'd driven the countryside looking for the white house with black shutters, surrounded by a white picket fence, but she hadn't found anything.

After taking a deep breath, she pulled the mortgage bill from the envelope. A mortgage she couldn't afford on her own. She'd barely signed the check when someone knocked at the door, and she hurriedly swiped at her puffy eyes. It had been almost a week since she'd even put any makeup on.

She looked through the peephole to see a uniformed man, a cop. The last time a police officer showed up at her door, it was to tell her that Ivan was dead.

She eased the door open, no longer concerned about her puffy eyes or the tears now streaming down her cheeks. "Yes?" She sniffled, pushing back a strand of hair.

"Ma'am, are you okay?"

She put her hand across her stomach. "I don't know. I guess it depends on what you're doing here."

"Lucy Turner?"

"That's me."

"I'm sorry, but this is a court summons." He pushed an envelope toward her before he slowly turned and walked away.

She closed the door, sat back down at the table, and stared at the unopened envelope, wondering which credit card was suing her. Katie Ann's gift hadn't come in time, and she wondered how she was ever going to make it. She'd called a realtor the day before, and even though the woman said she thought she could sell the house quickly, Lucy knew she didn't have enough equity to afford anything else—barely a small apartment to raise her child in.

She lowered her head and did something she rarely did. She prayed. But no sooner had she asked God to help her than a sharp pain seared across her abdomen, and within minutes she felt her water break. Gasping, she rushed to the phone to call her boss at the café, her only real friend. As she dialed the number, another sharp pain almost brought her to her knees.

She knew it was way too early to be in labor. She didn't know if God really existed, but if He did, this must be His punishment for her living with another woman's husband.

KATIE ANN WAS thrilled to meet some of the Amish women in Alamosa, and as she browsed through the shop owned by an Amish widow, she felt a sense of hope. Maybe someday she could own a shop like this in Canaan, even if on a much smaller scale. She could make all kinds of handmade items—pot holders, lap quilts, soaps, dolls, and even jams and jellies. Maybe her nephew David would put a few pieces of his furniture in her store. He'd recently acquired a furniture store in town, and he was a fine craftsman.

Katie Ann loved being a mother, but she couldn't help but fantasize about providing goods for the few tourists who found their way to Canaan, and perhaps even for the local *Englisch* folks.

"How long have you lived in Alamosa?" Katie Ann picked

up a business card holder with an Amish buggy etched on the front. Before the woman could answer, she asked, "Who made this? It's lovely."

"*Danki. Mei sohn* did."

Katie Ann put the card holder back on the shelf, wondering how old the woman's son was. By the time Jonas was old enough to help Katie Ann with a shop, she figured she might be too old to take on such a project. The woman excused herself to tend to another customer, and Katie Ann scanned the shop until she found Eli, who was carrying Jonas, and Wayne.

Her eyes stayed glued on Eli as she watched him tenderly shift Jonas from one shoulder to the other. But the longer she stared at him, the more she saw Ivan, and as the image of Eli returned, she reminded herself that no matter how wonderful Eli might seem, trust would not come easy for her.

And as hard as it was to trust Eli, she was having an equally hard time trusting God's plan for her life. She prayed the same amount of time that she always had, but she knew her communion with God was not the same. To hear Him, to know Him, and to understand the wonder of His love—one must trust Him completely.

"See anything you can't live without?" Wayne asked as he and Eli walked up to her. She cleared her thoughts and shook her head.

"No. But they have some finely crafted goods here." She smiled, focusing again on Eli with her precious Jonas. "Want me to take him?"

"Only if you want to. I think he's happy looking at the manlier items in the back of the store, like the workbench." He winked at Katie Ann before he looked back at the baby. "Aren't you, Jonas?"

Katie Ann couldn't help but smile at the tender tone of voice Eli used with her son. "Are you fellows ready?"

"*Ya.* Jonas is hungry." Eli grinned, and Katie Ann laughed.

"*Jonas* is hungry? Did he tell you this?" She glanced at the clock on the wall and knew it would be time to nurse him soon. And her stomach was growling more than normal for this time of morning.

Eli held his head close to Jonas. "*Ya*, I'll tell your mommy that you'd like some pancakes or maybe an early lunch. I think the *Englisch* call it brunch."

"Give me *mei boppli* before you confuse him with all your silliness." She gently eased Jonas from Eli's arms.

They were almost out of the store when Eli stopped and took a final look around. "I always wanted to own a place like this. Maybe something smaller, but still like this."

He smiled at Katie Ann, but she stood motionless. God's timing had never seemed more off.

MARTHA JOTTED DOWN the details of her surgery as the nurse on the phone rattled them off.

"Are you sure I can't eat breakfast? Because I'm not going to be in a very good mood when I show up at your hospital at seven o'clock in the morning hungry. I have cereal and a muffin every morning at six thirty. I really don't like to miss my breakfast."

She rolled her eyes when the woman insisted that she couldn't have breakfast that morning, nor could she eat anything the night before after midnight. Surgery was scheduled for the Wednesday after Thanksgiving, and even though her appetite had been declining, Martha didn't like to be told when she could eat.

"Fine." She forced herself to thank the woman for calling, since she was working on being nicer. If her time was coming, she wanted God's most recent memories of her behavior to be good ones.

After she hung up the phone, she got comfortable in her chair and thought about Katie Ann. She sure hoped that girl was having fun with Eli, and she wished there was some way to get that man to stay longer. She'd plotted and planned in her mind, but every time a lie for the good of all concerned came to mind, she was reminded that God was watching and her time was drawing to an end.

She arched a brow and glanced up. "I won't pull any tricks to get that man to hang around, but, Lord, I sure hope You can see Your way clear for him to stay. He needs to fall in love with Katie Ann and take care of her and that baby."

She picked up the newspaper and flipped the pages until she came to the obituaries. Using a red pen, she circled the ones that were nicely written and drew an X across the ones that didn't do justice to the deceased. She wanted to write her own obituary, to make sure it was done correctly, but that seemed a little over the top. Instead, she'd give her recommendations to Katie Ann and pray her friend could get it right.

"Lord, I'm going to miss Katie Ann and that precious baby."

She leaned her head back against the chair, resolved she wouldn't cry. If it hadn't been for Emily and David—and Arnold—she might not have found her way to God. She'd grown close to Emily and David last year when they were doing some work at her house, and those kids had such a strong faith, she couldn't help but be curious. Arnold drove it on home. The man's faith in God was amazing, and when Martha opened her heart to the Lord, nothing had been the same. She knew exactly where she was going when she left this world, but she sure was going to miss everyone here.

IT WAS NEARING dark when Wayne pulled into Katie Ann's driveway. Jonas was screaming, and had been for most of the drive back from Alamosa. They'd stopped twice during the short drive back—once for Katie Ann to change the baby's diaper, and the other time for her to rub his tummy, thinking maybe he was having stomach problems again. Nothing worked.

"I'll get the carrier. You get Jonas in the *haus*." Eli held the car door open while Katie Ann got Jonas out of his car seat, then stepped out of the car, thanking Wayne for driving. Eli settled with Wayne and followed her inside.

She paced the floor with the baby while Eli offered to get the percolator going. Jonas was soon fast asleep in Katie Ann's arms, and she worried that she shouldn't have had him out all day again. They'd hit several more shops in the area and eaten two meals while they were out. Tiptoeing, she eased down the hall to Jonas's room and laid him in his crib.

When she returned to the living room, Eli met her with a cup of coffee.

"I feel like a terrible mother. I shouldn't have had him out and about so much today."

Eli sat down on the couch, and Katie Ann sat down beside him.

"You're a *gut mudder*, Katie Ann. But I imagine the *boppli* is tuckered out."

She took a sip of her coffee. "It was probably too long a day for him."

"I hauled Maureen everywhere with me from the time she was born." Eli took a sip of his coffee. "Did you have a *gut* time today?"

"Very much." She'd brought back all kinds of knickknacks for Lillian, Vera, Emily, and Beth Ann, and of course something extra special for Martha—a quilt for a single bed, with scripture readings all over it. Katie Ann hoped Martha would take it to the hospital with her when she went to have her surgery.

She put her coffee on the table in front of them. "I need to light some lanterns before we're sitting in the dark."

Eli touched her arm. "You sit and rest. I'll light the lanterns." Then he rubbed her arm in a way that made Katie Ann want to curl up in his arms. It had been so long since she'd felt loved, she wished she could pretend, just for a while.

He knew where the lanterns were, and as she watched him light each one, she allowed herself a few moments to fantasize about what it would be like to have Eli around all the time. But before the vision could come full circle, she imagined him leaving her. They weren't even a couple, but Katie Ann could see him walking out on her.

Tomorrow he would go home, as planned. And Katie Ann was sure this was a good thing, before she got too attached.

A minute later, Eli sat back down on the couch. "Why are you looking at me like that?"

Katie Ann blinked her eyes a couple of times. "Like what?"

She hoped her expression didn't reveal her thoughts, how she wanted for him to hold her in his arms, even if it wasn't love. Even if it wasn't real.

Eli gazed into her eyes, and Katie Ann felt like she might cry, for reasons that confused and embarrassed her. As a woman, she found herself desiring Eli in a way that wasn't appropriate. She'd been a married woman for many years, and as such, she knew the comfort of a man's embrace. The kiss they'd shared began to replay in her mind, and she wondered if Eli was thinking about it too.

After a few moments Eli shrugged. "I don't know. You were just looking at me like . . ." He shrugged again, then smiled. "Never mind."

Katie Ann felt comfortable sitting on the couch with Eli as orange sparks shimmied up the fireplace and shadows from the lanterns danced around the room. It took everything in her power not to move closer to him. If only she could lean her head on his chest, listen to his heart, and have him wrap his arms around her. That was all she needed.

She felt a wave of goose bumps run the length of her body when he grabbed her hand in his.

"Katie Ann . . ."

His smile was sensuous, and for a moment she wondered if his intentions would exceed her needs. She couldn't allow him to kiss her again, but every part of her wanted him to. She swallowed hard as he finished his sentence.

"Meeting you has been the best part of my trip here." He gently squeezed her hand.

She knew she was in a dangerous place, longing and desiring

a man who wasn't available, but it would be hard to say good-bye to him.

"I've enjoyed our time together," she finally said. "*Danki* for taking me and Jonas on your sightseeing trips."

He eased his hand away from hers, stroked his beard, and locked his eyes with hers. Katie Ann braced herself for whatever he was about to say. She took a deep breath.

"Katie Ann . . ."

"*Ya?*"

"Are you hungry?"

She grinned, relieved, but slightly disappointed for some unknown reason. "I'm guessing you are, no?"

His smile broadened. "Maybe a sandwich?"

"I think I can do better than that. I have some leftover stew in the freezer that won't take long to heat up."

Eli rubbed his belly. "I can't believe I didn't eat it all when I was here before. Is it too much trouble?"

She stood up, a bit hungry herself. "Not at all. I'll just run it under some warm water and put it on the burner to heat."

"And I'll keep our fire going." Eli walked to the fireplace and glanced at the wood in the carrier. "Only one log left. I'll go carry in some more." He walked toward the door, and Katie Ann nodded as she moved toward the kitchen.

Twenty minutes later they were back on the couch with bowls of stew in their laps, both agreeing it was too cold to eat in the kitchen. Once they were done, the conversation turned to Katie Ann and Ivan, which wouldn't have been her first choice, but she found herself confiding in Eli in a way that surprised her.

"I'm not shocked about Ivan buying a house and not telling Lucy." She grimaced as she spoke. "Ivan was big on surprises, but also big on secrets."

Eli twisted to face her. "Katie Ann, I am so sorry for everything you've been through." He shook his head. "That's just so wrong."

She wasn't seeking his pity, and she was starting to wish she hadn't shared so much, so she shrugged. "All in God's plan, I suppose." She winced, as she could almost picture God staring down on her and shaking His head.

"I know it's hard not to question the Lord's plan for us when something so unforeseeable happens." Eli's brows narrowed as he sighed, and Katie Ann suspected he was referring to his wife's death. Then his face brightened, and he locked eyes with her. "But I'm thankful that it was part of His plan for us to meet. I'm grateful for this new friendship."

His presence gave her joy, even if she didn't understand the Lord's plan, or completely trust it. "Me too."

Eli shifted his weight and crossed one ankle on his knee, his body still turned toward her. "Katie Ann . . ." He paused. "I'd like to write to you. Would that be all right? I mean, I'd like to know how you and Jonas are doing."

"I'd like that." She playfully tapped him on the shoulder. "I want to hear all about your travels, the places you'll see."

He chuckled. "I know it's strange for an Amish man to take on such excursions, but I still plan to work hard too."

"You don't need to justify your intentions to anyone except God. I think you've earned some time to yourself."

"*Danki* for saying that."

"Where will you go first?"

"Indiana. Jake's wife, Laura Jane, has family there. They've invited me to stay with them, and I've never been to Indiana. Then I'll go back home and ready my land for planting. And after that, I plan to take a short trip to Florida."

Katie Ann knew envy was a sin, but the emotion surfaced just the same, and she fought the memories of all the times Ivan promised to take her on a vacation there. "I think that's wonderful."

"It will seem strange, being away from the *kinner*. Even now, being here, I can't help but worry about all of them." He chuckled. "That was the one thing the Lord couldn't have prepared me for with six children. No matter how old they get, I still worry."

"I can understand that."

Eli sat taller. "Do you have a phone?"

"I share the same phone that Samuel installed in the barn. We know lots of folks have cell phones these days or phone ringers in the *haus*, but I agreed with Lillian and Samuel that it's best to keep the ringers out of the house, especially when Jonas is sleeping. And Lillian wants her *kinner* to grow up without the invasions of the outside world."

"Can I call you sometimes?"

"I'd like that." She twisted away from him toward the table by the couch, found her small pad of paper and a pen. She scribbled down the phone number and address and handed it to him.

"Could you take my phone number and address down, in case you or Jonas need anything? I'm going to get a cell phone soon so I can be in touch with my family when I'm on the road, but for now I have a phone in the barn."

Katie Ann passed him the paper and pen. He handed it back to her with his phone number and address.

He glanced at the clock and grinned. "Time sure does fly when I'm with you. I guess I need to go." He stood up, and Katie Ann did the same. "My bus leaves early in the morning, and I'll have to catch a taxi ride to the bus station."

Katie Ann couldn't think of a single thing to say to get him to stay just a little longer, and she dreaded saying good-bye. She followed him to the door and waited while he pulled on his long black overcoat and put on his black felt hat. When he was done, he just stared at her. She didn't move, but as he inched closer her knees began to shake and her pulse quickened. He cupped her cheek.

"I've been dreading having to say good-bye to you," he said.

His touch was unbearably tender, as was the sound of his voice, sending a warm shiver through her. As his lips slowly descended to her cheek, she felt both relief and disappointment, then he kissed her again, this time closer to her mouth, and when his lips brushed hers there was an intimacy that she knew she would recall for a long time, and she was going to savor every second.

After what seemed like a long while, he eased away, picked up her hand, and pressed a kiss into her palm. "Take care, my friend."

Under any other circumstances, and with anyone else, it would have seemed a strange thing to say.

"You too." She fought the tremble in her voice. "Safe travels."

He smiled as he closed the door behind him.

Katie Ann watched Eli through the window as he walked

down the driveway to go back to Vera and Elam's, a light snow falling. She touched her lips and fought the urge to cry.

"Be blessed and safe, my friend," she whispered as he disappeared into the darkness.

Eleven

Middlefield welcomed Eli back with slightly warmer temperatures than he'd left in Colorado, but with snow just the same. He thanked the cabdriver, noticed all the buggies in front of his house, and wondered what was going on. Hurrying into the living room, he was surprised to see all five of his daughters inside.

"What in the world are all you *maedels* doing here?" He looked at each one of them. "And where are all my grandchildren?"

Hannah waved her hand in the air. "They're with Laura Jane."

"And why does she have all the *kinner* this fine afternoon?"

"Because we want to talk to you, *Daed*." Ida Mae sat down on the couch next to Karen and Frieda. "Sit down and tell us all about your trip."

Eli narrowed his brows. Something was up. His daughters all led busy lives, and he was going to see all of them here the very next day for Thanksgiving. "I could have told you all about it tomorrow, *mei maedels*."

"We couldn't wait!" Maureen was still standing, and she bounced on her toes as she spoke. "Tell us about . . ." She grinned. "Her."

"Who?"

"Katie Ann."

He glanced around the room at his five daughters. Why were they gathered here and asking about Katie Ann?

"*Aenti* Vera told us you spent a lot of time with her while you were in Canaan." Frieda pushed back a strand of dark hair that had fallen from beneath her prayer covering. "So we were just wondering . . ." She gave a little shrug.

Eli slowly took off his coat, then his hat. He hung them both on a rung by the front door and folded his arms across his chest. You could have heard a pin drop on the wooden floor beneath his feet. "And which one of you called *Aenti* Vera to check on me?" He tried to keep a serious voice.

Hannah laughed as she took a seat in a rocking chair in the corner. "We didn't have to call *Aenti* Vera. She called us. We're so happy for you, *Daed*. We've been praying that you would find someone to share your life with. You deserve that, and Katie Ann sounds wonderful, perfect for—"

"Whoa, whoa, whoa." Eli held his palm toward Hannah, whose expression dropped. "There is no romance between me and Katie Ann."

His kiss with Katie Ann flashed through his mind, and he knew it was the most romantic thing that had happened to him in seventeen years, but he wasn't about to admit that to his daughters. "We are friends. That's all." He looked at all of his daughters, one by one. "Now, why the long faces?"

Maureen was standing across the room, her expression

possibly the most forlorn of the group. "We were hoping you'd found someone special."

To insinuate that Katie Ann was not special caused a knot in Eli's stomach. "She *is* special. A special *friend*." Eli unfolded his arms from across his chest and put them on his hips. "Since when did all of *mei dochders* become so interested in *mei* personal life?"

"Maureen is married and out of the house now, *Daed*. We're all out on our own." Hannah walked closer to Eli. "It's time for you to find someone to grow old with."

Eli chuckled. "In case you haven't noticed, I *am* old." He walked to the coffee table and picked up his mail. "And none of you needs to be fretting about me." He flipped through the envelopes. "Besides, I told you girls that I planned to do some traveling."

"First of all, that's just not normal." Frieda scowled. "What sort of Amish man wanders the countryside?"

Eli put down his mail, rubbed his forehead, and wondered when his daughters all grew into such headstrong women. He looked at Frieda, stroked his beard for a moment, and then shook his head. "I've told all of you that I plan to take some time for myself."

"Well, that was before you met a woman who is perfect for you."

Maureen leaned back against the couch, her pouting expression reminding Eli of when she was a small girl.

"*Ya*. And you're going to blow it, *Daed*." Karen also leaned back against the couch, folding her arms across her chest.

"Perfect for me?" Eli faced off with all his girls, glancing around at each one of them in turn. "She is not perfect for me.

Katie Ann has a baby that is almost three months old. She is just now starting her family. I've raised six wonderful *kinner*, and I think I deserve a little time on my own."

Ida Mae huffed. "That sounds mighty selfish, *Daed*."

Hannah spoke up next. "Hush, Ida Mae." She turned to Eli. "It's not selfish, *Daed*. And we do think you should have some time for yourself, but—"

"*Danki* for your permission, Hannah." Eli smiled, but when Hannah's eyes teared up, he silently reprimanded himself for the comment. Hannah was his most sensitive child, even though she was the oldest daughter. "Girls," he said softly, glancing at each one of them. "If ever there was a time when I needed a *fraa*, it was when you all were young. I regret that you grew up without a mother for so long, and some of you not at all. So I'm going to say this one time, then that's the end of it. Katie Ann is a beautiful, wonderful person. We grew close while I was there, and we plan to stay in touch. As friends." He pointed a finger around the room. "Everyone clear about that?"

The girls all gathered near the door, nodding as they bundled up in coats and bonnets. They each kissed him on the cheek and rattled off what they were bringing for the Thanksgiving meal the next day. As the others scurried across the porch toward their buggies, Ida Mae hung back. She wrapped her arms around her father. "We just want you to be happy, *Daed*. That's all."

Eli eased away and cupped Ida Mae's chin. "I know you do, *mei maedel*. And hard work mixed with travel will make me happy."

She nodded, and Eli watched his very independent, strong-willed daughters hitch up their buggies to head home. Pride was something to be avoided, but Eli was proud of each one of them just the same.

He waved at the departing buggies, then walked back inside. Again his mind replayed his kiss with Katie Ann, the way it had been since the moment his lips left hers. She was as wrong for him as any woman could be. And it wasn't just Jonas and the new family she was beginning. Eli could tell from their conversations that Katie Ann was struggling to trust again. Maybe she had forgiven her husband and his mistress, but he sensed that trust was still a far cry away.

He didn't ever want to do anything to cause her to distrust him. What about the kiss? Shouldn't she have been able to trust him not to be so forward? Eli supposed he should feel guilty for both times that they had kissed . . . but he didn't.

Nothing had ever felt so right.

KATIE ANN BUTTONED her coat, tied her bonnet, and gathered up the extra-large batch of creamed celery she'd made to take for the Thanksgiving feast. She'd taken Jonas over earlier and was sure that Anna and Elizabeth were entertaining him. As she closed the door behind her, she stumbled, then grimaced when she saw what almost caused her to trip. *A dead mouse.* As she eased around the poor critter, she noticed he wasn't frozen, but freshly dead. Then something darted from underneath the house and raced toward the barn.

Mrs. Dash turned around once to look at Katie Ann before scurrying through a barn window and out of sight. Katie Ann looked again at the dead animal, then eased down her porch steps. She'd been feeding the cat leftovers most every morning and night. Katie Ann still couldn't get close to her, but perhaps this was Mrs. Dash's way of returning the favor—ridding the barn of mice.

She was almost to Lillian's front door when she heard a car. Spinning around, she saw that it was Martha. It was too cold to wait for her, so she headed into Lillian's large kitchen through a second door on the porch.

"It's toasty warm in here," she said as she put the creamed celery on the table. She scanned the room and saw everyone but the newlyweds. "Where're Emily and David?"

"They're here." Lillian pointed to the living room. "With Elizabeth, Anna, and Jonas."

Katie Ann peeked her head into the room and watched Emily and David fussing over Jonas. She smiled, sure that the couple was probably planning to start their own family soon. "Hello, everyone. Happy Thanksgiving."

After she'd hugged those in the room, she walked back into the kitchen just as Martha came through the door from the porch into the kitchen. Lillian disliked the fact that everyone used that door, but it was just so convenient. Martha elbowed her way through the crowd in the kitchen.

"I made a cheese ball." She handed it to Lillian. "Because that's just all the energy I could muster up this year."

Lillian took the ball wrapped in plastic wrap. "Martha, you didn't have to bring anything. I told you that." She tenderly rubbed Martha's arm. "How are you feeling?"

Martha shrugged. "As good as anyone who has a big tumor in their stomach could feel, I guess."

Katie Ann rubbed her forehead. Despite Martha's nonchalance, she knew her friend was scared.

"I want to know every little detail of your visit with Eli yesterday," Martha whispered in her ear. "You and I are going to your house directly this afternoon, and don't hold back any details."

"Martha, there isn't much to tell. We went to Alamosa, and—"

"Whatever. I want to hear it all anyway."

Katie Ann could feel her cheeks reddening just thinking about last night.

An hour later, a meal that took many hours to prepare was consumed in less than fifteen minutes, and the men retired to the barn while the women cleaned up.

"Oh, I need to tell you all, I got the details for my surgery next week." Martha handed Vera a plate to be washed. "They're cutting me open on Wednesday. I have to be there early in the morning, and . . ." She paused with a huff. "Can you believe I can't eat breakfast that morning? Not that I would have been thrilled to have cereal and a muffin as my last meal, but . . ."

Vera was running soapy water in Lillian's sink, and Emily handed her another plate as she turned to Martha. "Martha, first of all, it's not your last meal. Don't say things like that."

Emily's eyes were starting to tear up. Katie Ann knew how much the girl—and David—loved Martha. They all did. But Martha needed to be careful how she spoke about her upcoming surgery, especially around the younger folks.

Katie Ann patted Emily on the shoulder and whispered, "Everything will be fine. You know how Martha gets."

Emily nodded, but Katie Ann was as worried as the rest of them.

"Katie Ann?" David poked his head into the kitchen, grinning from ear to ear. "You have a phone call."

"A call? Who could be calling me?"

Everyone in the room turned to David, and Lillian spoke up. "David, who is it?"

His smile broadened. "It's Eli."

Katie Ann couldn't even look at the women around her, and the heat in her face was evidence of how red her cheeks must be. She tucked her chin as she moved toward the door.

"You go, girl!" Martha's voice boomed above the whispers in the kitchen, and Katie Ann kept her eyes down.

As she walked into the barn, the men began to scatter. Elam, Samuel, David, Jacob, and Levi all moved toward the door.

"I'm sorry. You don't have to leave."

"Sure we do," Levi said as he winked at her.

Katie Ann took a deep breath and watched as Samuel closed the barn door behind them. She wished she had thought to bundle up before she ran out the door. With chattering teeth, she said, "Hello."

"Happy Thanksgiving."

Her heart came alive at the sound of his voice. "And happy Thanksgiving to you." She put a hand to her chest, hoping to calm her rapid pulse, but it was no use. It hadn't even been forty-eight hours since he left her house, since the kiss, but her lips still tingled at the memory of his touch.

"I had to get away from the crowd for a few minutes. My girls have taken over my kitchen, which is fine. My son and sons-in-law have taken over my living room, which is fine. And my grandchildren are in my bedroom playing board games. That, too . . . is fine. But . . ." He chuckled. "I needed a few minutes of quiet. And I thought about you. Are you having a good day with everyone?"

"*Ya, ya*. We all ate too much, as expected." She held her breath for a moment, wondering if their conversation would be filled with small talk, in light of all the deep conversations they'd had over the past couple of weeks.

"I'm not going to keep you from family, but I didn't want the day to go by without wishing you a happy Thanksgiving. And you hug Jonas from me."

Katie Ann was glowing from the inside out, and she didn't even notice the cold anymore. "I will. And you give my blessings to your family as well."

It was quiet for a moment.

"Katie Ann, I'm feeling a little bad about . . ."

She heard him take a deep breath.

". . . about the way I kissed you Tuesday night."

"It wasn't like it was the first time." Katie Ann slapped a hand across her mouth, not believing what she'd said. She squeezed her eyes closed in horror and waited for Eli's response.

He laughed. "Uh, true. I was just thinking that maybe I somehow took advantage, and—"

"Eli, I'm a grown woman. You didn't take advantage of me."

"Well then, if it's okay with you, I'm not going to feel bad anymore. I'm highly attracted to my new best friend, and I had a weak moment."

"You had *two* weak moments." She squeezed her eyes shut again, but she couldn't stop smiling at how playful they were being with each other and how natural it felt.

Eli's familiar laughter warmed her heart. "*Ya*, I did. And trust me, I think about both. Often."

Katie Ann wanted to tell Eli that she thought about him too, but there was no way she was going to put her heart out there to a man she couldn't have. She thought about the way he always referred to her as his best friend. She liked that title. It was safe, but she wasn't sure what to say.

"Katie Ann, I'll let you go. Don't forget to hug Jonas for me."

"I won't. And *danki* for calling."

She waited for him to hang up, but she could hear him breathing. "Eli?"

"*Ya.*"

"Is there something else?"

"No. Not really."

Katie Ann waited.

"Okay, I'm hanging up now." Eli laughed. "Talk to you soon."

I hope so. "All right. Bye, Eli." And this time she hung up. She glanced around the barn for Mrs. Dash, but decided there was too much activity today for her to make an appearance.

Her cheeks warmed when she exited the barn and saw the men standing right outside, all shivering. She knew they had to have heard at least part of her conversation. But when she looked toward the house and saw all the women peering out the window at her, she knew what she was walking into.

It was nearing dark when the last of Eli's kin left. What a grand day it had been, and he felt like sharing the details with someone. Not just anyone. Katie Ann. As he kicked back in his recliner, he adjusted the lantern on the table beside him so he could see better. He searched his pile of papers and mail on the table until he came across a tablet of paper and a pen.

Dear Katie Ann,

He stopped and wondered if the details of his day would be of interest to her. After only a few moments of deliberation, he decided that they just might.

It's Thanksgiving evening, and everyone has gone home. It's quiet in the house. Just the way I like it (I'm chuckling here), but I wish you were here for me to tell you about our day. My oldest grandchild, Leah, sang to everyone in the living room after the meal, and I don't think I've ever heard anything so beautiful. She sang "Jesus Loves Me" and "For God So Loved Us." Do you remember me telling you about Leah? She's Jake and Laura Jane's oldest, my first grandchild. And also today, little Luke fell and bumped his head. It was a touching moment when his twin brother, Ben, touched his head and started to cry, as if he'd felt the pain. Seems like twins are always extra close. Luke and Ben are identical. Did I tell you that?

Sometimes, when it's quiet like this, I'll put out a small radio I have hidden in my bedroom and listen to country gospel music. Sometimes I turn it on really softly in the background when I pray. *Mei kinner* all know I have it, and I suspect that one or two of them might have a radio as well, but our bishop has a habit of showing up unexpectedly, so I keep it hidden in a drawer in my nightstand. I'm such a rule-breaker, no?

Eli stretched his socked feet out on the recliner and leaned his head back for a moment. He closed his eyes and let his last visit with Katie Ann play out in his mind for the hundredth time. When he'd relived the moment several times, he resumed his writing.

> I hope that when you receive this, it will put a smile on your face. You need to smile more. It's healthy. Or so I'm told (chuckling again). Either way, I love it when you smile.

Eli reminded himself not to come on too strong. He knew he should pray for Katie Ann to find a wonderful man to take care of her and Jonas, but he just wasn't sure he liked that idea. Actually, he was sure he didn't like that idea. *I'm a selfish man.* He scratched his forehead.

> What are your plans for Christmas? Will you celebrate First Christmas at Lillian and Samuel's *haus*, or will you go somewhere else? *Mei dochders* will take over *mei haus* again for First Christmas, then on Second Christmas we usually spend the day visiting friends and shut-ins. We always visit Annie Hostetler and her husband, John. Annie has Alzheimer's, and they don't get out much. That disease scares me. And we always end the day by having pie at Miller's Pantry. Best pie in the world, I think.
>
> I'll close for now. I hope to hear back from you. Sending blessings to you and Jonas.
>
> Best friends, in His name,
>
> Eli

He put the letter on the table, planning to mail it first thing in the morning. His fire was dwindling, and as he got up and threw another log on it, he thought about the fires he'd tended at Katie Ann's house and the time they'd spent talking while sitting on her couch. He shook his head and knew that he was going to have to clear his mind. It was fine to think about her. Just not all the time.

When he got cozy in his chair again, he thought about the next trip he'd be taking after Christmas. But he clearly needed to focus on something else besides Katie Ann.

On Tuesday morning Katie Ann helped Martha pack her suitcase to take to the hospital the next day. She worried her friend wouldn't bring what she needed, plus she was hoping Martha would take the quilt she'd brought back for her from Alamosa. She recalled her trip with Eli to the neighboring town, and she wondered what he was doing today. She hadn't talked to him since he called on Thanksgiving Day. Not that she expected to.

"Martha, I don't think you're going to need all those hair accessories at the hospital." Katie Ann watched as Martha loaded up a huge blow dryer, large pink curlers, several kinds of hair product, and of course . . . the butterfly clip.

"That's easy for you to say. It doesn't matter how your hair looks because it's always covered up by that prayer *kapp*." Martha grabbed Katie Ann's arm and pulled her to the bed. She eased her down on the pink and white comforter that Katie Ann had gotten her for her birthday last year. "Now, honey. Listen to me. I know you're scared about my trip to the hospital, but you've shown me the way to the Lord." She sat taller and raised her chin. "I'm not afraid to go."

As Martha dabbed at her eyes, Katie Ann knew that wasn't true, so she took a deep breath and tried to be strong for her friend. "You're not going anywhere yet. Everything is going to go fine, and you'll be home recovering in no time."

"I don't think so."

Martha lowered her head, but Katie Ann saw a tear trickle down her cheek. She looked up and swiped at the tear.

"I've never been knocked out. I know that's hard to believe at my age, but I just know I'm not going to wake up."

"Of course you'll wake up." Katie Ann was surprised to learn that this was Martha's biggest fear. Katie Ann was much more concerned about the surgery itself, and she planned to talk to the doctors as soon as she and Martha arrived at the hospital, something she should have already done. Had she not been so preoccupied with Eli . . .

"Where's that quilt you gave me, that lovely spread with the Lord's Word all over it?"

Katie Ann pointed to a chair across the room. "There it is."

Martha walked to the chair and picked up the small quilt. "We'll just carry it in, since it won't fit in my suitcase."

Katie Ann was thinking it might fit if there weren't so many hair supplies, but she didn't say anything. She glanced at the clock on the wall. Arnold would be arriving later in the afternoon.

Martha pushed the quilt toward Katie Ann. "You make sure I'm covered in this when they wheel me into surgery."

Katie Ann remembered when David had his kidney transplant. She was pretty sure they wouldn't allow the quilt to go into surgery with Martha, but she didn't say anything. At least Martha could sleep beneath it before and after.

"Let's pray for a while." Martha slowly eased down onto her knees and propped her elbows on the bed, folding her hands in front of her. Katie Ann slid down beside her. "And let's don't do it silently like you people usually do. Can you please pray aloud?"

Katie Ann blinked back tears. "Of course."

"Don't cry." Martha reached over and grabbed onto Katie Ann's hand. "Have I told you how much I love you?" Martha smiled. "Like you are my own daughter."

And no matter how hard she tried, Katie Ann couldn't keep the tears from spilling down her cheeks as she answered. "And I couldn't love you any more if you were my own mother."

KATIE ANN GRABBED her mail from the box at the end of her driveway on her way home from Martha's. She tucked it into her apron and went to Lillian's to pick up Jonas, who was sleeping soundly in a playpen in the living room. It wasn't until after she was home and had Jonas in his own bed that she saw the letter from Eli.

She wanted to enjoy every word, so she bathed, made coffee, got a fire going, and curled up on the couch. She was surprised that she hadn't heard from Arnold, but hopefully he had a safe trip and they would see him at the hospital tomorrow. She peeled the envelope open and read. Smiling, she could almost hear him chuckling as he wrote, and she felt a part of his life as he detailed memorable moments from his day. She couldn't wait to write him back.

Dear Eli,

I so enjoyed your letter and hearing about Leah and the twins. It sounds like you have such a wonderful family, and I loved hearing about them. Tonight, worry fills my heart, as tomorrow morning I will be taking Martha to the hospital to have the tumor removed. Lillian will keep Jonas for me. I've prayed hard about tomorrow, and I know that worry is a sin, but on this night I'm afraid I'm filled with concern. You probably only saw one side of Martha (now I'm chuckling), but I promise you, she has a huge heart, and she is very dear to me, as if she were my own mother.

Katie Ann tapped the pen to her chin as more visions of Eli's kiss raced through her head.

It has gotten much colder since you left, dropping into the single digits the last few days. I will be glad when spring is here. Last year, Lillian and I didn't have a garden. We weren't sure what to plant. The growing season is so different here, with only three months of frost-free weather. But after talking with some other folks, we have a plan. We will grow peas, tomatoes, sweet corn, potatoes, and onions. And we're told that cauliflower, cabbage, and broccoli will do *gut* in this climate. I'm looking forward to that, but our last day of frost will not come until mid-June.

Jonas continues to amaze me on a daily basis, and he smiles every time I say his name. What a blessing he is to me so late in life.

I've been quilting pot holders in the evenings, and I'm

> working on a cookbook. Someday I would like to have a small shop to sell things like that, something very small.

She recalled how Eli mentioned that he'd always wanted a shop, but she decided not to bring that up.

> I will close for now, as I want to spend extra time in prayer tonight. May this letter find you well in all the ways of the Lord.

She paused, thought for a minute, and decided to sign her letter the same way he had.

> Best friends, in His name,
> Katie Ann

She folded the letter, put it in an envelope, and found Eli's address on her end table. She'd drop the letter in the mailbox on the way to the hospital in the morning. She'd tried to get Martha to spend the night with her, but Martha was insistent that she wanted to spend her last night on Earth in her own bed.

Katie Ann closed her eyes in prayer.

Please, Lord, don't let Martha die. Please.

Twelve

"It stinks in here." Martha was dressed in a purple pants outfit, and Katie Ann could tell that her friend had spent extra time on her hair this morning. Not one strand was out of place, and it was tightly secured under the butterfly clip. And her makeup was perfectly applied, right down to her bright red lipstick. "And I don't even want to talk about how hungry I am."

"I'm sure they'll let you eat not long after the surgery."

They wound their way down the hall to admissions. Martha said she'd already preregistered at the hospital, so it wasn't long before she was shown to her room and settled into her bed. Much to her chagrin, it was not a private room.

"Katie Ann . . ." Martha motioned from her bed for Katie Ann to come closer, then she whispered, "Go find out why that person is in my room. I specifically asked for a private room, and I am paying good money to have one."

In the next bed, a woman was lying on her side facing the window, only her long blond hair visible atop the covers.

"All right." Katie Ann patted her on the arm, although she

wasn't as concerned about Martha's roommate as she was about finding the doctor and getting some details about Martha's surgery. "I'll be back in a few minutes."

She turned when she got to the door. Martha was wearing a white hospital gown and was tucked beneath the quilt Katie Ann had given her. "Do you need anything?"

Martha pointed to the bed next to her and mouthed, "I don't need a roommate."

"Okay," Katie Ann whispered as she left the room.

MARTHA TRIED TO calm her breathing. They'd be coming for her soon. She closed her eyes and prayed silently. *Please, Lord, if You could see fit to have me wake up and live a few more years, I'd sure be grateful to get to see my little Jonas grow into a small person. If I leave now, he won't remember me.* She sighed. *But if it's Your will to take me home, please take care of Katie Ann and Jonas. And, Lord . . . can You make this as painless as possible? You know how much I hate pain.*

Her prayer was interrupted when she heard whimpering to her left. She turned to face the back of the person in the bed a few feet from hers. Twisting her mouth back and forth, she watched the woman's body shaking.

"You all right over there?" When there was no answer, Martha asked, "Do you need me to get a nurse for you?"

The woman didn't turn around, but just shook her head.

Martha glanced around the room at all the equipment, wishing she could yank the IV out of her arm, but she figured that would hurt just as much as when they put it in. The woman in the next bed kept crying, and Martha hoped Katie

Ann would hurry back and get this person out of here. Last thing she needed was more sadness.

Martha sat up in bed, dropped her feet to the floor, then pulled the IV pole the few feet to where the woman lay. She tapped her on the arm. "Honey?"

"I'm fine, really."

Martha could tell by her voice that she was young, but she wasn't sure how young. Her body stretched the full length of the bed beneath the covers. Martha leaned closer, not sure what to do. "You don't sound fine," she finally said.

"Well, I am." The woman shifted a bit, but she didn't turn around.

Martha wanted to see the face of the person she was talking to. She gently tapped her on the shoulder again. "I'm going to call a nurse if you don't turn around and let me see that you're all right."

As the covers shifted, the woman slowly turned to face Martha, and Martha gasped.

"Do I look all right to you?" The woman could barely move her mouth due to the stitches across her lip, and Martha wasn't sure she'd ever seen a shiner like the one this young woman had. Her left eye was swollen shut, and another gash ran along the side of her cheek with more stitches. "Happy now?" She turned back to face the window.

Martha didn't move or speak for a few moments, then she took in a swift breath. "Whoever did that to you should be shot in the . . ." She bit her lip and remembered that the good Lord was listening. "Did a boyfriend or husband do that to you?"

No answer.

"Maybe a car wreck?"

The woman eased back around to face Martha. "I really don't want to talk right now. Can you please just leave me alone?" She rolled over again, just about the time Katie Ann walked back into the room.

"What are you doing out of bed?" Katie Ann moved toward her, and Martha reluctantly climbed back into bed. Once she was settled beneath her quilt, which, unbeknownst to Katie Ann, she'd had blessed by both a priest and Bishop Esh, she folded her arms across her chest.

Katie Ann leaned closer and whispered, "They'll be moving that woman out of here shortly, and you'll have the room to yourself."

Martha scowled. "What?"

Still whispering, Katie Ann leaned even closer to Martha's ear. "You told me that you didn't want to share a room, so they are coming to get her soon."

"Well, that's ridiculous." She waved her hand toward the door. "Go back and tell them never mind."

Katie Ann's mouth fell open as she cupped her hands to her hips.

"Oh, don't look so bothered. I'm the one about to get cut wide open. Just go now . . ." She waved her hand again, and Katie Ann shook her head all the way out the door.

Martha wanted to talk to the woman next to her. Actually, she was more like a girl, maybe sixteen or seventeen. But she wasn't sure how to start up a conversation without irritating her more.

Just then the door eased open. Martha glanced up, and she was sure her heart was going to beat out of her chest. "Arnold?

What in the world are you doing here? Now I'm *sure* I'm going to die, or you wouldn't be here."

The love of her life took off a black felt hat, similar to what the Amish folks wore, although Arnold was as Catholic as could be, and he shuffled toward the bed. "Hello, Martha. You should have told me you were ill." He leaned down, and to her surprise, he kissed her on the cheek. "I've missed you."

She swallowed back a lump in her throat. "How are things in Georgia?"

"I had my reasons why I needed to stay there after my son passed, but I am wrapping things up." He smiled. "I'm thinking about moving back here, to Canaan."

"Well, that's just peachy, Arnold. You decide to move back here *now*? When I'm about to kick the bucket?" She rolled her eyes, glanced up, and prayed aloud. "Lord, there is something unfair about this."

Arnold sat down in the chair by her bed, reached for her hand, and squeezed. "You are going to be just fine, Martha. I know it."

"Nope. I'm fairly certain that I'm not going to wake up once they knock me out." She squinted her eyes. "So, Arnold Becker, if there is anything you want to tell me, I suggest you do it right now." She raised her chin.

Arnold chuckled. "Still my same Martha."

His eyes twinkled, and Martha wished she could marry him on the spot.

"My, how I've missed you." Then he frowned. "Why wouldn't you let me come visit you?"

She turned to face the poor girl next to her, who was still facing the window. "I didn't want to have to say good-bye again."

She turned back to him. "But here you are, and I guess I'll have to say it anyway."

"I needed to be with my daughter-in-law and her family. We were all grieving, and I hated to leave them . . . and . . ." He pulled his eyes away from hers as he took a deep breath. "I didn't come back to stay because I couldn't provide for you in a proper manner. But I made some investments, and now—"

"Did the good Lord strip you of your senses?" Martha stiffened as she thought about all the months she'd missed this man. "I have more money than I'll ever spend in a lifetime. I thought you knew that."

Arnold stood taller. "But I wanted to be able to take care of you."

She stared into his kind eyes, never more touched—or frustrated. She pressed her lips firmly together for a moment. "On the off chance I pull through this, am I gonna have to tell you good-bye again?"

"Yes, we'll have to part ways once you are better. But I'll be back in a few weeks. To stay, if that's all right with you."

Martha shrugged, elated, but not about to let Arnold know just how much. "It's a free country."

Arnold chuckled again. "Yes, it is."

Martha narrowed her brows. "Who told you I was getting cut on today?" She waved her hand in the air. "Oh, never mind. I know who it was."

Right then, Katie Ann walked back into the room.

"My goodness, Katie Ann, look who showed up out of the blue!" She lifted one brow at Katie Ann, never more grateful to her friend.

"How about that, Martha. What a coincidence." Katie Ann smiled. She walked closer to Martha and whispered again. "The girl is staying, but I don't know why you can't make up your mind."

"Because I'm old."

Katie Ann grinned. "You visit with Arnold. I'm going to go find out when they are coming for you."

KATIE ANN WALKED to the nurses' station and asked to speak to Martha's doctor. She waited in a chair for almost fifteen minutes before a doctor walked up to her.

"Hi. I'm Dr. Lieberson. Were you asking about Martha Dobbs?"

Katie Ann stood and shook the doctor's hand. "*Ya*. I was." She took a deep breath, unsure how to ask the questions on her mind. "I was just—just wondering about . . ."

She recalled David's kidney transplant and how everything was always presented to them in percentages. Chance the kidney would fail, 33 percent, or chance of infection, 50 percent. Things like that.

"Can you tell me what Martha's percentage is?"

"Percentage?" The young doctor folded his arms across his chest. "Percentage about . . ."

Katie Ann bit her bottom lip and avoided his eyes. "What is the percentage that Martha will survive the surgery?" She glanced up at him as her heart thumped in her chest.

He paused. "Well, there are always risks when anyone has surgery, but I don't foresee any problems. Martha should be able to go home tomorrow afternoon."

Katie Ann gasped. "So soon? But won't she have a large cut on her stomach that must be tended?"

"No. It won't be a very big incision at all."

"But if her tumor is the size of a grapefruit, that seems like—"

"What?" Dr. Lieberson pulled off a pair of dark-rimmed glasses and squinted. "Martha doesn't have a tumor the size of a grapefruit. It's no larger than a pea."

"The kind you eat?" Katie Ann felt ridiculous the moment she said it, but she was more than confused already.

The doctor smiled. "Yes, like the kind you eat. We did a biopsy, and the cyst is benign, but it's causing her some irritation, so we're removing it. It's a very simple procedure that should take less than an hour, plus her time in recovery."

Katie Ann laughed out loud. "I'm sorry, doctor." She put a hand over her mouth to stifle further laughter as relief washed over her. "This is very *gut* news. Martha must have misunderstood her diagnosis."

She wasn't sure if that was the case, or if Martha did what she usually did when it came to medical issues . . . embellished a bit. Either way, Katie Ann was glad to hear this.

Dr. Lieberson narrowed his brows. "I'm sorry if Martha didn't understand. I spoke to her briefly after she met with her regular physician."

Katie Ann smiled. "It's all right. Martha must have been confused. I'll go make sure she understands."

"Do you want me to talk to her?"

"No." Katie Ann was anxious to get back to the room. "When will they be coming to get her?"

The doctor scratched his cheek. "They should have already been to get her. I can check and see—"

"Katie Ann!"

Katie Ann swung around to see Martha approaching on a gurney with her arm stretched out and Arnold by her side. An orderly was pushing her along.

"They won't let me take my quilt."

"It'll be in your room when you get back."

Martha shook her head. "*If* I get back."

"Martha, your cyst is very small. The doctor said this will be a very easy and quick surgery. You even get to go home tomorrow afternoon. Isn't that wonderful?"

"Big. Small. Whatever. I have a foreign growth inside of me." She scowled at Katie Ann, then turned to Arnold and batted her eyes. "I'm so glad you're with me during this difficult time."

Once again, Katie Ann put a hand over her mouth. She knew any surgery was risky, but she wasn't sure she'd seen Martha quite this dramatic before. She leaned down and kissed her on the cheek. "I love you. I'll pray that all goes well. And I'll see you shortly."

"Bye, Katie Ann."

Something about the way Martha spoke her name made Katie Ann terribly uneasy, and she didn't feel like smiling anymore. Instead, she stepped aside as Martha's gurney rolled past her, then she slowly followed. Once Martha was settled, she wanted to find the chapel.

TWO HOURS LATER, Katie Ann was growing antsy, and she could tell Arnold was too. He kept getting up, pacing in the waiting room, then sitting back down.

"Didn't they say it would only take an hour?" he asked Katie Ann for the third time.

She nodded. She'd found the chapel earlier and prayed for the Lord to place His healing hand on Martha, and now, as they waited, she prayed even more.

A few minutes later, Dr. Lieberson came out from behind the double doors that led to the operating rooms. Katie Ann stood up. When she saw him smile, she put a hand on her chest.

"Everything went just fine. She'll be in recovery for about an hour, then she'll be back in her room." He chuckled. "She mumbled something about food when she was first waking up." He stroked his chin. "I thought she said creamed celery, but I'm not sure." He reached out and shook both Katie Ann and Arnold's hands. "Anyway, she's doing just fine."

"Thank you." Katie Ann turned to Arnold and gave him a hug.

After a prayer of thanks, she and Arnold grabbed a bite to eat before heading back to Martha's room. Martha's roommate was still facing the window, so they were as quiet as they could be in case she was sleeping.

They'd barely sat down when the same orderly as before rolled Martha in.

Martha pointed a wobbly finger at the man. "Creamed celery is what I said."

"Yes, ma'am," he replied with a smile.

A nurse entered the room then, and together she and the orderly got Martha situated in her bed. Katie Ann quickly found the quilt and spread it on top of her.

"She's still pretty groggy." The orderly lifted the railing on the side of Martha's bed. "And I'm pretty sure she's hungry."

He grinned. "You folks have a good day." He waved as he left the room.

Katie Ann and Arnold each went to opposite sides of Martha's bed.

"Hello, sunshine." Arnold leaned down and kissed Martha on the cheek, but Martha turned to Katie Ann.

"I'm alive."

Katie Ann reached for Martha's hand and smiled. "*Ya*, you are."

"In that case, I'm hungry."

"I saw carts of food being wheeled around earlier, so I bet you will have some food very soon." Katie Ann brushed back some of Martha's gray strands that had fallen across her forehead.

"Creamed celery." Martha's eyes were closed as she spoke, and Katie Ann wondered if she would even be able to stay awake long enough to eat.

"I don't think the hospital has creamed celery, Martha."

Katie Ann heard movement to her left, and she turned to catch a glimpse of the battered young woman staring at all of them. The girl quickly turned back the other way. Katie Ann was wondering what happened to the girl when Martha squeezed her hand.

"Katie Ann, I think I need a nap . . ." Martha closed her eyes.

Katie Ann turned to Arnold. "The doctor said she would sleep most of today."

Arnold nodded, and even though Martha did indeed sleep most of the day, Katie Ann and Arnold both stayed with her until late in the afternoon and finally told her good-bye around four o'clock.

During their time at the hospital, Katie Ann prayed. And she laughed on the inside, wondering if Martha knew how loudly she snored. But Arnold never acknowledged it. Instead, he just mentioned every little while how much he loved his Martha. Katie Ann found herself longing for that kind of love.

MARTHA PUSHED THE nurse's call button for the third time in the past fifteen minutes. "What if I was dying in here?" she mumbled, glancing at the clock on the wall. Ten o'clock. She could vaguely remember Katie Ann and Arnold telling her good-bye earlier in the day, but foremost on her mind at the moment was the fact that she had apparently missed dinner, and she was sure she'd never been this hungry in her life.

"What can I do for you?" A young woman in blue scrubs walked into the room and spoke to Martha in a whisper.

"Food. I need food. I must have slept through dinner."

"The cafeteria is closed, but I can probably find some pudding, or maybe some chips. Something like that."

Martha hung her head for a moment. "I was thinking more like a burger and some fries." She looked up at the woman. "But I'd be grateful for anything you can round up."

"Sure." She picked up Martha's chart at the end of the bed and studied it for a moment. "No food restrictions. Let me go see what I can find."

After the woman left, Martha heard rock music coming from the bed next to her, then the girl answered a cell phone with a strained hello.

Martha lowered the volume on her television a bit.

"I don't know when I can go home. They haven't said. I think I'll be in here for a few more days." After a long silence, she said, "I know. That's what you always say." A moment later she clicked the phone closed and stared at the ceiling.

Martha studied the girl for a moment and wondered again what had happened to her.

"Why don't you just take a picture?" The girl turned to face Martha.

Her voice sounded like a reflection of the girl herself. Broken.

Martha took a deep breath as she gazed into the girl's one good eye. "What's your name?"

"Danielle." She dabbed at her lip with her finger and grimaced.

"I'm Martha."

Silence. Martha could tell Danielle wasn't in the mood to be friendly—and who would blame her?—but blatant curiosity drove Martha on. "Who did that to you?"

Danielle slowly twisted her head toward Martha. "Look, lady . . . *Martha* . . . I don't mean to be rude, but my situation is really none of your business." She closed her one good eye and winced, clearly in pain.

"Are they giving you something for the pain?" Martha shifted her weight slightly, thankful that she didn't seem to be experiencing near the discomfort as this poor child.

"I guess." Danielle opened her eye and stared at Martha for a few moments. "Is Arnold your boyfriend?"

"He used to be." She lifted one shoulder. "I don't know. I guess maybe he will be again."

"You're not very nice to him."

Martha pressed her lips together, raised one brow, and prepared to lambaste this child. But when the girl grimaced in pain again, Martha said simply, "I'm a lot nicer than whoever beat the snot out of you."

Danielle stared up at the ceiling, and they were both quiet for a while. Martha hoped the nurse would return with some food soon.

"So . . ." Danielle turned to face Martha again. She could barely move her swollen lips as she spoke, and Martha strained to hear her. "That woman who was here . . . she's Amish, huh?"

"Yes. Her name's Katie Ann."

Come on with some chow, nurse. Martha glanced toward the door and sighed.

"Those people are weird."

Martha turned to face her, semi-glad that a conversation was ensuing. "The Amish are the gentlest and kindest folks I know." She turned her attention to the door when it swung open.

The same young nurse smiled and entered. "The McDonald's downstairs was still open, so here you go." She placed a bag on the nightstand by Martha's bed.

Martha breathed in the aroma of French fries and wanted to hug the woman's neck. "Honey, my purse is right there inside that drawer . . ." She started to reach for the drawer of the nightstand, but gasped when she pulled against her incision.

"Now, now. You lie back," the kind woman said. "No need to pay me."

"Yes, I need to pay you. I insist." Martha opened the bag with the burger and fries. "You are my hero."

The woman chuckled. "I don't know about that, but just

pay it forward. Do something nice for someone else." Before Martha could respond, the nurse walked toward Danielle. "Can I get you anything, Danielle?"

Danielle just shook her head.

"Okay." She turned to leave. "I'm here until six in the morning, so let me know if either of you needs anything."

Martha dived into her burger and moaned with delight. Then she glanced at Danielle. "French fry?"

Danielle shook her head. "Those people are holy, aren't they?"

"What people?" Martha asked around a mouthful.

"The Amish. They're like all into God and everything, right?"

Martha swallowed. "They have a very strong faith." She popped a fry into her mouth. "Good folks, the Amish."

It was quiet for a while, only the low buzz of the television, some late-night talk show, and the beeps and sounds from the other side of the door. Normal hospital sounds. Martha was glad she was going home tomorrow, back to her own bed. And surely Katie Ann was at home making her some creamed celery. She smiled.

"I don't believe in God."

Martha snapped her head to the right. "What?"

"You heard me, Martha. There is no God, and people who waste their time praying to Him are doing just that . . . wasting their time."

Martha thought her heart might break. If this girl needed anyone, it was surely the Lord. "How old are you, child?"

"Seventeen."

"Not very smart for your age, are ya?"

Danielle squinted her eye at Martha and spoke slowly

through half-opened lips. "Just because I don't believe in God, that makes me stupid?"

"Correct." Martha shoved the last bit of burger in her mouth.

"You don't know anything about me. I used to make straight As in school, and I even graduated early."

"Micky D's wouldn't normally be my first choice for a meal, but this is the best burger I've ever had." Martha stuffed her trash into the bag and carefully eased it onto the nightstand, careful not to twist too quickly.

"Did you hear me? I'm very smart."

Martha didn't look at Danielle. "Yeah. I heard you."

"People just wrote all that stuff in the Bible to keep us from killing each other."

Martha turned to Danielle and lowered her chin. "Really? Wow, hasn't that worked well."

"You know what I mean. It's all made up, something to keep the masses in order."

"If that's what you choose to believe."

"It's the truth."

"If you say so."

They were quiet for a while, and Martha was starting to feel like she could sleep, but when Danielle spoke again, Martha heard the Lord calling her loud and clear.

"Why do you believe in God? What proof do you have that He exists?"

Martha took a deep breath, clicked the television off, and faced Danielle. "How much time you got?"

Thirteen

Lucy stared at tiny Benjamin in his incubator in the preemie nursery at Lancaster General Hospital. He was small but healthy, and Lucy missed Ivan now more than ever before.

Ivan, we have a beautiful baby boy.

Leaving him to go home would be the hardest thing she'd ever done, but the doctors had told her that he would have to stay in the hospital for at least two more months until he was closer to full term. He looked like Ivan with his big eyes, and like Lucy with his small pug nose. He was the most beautiful thing she'd ever seen, and she wanted more than anything to be a good mother, even though she and Ivan had never really discussed having a family. Ivan always said that if it was God's will, it would happen.

Lucy wondered what she could do to get on good terms with God. She'd never really had much to do with Him prior to her affair with Ivan, but she was sure God disliked her even more than she disliked herself. She'd been praying every day, asking for forgiveness and begging that God would show her how to be a good mother. She thought about Katie Ann a lot, sure that Ivan's wife was a wonderful mother. Lucy wondered if she and Katie Ann might have been friends in another life, but she knew the answer. Katie Ann was a good person. Lucy wasn't. But as she gazed down at the tiny miracle before her, she had this feeling that maybe there was hope.

MARTHA CLEANED UP in the small bathroom in her hospital room, moving slowly, but not in too much pain. Just glad to be alive.

Thank You, Lord.

She was brushing her teeth when she heard a nurse talking to Danielle. She turned off the water and pressed an ear to the door.

"Danielle, we have to discharge you today. We've let you stay an extra two days. Is there someone I can call to come pick you up?"

Martha held her breath and waited. No answer. The nurse started speaking again.

"Honey, are you sure you don't want to visit with that policeman who was here a few days ago? Are you sure you don't know who did this to you?"

Silence again. Martha scowled. That girl had to know who had done this to her. She listened as footsteps exited the room. She needed her butterfly clip from her small suitcase. Shuffling across the floor to her bag, she glanced up at Danielle. She was sitting up in bed, but staring at the floor. Martha had talked to her about God for almost three hours, and even told her some incredibly personal tales about her own faith journey, stories that would have made the average gal shed a tear or two. Not Danielle.

And when Martha had finished baring her heart in an effort for this lost soul to see the Lord for the hero He could be for her, Danielle had merely said, "Is that all you've got?"

Martha had fallen asleep in prayer, telling the Lord that she'd tried her best.

She located her clip and headed back to the bathroom. It took her longer than usual to secure her hair, since it hurt to lift her arms very high. She needed some help and wondered where Katie Ann and Arnold were. She thought they would have been here by now.

As she hadn't completely shut the bathroom door, she went to push it closed when she saw movement in the room. Peering through the tiny crack, she watched as Danielle tiptoed around Martha's bed. She kept watching as Danielle eased the drawer to the nightstand open. It didn't take her long to find Martha's wallet. Instinctively she opened her mouth to tell the little thief to step back, but she didn't.

Danielle had closed the drawer and was back in her bed in less than a minute, and Martha figured it wasn't the girl's first rodeo. She also figured Danielle probably needed the sixty dollars in Martha's wallet more than she did, but lies and thievery irritated Martha more than anything else. She wasn't sure how to handle this.

Once she finally had her hair semi-secure with the butterfly clip, she smoothed the wrinkles from her pink blouse. If she'd known Arnold was coming, she would have brought her matching pink earrings and necklace, but at the time Katie Ann was already scolding her for taking too much to the hospital.

She eased out of the bathroom and slowly lowered herself onto her bed. Now she just had to wait for Arnold and Katie Ann to get here. She gave Danielle an all-knowing smile, but the girl just sat on the edge of the bed, looking down at the floor.

"I heard you tell someone on the phone that you wouldn't be released for a few more days." Martha spoke firmly, tempted to tell Danielle that she was a thief *and* a liar. "But based on what I just heard the nurse say, that was a lie." She pointed her finger at Danielle and leaned forward. "You want to stay here in the hospital because it's *safe*. Right?" Martha couldn't hold back. "Who did this to you, Danielle?"

Danielle put her head in her hands for a moment, but when she looked back up at Martha, her one functional eye was wild with anger. "Are you always this much in everybody's business?"

Martha sat taller, as tall as she could without putting pressure on her incision. "If I need to be."

"Well, you don't even know me, so stay out of my business."

"Suit yourself." Martha felt sick to her stomach.

Pay it forward. Do something nice for someone. The nurse's words echoed in her head, but Martha figured she had done something nice. She was letting Danielle keep the sixty dollars she'd stolen from Martha's purse.

As the door swung wide, Martha turned to see Arnold and Katie Ann. "Katie Ann, please tell me that I'm going to a place where there will be creamed celery?"

Katie Ann kissed her on the cheek. "I have a fresh batch at home. I thought you might want to stay with me for a day or two until you're feeling better."

Martha didn't feel all that bad, but being catered to was

not something she was going to turn down either. "I guess I'd better." She turned to Arnold. "So what are your plans?"

"I'm going to see that you get settled at Katie Ann's, then I'll head home." He smiled. "To take care of some things. And pack."

Martha smiled.

"Yesterday I rented a small house." Arnold grinned. "Not too far from yours."

"My house is plenty big. You should have just picked you out a bedroom upstairs. I haven't even been up there in months. It'd be like having your own apartment." Martha braced herself for Katie Ann's rebuttal that was sure to come.

"Martha! That would have been totally inappropriate." Katie Ann raised her chin and glared at Martha, which only made Martha cackle.

"What? You worried about my reputation? At this age, Katie Ann?" She turned to Arnold. "Will we be having lasagna on Wednesdays, like we used to?"

Arnold moved toward Martha's suitcase and picked it up. "I sure hope so."

Martha pointed a finger at him. "Although something has changed since you've been gone, Arnold Becker."

His expression dropped. "What's that?"

"We used to go to your church in Alamosa, but since you've been gone, I've been worshipping with Katie Ann and her people." She glanced at Katie Ann. "I bet they'd let you come too."

Arnold smiled but didn't say anything.

Martha had enjoyed attending Mass with Arnold before he left, but his lack of response about the matter made her wonder if he'd consider a change to the Amish way of worshipping, which she tended to prefer these days. Martha had disliked the backless benches at first, but mysteriously several high-backed chairs showed up on the worship wagon shortly after she'd complained. She didn't understand most of the service, but after the noon meal, Katie Ann would translate whatever Martha didn't understand, which usually led to a lengthy discussion that Martha always enjoyed. Plus, the meal after worship was always a good one. And if there was another bonus to attending Amish worship, it was the fact that you only had to go to church every other Sunday. Probably because it was three hours long, but Martha was glad to have every other Sunday "off," as she called it.

"We checked at the front desk," Arnold said. "And you are cleared to go."

Martha pulled her purse from the drawer in the nightstand.

Katie Ann picked up the quilt and asked, "Are you sure you have everything?"

Martha shot a slow and coy smile at Danielle. "Probably not, but oh well."

"Guess we're ready then." Katie Ann moved toward the door with Arnold as he carried Martha's suitcase.

Danielle had lain back down on her bed and was staring at the ceiling.

Martha looked at her long and hard and chose her words carefully. "Danielle, I wish you well."

Danielle turned to face Martha and blinked her one eye several times. "You too."

Martha turned to leave before the girl could see the tears welling in her eyes.

Please, Lord . . . help her to see the wonder of Your love.

Arnold closed the door behind them.

Arnold left on Thursday afternoon after having lunch with Katie Ann and Martha at Katie Ann's house, and by Friday afternoon, Katie Ann could tell that Martha was ready to go back to her own home. She said she was feeling better and had gotten what she called her "Jonas fix." And while Katie Ann loved having Martha stay with them, she was exhausted from tending to both her friend and her baby. She wasn't sure which one was more demanding.

Arnold had driven Martha's car to Katie Ann's, then taken a cab to the airport, promising that he would be back soon and for good.

"Are you sure you can drive?" Katie Ann helped Martha get into her coat, hat, and gloves. It was snowing and cold outside. "I think it might be too soon, and the weather—"

"Katie Ann, you know how I feel about that extra bed of yours. I can only take it for so long. Besides, I'm only going around the corner." She kissed Katie Ann on the cheek. "Tell my baby I will see him on Sunday. I'm going to stay home out of this weather and rest tomorrow."

"I think that's a *gut* idea." Katie Ann waited until Martha's car rounded the corner before she closed the door.

Lillian came over later that afternoon with Anna and Elizabeth, and Emily stopped by also, thinking that Martha was still there. After all her company left, Katie Ann settled in front of the fireplace with Jonas in her lap and reread Eli's letter. She missed his smile, his laughter. As the fire crackled in the fireplace and the wind gently howled outside, Katie Ann wondered what he was doing. If he missed her at all.

The next morning, she heard a truck coming up the driveway. She finished feeding Jonas, laid him in the playpen near the fireplace, and went to the window. A Federal Express man was making his way through the snow and up to her porch.

"*Danki*," she said as she accepted the small box.

"You're welcome." The young man with a black stocking cap and heavy coat chuckled. "It's a cell phone, in case you didn't know." He paused, rubbing his gloved hands together. "It's been ringing in the truck on and off for the past two hours."

Katie Ann didn't know what to say, and the nice young fellow didn't wait for a response before heading back to his truck. Katie Ann hadn't even closed the door when she heard the faint ring from inside the box. Smiling, she walked to the couch and hurriedly worked to open the package. Only one person she knew would send her a cell phone.

SATURDAY MORNING MARTHA eased into her recliner with a cup of coffee, her thoughts on Katie Ann. She was starting to lose hope for Eli Detweiler. Hard to have a romance when the fellow was in another state. But at least the two were writing to each other, so just maybe . . .

She noticed a pile of bills on her end table. There wasn't a task she hated more than paying bills. She had plenty of money, more than the average person by far, but it was just a tedious chore. The piles seemed to be screaming at her as she sipped her coffee, so she eventually pulled her purse into her lap and took out her wallet, which also held her checkbook. She thought about Danielle. She'd been praying for the girl every night. That she'd be safe from whoever did harm to her, and that she'd put her trust in the Lord.

Martha hoped Danielle wouldn't steal from anyone else. Some folks might not be as understanding about it as she'd been. She opened her wallet, pulled her pen from its spot, and wrote out a check to the gas company. Then she curiously unzipped the money compartment, wondering if Danielle had taken all sixty dollars.

Martha pulled three twenties from inside and sat holding them for a moment. *Why didn't she take it?* She began to inspect the contents of her wallet, confused. Something had to be missing. What was it?

There were no checks missing. The cash was there. A book of stamps, several business cards she'd collected from local vendors. She drummed her fingers on the end table, holding the wallet with her other hand. She flipped through her credit cards, found her driver's license, her AARP card, and even two extra bobby pins clipped next to her credit cards.

She took a deep breath. Maybe her mind was going. Everything seemed to be just as it should be.

By the time Katie Ann ripped open the box, the portable phone wasn't ringing anymore. She picked it up and searched through the packing for a note, but the only thing besides the phone was what appeared to be an extra battery. She jumped when the phone rang again. She'd used a cell phone on rare occasions before, so she knew how they worked. This one flipped open.

"Hello."

"Katie Ann! *Gut, gut.* You got the phone."

"Eli?" She knew exactly who it was, but she was at a loss for words, so she waited for him to explain.

"I got your letter about Martha yesterday. I went right out and had this phone shipped overnight to you. I charged the batteries at the store before I shipped it." He took a breath. "I realized that by the time you got my letters, then I got yours, well . . . too much time was passing. How is Martha?"

"*Ach*, she's *gut*. It turned out to be a very small cyst." She still couldn't believe he had sent her a phone.

Katie Ann gave Eli the details of the past few days, even explaining about Arnold.

"Katie Ann, it's so *gut* to hear your voice. And I couldn't have you running out to the barn in bad weather to talk on the phone." He paused. "Is this okay? I mean, the phone?"

"Lots of people have cell phones. Our bishop isn't keen on the idea, but he doesn't make much of a fuss. But the money, Eli . . ."

He laughed. "They have this thing called the family plan. Only ten dollars! So now we're family."

Something about his statement warmed Katie Ann from head to toe. "I see." She brought her hand to her chest, closed her eyes, and pictured his face.

"Katie Ann, I'm going to Jake and Laura Jane's for supper. I just wanted to make sure you got the phone."

"*Danki* for the phone, Eli. You didn't need to do that." Katie Ann wondered how often he would call her, and if she would ever call him. She knew it would be easy enough to charge the phone at Martha's house.

"Can I call you when I get home later?"

She smiled. "I'd like that."

After they hung up, Katie Ann warmed up some soup. As she sat on the couch eating it, she eyed the box in the corner of her living room. It was an indoor swing for Jonas that Lillian had given her as a gift recently. Lillian had told her that she used a swing when both Anna and Elizabeth were babies, and that it was a lifesaver. Samuel had offered to put it together, but her brother-in-law was so busy that Katie Ann assured him she could do the job.

It was later in the evening, once Jonas was settled, when she started to put the swing together. She searched for the right nuts and bolts to attach the legs of the swing. Even though she'd sorted the parts into piles, she was confused about the directions and frustrated. She jumped when the cell phone rang on the kitchen counter.

"*Wie bischt?*"

Katie Ann smiled when she heard Eli's voice. "I'm *gut*, but I'm having trouble putting a swing together for Jonas. How was your supper with Jake and Laura Jane?"

"Laura Jane invites me to supper when she makes chicken and wafers, my favorite. What's the problem with the swing?"

"Too many nuts and bolts." She waited awhile for a response, but nothing. "Eli?"

Silence.

She pulled the phone away from her ear and realized the battery was dead. She picked up the extra battery Eli had sent but couldn't figure out where to install it. She tinkered with the phone, then opened the instruction book that had come in the box with the phone. After about fifteen frustrating minutes, she had the other battery installed.

Ten minutes later Eli called again. "Dead battery, no?"

His voice was light and cheerful, but Katie Ann was annoyed by her own inability to handle such simple functions in a timely manner. First the swing, now the phone.

"*Ya*. Sorry it took me so long. I had to get out the instruction book."

"I wish I was there to put that swing together for you. What about Samuel?"

"*Ach*, he offered, but I was sure it would be no problem." She sighed as she eased onto the couch and curled her feet beneath her. She pulled a small afghan onto her lap. "I'll finish it tomorrow."

From there, she and Eli settled into a comfortable conversation. He told her that he was not going to Indiana because of the weather, and had decided to go to Florida instead, but not until after Christmas. Katie Ann told him more about the pot holders she'd been quilting and a cookbook she was putting together.

"It keeps me busy late at night if I can't sleep." She leaned her head back against the couch, tired but knowing sleep wouldn't come anytime soon, and she would rather talk with Eli than sleep anyway. She smiled as she thought about what Lillian and Martha would think if they knew she was casually chatting on the phone with Eli.

"I have a hard time sleeping too." He paused. "I never used to have trouble sleeping. Do you think it's because we're getting old?" He chuckled.

"*Ya*. I guess so." Katie Ann pulled the phone from her ear for a moment, making sure it was still lit up. "How long will this battery last?"

"It should last a couple of days."

Katie Ann smiled.

And she spent the next several hours on the phone with Eli, discussing everything from his Florida plans to her desire to someday sell her handmade goods. Eli encouraged her and told her that she could do anything she wanted to do. Ivan had said that her efforts would produce little income and she'd be wasting her time. But finishing a handmade pot holder or throw quilt gave her a sense of satisfaction, like she was being fruitful. And she was building up quite a collection. It might not ever amount to much, but it made her happy, and Eli's encouragement warmed her heart.

She didn't think she'd ever enjoyed a conversation more than this one, and during the weeks to follow, their phone calls became a nightly thing. Every couple of days she would charge the phone at Martha's house, even if it meant taking a few minutes of ribbing from her friend. Katie Ann found herself sharing even the smallest details about her day. And when Jake and Laura Jane's baby was born—Eli's seventh grandchild—Eli called her from the hospital, more excited than ever about the new blessing.

He truly was her best friend, and while she knew friends had the capacity to hurt one another, there was something safe about her relationship with Eli. And every time she fantasized about something more than friendship with him, she forced the idea away because she realized that God was answering her prayers—in His way.

"Ask, and it shall be given you; seek, and ye shall find; knock, and it shall be opened unto you."

Katie Ann asked God to forgive her for doubting Him and for the distance she'd put between them. She sought to trust again, and the Lord had opened a new door. It might not have been what she expected, but her friendship with Eli was proving to be a gift from God.

WHEN ELI SHOWED up on her doorstep two days before Christmas, Katie Ann jumped into his arms without hesitation.

"What are you doing here?" She pulled from the embrace and coaxed him inside and out of the icy weather. "Why didn't you tell me you were coming?"

Eli's smile stretched across his handsome face. "Because I just decided to come this morning—I flew! Besides, it was worth it to see you so surprised."

Katie Ann laughed aloud. "I can't believe you did this."

She'd already mailed him a hand-stitched black vest for Christmas, which he had received and told her fit perfectly. He'd sent her a parenting book that focused on the toddler years, later laughing and telling her to be prepared—that it was a wonderful time but could be challenging. And he'd sent a Bible storybook for Jonas.

Eli moved across the living room to where Jonas was tucked into his swing and sleeping soundly. "I had one of those swings for Maureen. She loved it." He gazed down at Jonas, then back at Katie Ann. "I have to go back tomorrow. *Mei kinner* would be mighty upset if I wasn't there for Christmas. But I just had to see you." He pulled her into a hug and kissed her on the cheek. Katie Ann made no effort to leave the safety of his strong arms.

Finally he eased away and gazed into her eyes. "You look beautiful."

She covered her eyes with her hands. "I do not."

Eli gently pulled her hands away. "Trust me, you do."

Trust. Not so long ago, the word would have stung, been a reminder of all she'd lost.

As their eyes stayed locked together, Katie Ann wished she knew what was going on in Eli's mind and in his heart. They'd gotten so close that under normal circumstances, it would have seemed normal for them to take the next step past friendship. But they both knew that they were not going to make that leap.

"Do Vera and Elam know you're here?" Katie Ann walked to Jonas's swing and cranked the handle so that the swing would keep going.

"They do now. I asked the cabdriver to stop by there on my way here." He laughed. "I had to make sure I had a place to stay tonight."

By now everyone knew that the two of them talked on a regular basis. But Katie Ann wondered what Vera must be thinking about Eli's spontaneous trip to Canaan—by plane, no less.

Eli gently eased Jonas out of the swing. Katie Ann would have reprimanded anyone else for waking him up like that, but as Eli held Jonas up and gazed into his eyes, it was a precious sight that she knew she would cherish.

"How is *mei* little man?" Eli talked in the familiar baby talk to Jonas, and Katie Ann knew that Eli's arrival was by far the best Christmas gift she'd ever received.

They sat on the couch talking and drinking hot tea until the early morning hours, then Eli kissed her tenderly on the mouth and went to Vera's, telling her that he would be leaving early in the morning to catch a plane back to Middlefield. Katie Ann still couldn't believe he'd made the trip. Just to see her. He'd even sought permission from his bishop to do so, since air travel was normally frowned upon unless it was an emergency.

"It was an emergency," Eli had told her earlier in the evening. Although he admitted that the bishop in his district didn't have a stiff rule against flying.

She held her tears until the door closed behind him. And for the first time, she admitted to herself—she was in love with Eli Detweiler. In love with a man who wasn't available.

ELI HAD PLENTY of time to think on the plane. He thought back to yesterday morning when he realized he had to see Katie Ann. It was an unfamiliar sensation that he knew wouldn't go away until he laid eyes on her. He admitted to himself at that moment that he had fallen in love with Katie Ann Stoltzfus. And now that he'd spent more time with her, his feelings were confirmed.

He closed his eyes, the vision of her clouding his senses, blocking the roar of the engine and the light chatter around him. His heart ached, and for a few minutes he allowed himself to visualize a life with Katie Ann and Jonas. He was happiest when he was with her. But he'd made plans. And he'd had those plans a lot longer than he'd known her.

Fearing he'd taken too much of a risk with his heart—and possibly hers—he wondered if it might not be best to pull back some. She had to know they were in a dangerous place, to be as close as they were and not be able to move forward. Or maybe she was happy like this. Eli had thought it was the perfect arrangement. Best friends with a beautiful woman whom he was not responsible for.

Funny thing was—he felt as responsible for her and Jonas as he did any other member of his family.

He unzipped the backpack he'd carried onto the plane and pulled out a brochure about Florida, resolved that he would go there right after Christmas. He was going to need something to distract his heart, and what better way than to pursue the life he'd planned out. Flipping through the pages, he forced Katie Ann out of his mind.

Fourteen

CHRISTMAS CAME AND WENT, AND AMID THE FESTIVITIES Katie Ann missed Eli more than ever. It was a blessing to be able to share her first Christmas with Jonas, but she found herself quietly weeping at times. Sometimes because she missed Eli, and other times . . . because she still missed Ivan. Not so much the man as the memories from their early years. But every time her thoughts drifted to Ivan, they quickly shifted back to Eli, and it was Eli she wished were there to witness all Jonas's firsts. At four months Jonas was making a new sound, a gurgle when he smiled, and Katie Ann thought it was the cutest thing she'd ever seen. Eli would love it.

Lucy had written to say that she'd given birth to a boy and named him Benjamin. He was born very tiny, but healthy. Katie Ann found it strange that Lucy would write to her at all, until she got to the end of the letter—the part where Lucy asked if she'd heard anything about the house she thought Ivan had built or bought. Katie Ann didn't write her back.

Eli still called her, but Katie Ann could feel him pulling back on the friendship. Perhaps he had sensed that Katie Ann cared about him more than just as a friend. Or maybe she just shouldn't have trusted her heart to any man. But each time that notion reared, she'd remember how she and Eli had defined the terms of their relationship early on. So was it really rational to blame him because she allowed herself to get too close?

Either way, Eli was in Florida. He'd left a week after Christmas, with plans to stay until he felt like going home. In the past two weeks, she'd only heard from him twice. In fairness, Katie Ann had his cell phone number, and she could have called him. During his first call, he'd described the beach to her and said that he wished he would have come during the summer, but how the temperatures were still much milder than in Ohio this time of year. He'd read three books, done some sightseeing, and eaten at some fine restaurants.

Katie Ann told him how her inventory of homemade items was growing and how she'd talked to several shops in Monte Vista about taking her things on consignment.

And Eli always asked about Jonas. And if Katie Ann needed anything.

She needed *him*. But she always said that she and Jonas were fine.

Tonight she was waiting for Martha to arrive for their Saturday night meal together. Arnold wouldn't be moving back to Canaan for another week. Martha promised Katie Ann that nothing would change, but Katie Ann knew some things would change, as they should. She hoped that Martha and Arnold would get married. But every time she mentioned it to Martha, her friend changed the subject.

"I'm so tired of this cold weather." Martha walked into the living room, handed a pan of chicken lasagna to Katie Ann, and peeled off her coat, hat, and gloves. After taking a deep breath, she hung her purse on the rack by the door and said, "Now, where's my baby?"

Katie Ann nodded toward Jonas's room. "He's already asleep, but go peek in on him if you'd like."

Martha rounded the corner, and Katie Ann could hear her talking softly. A few minutes later she came into the kitchen where Katie Ann was setting the table. She plopped down in a kitchen chair. "You know, I think I might be losing my mind."

Katie Ann grinned. "Why is that?"

"I'm forgetful." She scratched her head. "I mean, I'm forgetting where I put things."

Katie Ann put two glasses on the table and filled them with tea. "That doesn't mean you're losing your mind."

Martha grunted. "Well, it sure feels like it." She leaned back in her chair and pointed to the chicken lasagna. "I was sure I bought a loaf of garlic bread to go with that lasagna, but I can't find it anywhere."

"No worries." Katie Ann put a loaf of her own homemade bread on the table. "I always have plenty of bread."

"That's not the point." She looked down at her hands. "I've also misplaced my jasmine vanilla lotion that I like so much."

Katie Ann took a seat across from Martha, and they both bowed their heads in silent prayer. Afterward, Martha scooped a large portion of lasagna onto her plate while Katie Ann helped herself to a piece of butter bread.

"I forget where I put things too." Katie Ann spread some rhubarb jam on her bread. "Especially my reading glasses."

Martha just shook her head as she chewed her food.

"Are you excited about Arnold moving into a house so close to yours?"

"Well, I'd be more excited if I could remember which day he was coming." She lifted her hands in the air. "See what I mean? He told me, but I can't remember. Something as important as that, and I can't remember if it's next Thursday or Friday." She took another bite and shook her head again.

"Just ask him again."

Martha twisted her mouth into a frown. "You haven't mentioned much about Eli lately. The two of you still writing letters?"

Katie Ann shrugged. They'd quit writing letters after Eli gave her the phone. "We talk on the phone, but he's in Florida right now."

Martha tapped her fork to the plate. "I just don't know what to think about the two of you."

"There's nothing to think about. I've told you over and over again . . . we're just friends."

"That man ever kissed you?" Martha glared at Katie Ann.

"Martha! That is not an appropriate question to ask." She avoided Martha's cool stare and focused on her plate.

"Well, you didn't deny it, so I'm assuming he has."

Katie Ann looked up to see Martha grinning. Katie Ann couldn't help grinning back.

"See, you're smiling. You've done some smooching, huh?"

Katie Ann stood up from the table and carried her plate to the sink. "I'm not discussing this with you."

Not only was it inappropriate to discuss such a thing with Martha, but Katie Ann had been training her mind not to think about those kisses with Eli. It was easier that way. Just then her cell phone rang on the kitchen counter. Katie Ann ignored it.

"Aren't you going to get that?"

Katie Ann started to run hot water in the kitchen sink, and although adrenaline shot through her body, she just shrugged. "No. I'm spending time with you."

Martha cackled. "Don't you dare let me interfere with your love life."

Katie Ann began to clear the dishes from the table. "I don't have a love life." She bit her bottom lip as she walked back to the sink. The phone rang again.

"Well, that's your fault."

Katie Ann spun around in time to see Martha raise her chin, so Katie Ann shot her a twisted smile. "Really? My fault?"

"Yep. That Eli would be a great catch, but you're afraid to let yourself be happy."

Martha huffed, and Katie Ann wanted to tell Martha she didn't know what she was talking about, but she was pretty sure she couldn't do that without crying. She kept her head down as she washed the dishes, hoping Martha would be quiet about it. Out of the corner of her eye, she saw her friend get up and put the jams in the refrigerator.

"Don't you think our little Jonas needs a father? And what about you? You can't tell me you wouldn't like to have a man to help you out around here."

Katie Ann stayed quiet as Martha shuffled around the kitchen, clearing other items from the table.

"And if you're still mourning that husband of yours—"

"I'm not," Katie Ann interrupted as she slammed a rinsed dish into the drain rack.

"I'm just sayin' that you should give Eli a chance. That's all." Martha walked up beside her and started to dry the dishes.

Katie Ann kept her head down as she chewed on her bottom lip. *Please let it go, Martha.*

"And one more thing . . ." Martha placed a dried dish in the cabinet as Katie Ann braced herself. "Don't you let what that husband of yours did keep you from loving again, because—"

"Martha, stop it! I love Eli. I love him so much it hurts." Katie Ann covered her face with her hands as she cried.

A moment later Martha was rubbing her back, and they were both quiet for a while. Then Martha spoke softly. "Honey, why didn't you tell me this?"

Katie Ann turned to Martha, then fell into her arms and sobbed, letting go of all the emotion she had built up where Eli was concerned. "Because I can't have him . . ."

Eli hit End on the cell phone as he walked to the balcony of his fancy hotel, feeling a bit guilty about the luxury he'd allowed himself for this trip. As much as he'd looked forward to some time alone, the sightseeing, and a new place—it just wasn't all he'd imagined. He'd spent his life working the land, raising *kinner*, and always having someone to take care of. Had he thought of those things as burdens at the time?

He stared out at the ocean as the cool wind threatened to pull his hat off, and he thought about his life. When had he been the happiest? Not a full second passed before he knew. When he was working the land, raising *kinner*, and having someone to take care of. As he contemplated why he'd looked forward to this time in his life, he supposed it was because these things seemed appealing at a time when they were not within reach. Now he could do anything he wanted. And all he wanted to do was go home.

Three hours later he was on a plane back to Middlefield, with more time to think. The bishop had agreed to Eli's request to fly to Florida and back, just as he had agreed to let him go see Katie Ann. But now Eli wondered if he was abusing the bishop's leniency.

As the plane prepared to take off, his thoughts drifted to Katie Ann. He'd tried again to call her from the airport, but she hadn't answered. Maybe she wasn't home or near the phone. Or maybe she didn't want to talk to him. He hadn't called her much the past couple of weeks, and their conversations were shorter these days.

Eli had wondered if—even hoped that—distance and time would help him stop thinking about her so much. Maybe once he got home and things returned to normal, he would. He couldn't help but wonder if his children were right—that it just wasn't normal for an Amish man to travel and shirk responsibility. But even when he considered a new path, one that possibly included Katie Ann, he knew he could never leave his family in Middlefield. He had never been more than a few miles from his children until recently.

He leaned his head back against the seat, closed his eyes, and tried to sleep, but Katie Ann's face was all he could see. She was her most beautiful when she was tending to Jonas, but she was a nurturing person by nature. The tender way she handled Eli, both in conversation and in touch, calmed his mind and soothed his soul. As was his duty, he'd provided for his family, but he'd also been caregiver for the children for many years after

Sarah died. A man should be strong and capable at all times, but with Katie Ann, he felt like he could let his guard down a little. And in return, he wanted to take care of her in every way.

Eli knew he couldn't leave his family. And it wasn't right to ask Katie Ann to leave the life she'd built in Canaan. And what about his plans to travel? What about loyalty to Sarah? His thoughts spiraled as they so often did recently. He just didn't see how it could work with Katie Ann.

But he wasn't sure he would ever stop thinking about her.

KATIE ANN HELD Jonas in her arms until long after he was asleep, enjoying the comfort of the one constant in her life. Her baby boy, who filled her with a love more profound than anything she'd ever known. Even when she'd heard the cell phone ringing for the second time today, she'd just sat holding Jonas, hoping the noise wouldn't wake him. Of course it was Eli. But her heart was hurting, and she wanted to blame him for that. Rationally, it wasn't fair, but over the past couple of months, she'd grown to love him in a way that was confusing.

It was late when she finally put Jonas in his bed, and after a hot bath she crawled into her bed, snuffing out the lantern before she tucked herself in. Loneliness settled in, the way it always did this time of night. She regretted that she'd let her emotions get the best of her in front of Martha, but it had felt good to just cry in her arms. Now she didn't feel like she had any tears left, nor did she feel like she could sleep. It was probably fifteen minutes later when she heard the phone ringing on the kitchen counter. Twice she'd ignored Eli's calls, and for him to be calling this late at night now made her wonder if there was an emergency. She leaped from bed and stumbled in the dark to the kitchen. A haze of moonlight lit the kitchen enough for her to locate the phone, but it wasn't ringing anymore. She carried the phone back to the bedroom with her, crawled into bed, and kept it in her hand as she wondered whether or not she should call him back. After a few minutes, she dialed his number.

"I miss you," Eli said before even saying hello. "I miss you so much I can't stand it."

She'd been wrong to think she had no more tears left. Instantly her cheeks were wet as she responded. "I miss you too."

"I've been calling, and I . . ."

She could hear him take a deep breath.

"I'm back in Middlefield."

"What?" She tried to control the shakiness of her voice. "I thought you were going to stay in Florida longer."

"I was. But I just wanted to go home."

Katie Ann bit her bottom lip. "Oh."

There was an awkward silence for a few moments.

"Katie Ann?"

The way he said her name caused her to hold her breath for a moment. "*Ya?*"

"What am I doing?"

"What do you mean?"

He waited a moment before he spoke. "I'm a middle-aged Amish man who dreamed for years about an independent life. And now . . ."

Katie Ann sat up in bed. "What is it, Eli?"

"Those dreams just don't seem important anymore."

One of the things that Katie Ann loved about Eli was his

joyful spirit. She'd never heard him sound so sad. "What do you want?" She closed her eyes, fearful of his answer.

"I don't know."

Another tear spilled down her cheek. What had she been hoping for? That he would say he loved her and wanted a life with her? It was too much to wish for, and anger quickly started to replace the hurt she felt. "I'm sorry your trip didn't go as you'd planned."

She knew her words were clipped, and as she raised her chin in the darkness, she knew that she was going to have to distance herself from Eli. She'd thought she could be happy with her best friend, but she needed more, and Eli sounded like a lost puppy. He didn't know what he wanted, and in truth, Katie Ann wasn't sure what she wanted either. She'd opened her heart to him, trusted again, and now . . .

"My life is here in Ohio, not out running around like I'm *ab im kopp*."

She pulled the phone away for a moment, took a deep breath, and tried not to sound like a woman on the edge. "I don't think you're crazy, Eli."

"I feel like it."

Katie Ann knew what she'd signed on for, and she knew that a friend should offer a sympathetic ear, but just hearing Eli's voice made her long to be with him. "It's late, Eli. I'm sure you'll feel better tomorrow." She closed her eyes, knowing her own emotions were putting limitations on her ability to soothe Eli's troubled heart.

Silence, until Katie Ann finally asked, "Eli, are you still there?"

"*Ya*."

More silence followed.

"Katie Ann . . ." He paused. "Can I come visit you?"

She put her hand over her mouth for a moment to keep from gushing in an inappropriate way. After composing herself, she said, "That would be nice."

"I have to take care of some things here, but what about next week?"

"I'd like that."

After they hung up, her heart fluttered like that of a young girl. Any decision she'd previously made to distance herself from Eli seemed as far away as he was. She couldn't wait to see him.

MARTHA EASED INTO her recliner late that evening, her heart heavy for Katie Ann. She should have known the girl's heart couldn't hold up to the boundaries she and Eli had set, and she wondered how Eli truly felt about her friend. She was tempted to find out, but Katie Ann would have her hide if she interfered in her business. Of course, Katie Ann had certainly interfered in Martha's business by calling Arnold. But Arnold would be coming home, and Martha was giddy as a schoolgirl about that. She sure wished Katie Ann's future looked brighter in the romance department.

She remembered the coffee cake she'd brought home from the bakery in Monte Vista yesterday. A slice of cake and some hot tea sounded like heaven right now. As she shuffled to the kitchen, she wondered if Arnold was going to ask her to marry him. Seemed the logical next step. She twisted her mouth back and forth, knowing she was mighty set in her ways. But she sure did love Arnold.

Scanning the countertop, she put her hands on her hips. *Where is that cake?* Finally she spotted it at the far end of the counter. She peeled back the foil and frowned. There was a large chunk missing that hadn't been missing before. She was sure of it. Or was she?

She scratched her head. *Is this what old age is like, Lord?*

She sliced herself a small piece and put it on a plate, then brewed a cup of tea. Once she was back in her recliner, she was wishing she had a nice fire in the fireplace, but that just seemed like too much work. She clicked on the television, put her feet on her ottoman, and savored the delicious coffee cake.

"Reruns. All reruns." She flipped between channels on the television, finally settling on an old John Wayne movie that was nearing the end. She had twenty good minutes of television before the movie ended, and after another round of channel changing, she turned the TV off. Too early to go to bed, but her eyes were heavy. Leaning her head back against the chair, she knew she needed to get to her bedroom before she fell asleep in the recliner. Suddenly, a noise upstairs caused her eyes to bolt open and sent a chill up her spine. She held her breath, trying to identify what she'd heard. Had something fallen over?

Her heart thumped, and she stared at the ceiling as her eyes followed the sound above her head. She recalled the time a squirrel had tried to take possession of her upstairs. She'd had to call David to come get the furry creature outside again. But this sounded larger. Maybe a raccoon. And she knew raccoons could be mean little fellows.

She eased out of her chair, quiet as a mouse, then tiptoed to the kitchen. Once she'd located the broom, she headed toward the stairs, armed and ready to meet her intruder. But when she flung the door open to her extra bedroom and flipped the light switch, she screamed at the top of her lungs.

And so did Danielle.

Fifteen

MARTHA EDGED FORWARD WITH THE BRISTLY END of the broom, poised and ready to pounce. As she made a hissing noise, she pushed the broom within a few inches of the girl.

Danielle stepped backward until she was standing up against the dresser. "Stop it! Are you crazy?"

Martha didn't lower the broom. "With all due respect, missy . . . you are the one who has broken into my house, and . . ." She saw her favorite jasmine vanilla lotion on the top of the dresser . . . next to a half-eaten loaf of garlic bread. She narrowed her brows and scowled. "What are you doing up here?"

Danielle shifted her weight, and Martha noticed that both eyes were wide open and the stitches on her cheek were gone, leaving a red mark down the side of her face. Her bottom lip was still swollen on one side.

"If you'll just move that broom, I'll leave."

Martha raised her chin. "No. You answer the question. What are you doing up here?" Now Martha noticed a bag of Fritos, two of her colas, and three dirty dishes on the floor by the bed. "And exactly how long have you been here?"

"I—I don't know. Maybe a few days. Maybe longer."

Martha thought she might fall over. "So I've been sleeping in my bed downstairs while a thief has been living above me." She shook her head. "Unbelievable."

"I'm not a thief!" Danielle clenched her fists.

Martha nodded to the pile by the bed. "Oh, really. Then what do you call that? Were you gonna leave an IOU?"

"I'll pay you for it."

Martha lowered the broom and held it like a pitchfork by her side. "Fine." She held out her free hand, palm up. "Pay up."

"I—I'll have to go get the money and bring it back to you."

Martha laughed. "Sure you will." She walked to the bed and sat down atop the pine green bedspread she'd had since the sixties. She rubbed her forehead for a minute. "How'd you know where to find me?" She sat taller and frowned. "And *why* did you come here?"

Danielle shrugged. She was a petite little thing, and leaning up against the dresser, her wounds still not completely healed, she didn't seem very threatening. But surely Martha deserved to know why the child had taken refuge in *her* upstairs.

"If you don't want me to call the cops, I suggest you start talking."

"I'll leave. I'm sorry." She edged toward the door.

"Danielle, wait." Martha stood up, and slowly Danielle turned around. "Are you hiding from someone? From whoever did that to you?"

"I gotta go."

Danielle rounded the corner, and without giving it much thought, Martha yelled the first thing that came to mind.

"You can stay if you want!"

Martha waited, and she heard the footsteps on the stairs stop. A moment later Danielle crept back over the threshold. "Why would you let me stay?"

"Why did you come here in the first place?" Martha had suddenly realized what was missing out of her wallet. An ID card that she carried, which listed her address.

Danielle shrugged, eyes to the floor. "I dunno."

"Sure you do. Something sent you my way."

She kicked at the corner of the doorway with her scuffed-up white tennis shoe. "I heard you say no one lived up here."

Martha fought the urge to make a smart remark. Instead she took a deep breath. "I'm going to bed. It's late. I suggest you do the same." She pointed to the pile of dishes on the floor. "This is not how we do things around here. First thing in the morning, I expect to see this room cleaned up." She glared at her lotion on the dresser. "And my lotion back downstairs on the table by my recliner, where I've kept it for years."

She stood up, walked past Danielle, and was almost to the stairs when Danielle called her name. She turned around. "What?"

"Are you going downstairs to call the police?"

Martha pushed back a strand of hair that had fallen forward and sighed. "No, Danielle. I'm not. Now get some rest."

Good grief. Lord, what have You got in store for me now?

WEDNESDAY AFTERNOON THE air was a bit chilly, but the sun was shining. Katie Ann bundled up Jonas and took him out to the barn with her, thinking he could use some fresh air.

She had some leftover ham for Mrs. Dash, who'd left two more mice on the porch.

She eased into the barn and saw the cat curled up in a big ball in the corner on the quilt. She squatted down with Jonas. "She's going to have a *boppli*, Jonas. Probably several."

She reached into her pocket and pulled out a baggie half-filled with pieces of ham she'd torn into bite-sized pieces. Expecting the cat to bolt, she was surprised when Mrs. Dash just stared at her. And this time her ears weren't flattened to her head.

"Here you go, girl." She tossed some of the ham closer, then waited. "Mrs. Dash is learning to trust us, Jonas."

She nuzzled Jonas's nose with hers, and he made a strange cooing noise. Katie Ann waited for the cat to sprint around the corner. But instead, Mrs. Dash rose from her spot, arched her back in a stretch, and moved closer to the ham. Katie Ann didn't move. After a few moments, Mrs. Dash was within a foot of her, the closest the cat had ever come.

Katie Ann thought about all the prayers she'd said, asking God to help her trust His plan for her, whatever that might be. Figuring cats don't pray, she silently prayed that God would take care of this big black cat and that she would deliver healthy little kittens.

And maybe you could send a Mr. Dash to help her.

It was a strange ending, and probably even odder to be praying for the cat, but her father had always said there was a place in heaven for animals.

She rose slowly, so as not to spook the cat. Once she was standing, Mrs. Dash looked up, but quickly lowered her face and finished off the ham. She hadn't even finished chewing her last bite when she went around the corner, but it was progress.

When she got back inside, Katie Ann put Jonas in his swing, which he enjoyed more all the time. She cranked the handle, then went to the kitchen to make sure she had everything she needed to cook supper for Eli that evening, and she tried to keep worry from her heart. She wanted to enjoy her time with him, and she was going to do everything she could to keep things in perspective and to see their relationship for what it was.

Her excitement about his coming overrode everything else. Even Martha's situation with her new houseguest. Martha still came by daily, and twice she'd brought Danielle. The teenager didn't say two words either time, and mostly sat on the couch fidgeting.

Katie Ann had asked Martha privately if she should be housing a child without the parents' permission, but Martha said they weren't very good parents if they had let something like this happen to their daughter. Katie Ann didn't know what to think. Arnold was due back tomorrow, and Katie Ann knew he'd keep an eye on the situation.

She heard a knock and looked at the clock, knowing it was much too early for Eli to arrive. When she opened the door, she saw Lillian.

"Come in out of the cold."

Her sister-in-law didn't take off her coat or bonnet, but instead handed Katie Ann a letter. "The postman brought this to our *haus* instead of here, so I signed for it. It's from Robert Dronberger. Isn't he a lawyer back in Lancaster County?"

Katie Ann took a deep breath. "*Ya*. I believe so. Do you want some tea?" She walked toward the living room.

Lillian followed, still in her winter gear. "Why is he sending you a certified letter?"

Katie Ann turned to face her. She knew exactly why Robert was sending her a certified letter. Most likely because she hadn't responded to his other three letters.

"I—I think he is handling some things." She took a deep breath. "Things for Ivan. I mean, things of Ivan's. I don't know." She shrugged. "I think I am the owner of anything that was Ivan's, since we were still married."

"Oh." Lillian bit her bottom lip and stared at Katie Ann for a moment. "Do you have to go to Lancaster County?"

Katie Ann thought about the past three letters since Ivan's death, all requesting her presence in Lancaster County. "I think so."

"When?"

"I don't know."

"Hmm . . . I wonder if you will have to go get anything of Ivan's from Lucy's house?"

Katie Ann folded her arms across her chest. "I don't want anything of Ivan's. Besides, if you'll recall, Ivan left here with almost no money. Any money that he made while he was with Lucy, well, I suppose it should go to Lucy."

Just then Katie Ann had a horrible thought. What if there was money or a house or something that was tied up legally, something that should go to Lucy and her baby? She didn't want anything to do with Lucy, but if there was money that was rightfully Lucy's, Katie Ann didn't want to be the one holding things up. "I'll go soon."

"Well, uh . . . Ivan's been dead for, uh . . ."

"*Ya*, I know. Seven months." Katie Ann recalled the first

letter, which had arrived about a month after Ivan's death. At the time she had scanned it, but knew she couldn't face a trip to Lancaster County. The second letter arrived a month after that, and the third had come last month. Each time she read the letters, she'd put them away . . . to deal with another time. Now time must have caught up with her.

"Eli is coming for a visit." She was anxious to change the subject, even though she knew her comment would spark questions from Lillian.

Her sister-in-law smiled. "*Gut* news. How long is he staying?"

"He told Vera he would be staying for a few days."

Lillian shook her head. "I don't know why he doesn't just pack up and move here." She grinned.

Katie Ann frowned. "Lillian, that's impossible. His family is there. And as you know, we are just—"

"*Ya, ya* . . . I know. Just friends. That's what you keep saying." Lillian sighed. "I have to run. Enjoy your supper." She winked at Katie Ann before she closed the door behind her.

Eli chatted with Vera, Elam, and Levi until he thought he might explode from politeness. All he wanted to do was get to Katie Ann's house. Betsy bounced in and out of the living room, usually with a book in her hand. She'd read for a while, then share something about what she'd read, then mosey back upstairs. January was generally slow for all Amish folks, so it wasn't surprising that Elam and Levi were inside with Vera and Betsy on this cold Wednesday afternoon.

"*Gut* to have you back for another visit." Vera handed him his second cup of coffee.

"*Danki*, Vera." He smiled.

"Stay as long as you like." Vera folded her hands in her lap from where she was sitting across the room from Eli. Then she asked about all of Eli's children, how he enjoyed Florida, and what he planned to plant this spring. But she must have caught him looking at the clock.

"I imagine Katie Ann has supper almost ready. You don't want to be late."

Eli looked at the clock again. It was only three thirty, too early for supper, but he was going to take his cue and go. He stood up, and Elam walked him to the door.

"I'll help you get the buggy hitched up." Elam pulled on a heavy coat and gloves.

Eli pulled his hat and coat from the rack by the door.

"*Danki*, Elam," Eli said once the buggy was ready. His cousin stroked his beard, clearly with something on his mind. "What is it, cousin?"

"I'm not sure there is anything more fragile than a widow's heart, Eli."

"Except maybe a widower's heart," Eli quickly responded. But he knew what Elam was saying. "Are you afraid I'm not doing right by Katie Ann?"

"I didn't say that. I'm just reminding you that she is fragile." He backed up a few steps, waved a gloved hand, and said, "Have a *gut* time."

Eli thought about what Elam said as he drove through a flurry of snow to Katie Ann's house, and he wondered if being so close to Katie Ann was a good idea. But it wasn't like it was something he could control. He loved her, and he felt led to be here. Despite his own plans for his life, God seemed to have something else in mind. But even if he did trade in one dream for another, how could God expect him to leave his family to be with Katie Ann? It wasn't fair to ask her to leave the home she'd built in Canaan either. He'd have to go home at some point, and how would they both feel?

He shook his head, deciding not to worry about leaving her before he saw her. He parked the buggy, then made his way up the porch steps. She was opening the door just as he held up a hand to knock. He pulled the screen open and stepped across the threshold into the warmth of Katie Ann's home.

"It's *gut* to be here." His teeth were chattering as he pulled off his coat and hat.

Once they were hung on the rack, he pulled her into a hug, wishing he could stay in her arms for the rest of his life. He cupped her face in his hands and kissed her, the way a man kisses his wife, and as the passion built between them, Eli felt her trembling. He eased away and gazed into her beautiful brown eyes. "I—I . . ."

Eli wanted to say it so bad, tell her how he felt. But Elam's words rang in his ears. Katie Ann's husband hadn't been gone a year, and unless Eli was ready to leave his home in Ohio and be a husband to Katie Ann and father to Jonas, he knew that he would have to keep his feelings to himself. Anything else would be selfish and unfair.

"I know friends aren't supposed to kiss like that," he said after a moment. "But I missed you."

"I missed you too. Very much."

Her eyes twinkled as she spoke, and Eli felt torn between taking her in his arms again or running out the door. There was a struggle going on inside of him—between what he thought he wanted and what seemed to be playing out in his heart. And all the while a passion burned inside of him for Katie Ann that made it almost too much of a temptation for him to even be there.

KATIE ANN SMOOTHED the wrinkles in her black apron as she took a slow deep breath and wondered if her heart would ever stop pounding against her chest. She released the air in her lungs only after Eli had turned away and walked toward Jonas's playpen in the living room. He eased his hand down and touched her sleeping baby on the head with a tenderness that Katie Ann could hardly bear.

A few minutes later Eli was stoking the fire and Katie Ann was brewing coffee. By the time they settled onto the couch and began talking, it was as though no time had passed. Once again, they ate supper on the couch in front of the fireplace, and Eli raved about Katie Ann's chicken and rice casserole. Eli told her all about his trip to Florida, but not with the excitement that she expected.

"I don't know. It was nice, I guess." He set his empty plate on the coffee table and took a sip of coffee. "I felt . . ." He sighed. "I felt guilty. So much luxury and things that just aren't necessary. You should have seen how many different kinds of soaps, shampoos, and lotions were in the bathroom at the hotel." He chuckled. "I did enjoy the television."

Katie Ann smiled, glad to hear the laughter back in his voice. "I don't think you should feel guilty, Eli." She wasn't completely sure how he should feel, since she'd never known an Amish man to travel.

He looked down, rubbed his forehead, then locked eyes with her. "It just wasn't as much fun as I'd always pictured it."

"I'll be taking a trip soon."

His ears perked up. "Really? Where?"

"Lancaster County. I have to handle some things for Ivan. A lawyer has sent me several letters."

"What about Jonas?" Eli narrowed his brows as he glanced toward the playpen. "Will you take him?"

Katie Ann shook her head. "*Ya.* He's not even five months old yet. I couldn't bear to leave him."

Eli squeezed her hand. "Do you want me to go with you, so you and Jonas don't have to travel alone?"

While she was touched, she also knew that she needed to do this on her own, find some closure with Ivan. She shook her head. "No. I've traveled by plane before. But *danki*."

"When will you go?"

"I'm waiting until after Arnold gets here. I'll feel better leaving Martha." She raised her brows. "You'll never believe what is going on at Martha's house." Katie Ann told Eli about Danielle and how Martha found her living upstairs.

"And she's still there?" Eli sounded as shocked as Katie Ann had been when she found out Martha was letting the teenager stay with her.

She laughed. "*Ya*, she is. And I'm not sure who is having a harder time of it. Martha is a bit"—she paused—"set in her ways. And Danielle is . . . how should I say this, since I don't know the girl well?" She sighed. "She's a bit . . . messy. Martha said she leaves plates in her room upstairs, throws her clothes down on the bathroom floor, and never offers to help clean anything up. And . . ." Katie Ann grinned. "Martha threatened to wash her mouth out with soap if she didn't clean up her language."

"Where are the girl's parents?"

"Danielle says her parents are dead, that she graduated school early while living in foster care, and that her boyfriend is the one who beat her up."

Eli shook his head. "That's terrible. How long will Martha let her stay there?"

"I don't know. Martha has a huge heart, so I suspect it could be awhile."

MARTHA PUT HER hands on her hips and eyed Danielle as she stepped out of the dressing room. They were in a store Martha had never heard of. "You are out of your mind if you think I'm going to buy you that."

"Why? What's wrong with it?" Danielle faced off with her, mirroring Martha's stance.

Martha started to tell her that she looked like someone who should be standing on a street corner, but she decided a more tactful approach would be better. "You look like a tramp."

"What?" Danielle shifted her weight, which Martha was impressed with given the skintight pink leggings. "This is what everyone wears."

Martha pointed at the two inches of skin showing between Danielle's sprayed-on pants and matching pink crop top. "And that is not going to fly." She glanced around at the sales staff, most of whom were dressed similarly to Danielle, and shook her head.

"But I like this."

"I told you that if you were going to live with me, you have to get a job. What kind of reputable company would hire you dressed like that?"

"Well, I wouldn't be caught dead in what you're wearing."

Martha gasped, looking down at her red-and-white-checked pants outfit. One thing Martha knew for sure—she was a snappy dresser. She was at a loss for words.

"And why do you always wear that dumb butterfly clip in your hair?"

Martha's eyes rounded with rage as she reached up and touched the precious clip that she'd had since she was married to Herbert many moons ago. "This *clip*, my dear, will never go out of style."

"Whatever."

If that girl said *whatever* one more time, Martha thought she might snap. "I think we'd better try another store."

"Whatever."

Danielle marched back into the dressing room and slammed the door. Martha leaned her head back and looked up. *I have no idea what You want me to do with this girl, Lord, but help me keep my cool.*

Martha raised her chin, then glared at the clerk to her left. She shook her head, amazed that her mother would let her out of the house dressed like that. A few minutes later Danielle popped out of the dressing room. But instead of returning to the jeans and T-shirt that she'd had on, she tried on another outfit.

"What about this one?" Danielle raised her brows and stood taller, which only caused the tiny blue blouse to show even more of her tummy.

Martha shook her head, and Danielle stomped back into the dressing room. She couldn't wait until Arnold arrived tomorrow morning. Maybe he knew more about teenagers than she did.

Sixteen

Katie Ann was thankful for the four days she had with Eli, even though her feelings were more unresolved than ever before. They had spent each day together and into the evening. At night, Eli would kiss her tenderly and go to Vera and Elam's house to sleep. It had been magical.

But right now, Lillian was watching Jonas, and Katie Ann's furry friend needed her help. Katie Ann had witnessed enough calf births to know that things were not going well for Mrs. Dash. As she knelt down on the hay in the corner of the barn, she stroked the cat's head and spoke softly. It was the first time Mrs. Dash had let Katie Ann touch her, and the animal's eyes were glassy, barely open.

"It's okay, girl. You can do this."

When the first kitten was born, Katie Ann watched Mrs. Dash clean the animal, but Katie Ann's stomach lurched when she realized that the tiny creature wasn't breathing. Mrs. Dash worked to free the new baby of afterbirth, but when it was time to deliver the next one, she simply pushed it aside. Katie

Ann tried massaging the small kitten's stomach, unsure what to do. Nothing. The second kitten and the third kitten, also lifeless. *No, no.*

When the fourth kitten, the smallest one of all, solid black like its mother, was born, Katie Ann watched Mrs. Dash work to clear the mucus from the animal's face. Katie Ann started to cry when this animal also lay lifeless before her. "I'm so sorry, girl. I'm so very sorry."

She stared into the cat's eyes, wondering if the pain of death was as horrible for an animal as it was for a human. If the tale were told through the eyes of Mrs. Dash, Katie Ann would have to say yes. The new mother nudged each of her babies over and over again. She cleaned them as their little bodies tumbled at her touch, as if she could bring them to life with love. Katie Ann prayed silently for all of them.

Even knowing she had to pick up Jonas from Lillian and catch a plane, she couldn't bring herself to leave. She didn't want to leave the cat—with all of this. She rubbed Mrs. Dash's head, and the cat leaned in toward Katie Ann, then looked up at her. Katie Ann rubbed her head as flashes of her sister lying still and lifeless in the crib shook her.

Then there was a movement. The tiny black kitten moved. Or did it? Katie Ann picked up the little body and moved it closer to its mother. Mrs. Dash worked her tongue across the new baby, and seconds later the little one breathed in life. She watched for as long as she could without missing her plane. "Take care of your little one," she said as she gently touched the new mother on the head.

Mrs. Dash leaned her head back and found the top of

Katie Ann's hand. Katie Ann stayed perfectly still as the cat's tongue, like sandpaper, swept across her hand in loving strokes of thanks.

KATIE ANN SAT on the plane headed toward Lancaster County with Jonas in her lap, her mind reeling with what-ifs.

Eli had told her that he would see her again soon, and he'd also invited her to visit him in Ohio. She'd declined, for the moment at least, knowing she had this trip to Lancaster County to make and unsure how she was going to feel when she returned. She was hoping to get her business taken care of in a couple of days, although she was looking forward to seeing Ivan's brother and two sisters, along with their families.

Arnold had arrived in Canaan before Katie Ann left, and Martha was busy helping him get settled in his new home. And Martha and Danielle were getting to know each other, and although Katie Ann couldn't imagine the two living together, Martha said she felt called to watch over the girl, at least for a while.

She'd tried to ignore the curious stares at the airport, and even now on the plane. Once she got back in Lancaster County, heavily populated with Amish folks, there wouldn't be as many curious sets of eyes. Katie Ann had flown twice before, both times for funerals. The bishop in Canaan frowned upon air travel, unless it was necessary. She found it curious how lenient Eli's bishop was about his travels.

As she laid her head back against the seat, she realized that Eli hadn't mentioned taking any more trips. She wondered what his home in Middlefield looked like and if she'd ever see it.

And she wondered when she would see him again.

ELI SPENT THE days following his return from Canaan staying busy around his house. He'd made repairs to the fence in the far pasture, put a fresh coat of paint on the woodshed, cleaned the barn, and repaired the passenger door on his buggy.

Busy. He had to stay occupied to keep his mind off Katie Ann. He'd come mighty close to telling her how much he loved her more than once, especially when they parted ways this last time. But Katie Ann had much on her mind, and he knew it would be difficult for her to travel back to Lancaster County to settle her husband's affairs. So many times he'd wondered what kind of man would leave a woman like Katie Ann. He would spend the rest of his life loving her, given the chance. But he knew his children and grandchildren wouldn't hear of him leaving, and she had created a new life for herself in Canaan. He wondered if she would consider moving to Ohio.

Even though these thoughts filled Eli's mind, the plans he'd made for years kept bumping around in his head.

He carried a bucket of feed across the snow toward the barn. It was a dreary day, filled with gray clouds and the threat of more snow. He thought about Canaan and how the sun was always shining there, even after a hard snow, lighting the white peaks as if by rays from heaven. And something about the way the Sangre de Cristo and San Juan Mountains hugged the San Luis Valley in a protective embrace made him see why folks would want to live there. The Amish community in Canaan was small, but Katie Ann had told him that the population had more than doubled in the past year, with more and more folks migrating to the area for cheaper land and more room to spread out.

Eli was walking back to the house when he heard hooves padding up the driveway. He turned to see three buggies pulling in, the first of which he recognized as his oldest daughter's. Hannah's horse, Midnight, was a fine animal and easily recognizable with his tall steady gait and coat so black it looked almost midnight blue. Eli pushed back his black jacket and looped his thumbs beneath his suspenders.

Ida Mae was in the buggy with Hannah, and Karen and Frieda were in the next one. Bringing up the rear was his baby girl, Maureen. Whenever all his girls convened like this, something was afoot.

"*Wie bischt,*" he said, greeting them as they made their way across the yard to the front porch, each one toting a casserole dish or bag. It wasn't unusual for his daughters to keep him supplied with casseroles and freshly baked goods, but they didn't make a habit of all arriving at the same time. "Dare I ask what brings all my lovely *dochders* here today?"

Hannah glanced at Ida Mae and shrugged as they brushed past him and toward the porch steps. "Just wanted to visit our *daed.*"

Sure you did.

He walked alongside his other daughters toward the house. Was Jake ever invited to these sessions, he wondered, or did his son just have enough *gut* sense to decline?

"I brought you a chicken and rice casserole," Maureen said as she placed a dish on Eli's kitchen table.

Flashbacks of eating the same casserole with Katie Ann on her couch played in his mind.

"And I made you some fresh granola, *Daed*." Karen put a Tupperware container next to the casserole.

His other three daughters all unloaded more food—chicken noodle soup that Frieda said could be frozen, two loaves of bread from Ida Mae, and a chocolate shoofly pie from Hannah.

"*Danki, danki*. I won't go hungry, no?" He smiled at all his girls, knowing something was coming.

Hannah must have been awarded the job of speaker. "*Daed*, *Aenti* Vera called, and . . ."

Eli shook his head. He loved his cousin's wife, but that woman could stir things up more than any female he'd ever known, except maybe for his own daughters. "And what did *Aenti* Vera have to share?" He eased into a kitchen chair, sighing as he waited.

Hannah sat down across from him. "*Daed*, she said you've become very close with Katie Ann." She glanced around the room at her sisters. "And we were just wondering if you are going to end up moving to Canaan."

Eli was smiling on the inside, even though he tried to stifle his joy in front of his girls. They *did* need him. He should have known they would be afraid that he would leave them to move to Colorado.

"No worries, *mei dochders*. I'm not going anywhere." Although the moment he said it, his heart sank. Confusing. He glanced at each of his girls. Also confusing. Each one of them was frowning. "What is wrong with all of you?"

Frieda and Karen sat down too, and Karen spoke up. "We

were just hoping you'd found true love." She batted her eyes a few times, and Eli wasn't sure what to say. "We want you to be happy, *Daed*. We thought maybe Katie Ann was the one."

"You want me to move?" Eli recalled how he'd raised each and every one of them. Now they didn't need him anymore?

"Of course we don't *want* you to move, but we don't want you staying, either . . . because of us." Karen reached over and touched his hand. "We all have husbands to take care of us now."

The statement hurt, but he forced a smile.

Maureen, the newest bride and still filled with romance, spoke next. "Do you love her, *Daed*?"

It was a conversation no Amish man should be having with his grown daughters, but he answered truthfully. "I love her very much."

"Yay!" Maureen jumped up and down, and all his girls laughed and clapped.

"We're so happy for you, *Daed*," Ida Mae said. "We didn't think you would really travel the world like you planned."

"I did," Eli mumbled, even though traveling didn't hold the allure it once did.

"Do you think Katie Ann and her son would consider moving here to Middlefield?" Maureen brought her hands to her chest.

Katie Ann had been through so much, and she seemed settled and happy in her new world. Eli envisioned a life with Katie Ann, surrounded by the mountains, sunshine most days, and—the baby. He would be Jonas's father if Katie Ann would have him. With his children's blessings all around him, he couldn't help but get excited about the possibility of being with Katie Ann and Jonas in Colorado. "I think we would be best to live in Canaan."

"We would miss you so much, *Daed*," Karen said. "But you've given to each and every one of us, over and over again. We will support any decision you make."

"*Danki*, girls." Eli narrowed his brows. "And what does your *bruder* think about this?"

"Jake agrees with us," Hannah said.

Eli rubbed his chin and wondered how hard it would be to be away from his children—and his grandchildren. Could he really do that?

But could he really live without Katie Ann?

MARTHA KNOCKED ON Arnold's front door.

"Why don't you use the key I gave you?" Arnold lifted one eyebrow as he stepped back so Martha could enter.

"Easier to knock." Truth was, it felt odd to walk into Arnold's home unannounced. Rumors were flying that Arnold was going to propose. He'd been caught browsing among the rings at a jewelry store in Monte Vista. Vera told Martha she'd seen him when she was on her way to the post office, and from that point, everyone in the Amish community seemed to know. And that was okay. Martha didn't mind being the center of attention. But she wondered how Danielle fit into this scenario. Poor girl didn't have any parents, and her ex-boyfriend was certainly a thug. She couldn't turn her out on the street. While she couldn't say she was bonding with the girl, she did feel protective of her.

"How is it going with Danielle?" Arnold sat down on the

couch while Martha sat down in Arnold's recliner. She loved the way he always insisted she sit in his favorite chair.

"Funny you should mention that." Martha squared her jaw and leaned her head forward a bit. "Do you know I think that girl could sleep fourteen hours a day if I didn't get her up? And, Arnold, you know I like my junk food, but she survives on it. She ate all my Fritos before I even had a one. And sodas . . . she'll drink them back-to-back all day long." Martha took a breath. "And she's a slob. Throws her clothes everywhere, leaves plates and food in her room, and her clothing . . ." Martha rolled her eyes. "And did I mention that she's lazy?"

Arnold chuckled. "Sounds exactly like most of the teenagers I've known."

"None of my Amish family has teenagers that act like that."

Arnold nodded. Martha knew that Arnold and his son had fallen on bad terms until shortly before Greg died. Arnold said he would be forever thankful that they mended their ways.

"Were you a part of Greg's life when he was a teenager?"

"Yes. I was. They are difficult years."

He shook his head, which made Martha wonder if he'd take on Danielle in the marriage proposal too. She wasn't about to ask.

"Where is Danielle at now—home?"

Martha sighed as she rolled her eyes. "Yes, I suppose her home is my home. And that's where she's at. I'm hoping she'll look for a job. Not that money is an issue. But I need her out of the house sometimes. She interrupts my schedule." She crossed her legs. "I have my certain shows that I like to watch on TV. I like to eat supper at exactly seven o'clock. And I don't like anyone else running bathwater at the same time I am. I lose water pressure."

"How long are you planning to let her stay?"

Ah. There was the question. Maybe Arnold was waiting to propose until he found out exactly how long she'd be housing the teenager.

Martha shrugged. "I have no idea."

DANIELLE KICKED HER feet up on Martha's ottoman while she stretched out in Martha's comfy chair. She was sure the woman would have a heart attack if she saw her sitting so smug in the worn-out recliner. After rubbing some jasmine vanilla lotion on her hands, she clicked the television on. For such a big house, this was the only TV, and Martha always controlled the remote. She flipped through the channels, but after a few minutes she hit the Off button. There wasn't anything good on this time of the afternoon, and besides . . . she couldn't concentrate.

It was only a matter of time before Martha found out she was lying, and then she'd throw her out for sure. And there was no way she was going back to her old life. She reached up and touched the scar on her cheek. The doctor said it would fade over time, but Danielle wasn't sure she'd ever really heal.

She replayed the scene in her mind, wondering what she'd done to provoke it. Closing her eyes, she could almost feel the blows to her face, particularly the curled fist with the chunky gold ring that caught her upper cheek and eye. She'd known when she smelled the whiskey and saw the staggering, she should have run. As she'd done more than once before.

She glanced around Martha's house. The woman annoyed

her to no end with her rules about housecleaning and eating at a certain time, and she had zero sense of fashion—evidenced not only by her own bizarre clothing, but also by her house décor. Danielle looked at the picture of the owls hanging above an outdated red and gold couch and shook her head.

But Danielle liked being here better than any other place on Earth. It was the only place she'd ever felt safe. So even if she wanted to yank that ridiculous butterfly clip from Martha's scraggly hair sometimes . . . or just for once have the remote control, eat in her bed upstairs, or not be restricted about when she could bathe—some things were worth forgoing. And one thing Danielle knew for sure. Martha would never hit her. She could just tell.

The woman was crabby and a nuisance, but Danielle hoped she wouldn't send her away.

She jumped when someone knocked at the door, then panic set in. She figured she would spend the rest of her days here worrying that she'd been found. It was bound to happen sooner or later, but when she peeked around the curtain in the living room, she saw a buggy and a horse, so she knew it was one of those Amish people coming to visit Martha. They were as strange as Martha, dressed in their funky clothes and living in houses with no electricity. She'd never seen an Amish person until some of them visited Martha in the hospital. She'd also gone with Martha to Katie Ann's house a couple of times. Danielle couldn't believe they lived like that.

"Martha's not here," she said when she opened the front door. Then she studied the figure before her. If ever there was a hot Amish guy, he was standing in front of her in his black pants, black coat, and one of those funky black hats.

"That's okay. Can you give her this?" He held up a brown paper bag, but Danielle was still summing him up. He reminded her of some of the hockey players back home—tall and athletic, although he wasn't missing any teeth.

"Sure," she finally said as she accepted the bag.

"I'm Levi Detweiler." Mr. Handsome extended his hand, and Danielle slowly latched on. "My mom is a friend of Martha's, and she asked me to bring her this rhubarb jam. I think Martha goes into withdrawal or something if she runs out." He almost smiled. One side of his mouth curved up, but it was brief.

"You wanna come in?" Danielle paused. "I mean, Martha will probably be back soon, if you want to wait."

He grimaced a little. "Is anyone else here?"

Danielle felt her heart skip a beat. Why would he ask that? Would he hurt her in some way if she said no one was home? "Uh, no. But I just remembered Martha will be back *any* minute."

"I gotta go. Nice to meet you."

Danielle watched him leave. He was intriguing, almost in a creepy sort of way. He had those weird clothes that soft voice, and his mouth was crooked in a way that made it hard to tell if he was smiling or angry. But she didn't think she'd ever seen a hotter-looking guy.

"LEVI'S THE QUIET one," Martha said as she plopped a bag of groceries on the table. "A fine fellow. His brother, Jacob, got married about a year ago, and his sister Emily just got married this past November. I guess Levi's still looking for his someone special." She pulled a frozen pizza out of the bag, along with some Fritos and a six-pack of soda, and put them all on the table. "We're splurging on junk food tonight, but don't get used to it, missy. I just don't feel like cooking."

"I'll be his someone special," Danielle said as she pulled the bag of Fritos open. "He's hot."

Martha put her hands on her hips. "That is no way for a nice girl to talk, Danielle."

Danielle chuckled. "You're kidding me, right? Just yesterday I heard you say the mailman had nice buns."

"Are you familiar with the expression 'Do as I say and not as I do'?" She reached up and tightened her butterfly clip.

"Well, the Amish guy sure was cute. Levi. I asked him to come in, but he got kinda weird about it. Then I thought maybe he might be dangerous or something."

Martha cackled. "Dangerous? Levi? Uh, no. He didn't come in the house while you were here alone because it wouldn't be proper."

"I think Amish people are weird."

Martha pointed a crooked finger at her. "There will be no talk like that in this house. There's no finer group of folks."

Danielle shrugged. "Whatever."

Martha stared at her for a moment, then shook her head. "I'm going to heat this pizza. Now would be a good time to shower if you want."

Danielle started to argue that she'd prefer to take a shower closer to bedtime, but the woman had bought pizza, Fritos, and soda for dinner, so she'd go along with her on this. "Okay." She crossed through the living room toward the stairs, then turned around. "Martha?"

"What?"

Danielle waited until she turned around. "Thanks for letting me stay."

Martha rolled her eyes. "Whatever."

Danielle grinned as she headed up the stairs.

MARTHA WAITED UNTIL the oven heated up before she popped in the frozen supreme pizza. Arnold was going to the gym in town this evening, something he'd started doing twice a week. He said it helped his arthritis. She'd made it pretty clear that she had no plans to join him in that particular activity. Exercise made her nauseous. Besides, she was hoping maybe she and Danielle could chat a little. It bothered Martha that Danielle had no interest in God. Only once since their stay in the hospital had Martha broached the subject, and the girl turned red and marched upstairs. Danielle seemed angry with God. A few years ago Martha would have let it go. But when Arnold, Emily, and David opened her heart to the Lord, her life had changed. She wanted that for Danielle too.

But one thing she was learning about teenagers—if they think you want them to do something, they will do the exact opposite. So Martha knew she needed to approach the subject carefully. She smiled, recalling how she had to find the Lord in her own time, knowing that everything ultimately happens on God's timetable.

She'd just shoved a handful of Fritos into her mouth when she heard a car pull up. No one she recognized, and from the looks of it . . . no one she knew. A woman dressed in tan slacks and a dark brown coat held her hand in front of her face to block the light snow flurries. Martha had the door open by the time she was about to knock.

She was an attractive woman, midthirties, Martha guessed. She wasn't smiling.

"Are you Martha Dobbs?"

Martha gave her a critical squint. "Who wants to know?"

"I'm—I'm looking for someone. I think she might be here. My name's Vivian Kent."

Martha raised her chin and eyeballed the woman for a moment. "Who ya looking for?"

Vivian pulled a photograph from her purse. "Have you seen this girl?"

Martha stared at the picture of Danielle. "Who are you to her?"

"I'm her mother."

Seventeen

MARTHA PULLED THE DOOR WIDE. "COME IN. YES, Danielle is here." She wasn't sure what she was most upset about, the fact that the woman might have her arrested for harboring a runaway, or that Danielle had lied to her. "Danielle said her parents were dead."

Vivian folded her hands in front of her and sighed. "I'm not surprised. We've had a lot of trouble with Danielle."

Martha could believe that. The girl was willful.

"She's upstairs taking a shower. She should be down in a minute."

Martha felt a wave of relief. Apparently she hadn't been called by the Lord to straighten out young Danielle. And she wouldn't have to worry about her and Arnold taking on parental roles at their ages. What a mess that would have been.

"Can I get you a soda? Some tea?"

Vivian sat down. In Martha's recliner. Martha fought the urge to ask her to move.

"No, I'm fine. How long has Danielle been here?"

"Oh, a week or two." Martha scowled. "How long has she been missing?"

"Since the hospital. We traveled here from Wisconsin to visit a friend, and then Danielle ended up in the hospital." Vivian hung her head and sighed. "When I couldn't find her, I eventually had to go home."

"Did you call the police, report her missing?" Martha was sitting on the edge of the couch, hands folded in her lap, wondering how Vivian could have left the state not knowing where her daughter was.

"I—I couldn't really call the police. Danielle's been in trouble with the police before."

"Why does that matter? Someone beat the life out of her." Martha leaned forward. "Who did that to her?"

Vivian swiped at her eye. "I don't know. I went out with friends, and when I got back to our hotel room, she—she . . ." The woman folded an arm across her stomach as she looked at the floor.

Martha wasn't sure what to say, but trouble or no trouble, someone should have called the law.

Vivian straightened. "I'm sorry. I'm so sorry that Danielle showed up here and bothered you."

"She's no bother," Martha said. "How did you find me, anyway? I mean, I know how Danielle found me. She took an identification card out of my wallet. I was her roommate in the hospital. Hey—I don't remember seeing you at the hospital."

"I was there." Vivian smiled.

Really? "I never saw you."

Vivian fumbled with a button on her coat. "You—you were sleeping."

"Oh." Martha was thinking that if it had been Katie Ann in that predicament, she'd have never left her side. But she sighed, knowing that everyone wasn't so thoughtful.

"And Danielle eventually called a friend of hers back home and told her where she was. The friend's mother knew how frantic I was, so she phoned me right away." Vivian dabbed at her eyes. "All I knew was that Danielle was here in Canaan. I've been asking around and showing her picture for two days, and finally someone recognized her—an Amish girl named Beth Ann said she was staying here."

Martha nodded, then pointed to Vivian's ring, a big gold thing on her right ring finger. There was a time when Martha used to adore big, clunky jewelry. "Nice ring."

"Thanks. It was a gift."

Martha stood up when she heard footsteps heading down the stairs. So did Vivian.

"You've got company, Danielle," Martha said, ready for her lying houseguest to go. *What kind of kid says her parents are dead?* She shook her head.

"Hi, Dani."

Vivian didn't run up to Danielle as Martha expected, and Danielle turned pale as a ghost, her feet rooted to the floor at the bottom of the staircase.

"Hi, Mom."

"Get whatever things you have here and let's go. You've inconvenienced Martha enough." Vivian readjusted her purse on her shoulder. "Be quick."

Danielle turned around and ran upstairs.

"She really wasn't any trouble." Martha edged toward Vivian.

"I sure hope you can find out who did that to her, and prosecute that"—she took a deep breath—". . . person."

Danielle was back, carrying a plastic bag, which Martha assumed contained the two changes of clothes Danielle had brought with her, plus the four outfits that Martha had purchased for her, ones they'd finally agreed on, plus some undergarments.

"Good luck to you, Danielle." Martha lifted her chin, feeling unappreciated, but still relieved. *The unruly teenager lies and breaks into people's homes.*

"Thanks for the clothes." Danielle's eyes were locked with Martha's as she blinked back tears. The girl had to be worried about the trouble she was in for running away, but surely Vivian would let it all go, after everything the child had been through.

"I forgot to ask. Where's your dad, Danielle?"

"He died. About six years ago." Vivian bit her bottom lip, then smiled. "So it's just been Danielle and me since then."

"Oh." Martha walked them to the door.

Vivian reached into her purse and pulled out her wallet. "I'd like to pay you for any expense or trouble you went to."

Martha waved a hand in the air. "No, no. Just get Danielle home where she can finish recovering. I still hope you find whoever did this."

Vivian tucked her wallet back in her purse and smiled. "I just want to get Danielle home."

"Bye, Danielle." Martha held the door open for them, but Danielle didn't look at her. As Martha closed the door, she sighed, then watched them through the window, until a chill ran up and down her spine. There was something about the way Vivian was manhandling Danielle to the car. Martha's stomach seized up, a pang in her gut that something wasn't right.

As she watched Vivian dragging Danielle by her arm, the girl stumbled, but Vivian just kept pulling her toward the car.

Martha flung the door wide and stepped onto the porch. "Vivian, you wait just a minute! Do you hear me?" Martha marched down the snowy porch steps, certain that she could take on Vivian if it came to that.

IT WAS AFTER ten o'clock when Katie Ann heard the cell phone ringing. She'd talked to Eli earlier in the evening, but it was a short conversation, and once again . . . she felt like Eli was pulling back. She knew he had feelings for her, and maybe it was just getting too hard for him to keep saying good-bye. Katie Ann felt the same way.

But it was Martha's name flashing across the display screen. She quickly flipped open the phone, hoping Jonas wouldn't wake up. She'd just gotten him settled in a playpen next to the bed.

"Is everything okay?" She sat up in the extra bedroom at her sister-in-law's house. Mary Ellen, Abe, and their children were already asleep.

"Everything is fine. I guess."

Martha told Katie Ann a bizarre story about her day. In the darkness Katie Ann listened quietly, her heart breaking for poor Danielle. "You think her mother did that to her?"

"She won't say, but I think so. She wouldn't eat any supper, and she's been up in the extra bedroom for most of the night. I keep checking on her, though. She's not her smarty-pants self, which kinda worries me."

"She's still there? For how long?" Katie Ann wasn't sure she understood all this.

"I have no idea. When I walked outside and told them to wait, I looked at Danielle and asked her if she wanted to stay. Vivian tried to argue, but I told her to shut her mouth. Danielle ran to me."

"*Ach*, Martha. That's horrible. Poor Danielle. But what are you going to do now? Call the police? Report Vivian?"

"I don't know. I'm going to give her some time. If her own mother did this to her, don't you think she might be kinda messed up?"

"I'm sure of it."

"How are things going there?"

"I meet with the lawyer tomorrow morning at ten o'clock. It's been nice visiting with friends and family, and they love spending time with Jonas."

"Well, I miss my baby."

"I know. And he misses you too."

"I hear Danielle coming downstairs," Martha said in a whisper. "I'll call you tomorrow and see how the lawyer went. I love you, sweetie."

"I love you too."

Katie Ann lay back down and closed her eyes. Being back in Lancaster County had felt so familiar. Now that Ivan was gone, everyone kept asking her if she would move back to Paradise, and she was considering it. She'd left Lancaster County for a fresh start with Ivan, which didn't work out the way she'd planned. Maybe another fresh start was in order.

THE NEXT MORNING she had breakfast with Mary Ellen's family, and Mary Ellen convinced her to leave Jonas while Katie Ann went to meet the lawyer. She didn't want to be away from her baby, but she knew he would be better off with Mary Ellen, as opposed to going into the city. Mary Ellen had arranged for a driver to pick her up and take her to Robert Dronberger's office.

It was almost ten o'clock when she arrived, and within a few minutes a woman ushered her down a hallway to an office at the end of the hall.

The lawyer rose from behind a large oak desk and extended his hand. "So nice to see you, Katie Ann. It's been a long time." He pointed to two tan chairs in front of his desk. "Have a seat, please."

Katie Ann sat down, her heart thudding against her chest. She'd been dreading this visit, a summary of recent events that she didn't care to revisit.

"I'm so sorry about Ivan." Robert put on a pair of reading glasses and thumbed through a thick file folder on his desk, keeping his eyes down. "As you'll recall, you and Ivan came in here before you moved to Colorado and had a will prepared." He looked up at Katie Ann. "Everything that Ivan owned belongs to you."

"How can that be? He was living with—with another woman." She hung her head. No matter how much time had passed, humiliation still soared through her.

"That's just the way the law works." He sat back in his chair, pulled off his reading glasses, and rubbed his chin. "You are still legally his wife."

Katie Ann knew that prior to his death she hadn't really been his wife for a long time. "There are papers for me to sign, no?" She folded her hands in her lap and hoped this wouldn't take long. She'd asked the driver to wait for her.

"Yes, I have paperwork for you to sign, but I need to explain a few things to you." He sighed. "Whatever money Ivan had, Lucy has now. They had a joint account, which Lucy has closed, so I'm afraid there aren't any liquid assets. But Ivan's personal belongings technically belong to you."

Katie Ann shook her head. "No. I don't want any of it. Lucy can have it all, whatever there is."

Robert stared at her for a few moments. "Katie Ann, there is a house involved. Ivan invested all of his money to build a house about ten miles outside of Bird-in-Hand. He'd hired a builder, and they'd just finished the home a week before he died."

Katie Ann fought the tremble in her voice. "I do not want any house that Ivan was building for him and Lucy to live in."

"I understand. But you can sell the home."

She shook her head, knowing she should have settled all this way before now. "No. Give the house to Lucy."

Robert shifted his weight in the high-back chair, rubbed his forehead, and locked eyes with Katie Ann. "I went to the house, Katie Ann. I think you should go look at it before you make that decision."

Again she shook her head. "I am not in a position of financial need. Ivan was living with Lucy, so she should have the house."

Katie Ann had realized right away that this would solve Lucy's money problems. It wasn't at the top of her priority list to help Lucy, but there was a child involved. Ivan's child.

"Katie Ann, there's something else." Robert sighed. "There's a mortgage owed on the house. In addition to the cash Ivan put into the house, he also took out a mortgage. Lucy will need to keep up with the payments, which are already behind since we had these legal issues to work out."

"But Lucy can't afford to . . ." She stopped, knowing it was not her place to air Lucy's business.

"Ivan was optimistic about his business expansion, and he built a fine home." Robert paused. "I think you should go and see the house before you make any decisions. Legally, it's yours."

In a self-destructive way, she couldn't help but be curious about the kind of house that Ivan would build for him and Lucy to spend the rest of their lives in. Were there rooms for children? Did it have an extra-large fireplace, the kind Ivan had always wanted? Was there room for a garden? How big was the kitchen?

One thing she knew for sure. She was not going to make mortgage payments on a house that Lucy would live in. "All right," she finally said.

Robert gave her the address after offering to drive her to the house, but Katie Ann declined. She'd rather be alone when she saw it. If she sold the house, she would give the profits to Lucy. It might not be much, but Lucy deserved whatever money Ivan had earned while they were together.

It was a forty-minute drive from Lancaster to Bird-in-Hand. As they drove down Lincoln Highway through Paradise,

Katie Ann glanced at the bakery on her left, the location of her first coffee date with Ivan. To her right was the street that led to Noah's clinic. They passed Black Horse Road, the street she and Ivan had lived on. So many memories. And most of them good. She wondered if moving back to Paradise would be a good move for her. As much as she loved Colorado, the rolling hills of Lancaster County beckoned to her.

She'd been guilty of picturing a life with Eli in Colorado, a fantasy that often made her regret ever meeting him. And he'd seemed distant since his last visit. It was hard having to keep saying good-bye to him. But could she really say good-bye to Martha, Lillian, Samuel, David, Emily, and all her friends in Colorado?

A few minutes later they passed the sign that read Bird-in-Hand.

When the driver pulled to a stop in the driveway, she recognized the white clapboard house with black shutters surrounded by a white picket fence, and instantly bitterness stabbed at her heart. She'd always wanted a house like this, high on a hill overlooking the valley.

She asked the driver to wait, and she slowly walked up the cobblestone path, then unlocked the door with the key Robert had given her. As she eased into the living room, the smell of fresh white paint hit her, and shiny new wooden floors met with the sun's rays as she slowly walked to the middle of the room.

There wasn't any furniture in the room except for a small desk and wooden chair next to a very large fireplace. Ivan's desk. He'd had the piece of furniture since Katie Ann had known him, a gift from his father when he was just a boy.

She could see a large and welcoming kitchen through a

doorway to the right, and again she fought the bitterness in her soul. She'd always wanted a kitchen like this. She ran her hand gingerly along the white countertop. Peering out the window, she saw a nice spot for a garden, then forced herself to see how many bedrooms were in the one-story house.

The master bedroom was roomy and filled with windows. Farther down the hall were three more bedrooms. She grabbed her chest when she walked into the last bedroom on the right and struggled to stay on her feet. There, in that room, was everything she'd ever envisioned for a nursery. A beautiful crib up against the wall, filled with blankets and two stuffed bunnies. And a changing table, dresser, and baby carrier were also in the room. She couldn't stop the tears from coming. Ivan died before he knew that Lucy was pregnant, but they were clearly planning on a family.

She thought about how Jonas would never know his father. Lucy's baby would never know Ivan either. Her heart ached as she eyed the room, feeling a level of pain for Lucy she didn't expect. Lucy didn't even know about the house. It was a surprise for her, and as much as it hurt Katie Ann to witness Ivan's plans for his future with Lucy, she wondered if Lucy's loss was as great as hers had been. Maybe greater.

Swiping at her eyes, she walked into all the rooms several more times, knowing that she would have to tell Lucy about the house, about the nursery. Or maybe she'd ask Robert to do it. Lucy could make arrangements to pick up the baby furniture for Benjamin. And Ivan's desk.

She walked to the wooden chair and sat down, leaning on her elbows and supporting her head with her hands. After a few moments she lifted her head. And that's when she saw the envelope addressed to her in Ivan's handwriting. Picking it up, she feared Ivan's last words to her and the level of hurt she'd endure reading anything he'd written to her. But she slid her finger beneath the seam and pulled out a piece of white paper.

Dear Katie Ann,

I hope that this letter finds you well. I wanted to talk to you in person and hope to do so soon, but the distance between us, both physically and emotionally, has made me choose to write you this letter instead.

I know you're pregnant, and my heart jumps with joy about this.

She gasped as she slapped a hand to her chest, clamping her eyes shut. She took a deep breath and went on.

In a community our size, I was bound to find out that you are with child, but I can understand why you would be fearful about telling me, scared I would return out of obligation. I know you so well. But before I found out this news, I was already praying that we could find our way back to each other. I think of you, dream of you, and my regrets are many.

My heart longs to be with you . . . and our child. I want us to be a family again.

Katie Ann sobbed so hard, she was having trouble reading. She dabbed at her eyes and went on.

I hired help to build a house outside of Bird-in-Hand, and it is my dream for you and our child to live there with me, if you can ever find a way to forgive me. I have shamed you, shamed myself, and shamed God.

Please, Katie Ann. I want to make things right for you . . . and the baby. I have always loved you and continue to love you.

In His name,
Your husband, Ivan

She put her head down on the desk and cried until she was sure there were no more tears. Lucy's words hung in the air like a thick fog that was choking her. *"I always wondered if he was going back to you."*

"How could you do this to me, Ivan!" she cried when she finally raised her head. Dangling the letter by her side, she got up and walked to what might have been Jonas's room. She leaned against the wall, but the gravity of this news caused her to slide down until she was sitting on the cold wooden floors. She looked around the room and realized that she hadn't noticed until now—no electrical outlets or lighting fixtures.

She stayed on the floor for the next hour, her legs extended in front of her, the letter in her lap. In a daze, she tried to sort out feelings that had nothing to do with Eli, yet it was his face that kept flashing into her mind.

What would she have done if Ivan hadn't died? Would she have received this letter months ago and reunited with him? Would she be living in this house now? A house he'd built for her—behind Lucy's back.

She thought about Lucy and Benjamin. Would Ivan still have left Lucy once he found out that Lucy was carrying his child? Did Ivan suddenly long for a family and either woman would do?

Then it hit her. Ivan was doing to Lucy the same thing that he'd done to her. He might be a man full of surprises, but this house wasn't just a surprise for Katie Ann—it represented betrayal. Again. This time he would slither away from Lucy, just as he'd done to Katie Ann, leaving her without any money or future to look forward to. He might not have taken money for himself, but he'd certainly left her in a bad financial way. Just as he had planned to do to Lucy. He was a selfish man, but Katie Ann still wondered whether or not her love for him would have been enough to open her heart to him again.

After only a short while, she decided not. She stood up, took a final look around, and knew exactly what she was going to do.

She asked the driver to take her back to Robert's office. He was busy with someone else when she arrived, but after about thirty minutes, she was escorted back to his office. She didn't sit down.

"I would like to pay off the mortgage on the house." She raised her chin, determined not to cry.

"Really?" Robert scratched his chin. "So you're planning to move back to Lancaster County?"

She fumbled with Ivan's letter in the pocket of her apron. "No. I would like the house deeded to Lucy."

Robert stood up and walked around his desk. "Katie Ann, are you sure?" He paused, brows narrowed.

"Lucy has a baby now. Ivan's child. And Ivan probably would have left her and the child the same way he left me."

"You're being very generous."

Katie Ann didn't feel generous. In addition to wanting to do the right thing on Ivan's behalf—since Ivan had earned all the money for the house while with Lucy—she was hoping to never hear from the woman again, to finally have closure on all this.

But then she recalled the way Lucy was at Ivan's funeral months ago and the way she was when she came to Katie Ann's house, still stricken with grief.

"He built the house with money he made while he was with Lucy. It only seems fair that she should have it."

"It doesn't seem fair—to you." Robert folded his arms across his chest. "There's a considerable amount of money owed on that mortgage. I'm not sure why you would do this, but all right."

"Thank you."

"I'll let Lucy know what you've done, and—"

"No. Please don't."

Robert locked eyes with her. "Don't you think it's odd that Ivan would build a house without any electrical outlets or fixtures?" He rubbed his chin. "Everything is fueled with gas or propane too." Robert paused again, the hint of a smile in his expression. "Certainly resembles a lot of Amish homes I've seen. And Ivan wasn't Amish anymore."

Katie Ann pulled her eyes from his and shrugged. "Do you think you can make arrangements to have the electricity hooked up before you make mention of this to Lucy? I don't want her to have any doubt in her mind that Ivan built the house for her."

There was no reason for Lucy ever to know the betrayal that Ivan had planned for her. And as for Katie Ann, she just wanted to go home. To Colorado. Her life here was behind her. Now she just wondered what God had in store for her future. But one thing was for certain. There was no room in her heart for more heartbreak.

As she walked out of Robert's building toward the driver's car, she wadded up Ivan's letter and tossed it into a nearby trash can.

Good-bye, Ivan.

Now she just needed to say good-bye to Eli.

Eighteen

Eli sat down at the kitchen table with the package that had arrived in the mail. He stared at it, knowing what it was, but not wanting to admit that his friendship with Katie Ann was over.

Finally he forced himself to open the box and unwrap the cell phone. She hadn't been back in Colorado for twenty-four hours when she called to tell him that she was sending the phone back. Eli wasn't sure what happened in Lancaster County. Maybe she was still grieving for her husband, and being back there made her feel like she was betraying Ivan by being friends with Eli.

But who were they fooling? Katie Ann knew that they were much more than friends, just as Eli did. He had tried to talk her out of sending the phone back, but she was insistent that it was a luxury she shouldn't have. When he asked to visit her, she declined.

Over the next few weeks, he left several messages on the barn phone. She never called him back. He stayed busy planting the fields, but as the seasons began to change, Eli's feelings began to change too. His hurt turned to resentment. Before Katie Ann, he'd been a happy fellow with his entire life planned out. Now he was lonely and bitter. He didn't even want to travel anymore. He missed her so much he could hardly stand it.

It was the first of April when all his daughters once again came to see him. He was out on the plow when he saw their buggies pulling in. He was tempted to stay right where he was, but his strong-willed daughters would only wait him out.

As he walked across the fields, he pulled off his hat and wiped sweat from his brow. Four of his six grandchildren scurried about in the yard among their mothers, and Eli smiled, feeling angry at himself for his bitterness about Katie Ann. He knew that he was blessed more than most men. He'd loved two women with all his heart, and he had a wonderful family and these beautiful grandchildren. He told himself that he would enjoy the Lord's blessings, and he would joyfully endure another intervention from his daughters. Wondering what it would be this time, he recalled the girls' many attempts to cheer him up over the past month. There had been several conversations about Katie Ann. His daughters were convinced he should travel to Canaan and tell her how he felt.

But it was Jake who convinced him otherwise. "If she wanted to be with you, *Daed*, wouldn't she be?" he'd said.

As he got closer, he hesitated for a moment. Jake was sitting on the porch. All of his children were here, and by their expressions, Eli knew this wasn't just a social call or a planned visit to boost his spirits.

Katie Ann added another pot holder to her pile. Her days were long, spent tending to Jonas and working on her handmade items. Turning out lap quilts, pot holders, and knitted items kept her hands busy, if not always her mind. So often her thoughts would drift to Eli, but in her effort to guard her heart, she focused on being a good mother to Jonas and on more tangible goals that had nothing to do with Eli.

Vera paid a visit to Katie Ann every time she heard from him. Katie Ann looked forward to hearing what Eli was doing and how he was, although that same evening she would usually cry herself to sleep. The past two weeks had been better, though, because someone else's love life was the focus of everyone's attention. Martha and Arnold were getting married the first of May.

She smiled as Jonas pulled himself up in the playpen; she couldn't believe he was seven months old already. An April breeze filled the house with the scent of spring, and Katie Ann was looking forward to Martha coming for supper, the way she always did on Saturday night. Katie Ann had said repeatedly that Martha should bring Arnold, but Martha always said this night was reserved for just the girls, which now included Danielle. The teenager was always pleasant, but a bit guarded. Martha said she was just the opposite at home, always rambling on about something. But apparently "Amish folks" made Danielle nervous.

Danielle had finally talked to Martha about her mother, a troubled woman with a drinking problem. Evidently that was not the first time her mother had hit her, but it was the worst. Katie Ann couldn't believe they had not heard one word from the woman since the day she left Danielle there.

And Danielle was a handful for Martha. Twice Martha had awakened during the night to find that Danielle wasn't home. She'd gone for a walk—or so she said. Then there was the loud music, the need for a cell phone, arguments about clothes. And Danielle still didn't have a job, something Martha insisted upon when she agreed to let her stay.

"Where's my baby?" Martha said when she arrived later that afternoon. She handed Katie Ann the casserole dish she was carrying before she marched to the playpen, leaned down, and smothered Jonas with kisses. "Oh, and by the way, I didn't cook that. There was a woman in Monte Vista selling tamales out of a little shack. There was a long line, so I figured they must be good."

Jonas raised his arms, always excited to see Granny, as Martha was now calling herself.

Katie Ann nodded. She'd never had tamales before, but she knew there was a big Latino influence in the area, and she was eager to try something new. "Where's Danielle?" she asked as she peeled back the foil and breathed in the scent of pork and spicy seasonings.

Martha stood up, put her hands on her hips, and huffed. "You know that girl is as smart as a whip. Graduated from high school early before she ended up on my doorstep. But I'm not always sure her choices are as smart. She seemed to think that going to the movies with Angie was more important than our girls' night out."

"Who is Angie?"

"A girl she met in town when I sent her shopping for me. And Angie has a *car*." Martha rolled her eyes. "I wish she could get friendly with some of the Amish young people around here. I'd feel a lot better. Her new friend's nose is pierced, for goodness' sake." Martha threw her hands in the air. "What kind of girl pierces her nose?" She plopped down on the couch. “And I’ve told Danielle that she needs a job before we kill each other.”

Katie Ann smiled. “You care for her a lot, no?”

“I guess,” Martha said with a pout. “But I wouldn’t want to have three or four more just like her.”

“Tell me about the wedding. Is everything ready?” Katie Ann sat down beside her.

“Everything is ready except for confirmation from Bishop Esh. I visit him regularly, even though I’m not Amish. I figure he can bless our union and stand right up there next to Father Jim, who I also visit often, even though I’m not a Catholic.”

Katie Ann grinned every time she pictured Bishop Esh standing next to the priest from Arnold’s church—both presiding over a wedding that was neither Amish nor Catholic. She didn’t think their bishop from Lancaster County, Bishop Ebersol, ever would have done such a thing, but Bishop Esh was a bit more liberal.

Katie Ann used to think that maybe Martha was considering conversion to their faith, but Arnold was a devout Catholic, so that seemed unlikely now. Martha had a good relationship with both the bishop and the priest. She said it didn’t matter what religion you were as long as you were fully committed to the Lord.

“Someone’s here,” Martha said as she sat taller. “It’s a buggy. I can hear it coming up the driveway.”

“It’s Vera.” Katie Ann peered out the window, surprised that Vera was coming so close to the supper hour.

A few minutes later Vera walked into Katie Ann’s living room. Her expression was strained, and she didn’t even bother with polite small talk or come more than a few feet into the room. “I’m sorry to come this time of the evening, Katie Ann, but I got a phone call from Eli awhile ago.”

"What is it, Vera?" Martha asked.

"It's his daughter Hannah, his oldest girl. She had the cancer awhile back, and they just found out it's back." She hung her head, then looked back up. "I thought you'd want to know, Katie Ann."

"*Ya, ya. Danki*, Vera." Katie Ann touched her on the arm. "Do you want to stay?"

"No. I have to get home and feed everyone, but I just wanted you to know."

Katie Ann swallowed back the lump in her throat. She forced a smile.

Vera wasn't even around the corner in her buggy when Martha reached into her purse and handed Katie Ann her cell phone. She took it, walked outside, and sat down on the porch step. She dialed his number, and he answered on the first ring.

"Eli?" She hoped she had dialed correctly. It had been so long since she'd heard his voice, she wasn't sure it was Eli who answered.

"Katie Ann?"

"*Ya*, it's me. I—I just wanted to call and tell you how sorry I am to hear about Hannah. I'm so very sorry." She struggled not to cry, knowing how hard this must be for him.

"*Danki*, Katie Ann. The doctor said they caught it early, so we are very hopeful. How are you? It's *gut* to hear your voice."

It took everything in her power not to break down and tell him how much she missed him, but now was not the time. "It's *gut* to hear your voice too." She sat taller and took a deep breath. "Please tell me if there is anything that I can do for you or your family. I will be praying for all of you."

"I pray for you and Jonas every night. I miss you, Katie Ann." His voice was soft and sounded so sad.

She felt a tear roll down her cheek. "I pray for you too." She covered her eyes with one hand.

"Do you miss me?"

"I—I don't think this is—is the time to be . . ." Her voice cracked as she trailed off.

"It is the time, Katie Ann. I need . . . I need my friend more than ever right now."

A faucet of tears trailed down her cheeks. "I will always be your friend, Eli. Always."

"Really? Because it hasn't felt like that."

She could hear the anger in his voice, and while part of her wanted to lash out at him for breaking her heart in the first place, she knew his pain was great, and she wasn't going to do anything to add to it. "I'm sorry, Eli. It was just—just getting too hard."

There was silence, and Katie Ann assumed that Eli knew exactly what she was talking about. "Long-distance relationships." He let out a lighthearted chuckle. "Hard work, no?"

She was glad to hear his voice a bit brighter. "*Ya*. Hard work."

They stayed on the phone for another thirty minutes, not saying much, but not wanting to hang up either. Katie Ann offered to pray quietly with Eli before they said good-bye, and as was always the case, she cried for quite a while after they hung up.

"That's just terrible," Martha said about the call, shaking her head as they ate supper later.

Katie Ann placed some peas and ham on Jonas's highchair

tray, having decided the tamales were too spicy for him. "*Ya*. It is." Despite her resolve, she was starting to cry again.

"Honey, I don't know why you don't tell that man how you feel about him."

"I'm not going to push him into a life he didn't plan for, Martha."

"Vera said Eli hasn't traveled anywhere. If that was the life he wanted, then why isn't he living it?"

"I don't know, but I'm not going back to how things were. Being so far away from each other was too hard." She shook her head.

"Well, I say life is too short."

Katie Ann was quiet. She didn't know what else to say.

Over the next couple of weeks, Katie Ann slipped into a comfortable routine. After she had Jonas in bed, she'd go out to the barn and call Eli. After their first conversation about Hannah, he'd asked her to call him the next night, and at the end of each call, Eli would make the same request, for her to please call the following night. She carried the baby monitor to the barn so she could hear if Jonas woke up. Both she and Eli avoided any more mention about their own relationship, and in some ways, it was like old times. Hannah had a good prognosis, and the doctors had removed the small lump in her breast and anticipated a full recovery without Hannah needing to have chemotherapy or radiation. Eli returned to his old self, laughing and being positive.

Katie Ann had to admit, she was happier talking to him than she was not talking to him. Twice he'd mentioned seeing her, but she sidestepped the idea. Besides, he couldn't leave his family right now, and Katie Ann was much too busy keeping Martha on an even keel with the wedding only a week away. But there was a huge part of her that longed to feel his lips against hers, the feel of his arms around her. So much so that she was almost willing to endure another good-bye just to have him hold her one more time.

MARTHA SAT ON the edge of her bed eyeing her wedding dress on a hanger across the room. It was a beautiful ivory-colored gown that the lady at the bridal boutique said was tasteful and elegant. Danielle said it looked like an old lady dress, so Martha reminded her that she was an old lady. Martha and Danielle were starting to adjust to each other's ways, but she worried how Arnold would fit into their routine. In a week, they would vow to love each other forever, and he would move into her house, since his was only a rental. She loved that man with all her heart, but she was having some prewedding jitters on this Tuesday afternoon when Danielle knocked on her door.

"Come in."

Danielle walked in, her long blond hair in a ponytail and wearing her usual blue jeans and a T-shirt. "I have some news for you."

Martha crossed herself and looked up. "Please, Lord, let it be good news."

Danielle smiled. "I got a job."

Martha crossed herself again, brought her hands together in prayer, and looked up again. "Thank You, God."

"I'm going to be a waitress at the Mountain View Restaurant in Monte Vista."

Martha smiled. "That's a nice place. They have the best burgers on the planet."

Danielle tucked her chin as she raised an eyebrow. Martha knew what was coming next.

"I'll be working at night, and you'd have to take me there, and I know you don't like to drive at night, so . . ." She raised her shoulders, then let them fall slowly.

"Yeah, I knew this would be coming. You want a car."

Danielle sat down beside Martha on the bed. "It seems weird to say that. I mean, you're not my mom or anything. And you've already done so much for me."

It wasn't often that Danielle acknowledged Martha's generosity, so it always touched Martha when she did. "Still no word from your mother?"

"No." Danielle stared off into space the way she usually did at the mention of her mother.

They were quiet for a while, then Danielle turned to face Martha. "You're not going to wear that butterfly clip in your hair when you get married, are you?"

Martha frowned, twisting to face her. "Yes, I am. It matches my dress perfectly."

"I don't think so. It's pink." Danielle shook her head, smiling, but she stopped and tipped her head to one side. "Do you think it's okay with Arnold that I'm living here?"

"You two seem to get along well." Martha grinned. "And he knew we were a package deal."

"Arnold *gets* me. He's a good guy." She reached up and pulled her hair tight within the ponytail. "You don't *get* me sometimes."

Martha glared at her, but Danielle just chuckled and did the unexpected. She reached over and hugged Martha. At first Martha just sat there. After a moment, she put her arms around Danielle and they held each other for a while.

"I guess I'll go take a bath." Danielle eased away and started toward the door. Then she laughed. "I wonder when Arnold's allocated bath time will be."

The sound of the girl's laughter warmed Martha's heart, so she decided to ignore her reference to Martha's most-reasonable rules. "I'll tell you what . . ." Martha reached up and tightened her butterfly clip as Danielle turned around at the doorway. "I have a deal to make with you."

"Really?" She eyed Martha, squinting one eye. "And what's that?"

"You go to worship with me every other week, and I'll buy you a car."

"To that *Amish* church?" Her eyes grew round.

You'd think I just asked her to make a deal with the devil himself.

"Yes, to that Amish church." She pointed a finger at Danielle. "It's either my church people, or you can go to church with Arnold, but he goes every Sunday, and they don't have food afterward."

"But his church is only an hour long. You're gone like half the day when you go to the Amish church."

"Well, Arnold's church is almost thirty minutes away. So let's see . . . thirty minutes there, thirty minutes back, an hour for Mass, no meal, gotta go every Sunday . . ."

"Fine! I'll go with you." She folded her arms across her chest. "That doesn't mean I'll change my mind about God.

Besides, you said it's mostly in German anyway. I won't even understand anything."

"The Lord has a way of getting through to us when it counts." Martha smiled, glad she remembered some German from her college days to combine with the Lord's efforts.

"What kind of car?"

Martha cackled. "An old clunker, just like I had for my first car."

"What?"

"Take it or leave it."

Danielle sighed. "Fine. I'll take it."

Martha smiled as Danielle headed out the door and down the hall. The three of them were going to be a family.

Now she just had to figure out what to do about Katie Ann, who would always be like her daughter—but the girl deserved happiness. The kind of happiness that comes from a family who lives together under the same roof—loving, arguing, and growing together.

Hmm . . . She could feel the wheels spinning in her head.

Nineteen

KATIE ANN DIDN'T THINK GOD COULD HAVE BLESSED Martha and Arnold with a better day to get married.

Their wedding was a conglomeration of compromises. Arnold thought they should get married indoors, and Martha wanted an outdoor wedding. Arnold wanted a small gathering, just family and closest friends. Martha wanted to invite every single person she knew.

"It's not like I get dressed up like this every day," she'd told Katie Ann. "Seems everyone I know should see me at my best."

Arnold wanted the priest to preside over the entire ceremony. Martha insisted the job be shared with Bishop Esh, who had agreed with some reluctance. Katie Ann figured the bishop went along with Martha's request because Martha was as close to being Amish as any *Englischer* they'd all ever known—with regard to her faith only. Her flashy ways hadn't diminished in the least.

Martha's husband-to-be didn't see the need for attendants, but Martha was clear about having Katie Ann by her side.

Arnold wanted an evening wedding, but Martha said it would be an all-day affair beginning at eight o'clock in the morning.

"That way we get two meals out of the deal," she'd said. "Like the Amish."

In the end Martha won out on every detail, and Arnold had just smiled. "Whatever my Martha wants," he'd said.

Emily and David offered to host the wedding. They'd recently moved into their new home, and they said they wanted to do this for Martha and Arnold. Martha had played matchmaker between them, and they both wanted to do something special for her. The newlyweds lived on property that Samuel and Lillian had given to their son, and the spacious house was high on a hill with the Sangre de Cristo Mountains to the east and the San Juan Mountains to the west.

Katie Ann tethered her horse amid the other buggies and cars. They'd invited over a hundred people. She took Jonas from his car seat and gazed across the field dotted with the occasional burst of color from the earliest of the wildflowers, an orange glow lingering behind the mountains. Not far into the field, white chairs were lined up on either side of a white runner that led up to an archway that David had built for the occasion. Martha had asked David to walk her down the aisle, and Bishop Esh had agreed to Martha's request.

Katie Ann moved toward the house, and the smell of *roascht* filled her nostrils. That was another tradition Martha wanted for her special day. The chicken and stuffing were always served at Amish weddings. People were scurrying about, and Katie Ann spoke to those she passed as she made her way into the kitchen.

It was nearing eight o'clock when everyone gathered outside for the wedding. Emily took Jonas, and Katie Ann stayed behind, as did David. Martha didn't want Arnold to see her before the wedding, so she'd been hiding upstairs in Emily and David's bedroom. Katie Ann walked upstairs to get her.

"It's time, Martha." Katie Ann walked toward her, surprised to see Martha's hands trembling. Katie Ann picked up the bouquet of flowers on the bed and handed them to her friend. "Here you go."

Martha took the flowers, bit her bottom lip, and blinked a few times. "Katie Ann . . ." She let out a deep breath. "I don't know why the good Lord saw fit to bless me with Arnold this late in life, but I feel like the luckiest woman in the world. Do you think I deserve all this?"

Katie Ann swallowed hard, thinking Martha had never looked more beautiful, or more vulnerable. She touched her on the arm. "You deserve all this and more, Martha. And you look beautiful."

Martha reached up and touched the butterfly clip. "Danielle said this doesn't match, but I don't go anywhere without it. What do you think?"

"I think it's lovely."

Martha held the flowers with one hand and reached for Katie Ann's hand with the other. "The wonder of the Lord's love is an amazing thing, isn't it?"

"*Ya*. It is." Katie Ann blinked back tears.

Martha cleared her lungs of the breath she'd been holding. "Well then . . . let's get this show on the road."

Once they were downstairs, Katie Ann gave Martha a final hug and told David to watch for their cue from their spot on the front porch. Then she went and found her place on the front row. As was customary for Amish weddings, the men were on one side, the women on the other, even though here folks were facing forward instead of toward each other. It was the strangest setup for a wedding that Katie Ann had ever seen. She smiled, knowing she wouldn't have expected anything less from Martha.

Katie Ann's own marriage to Ivan flashed in her mind and, refusing to let anything put a damper on this day, she was able to recall her wedding day with fondness. She'd been so in love. It was a shame that over the years so many bad memories had stamped out many of the good ones.

Then she thought of Eli. They'd continued to talk every night until the past two. Katie Ann had called from the barn phone, but there hadn't been an answer either night. When they talked in the evenings, the conversations ranged from light-hearted to intense, especially when things like Hannah's cancer came up. But they steered clear of any talk about their relationship. Eli ended each call with, "Sleep with the angels," and Katie Ann said the same to him.

Someone Katie Ann didn't know, a woman about her age, was in charge of the music, and Katie Ann watched her get up from her place on the back row and walk a few steps to a CD player. She pushed a button, and as Martha had instructed a hundred times, Katie Ann rose and went to stand beside Bishop Esh, then motioned for David to walk Martha across the field to the white runner.

Bishop Esh had agreed to recite some prayers at the wedding, but he'd drawn the line when it came to officiating the ceremony. Katie Ann was shocked that he'd agreed to as much as he had already. She turned her eyes to Martha as she and David stood ready to walk down the makeshift aisle, then she scanned the crowd for Jonas, expecting him to be in Emily's lap. When she didn't see Jonas, her heart pounded and her eyes started going row to row until she spotted him. In Eli's lap near the back. *Eli's* lap?

When their eyes locked, he smiled and lifted Jonas's arm like he was waving to Katie Ann. As if the sight of Eli didn't warm her heart enough, the vision of him holding her son filled her with so much joy she went weak in the knees. Why hadn't anyone told her Eli was coming? She bit her lip to keep from grinning, and she forced her eyes back to Martha, who glided down the aisle with the dignity of someone entitled, her chin raised slightly, bowing her head to the attendees on either side. Any other behavior simply wouldn't have been Martha, Katie Ann surmised as she struggled to keep her grin from growing to a large smile.

What a wonderful day this is.

Most of the ceremony seemed to Katie Ann to be Catholic, but then occasionally Bishop Esh would interject prayers. The ceremony seemed to fit both Martha and Arnold perfectly. It was shorter than an Amish wedding. Arnold and Martha took their vows after the Catholic folks took Communion, about forty-five minutes into the ceremony. As Martha had instructed, Katie Ann stood up and joined Martha at the front. As Arnold and Martha vowed to love, honor, and cherish each other for the rest of their lives, Katie Ann's eyes involuntarily drifted to Eli. He was still holding Jonas on his lap, and his gaze met hers. Then his mouth silently formed words, but Katie Ann could make them out quite clearly. *I love you.* She held her breath for a moment, then forced herself to release it for fear she might pass out.

She pulled her eyes away and focused on Martha, who was now crying buckets. She kept her attention on the new couple. Next thing she knew, Martha and Arnold were walking back down the aisle and everyone was clapping. She looked at Eli, and this time he just smiled, his eyes bright, and he was standing with Jonas on his hip. She didn't know an Amish man alive who would tend to a youngster during a wedding, or any other time for that matter. She watched as everyone made their way across the grass toward the tents set up in the front yard. A dozen women were already setting out food. She watched Eli hand Jonas to Emily as she walked by. Katie Ann's feet were rooted to the ground beneath her. A few minutes later, everyone was in the front yard, and Eli and Katie Ann stood alone. She knew he wouldn't kiss her with so many eyes nearby, but she'd never wanted anything more in her life. He hugged her, though, then just eased away and stared at her.

As the sun warmed her cheeks and the smells of spring swirled around them, Eli took her hand in his and squeezed, smiling tenderly. "I love you, Katie Ann." He shook his head and looked down for a moment, then back up at her. "I've wanted to tell you that a hundred times. I love you." He gazed into her eyes, and she could feel the sincerity behind his words. Letting him go this time would surely leave her with little room to ever recover, but she knew that she had to tell him what was in her heart.

"I love you too, Eli."

"I know." Then he chuckled, and Katie Ann smiled, filled with love, but so many questions. "We have a predicament." He kept hold of one of her hands tightly, as if he feared she might flee. He stroked his beard. "I can't leave my family."

Tiny cracks in her heart spread like vines, but she knew this was coming. "I know," she said softly, knowing he was going to ask her to leave Canaan, a place that had become home. And her family was here. She lowered her head and waited.

MARTHA MOVED THROUGH the crowd, making sure that every person here had an opportunity to hug her, but if anyone thought she wasn't watching the events around her—they were wrong. Everyone had gathered outside after the meal, and she'd already spotted Danielle and Levi underneath the big oak tree on the west side of the house. The two young people were deep in conversation, and Martha was thrilled. But when she saw Vera standing a few feet away from what Martha hoped was a blossoming new friendship, Vera stood with her mouth turned down and her arms folded across her chest, pretending to listen to Lillian but staring at Danielle and her son.

Hmm . . . Martha had wanted nothing more than for Danielle to find some nice Amish friends, mostly because the kids were just good folk, with a strong faith in the Lord. And none of them had their body parts pierced. But she felt a little protective of Danielle. Was Vera thinking that Danielle wasn't good enough to be friends with her son? True, Danielle was a work in progress, but the girl had gone through a tough time.

Martha didn't care if it was her wedding reception, she was going to find out if maybe she was wrong. She waited until Lillian walked away before she approached Vera.

"Glad to see Danielle is making some friends." Martha nodded toward Danielle and Levi.

Vera smiled. "*Ya, ya.*" She paused and raised a brow, her voice unusually hopeful. "Has she made any friends with her own kind?"

Never before had Martha felt the invisible lines that divided them as strongly as she did in this moment. A taut reminder that, no matter the love and friendships—Martha and her people were not Amish. And for a group so dedicated to not passing judgment, Vera's eyes were expressively judging Danielle for the Amish person she was not.

"She's made a few friends," Martha said casually. "But I was hoping she'd make friends with some of the Amish folks. You people raise good kids." She grinned, hoping the compliment would make Vera lighten up a bit.

"We believe in hard work and discipline." Vera pressed her lips together as she glanced over at Danielle and Levi.

"Danielle got a job at the Mountain View Restaurant." Martha felt defensive, a place she didn't like to be. "She'll work hard, I'm sure."

Vera smiled. "I'm sure."

Martha wanted to give Vera a little shove and tell her to quit being so judgmental, that Danielle was just as good as Levi. But today was her wedding day, so she wasn't going to let Vera spoil it.

"Where're Eli and Katie Ann?" Martha scanned the crowd around her and didn't see them. She looked back at Vera, who was now grinning from ear to ear.

"It was a wonderful idea for you to invite Eli. And with Hannah doing so well, he was thrilled to come." She pointed toward the field where Katie Ann and Eli were still standing. "There they are."

It warmed Martha's heart to see them together. It was a picturesque setting as an orange glow rose into a deep blue sky, mountains in every direction. She took another look. *Is Katie Ann crying?*

KATIE ANN SEARCHED her heart, and she knew that she would travel to Ohio to be with Eli if he asked her to do so. It would break her heart to leave Canaan, to leave Lillian, Samuel, and the children. They were her family. And what about Martha?

"I can't keep doing this, Eli." She lowered her head as a tear trailed down her cheek. Eli lifted her chin and brushed away the tear with his thumb, keeping his hand on her cheek.

"I don't want to be without you either, Katie Ann."

She was surprised when he leaned in and kissed her, but time stopped for a moment as she allowed herself a few moments in his arms. He kissed her again, then kissed her on the cheek, cupping her face in his hands.

"I love you, Katie Ann. I don't want to be without you, but I'm not going to ask you to leave your family here. I wouldn't do that."

The tiny webs in her heart thickened and spread wider, enough so that she was sure she would never survive what was coming. She stared out into the open field toward the majestic mountains and silently prayed for strength. Eli smoothed back a strand of hair that had fallen forward and kissed her again.

"Marry me, Katie Ann. Spend the rest of your life with me." Eli smiled. "Let me be a *gut* husband to you and a father to Jonas."

She was confused. "But how can that be, Eli? What about your plans—"

Eli gently put a finger to her lips. "*Mei lieb*, God had other plans for me. I have spent my entire life taking care of others. And it's not a burden, but a blessing. I want to take care of you and Jonas. God's plan was for me to fall in love with you, Katie Ann. And nothing would make me happier than living out my life with you and the two of us raising Jonas together."

She looked deep into his eyes, silently begging for the Holy Spirit to guide her. Then she knew. "I will go anywhere to be with you, Eli. I love you."

He smiled. "You don't have to go anywhere, Katie Ann. I'm staying here."

"But . . . I don't understand. You said you could never leave your family."

"It would hurt me deeply to have to leave all of them."

She shook her head. "I would never ask you to do that, Eli, but I don't understand."

"Do you know how much an acre of land costs here compared to Middlefield?" He stroked his chin. "Much cheaper here." He paused again. "And have you ever noticed how there isn't a camera in your face everywhere you go here? Not nearly as many tourists. And there is plenty of room."

Katie Ann's eyes widened.

"You'll be meeting most of your extended family this fall when they move to Canaan, a decision they made on their own. They want the freedom to spread out and grow here in Canaan—with us."

Katie Ann threw her arms around him. "Eli! I love you so

much. This is wonderful news! I can't wait to meet everyone—Jake, Hannah, Ida Mae, Karen, Frieda, Maureen, and all their families and—"

Eli eased her away for a moment. He pushed back a strand of loose hair that had fallen across her face, then cupped her cheek. "They aren't *all* coming."

Katie Ann didn't understand. "What do you mean?"

"Maureen . . ." Eli lowered his eyes for a moment. "Maureen won't be coming. Her husband has taken over his father's blacksmith business, and he said they will be staying in Middlefield."

She knew that Eli held a special place in his heart for his youngest daughter. "*Ach*, Eli, I—I don't know what to say."

"Say that you love me." He pulled her close.

"I do. And we will visit Maureen often." She pulled out of his embrace slowly. "Are you sure this is what you want, Eli?"

Then Eli did the unthinkable. He picked her up around the waist and swung her around until all the wildflowers molded into a blurred rainbow of sheer beauty. "I've never wanted anything more in my life."

Katie Ann saw Martha stomping across the meadow, lifting her white heels high as she walked. She wiggled free of Eli's hold but could hardly contain herself as tears of joy poured down her cheeks.

"What in the world is going on out here?" Martha put her hands on her hips. "First I saw you crying, and now . . ." She grinned. "Are those happy tears?"

"Eli and I are getting married!" Katie Ann bounced on her toes.

Martha threw back her head and laughed. "Just had to go and steal my glory today, didn'tcha, honey?" Then she pulled

Katie Ann into a tight hug. "I don't know how I'm going to live without you here, though."

Katie Ann had to pry herself from Martha's embrace. "You don't have to. Eli is staying here, and . . ." She smiled at Eli. "His family—all but his youngest daughter—are moving here."

Martha looked at Eli, her eyes wide. Then she laughed. "That's the best wedding present I could have asked for. This makes me very happy!" She kissed Katie Ann on the cheek and hugged Eli. "Now I have to go find my new husband before he starts missing me." She turned to leave but then turned back around. "Just think of all the fun we're going to have here in Canaan with such a big family."

Katie Ann closed her eyes and thanked God for the wonder of His love. Then she kissed Eli on the mouth—right in front of Martha.

Martha shook her head, mumbling as she turned to head back toward the house. "Good grief. *My* wedding day, and I can't even hold on to the spotlight." She twisted her head around and winked at Katie Ann. "But you go, girl!"

Acknowledgments

There is always a mild level of anxiety when I write my acknowledgments, for fear of forgetting someone. With each book, more and more people are involved in the process, and getting the book on the shelves is a huge combined effort.

I'll start by thanking God, who continues to bless me with stories to tell. Without Him, there would be no books. Thank you, Lord, for guiding my hand in my effort to deliver stories that both entertain and bring folks closer to you.

To my husband Patrick—you are the constant in my life that keeps me on an even keel despite the chaos sometimes. Thank you for making me laugh, for loving me, and for reading every single book I write, like you promised . . . ha ha. ☺ I love you with all my heart.

Sherry Gregg, it is an honor to dedicate the book to someone whom I admire in so many ways. I've always said that sometimes God drops people in our paths for a reason. He sure knew what He was doing when he introduced us. Okay, I better mention your husband, too, since I've known him since

I was a kid . . . ha ha. Tim, you're the best! Thank you both for your hospitality and your friendship. Despite the many places Patrick and I have traveled, we often recall our trip to Colorado as one of our very best vacations. Love you both!

To my very best friend and kindred spirit, Renee' Bissmeyer. You are a walking journal of my life, the one who knows the me I sometimes don't even know. All these books later, your encouragement and love still keeps me going even when I doubt myself. You continue to be the wind beneath my wings. PEACE and love always.

Janet Murphy, you rock! We make a great team. Thank you for walking one step ahead of me and keeping me on track. You're an awesome assistant, publicity coordinator, listener, encourager, and friend. Cheers to an ongoing journey!

To my editor, Natalie Hanemann, and my Thomas Nelson family—I am incredibly blessed to be traveling this road with you all on my team. Thank you for everything, both professionally and personally. You guys and gals are the best!

Mary Sue Seymour, my friend, my agent—thank you for guiding my career and for the friendship we share.

Barbie Beiler, I sure do miss you, and I hope to visit soon! Your input—based on your own Amish background—continues to strengthen my books, keeping them authentic. Sending you big hugs, my friend.

To my line editor, LB Norton—Wow! You jumped in at the 11th hour on this book, and what a fantastic job you did. Thank you for all your hard work and willingness to push a step further to make the book a better read. Hope to meet you in person soon. Blessings to you.

To friends and family not mentioned here, please know

that they only give me so much space to write acknowledgments, or otherwise, I could go on forever and ever about how much each and every one of you means to me and how much I appreciate your encouragement, support, and love.

And last, but certainly not least—to my readers. A huge thank you for reading my books. If one of my stories brought you a step closer to God, or perhaps got you off of the fence where He is concerned, possibly gave you hope or a better understanding of His grace—please let me know by sending me an email at author@bethwiseman.net.

Reading Group Guide

1. In the beginning of the story, Katie Ann doesn't think Eli is her type. Why? What are some of Eli's characteristics that Katie Ann ultimately finds charming and is attracted to?
2. Katie Ann struggles to forgive Ivan for his infidelities. How does her inability to forgive set roadblocks along her own life path? Who are we really hurting when we can't forgive?
3. Eli has his life planned out, and he feels as though he's earned some time off. When do his big plans to travel start to fall apart and lose the allure? Why do you think that happened?
4. Katie Ann admits to herself that her relationship with God is not what it used to be. What happens when Katie Ann finally accepts that God is in charge and submits to His will without second-guessing His plan for her?
5. As in real life, there are several 'gray' areas mentioned in the book, things or a way of life that aren't traditionally part of Amish living. One of those is the use of cell phones. What are two more instances where rules are bent?
6. Eli notices early on that Katie Ann and Martha's friendship is special, if not unlikely. But despite their many differences,

Katie Ann and Martha are more alike than they may seem. How so?

7. What do you think will happen to Lucy? Do you think that she and Katie Ann will cross paths again someday? Will Jonas and Benjamin ever meet each other? If so, how do you think that will go?
8. Martha is a large presence in the book, and her heart is as big as her outspoken personality, which explains why she took Danielle in. As Martha begins to take on a parental role, how do you see her changing with regard to Danielle?
9. Early on, Katie Ann and Eli agree to just be friends. Have you or anyone you've known fallen in love with their best friend? How did it turn out?
10. Katie Ann and Eli share one similar quality. They are both unselfish. What are several instances when this shines through for each of them, and when does this endearing quality sometimes block God's efforts for their future together?
11. Danielle tells several lies—to her mother on the phone in the hospital, to the nurse and others about not knowing who hit her, and to Martha when she tells Martha that her parents are dead. Is it ever justifiable to tell a lie? How might things have turned out differently if Danielle had always told the truth? Would things have turned out better or worse for her?
12. Often God has a plan for us that we can't see or understand, putting us on the right course for the life He wants us to live. What are some examples of this in your own life? Have you ever unknowingly blocked His efforts? Or do you believe that it was always God's will for things to have happened exactly the way that they did?